Love So
of the Ton

Asher Brauner

Leon,

During the writing of this fine work I listened
to accessible Beethoven sonatas almost
exclusively — Appassionata, Moonlight, etc.
Seek the patterns of those works within
these words.

It's a fool's errand, but it will keep you busy,
and it will certainly be more entertaining than
the book itself qua literature.

Best Wishes

As B

Cover design by Zachary Goodman
Cover photograph of police © Hamish Reid

Love Songs of the Tone-Deaf
© 1997 Asher Brauner. All rights reserved.

BROWN
BEAR
BOOKS

For information contact:
Brown Bear Books
325 High St., Santa Cruz, CA 95060

Library of Congress Catalog Number 99-94657

ISBN 0-9670861-0-8

Printed in the United States of America

10 9 8 7 6 5 4 3 2 1

Love Songs
of the Tone-Deaf

Asher Brauner

Preface

I wrote this tale a few years ago, when I was younger than I now am. I did so in large measure because I could not possibly have written it when I was older than I now am.

I believe I may have scribed my story in an effort to trace the trajectory of that gentle, fierce creature I call my soul — but that's just a guess.

But a warning is due you, kind or unkind reader. At times in the following narrative I may appear to you a lout, or a boor, or a caustic fraud, providing you have the capacity for reason.

I can counsel only patience, and as hope offer only this reminder: a caterpillar is not a lovely creature. Dull and worm-like, an eater of dust and leaf, it inspires no poetry. It is a creature so full of self-loathing it must spin a cocoon to hide from itself.

But transformed it emerges, a fluttering floater in violet skies. And what fascinates me most is this question: at precisely what moment does dawn become day? When and how does loathsome larva become winged wonder?

This story is, in part, my attempt to answer that question. The other parts are just extra stuff I made up.

-- R. S.

Chapter 1

If you're like me, you've never lost an argument. If you're like Karen, you've never been in one. And if you're intrigued and amused by the oddities of human attraction — well, pull an armchair up to the dessert table.

"Give me one good reason why I should care," I said, wishing I hadn't.

Karen eyed me with a complex expression that was at once wary, defiant, and earnest. I liked her face.

Christ, I liked her face.

"You should care because they were people," Karen said, with the endearing enthusiasm of those who labor under the mistaken impression that the purpose of argument is persuasion. "Because they lived here for thousands of years, and now they're gone, and it's tragic."

"Yes," I said. "Quite tragic."

I tried not to look her in the eye when I said it. Renegade laughter struggled to emerge from my judgmental jaws. I clenched them tight, grinding the giggle between my molars. I could see my face reflected in the glass partitioning the restaurant booths. I looked like a constipated anchorman, with a highly unprofessional goatée.

"Tragic," I repeated, for effect.

I was trying hard. You have to give me that.

"You don't think it's tragic," Karen said. "I can totally tell."

"I *do* think so, baby."

"I told you not to call —"

"— right, sorry."

Christ.

Karen was a human obstacle course. Duty demanded that I empathize with her twenty-one years of accumulated feelings and understand where she was *coming from* and hurdle my grammar and vocabulary over every hostile new barrier she could erect. The exercise irritated me beyond measure.

So why was I bothering? Hey, nothing original. Nothing new under the sun, mama. I wanted to get my hands on that spongy ass of hers one more time.

Christ.

Perhaps you've had sex before. Perhaps many times. Perhaps with a wide variety of partners. Perhaps with a wide variety of genders, too. I don't care.

The point is, how many times did you really enjoy it? No bullshit, now. No bluffing. No macho swaggering. Girls, no faking it. Because that fearful, sweaty thing they call lovemaking is never as good in real life as in the movies, and we all know it, so let's stop pretending.

I mean, tell me honestly: how many times were you too drunk, or stuck in the back of a freezing cold Chevy Impala, or embarrassed by the sight of your own awkward, blemished body standing stark naked, reflected in a stranger's bedroom mirror? How many times have you taken a good look at the person you found yourself in bed with and felt like you didn't have a clue what you were doing there?

In short, to employ the cliche — how many times was it good for you?

Wait, are you counting the time when you were just about to graduate high school and your parents were at the movies and you humped your little sweetheart on Mom's favorite green couch with the little white doilies? Forget that one. Take points off for the fact that you were picking forbidden fruit. It was your First Time, too, wasn't it? I knew it. That doesn't really count. You'll never duplicate that awkward but blessedly frenzied moment, when surge and fear, innocence and guilt smash headlong and flood the senses with those charmingly incomprehensible messages.

After the First Time — after the first good one, that is, we are doomed and damned. We know what to expect, and all our nocturnal innovations and gymnastics are like new versions of "Wild Thing": the same three pathetic chords no matter how fast or slow we play them. And all the lovers who wander through our lives are just a long line of imposters in a brutal parade.

Except Karen.

You see, I keep asking myself why an intelligent college goddamn graduate like myself and a freaked-out chick who actually believes in astrology ever bothered staying together for more than five minutes.

Mostly, I come up empty. I'm perpetually snide; she's perpetually earnest. I enjoy hostile arguments; she likes herbal tea.

Only one thing bound us together. That beastly, rutting thing that makes rock 'n' roll stars rich and supermodels richer: we had absolutely goddamn fantastic sex.

I'm not sure I can even explain it to you. I know it made no sense to me.

"Fantastic sex" doesn't even come close to describing it. An adjective and a noun and out the door, but what does it really convey? Have you ever penetrated beyond your fears to the endless golden space where pleasure resides in sun-drenched comfort? Have you ever lain on a blanket on a grassy riverbank for hours in the balm of wildflowers smelling so sweet and burning so beautiful they not only surpassed the limits of your imagination but made you laugh out loud?

Have you ever eaten a banquet feast so perfect, so full and so rich that even the tiniest silver spoonful of chocolate mousse would have left you dancing on the brink of excess?

Have you ever had sex with a woman whose logic seemed to lead nowhere, but whose breath of love's promise seemed to lead everywhere? Have you ever been touched so delicately yet passionately that your tender neurons didn't know if they were living lava or a pool of Arctic-blue water? Have you ever kissed your lover's eyes and cupped her breast like it was the Holy Grail glowing gently in your trembling hands?

So don't talk to me, alright? Because I've been in that otherworldly netherzone for long hours through a sweaty night, forgetting to breathe the whole time. I've lived in that limbo where rational thought gives way to the impulses of the body, where the cerebral cortex lets the spine do the thinking, like some lower-order proto-mammal for whom sensation is everything and the future does not exist. I've snuggled, giggled, throbbed and petted with neither conscience nor guide. Where there are no words I have met another being, touched another soul. Against my better judgment, against everything I think I am and everything I know other people are, I have finally and utterly fallen in — what's the word?

Well, maybe.

The thing is, Karen is a hippie, and hippies are bullshit in my book. I mean 90's hippies. Real hippies were a 60's thing, now long dead or burnt out or both. Most transmuted into yuppies. Aboriginal hippies thought up the whole hippie thing. They had a big ol' war to protest and cops to call pigs. They had something novel going on, and I can respect that.

But when I walk down a city thoroughfare and some yokel with his battered guitar case flapped open to indicate that begging season is nigh assaults me with a tuneless tune about Kent State, warbling even worse than the original crooner about mother nature on the run in the 1970's; well, let's just say there's little danger my laundry quarter might leap out of my pocket.

Hm. Problem. Potential comprehension gap. Maybe you're from

the East Coast, or from one of those states they put in between the coasts for some reason. Perhaps your roots have found soil more fertile than the black loam of the agricultural wonderland where I now reside.

Mine are not particularly tenacious roots. I am a weed, sunk in this particular spot at this windborne moment. A chance gust, an unseasonable rain, and my spores might carry me well away from this hippie haven and down the block from you. Count very carefully every one of your blessings.

Perhaps you actually know why you live where you do. I have heard such people exist. But if your home is nowhere near mine, then you probably don't even know what I'm talking about when I mention mendicant hippies still walking the earth, because to you hippies are nonexistent, or very old news resurrected only in TV retrospectives about the Summer of Love, or quaint little elves and sprites who mean no harm.

The problem is, that's exactly how they think of themselves. These dreadfully dreadlocked, multiply-pierced little misfits while away their hours goofing, grinning, and grooving. Their self-appointed mission is to guide this sadly deprived world to desination: bliss through the rigidly circumscribed steps of their carefree, uninhibited tribal dance. Hippies conceive of themselves as anti-establishment rebels, but the sad and ugly truth is that their passive-aggressive little act disguises a subculture that is as insular and judgmental as any. For my money hippies are no different from Jehovah's Witnesses or Mormons or any other brainwashing outfit. Just replace Jesus Christ with Jerry Garcia, Muhammad with Bob Marley, or Brigham Young with Neil Young, and you've got yet another meaningless religion blessed with edicts the followers adore but ignore.

Hippies pretend a childlike purity, posturing an innocence they have long ago lost. They gambol and frolic with a carefree self-consciousness that's hideously embarrassing to those who can see behind the mask. They impose on the generosity of others shamelessly, even proudly. For what are material goods but a barrier between one human soul and another, and could I borrow a couple of bucks for some rolling papers, man?

Come on out to Santa Cruz, California sometime. You'll get a whiff of what I'm talking about. Think of yourself as having joined the Audubon Society. I'll be your field guide. You can chalk up points whenever you spot a new species of hippie. Bring binoculars. And insect repellent. Here we go:

4

The Deadhead. Uniform: tie-dyed anything. Hair: long, dreadlocked. Smell: patchouli oil, incense, body odor. Distinguishing characteristics: Still shocked, simply shocked at the unexpected death of aging overweight diabetic heroin addict Jerry Garcia. Absence of discernible income. Presence of drum. Owns hundreds of bootleg Grateful Dead tapes. Drives anything constructed in a VW factory before 1970. Preferably a green microbus. Yeah, they still do that. With all the requisite Dead stickers and a garden variety of inscrutable leftist slogans. VW starter generally shot, needs push-start. Watch for the telltale puppy on a rope, eventually abandoned to the pound.

The Earth Mama. Uniform: loose, flowing skirt made of natural fibers. Paisely or batik blouse. No bra, but don't get excited, boys. Earth Mamas are either lesbians, unattractive, or definitely not interested in you. Generally all three. Distinguishing characteristics: armpit and leg hair. Listen also for the munching of: granola, trail mix, tofu, tempeh, wheat grass, and other inedible health food crap. Especially rice cakes, which resemble cake as nearly as I resemble the Dalai Lama. The Earth Mama is a close relative of

The Earth First! Hiker Guy.

Uniform: khaki shorts, long-sleeved flannel shirts and sturdy boots. Distinguishing characteristics: Tall, thin, with wiry leg muscles and most importantly a taciturn nature. Don't ask me why. These guys have nothing to say, with one frightening exception: do not, repeat, do not lure them into a conversation about organic farming.

The Political College Kid. Uniform: varies, but watch for the protest commemorative T-shirt, the telltale clipboard, the shoes worn out from walking door-to-door. Distinguishing characteristics: Obsessed with, and converses endlessly about Important Ideas. Worried sick about depletion of the ozone layer, sexist language, and Eurocentric academic curriculum.

Oh, I could go on and on, but the point is, we're dealing here with a subspecies of the counterculture I find particularly repulsive for its unctuousness, self-righteousness, and poor grooming habits.

And Karen was ever one of them. That is the cross I bear. Precisely what variety of hippie was Karen? Good question. She was hard to pin down. She wandered among the various tribes like Jimmy Carter in the Third World: welcome everywhere, belonging nowhere.

And so we sat in our diner and bickered, as was our custom. Karen was lecturing at length about the tragic demise of the Ohlone Indians, who were apparently the former occupants of the very spot, the very land where now stood the very Golden West pancake house in which I was about to undertip.

Karen gripped my forearm with razor nails. "Try to listen to me, O.K., Ronnie? We can't do anything about the past. But this is now. It's our responsibility. Something deadly serious is happening," she said, "right here, in our town. We have to stop it. All of our lives depend on it: yours and mine and little kids who haven't even been born yet."

I blinked. Under ordinary circumstances Karen's voice was so devastatingly sweet and cheerful the FDA was fast-tracking it as a safe sugar substitute. But for a weighty moment there had been a hard, unfamiliar edge to it.

The invasive tone was so uncharacteristic I had trouble placing it. A sinister timbre, that's what it had been. A signal of danger and menace. I didn't even know she possessed those volatile vocal cords. I found it a curious discovery.

Was it possible Karen was a more complex Web page, of which I had glimpsed only the first colorful images, awaiting the entire text?

Pursuing the metaphor, one is forced to admit that download time is usually more a reflection of the capacities of the observer, and not the observed.

But such thinking leads to some rather unlikely, counterintuitive conclusions about the nature of Karen's continuum, and my place upon it.

It seemed a bit much to base such thinking entirely on a simple vocal volatility, a trembling of the treble, a quiver of the bass.

I decided it was all rather excessive extrapolation on my part, induced by a few perplexingly peppery phrases sprinkled along a honeyed tongue. By the time I had analyzed the semiotics of the sound, it had already evaporated into the ether.

I peeled her fingers off my arm. "I need coffee," I said. "Then I'll help you worry about the world coming to an end."

Karen shook her head at me with a penetrating look of disappointment and resignation. It came either from the very depths of her soul or from the very surface. With Karen one could never be sure.

"I need coffee," I repeated, twisting wildly in my seat to search for the waitress.

Karen shook her winsome head again, and in that instant her usual playful self returned. She gave a goofy grin at my gyrations.

"Sit still, would you? You look like a two-year-old kid who misses his mommy."

The waitress was doing her best to meet my diminished expectations of the work ethic in the food service industry. I had spent the last ten minutes gesturing for more coffee in every sign language variant known to me. By this point even Koko the talking goddamn gorilla would have gotten the picture and poured me a nice steaming cup of joe.

"Let us bow our heads," I urged Karen. "Hold my hand and share my grief. We are gathered here today to lament the passing of our dear departed waitress."

"Come on, Ronnie," Karen said, "cut it out. You're not nearly as clever as you think, and the rest of us aren't nearly as dumb as you think."

"Christ, Karen, all I'm asking for here is some powdered bean with hot water all over it, and maybe a little cream. Fucking Golden West. Where's the fucking waitress?"

"Do you have to swear all the time?" Karen blissed at me.

"No, I don't. Where's the fucking waitress?"

"It's not cool to be so mean to them. She's just earning a living, you know."

"Not at this rate she isn't. Hey," I called out to the waitress with a gentle tone of persuasion. "Hey! Who do I have to kill to get a cup of coffee around here?"

Without responding nor even making eye contact the waitress poured the treasured liquid and vanished.

"You shouldn't joke about that," Karen said.

I swallowed the first sip of the nuclear fluid and scalded my tongue, palate and throat. The caffeinated revenge of a homicidal waitress.

"Shit, that's hot! Joke about what?" I asked. "And why not? I joke about everything."

"I know, that's just the problem. You shouldn't say things like who do you have to kill to get a cup of coffee."

"Oh? And why shouldn't I? Edify me, please."

"Because it's not funny. Violence isn't funny. It's immature to joke about it."

Arrgh, immaturity. This was a staple of Karen's accusation diet. It was the Texas School-Book Depository of her incessant character assassination. As the object of said accusation and assassination, I felt more than anything like a character in an absurdist play. Consider: Karen, hugging and drugging Karen, spinning and grinning Karen, feathery, anti-leathery Karen Anne Bellamy calling me immature. The mind reels. Salman Rushdie observed in *Midnight's Children*, which by the way I read before he ever got that famous *fatwa* flung at him, so don't go thinking I'm some wanna-be, Johnny-come-lately, rubberneck-at-the misery-of-celebrities type of guy; anyway he observed that there's nothing so humiliating as being condescended to by dolts.

Not that Karen was a dolt. I will grant as much gladly, because I am nothing if not generous in my praise of others. It is a defining characteristic of my humble personality.

Understanding Karen was like looking at a prism through a kaleidescope. Light there was, and plenty of it, but what the original image looked like one could only guess. Clever she could be, when it suited her. Charitable, certainly. Blissed out, constantly. But the very notion of Karen calling me immature from some vantage point high in the sky was so hideously contrary to all objective reality I confess I found myself at a loss to conjure up the necessary hyperbole to express my indignation. Mightily I was miffed.

"Immature? Do you really think it's advisable to go back over that well-explored terrain?" I asked Karen. "Because, frankly, I don't think it's a stone you want to throw, living in a house as glassy as yours."

Puzzled by the remark but ready for battle, she leaned forward and set her chin defiantly into one small palm, thereby squishing her features into an unexpectedly charming reincarnation of a Karen of a chubbier yesteryear. She gazed at me with objectionably attractive defensiveness.

"Why are you in such a grumpy mood?" she asked. "Just admit it wasn't a very nice thing to say."

I shifted uncomfortably in the sticky vinyl seat, painfully and regretfully adoring her perpetually moist lips and downy cheeks, which unmercifully exuded a softness and delicious innocence which would undoubtedly have been palpable from across a crowded ballroom.

"Sherpa," I said, invoking a pet name, the evolution and etymology of which is too intricate to explain in one volume, "Sherpa, baby, you must believe me that I did not actually intend to kill anyone for the coffee. We could have stayed here all night, perhaps for the rest of our lives, and I would not have killed anyone for that cup of coffee. I am a coffee pacifist. I am the Mohandas K. Gandhi of the java world. I am the Martin Luther King, Jr. of the espresso set. It's an expression, Sherpa. I wouldn't actually kill anyone."

"Well, it's impolite to say you would, and I wasn't making a big deal but you're the one making a big deal so now it's a big deal."

"Christ," I groaned, probing my burnt and dangling palate with my tastebud-tortured tongue to assess the extent of the internal damage. "Sorry I said anything."

Karen was mildly mollified. "Apology accepted," she said sweetly, curling a tendril of hair about an absent-minded forefinger.

"Of course," I hastened to add, "you understand that having been raised from infancy by a pack of well-meaning but wild wolves, I lack the table manners and grace which you ooze ever so effortlessly."

"Oh, fooey on yooey," she oozed, ever so effortlessly.

Chapter 2

Out to the godless cement of another endless American parking lot we wended our witty way. Karen did not own a car. I believe she considered them an unconscionable concession to the crass consumption imperative our bourgeois society dictates and demands, but I could be wrong about that. She never expressed her objection in those terms. I believe she did at some point stake out some superior moral high ground to the effect that cars are evil monsters whose sole role is to pollute by burning precious, irreplaceable fossil fuels.

And yet she was more than happy to con me into giving her rides all over town in my car. Her house was miserably far away from the university. There was a bus stop near her house, but the local transportation system was so woefully inadequate, it took her an hour and a half and two transfers to travel ten miles to school. Karen rode the bus only as a last resort. In the main she relied on housemates to get around — and for the last few months, on me.

I was the proud owner of a huge white 1972 Buick station wagon, a rickety, rattlesome jalopy that coughed its way around corners, black smoke pouring out its pores. It had an unreliable starter, a poorly rebuilt engine, chronic carburetor fatigue syndrome, and a bashed-in passenger door with a loose window which had slipped its moorings and now moved up and down quite independent of external stimuli. The driver's door never closed quite right unless you had the touch, which took me several months to master. The car was an eyesore, an environmental hazard, a bottomless money pit, and an endless pain in the ass, God bless it.

The car guzzled gas like a fish, which was why my good, goofy friend Hal originally dubbed it Great White. I bought it for fifty bucks off a family of migrant workers who had been living in it. It was a monstrous eight-cylinder power-steering beast, but it had character, presence and charisma. Other cars sensed its force immediately, and tended to get out of its way as soon as safely possible. When Great White would fail to start up again after stalling at an intersection, which happened so frequently I considered it just another part of the trip, it took several carloads of volunteers to jump out and push it to the nearest gas station.

Karen, oddly enough, adored Great White. She liked the bench seats, she liked the quaint staticky AM radio, she liked the serapé the previous owners had thrown over the front seat's exposed springs and decayed yellow foam. Karen loved to steer when I jumped out to push. Perched behind the massive steering wheel, her head bobbing and swaying to the AM music, or to none at all, she was adorably in charge. I suspect she enjoyed the sensation of motion *sans* motor, and actually created detours to the gas station to prolong her enjoyment.

Great White's rear bench folded down so that the entire back of the car became a bed. I kept foam pads and a sleeping bag back there. This was the feature that Karen liked most of all. As evening fell, she would encourage me to park in a natural setting; a woodsy turnout or a beach cliff parking spot were best. We would clamber like children into the way-back, pull out the sleeping bag, and then ...

... yes, and then Karen would conjure forth the mythological transformation that turned her pedestrian daily self into a latter-day Aphrodite: sublime, intoxicating and wet.

The saliva of memory chokes my throat. The perfect proportions and languid sensuality of Karen's body, shimmering and glistening in the moonlight, were an impossible fantasy of an utterly beautiful, purely sexual woman, who wanted only to touch and to be touched, to forget fear, and to laugh at mortality with a deep, prolonged, ecstatic twitch of the soul. In those magical hours, I became aware that lovemaking was Karen's most natural, most comfortable state of being, the activity on which she concentrated best. In those early days, it often seemed to me that Karen owed her entire existence solely to the amazing powers of my own delirious imagination.

Upon Karen's graceful belly fluttered a beautiful tattoo of a red, green and gold butterfly, its gossamer wings pointing both north and south in tempting allure. Karen's belly button formed in negative space the place where the head would have appeared. Just above, tiny, jaunty black antennae sprang forth.

It was a lovely, shy butterfly, seldom revealed to the outside world, a gorgeous chrysalis the wings of which were spread only for the privileged few who were permitted on the inside.

With Karen aboard, Great White's interior was transformed. The air became thick with the uncompromising funk, the humid stench of repeated sexual activity. It was a motorist's Garden of Eden, in which Karen and I were Adam and Eve, in that briefest of moments of timeless possibility, before the appearance of the evil serpent. The role of the serpent was played by the police on their nightly rounds, shining their headlights and flashlights into the car, carrying out the vital societal function of transforming impassioned lovers into shamed criminals.

We were cast out, fig leaves firmly affixed. Natural settings became forbidden for natural activities. We had to leave Great White to the loneliness of parked life. Like hibernating bears unclear on the concept, we headed indoors in the spring. Over the hills and through the woods, to Karen's house we go.

I did not feel at home there. I don't particularly feel much at home anywhere on this particular planet of yours, but Karen's hippie headquarters was an overcrowded, stultifying social greenhouse, hyperoxygenated and dense, and I am, socially speaking, a cactus.

Whenever possible, therefore, I lobbied Karen to spend the earlier hours of an evening's entertainment away from her resplendent residence, while inwardly strategizing a return to her nest of intimacies for the final act.

"Ronnie," Karen said as we got into Great White, "can you give me a ride somewhere?"

I didn't like the sound of that. I had a pretty good idea of how I wanted the evening to end, and a ride somewhere wasn't it.

"Where to?" I asked.

"The E. Club meeting," she said, slamming Great White's extremely fragile passenger door like Charles Atlas on a vision quest.

"Whoops," she said lightly, "I forgot, sorry."

"That's alright, Sherpa," I sighed. "I can't fault you for your natural exuberance."

She leaned over unexpectedly and kissed me on the cheek, one delicate hand sweeping the hair off my forehead.

"You try to be a big old bear, but I see right through you," she said, mixing me a metaphor.

"I am rather transparent," I admitted.

"Wait, no, you know what you are?" Karen asked.

"I have no idea," I said. "What am I, Karen?"

"You're an artichoke," explained the reigning world champion of the unexpected remark.

"An artichoke?"

"Yes, exactly. You're like a thorny thistle with a sweet heart."

I imagine I was supposed to take this as a compliment, but being as I could not help but imagine my own dripping red heart, dipped in your choice of either mayonnaise, clarified butter or balsamic vinegar, it was hard to feel touched.

I shot Karen the expression in my arsenal which most closely approximates a human smile.

"What is this E. Club of yours?" I asked.

"The Environmental Club, on campus?"

Listen: I've tried to train Karen not to pose declarative statements as questions. Truly I've labored. I despair of making any progress. You try it for a while, you'll see.

It's no small matter to bear the burden of linguistic superiority. My mother, who was born in Sweden, has always insisted on accurate use of the English language. She worked as a translator for a time, Swedish-English, English-Swedish, simultaneous on occasion.

I have always had an intimate relationship with words, irrigated in me through amniotic osmosis. I learned to read when I was three years old, and have never stopped. I liked to banter, debate and pontificate at an age when most of my peers were eating dirt recreationally.

"I didn't know you belonged to an Environmental Club," I said.

"I don't."

"Then why do you need to go to this meeting?"

"Because they're organizing the protest," Karen said.

"What pro — never mind," I sighed. "Sure, I'd be glad to give you a ride up there."

"It won't go on all night," she said, sliding her hand on my knee with charmingly suggestive innocence. "Probably like an hour. Maybe you could stick around and give me a ride back to my house."

"Maybe," I said. "Maybe not. Maybe I'll just head back to my apartment. Care to come over?"

"Gross."

It was difficult to dispute that eloquent point. "You want me to just wait around an hour? What shall I do, monitor the hall?"

"Ronnie," Karen said, leveling the eyes of the demon upon me, "I think you'll want to be there when I get out. I think you'll want to drive me home."

"Oh?"

"Yes," she said sweetly. "Oh, yes. I think I can guarantee that."

"Guarantee? That's pretty impressive. Is that a 100% guarantee?"

"100%."

"Hmm. 100% guarantee. Money back?"

She smacked my arm. "Just drive."

I drove.

Karen was a junior at the University of California at Santa Cruz, the selfsame institution which two years earlier had hurled a valueless diploma in my direction and unceremoniously kicked me out the front door like an authoritarian parent practicing tough love on a shoplifting son.

Karen and I originally traced different paths to UCSC. I came only because it squatted indifferently atop a short list of mediocre options for life after high school. College, living at home, menial labor, the armed services, crack salesman: pick your poison. As a state school, UCSC offered a relatively cheap education, and with my sister Eva already in school my parents were not eager to privatize me. It was also the best of the schools that accepted me, and it fit my other criteria: it was far enough from home to breathe, it was not excessively urban — quite the opposite — and it had a sizable literature department.

I initially conceived of myself as a literature major, a mistake I quickly corrected after my first literature class. The lit kids were big on pointless symbology, pathos, and ferreting out shrapnel of objectionable sexism and racism in century-old texts. A bonus was awarded for any evidence of homosexuality gleaned from the insipid crap. Things bottomed out when three earnest young women, each clearly weighing an intellectual conversion to lesbianism, presented a joint oral report on the watery suicide of Virginia Woolf in the form of a tragic play during which they did not speak. Not one word. The bewildered class applauded wildly. The jittery teacher actually wept. I ran my bayonet through a dummy in a daydreamed basic training exercise, and asked myself, "Self, what are we doing here?"

Karen, on the other hand, originally came to UCSC with a giddy sense of purpose, absolutely certain it was the right school for her. It represented everything good she could imagine. It has a national reputation as a haven for liberals, leftists and assorted fellow travelers. It positively radiates a counter-culture aesthetic, which Karen naturally craved.

Living museum relics haunt the campus. Dinosaur professors, bearded and bisexual herbivores from the 60's, forage through hipster departments like Environmental Studies, Women's Studies, and the History of Consciousness, whatever the hell that may be.

Oh, dear God, I almost forgot to mention: Jello Biafra, lead singer for the seminal punk band the Dead Kennedys, once attended UCSC for a whole quarter before he wised up, dropped out and took off for San Francisco. The kids at UCSC still bristle with pride at their brush with greatness. Maybe he was sitting on that bench — right over there, under the redwood tree — when the concept for *Too Drunk to Fuck* first germinated. Brrr. Doesn't the sheer creativity just make you shiver?

With all that going for it and the added attraction that it offended the sensibilities of her conservative parents, UCSC drew the little metal filament Karen like a multi-ton magnet.

And, of course, the natural setting is unparalleled. Karen and I agreed on that much, as has anyone else who has ever visited the place. I'm not much of one for the outdoors — no tree-hugger I — but I must admit that the majestic UCSC campus pained me with its beauty from the first time I visited it, years ago.

I was seventeen years old, a high school senior, sneeringly touring the state's campuses at Mom's side. Studiously, stubbornly I avoided the embarrassing appearance of enjoying anything whatsoever, but I had to admit that the vistas at UCSC were stunning.

Mom and I, along with fourteen other similar pairs and a tour guide, paused for a long moment in the courtyard of a pastoral little college. It was one of a set of nine or ten colleges, nestled like a necklace of some kind of fancy jewel my sister Eva would know the name of, deep within 2,000 acres of redwood forests and meadows. The gorgeous waters of the Monterey Bay, placid and welcoming, stretched out far below us, the white foam caps of the distant waves crashing in silent thunder, the glistening sun reflecting on the vast expanse of water like an incomparable Swedish sunset.

At least that's what Mom said, babbling on about the beautiful North Sea of her native land, her enthusiasm gushing like a geothermal Scandinavian geyser.

I liked the school even though Mom did. I couldn't help it.

A year later I stood in the same spot, enrolled and alone, wondering if it was raining in Eugene, Oregon, and if so, whether my sister Eva was using the stylish James Bond British black umbrella I had bought her when she first left for college two years before I did. I sat there in the oceanic sunshine, squinting, and composed what seemed to me a college and adult invitation to Eva to come visit me in my new digs. The photo side of the postcard was a black-and-white James Dean reproduction from the set of "Rebel Without a Cause". Can't go wrong with ol' Jimmy Dean. I've never met a woman, young or old, hip or prude, straight or dyke, living or dead, who didn't have a thing, however small or fleeting, for James Dean.

Eva he had always melted to a puddle of girly mush, but this time he didn't perform his usual magic. It took Eva a whole year to come visit me, and by then it was too late.

For what, I cannot say for certain.

Chapter 3

I drove Karen up to campus with the benighted aplomb of an aloof alumnus. We approached customs and Karen dug through her patchwork quilt sack for identification. The campus has only two vehicular entrances. After dark, fake cops armed to the teeth with imposing black flashlights guard the entrances with fearsome, potentially lethal orange traffic cones, permitting access only to wayfarers who can present student identification or some other compelling reason why they should be admitted — perhaps relatives already residing in the country.

The campus immigration policy has always amused me. I am sympathetic with the goal of protecting the tender young residents of the campus from outsiders of malicious intent, but there are so many holes in the system, it would make a good colander. There is nothing preventing would-be rapists from driving onto campus any time before the gates shut at dark. Perhaps the reasoning is that they are still in their coffins during the daylight hours. Busses also regularly storm through the blockade without scrutiny, offering those arsonists and assailants who are burdened with a sense of civic responsibility the opportunity to reduce pollution by enjoying the benefits of public transportation on their way to work. Finally, the school is ringed with approximately five hundred perimeter acres of trespassable lands with neither roads, blockades, nor fences, an easy climb through nighttime fields for a felonious bicyclist or cannibal hiker.

I have always suspected that the invisible masterminds of campus security are familiar with these flaws, but operate under the principle that the appearance of security is at least fifty per cent of the battle to deter it. This same theory is in operation at airports, World Cup stadiums, or anywhere large groups of people are threatened by smaller groups. And yet, the empirical evidence, readily acknowledged by experts, shows that no effort, no pre-positioned phalanxes of security guards, no stockpile of weaponry, no growling, sniffing German shepherds can truly do a thing to stop human beings from harming one another if that's what we truly desire.

Karen flashed her I.D. and we were waved through. Great White trolled up the long hill, thirsty for gas on a dry night. Campus cows stood under mothy lamplight in the corner of a large field, chewing their cuds contentedly and contemplating the coughing car. Karen managed to roll down her window, stick her head out, her hair flying in the wind, and yell out, "Hello, cows! Moo! Mooo! Hello! Hi! Hi, cow!"

Yes, she actually said that. I know, I know, you think I make this stuff up out of some malicious misogynistic impulse, but I'm just reporting the facts as they unfolded. Karen didn't merely greet the cows. She didn't just comment in passing on their placid, pastoral presence, or pause to admire their balletic grace. No, she felt compelled to commune with them, to merge her soul with their infinite bovine karma. In a way, I felt relieved. I had been spared considerable airfare. I no longer needed to fly to India to witness the spectacle of cows being revered as holy.

Our destination was the Student Center, a sparsely populated, nondescript building plopped in the middle of some gorgeous meadow or other. The first and last time I had been there was just after my arrival six years earlier. I had spent four of my first twenty-four collegiate hours standing in a long line for freshman identification card processing. I don't believe I had been in the building in the interim. It houses the do-gooder organizations, the save-the-world types, the protest-of-the-month clubs. Nobody with a life goes there.

I parked Great White and hesitated. I truly did not want to go inside. My motivation for waiting for Karen was clear. The concept of picking her up later was solid, but I had not yet fleshed out the details of the waiting-for-an-hour part. Various srategies for whiling away my hour as I avoided the den of horrors sprang into my mind and were discarded in turn. I could wander over to a coffee shop on campus, swallow some stale baked goods, and suffer through whatever the hip college music of the moment might be. But Karen didn't know precisely when she would be done, and it was in my own enlightened self-interest not to keep her waiting. Nor did I really want to go to any of the coffee shops on campus. I knew them all well, having been a habitue of each in my time. There's nothing more depressing than the graduate who keeps coming back to the familiar haunts, who can't move on. Better to emulate *The Graduate* and sink to the bottom of a silent, sarcophagal swimming pool.

I could sack out in the back of Great White, but that would involve clearing a space between all the fast-food bags and assorted other garbage accumulated in the weeks since Karen last lay there, or worse yet, cleaning the beast out. Karen suggested that I might go for a walk amid the natural splendor, but I am spiritually opposed to any form of exercise.

Karen sprang lightly out of Great White, slamming the poor door and humming a Crosby, Stills and Nash tune. "Suite: Judy Blue

Eyes," to be precise. Evie and I used to sing it together in our shared bedroom when we were kids.

"Change my life/make it night/be my baby," sweet Karen brown eyes beckoned, mangling the lyrics and extending her open palms to me, and there was nothing more for it. I followed like a meek little lamb. Baa. Baa.

Hello, lamb! Hello, hello there, little lamb, hi!

Bah.

We went in. The meeting was held in the large multi-purpose room. Protest planning for the cause *du jour* was in full swing. Large banners of blank butcher paper hung on the walls, aching to be scrawled upon. Purposeful young protesters went about pinning green ribbons on all comers. I did not want a green ribbon. I said so, but the yearning young face behind the ribbons launched into a lengthy explanation of their meaning and importance. I did not care one whit, but after a brief scuffle I permitted the intrusion, hating him and myself in equal measure.

Not very long ago I finally learned the hard way that I can either change the whole world to my way of doing things, or go along with behavior in which I do not find merit. Life is full of these unhappy little compromises. The battle to destroy personal liberty and individuality is not waged in a grand public arena by a fiendish, totalitarian government. It is waged on a daily, dreary battleground of pointless private decisions, the net effect of which is to bludgeon into submission any natural instincts for individual differentiation we may once have had. When I permitted the green ribbon to be pinned to my sweater, I permitted a tiny little piece of my true self to be crucified by the same pin.

There were far more of the yammering youngsters filing in than I had expected. I know how this sort of thing usually works: they put up some flyers, they make a few class announcements, and at the appointed hour, five or six true believers gather to convince one another of the righteousness of the cause and of the dire need to recruit new converts.

This particular protest meeting, however, was turning out to be a wholly different stripe of zebra. The head count, by my rough estimate, had already reached one hundred and was nearing the fire marshal's legal limit for standing or dancing occupancy. It was hard to imagine the serious, intense, beribboned youngsters breaking into dance, but then again these were hippies, and anything was possible. More eager beavers were spilled out into the courtyard, straining to see past the bottleneck at the door.

There followed a few minutes of good-natured jostling for seating, some rapid-fire, incoherent leaflet distribution, and crucial announcements that went unheard. In the confusion, I lost Karen. Like a disoriented victim of a flash flood, I concentrated on my own survival and abandoned Karen to her own fate. I found a solid perch on a broad, dry window-sill, well above water-level, inaccessible to ribbon-pinners, and surveyed the scene.

The chairs in the room, originally arrayed in a cheery, egalitarian circle, had now become a nuisance. Jumpy strong guys eager for some sort of action stacked the chairs along the walls. Sitting cross-legged on the floor soon became the order of the day.

Fifteen minutes late, the meeting began. It was called to order by a short, barefoot, poorly shaven kid wearing bicycle shorts. He squatted on his haunches on a table in front of the congregation, balancing on his toes like a baseball catcher. Squatting was a clever strategy which served several purposes. It made him seem down-to-earth and yet ready to spring into action. It set him high enough above the crowd to see and be seen, and most importantly it showed his bicycle leg muscles to good effect. He really did have spectacular bicycle muscles.

"My name's Gregory," bicycle-man said, "I'm the Chair of the E. Club."

I was tempted to answer, "Hi, Gregory" in mock Alcoholics Anonymous fashion, but I bit back the autonomic response. The last thing I wanted was to draw any kind of attention to myself. And the truth is, I've only seen parodies of 12-step programs, but never witnessed the real thing, and a mockery based on parodies skates on very thin ice.

"It's great to see so many of you here," Gregory said, thereby coining a brilliant phrase which will likely be emulated by meeting convenors for decades to come. Listen for it.

"I'm going to facilitate this meeting, if that's O.K. with everybody."

The point was hotly debated for a few minutes. A corner contingent contended that it wasn't right for men to have the position of power always, and that having a formal leader only served to replicate the exact sort of hierarchy against which we were fighting. Worse yet, Gregory was white. Further explanation of the relevance and importance of this damaging point was not deemed necessary. It was self-evident.

So some chick, some babe, some broad — it's my chronicle, I'll render it as I please — some token young woman by the name of Marcia was pressed forward into public service. She too was white, but the corner contingent tacitly permitted the transgression as the half loaf that is preferable to none. We were given to understand, courtesy of some not-very-subtle body language on the part of the corner contingent, that overlooking Marcia's pigment deficiency was an act of bountiful generosity. It was an extraordinary expression of their reasonable goodwill and willingness to compromise just this once for the good of the group. I scrutinized the room. Not surprisingly, everyone I could see was white. How shocking. It's a white town, a white school, and this, after all, was environmentalism, the whitest movement since the Ku Klux Klan.

"O.K.," Gregory said, his authority a bit shaken but his haunches still bulging, "Marcia is going to co-facilitate and be the timekeeper. Is that O.K. with everybody?"

That was O.K. with everybody.

"I guess a lot of you don't know the full story of what's gone on until now, so I guess the first thing we're going to do is go through that."

"Introductions!" he was heckled.

"Oh, right, introductions. O.K., why don't we go around the room and everybody say their name and add something, anything, whatever, about themselves?"

This was a very bad idea. It took sixteen minutes, by my close accounting, and served no purpose other than to help me locate Karen. She was leaning against a concrete pillar with her peerless derriere, supporting the structure like a sybaritic Samson.

Most of the introductions were on the order of, "Hi, I'm Kelly, I'm a freshperson —" more on the controversy of class designation in a moment — "and I just think this whole development plan really sucks."

There were a few of the oratory variety: "I'm Bernard, I'm a senior, uh, sort of. I was last year. I think we should strike, right now, the whole school, shut this fucking place down. I've got some leaflets here, if everybody could pass them around, thanks, here, and pass these around too, and there's a strike meeting right after this meeting for people who are willing to get arrested, to learn how to do civil disobedience, so stick around because we have to ACT if we want to get something done, not just talk about it!!"

Moments later: "I'm Karen, I'm a junior, and I think it's beautiful that we've all come together for this cause, and I just hope the energy can stay great the way it's been so far."

Yes, sir, that's my baby. No, sir, don't mean "baby".

More names, more faces. Many freshmen, more than I would have expected. Ah, yes, now, the proper term for a new student, one who has not yet become a sophomore. This is a point of hot contention at UCSC. Entire symposia are devoted to such subjects. Hey, don't laugh. This stuff matters, dammit!

"Freshman" is clearly out of the question, for reasons I shouldn't have to explain to a sensitive, educated adult like yourself. "Freshperson" is a terribly awkward substitute, an insult to the ears. Now and again one hears the truly peculiar term "frosh", but I suspect it's an East-Coast preppie import, a transplant which has definitely not taken. "Incoming student" isn't accurate once school begins, and one can be also an incoming student as a junior transfer, compounding the confusion. "First-year student" generally seems to win out. I'm proud to say I have never once uttered that absurd term. Hal and I once coined the term "freshmeat", but in an entirely different context.

My turn.

"I'm Ron. I'm an alumnus. I enjoy the company of my inflatable sheep."

I scored a few laughs, a few scowls, but mostly looks of confusion and concern for my well-being. Leader Gregory was not amused, but now Karen had finally located me, and beamed a proprietary grin across the room at me.

Presently Gregory regained the floor. He shifted his weight. His great, tireless haunches flexed once, in a mighty, indifferent gesture which I interpreted as a flawless nonverbal expression of his grand contempt for anyone unable to squat like a baseball catcher for hours on end.

"So now I'll kind of fill everybody in on what's been going on, then we'll talk about what to do about it. So," he rushed on, having learned the hard way not to wait for the group to concur with his process, "you all probably know that the A.U.E, that's American United Electrical Co., has filed plans to develop what they call a 'science research park' on Deerpark Meadow, behind College Nine."

Boos, hisses and jeers.

"Right. And I guess you know the U.C. Regents have given preliminary approval to the plans. So now they've issued what's called a Draft Environmental Impact Report ... "

There followed a lengthy logistical lecture, which I did not bother to follow. Having spotted me, Karen decided to mosey on over. As Gregory spoke, she was the only creature in motion in the whole room. All eyes followed her with listless curiosity, modulated only by the sharper inspections of a few avid young gentlemen with excellent taste.

Karen crawled up and eased herself behind me on the window sill. At first her intrusion was an innocuous one. But then, in the darkened shadows of the windowsill, she leaned forward, her hot breath on my throat, and began to knead the inside of my near thigh with an obscene, caressing fist.

Within a few moments this kneading resulted in a maddening but predictable physical response, one I found highly inappropriate for the time and place.

"Sherpa," I whispered huskily, "stop it. You're killing me."

"Oh dear," she whispered back, close into my ear. "I'm so sorry, baby. Of course I'll stop. I wouldn't want to make you uncomfortable."

She leaned back, smiling coyly, and traced a floral pattern on the window. The room was damp from the humid presence of one hundred humans in close proximity. Beads of precipitation were forming on the ceiling.

"Hey," I whispered to Karen, "you just called me 'baby'. I thought I told you not to do that."

"Ronnie," she leaned forward, growing serious, "what's this guy saying?"

"If you'd listen instead of distracting others with your feminine wiles, you might learn something," I said.

"Wiles?" she asked.

"Ssssshh," we were instructed.

Chapter 4

Gregory's voice came back into focus. "As far as I can tell, the City Council is on our side. The County Board of Supervisors is definitely not, but it's not really clear if either body has jurisdiction. The University of California is its own state entity, so it doesn't really have to have things approved by local government. Other questions?"

A pale kid with an appalling monstrosity of a nose stood up. His head was shaven. Anyone with a beak like that should have hair as long as possible, as a form of damage control. For proof of this theory, I offer Howard Stern.

"My name's M'Bopape, and I heard that what they're calling a 'science research park' is really a plutonium processing facility."

I know, I know, you're wondering how a white kid from Berkeley ends up with an unpronounceable African name. I could explain it to you, but the effort would wear us both out. I beg you, try to have more faith in my stereotypes: he was a hippie, plain and simple. Further explanation should no longer be necessary.

Gregory said, "I've heard a lot of people saying that about the plutonium, but until we get some hard evidence, I think we should consider it a rumor and not spread it."

"Check it out," M'Bopape continued, undeterred. "The University of California manages the Lawrence Livermore Laboratory, which has done 90% of the research for nuclear weapons in the history of the country, right? And ever since the collapse of the Soviet Union, end of the Cold War, all that, they've been getting a lot of pressure to change their mission, right? So they start converting to standard civilian research up there, which means they need a new place to process the plutonium. I mean, you know they're going to keep doing that somewhere. It's not like they're ever really going to give up on that part of their mission. But they've been under public and media scrutiny up there for years now and they're sick of it. Best place to go? Off in the deep woods in little Santa Cruz, where no one can see you."

These unfounded, paranoid remarks precipitated a sudden hubbub, like an angry beehive stirred by a bear's paw. Gregory called for attention once, twice, and then rapped on the table with knocking knuckles. The hive continued its undiminished buzzing until co-facilitator Marcia said, "O.K., people," quietly and distinctly. The little twerps all shut up, falling all over themselves to support a woman in a leadership position, however minor or unearned.

"I think we should hear from people who haven't spoken," Marcia said, "and that guy in the way back, yeah, you with the red flannel, he's had his hand up for a long time. Go ahead."

The guy with the red flannel stepped forward. He had very straight, very black hair gliding smoothly down in back, well past his shoulder blades without a ripple or curl. His face was hard to read, with olive skin I associate with Latin America, but that ancestry didn't seem quite right. He was dressed without affectation, which was quite an achievement in that crowd. Under the aforementioned red flannel was a simple blue T-shirt. Standard jeans and sneakers completed the outfit. He studied the crowd for a moment through round wire-frame glasses. He was a good-looking kid.

"My name is John Lone Pine," he said, in a voice curiously devoid of inflection.

Ah, I thought, an Indian.

Ah, Karen thought, a Native American.

"I'm with Friends of Big Mountain," he said quietly. So quietly, in fact, that I misunderstood him and had to have Karen repeat it for me. I was sure I had heard him say "I'm friends with this mountain." That might not have been such an outlandish remark, given that I was in the Land of the Hippies, but I wanted to be sure. I liked this kid. I didn't want to have to write him off so quickly. I didn't know what Friends of Big Mountain was, but Karen seemed familiar with it. I leaned forward a bit to catch his next subdued remarks.

"I don't know much about environmental impacts and city council meetings and lawsuits and all of those things people were talking about. None of that is important to me."

Nor to me.

"What is important is that the place where they want to build this building is a sacred place. It was a burial ground for the Ohlone tribes. It would be the worst kind of desecration to build this evil project there. White people enslaved the Ohlone, lied to them, gave them diseases, and killed them. Now they want to dance on their graves. Even in death their spirits have no peace. This is a sacred place, and I'm ready to give my life to defend it. Are you?"

He sat down. There was a scattering of guilty applause which crescendoed into a thunderstorm. Abruptly I realized this was the second time that evening I had heard something about the Ohlone Indians. Maybe Karen had mentioned them. I turned to her to verify my memory. Her eyes were misty and her face angelic. I didn't bother

her.

"Alright," said Gregory, our fearless leader, "If anybody came here unsure how they feel about this fucked-up project, I think we've now heard about twenty excellent reasons to oppose it. So now I think we should move into figuring out how exactly to do that. There's some stuff that has to get done right away, and some stuff that's more long-term, and everybody can do something to help out. I propose we break up into groups and split up the work that needs to get done."

He pulled out a sheet of paper with a list of the committees to be formed. The little bastard. He had planned the whole thing in advance. I could readily see that the first hour of the meeting had been a charade, a pep rally designed to inflate Gregory's massive ego and then funnel us down his predetermined path.

He read from his list: "Campus organizing, petitioning, downtown organizing, faculty and staff recruitment, media, publicity, project research. Anything else?"

"Fundraising," someone yelled out.

"Fundraising, good point. We're up against a multi-million dollar establishment. We're going to need whatever we can get, especially if we decide on the lawsuit. Anything else?"

A frail young woman spoke up. She was an unctuous little Karen-clone, with the same hairdresser, haberdasher, and general aesthetic sensibility, but without a trace of the grace and sensuality of the original.

"I can't believe no one has, like, said this?" Karen Junior said. "We absolutely have to totally have a committee to like, work as a liaison, like with groups of color? I mean, look around you. Everybody's like, white?"

I found this a particularly odious remark. It was trivial, irrelevant and stupid, and it was old news. Moreover, if John Lone Pine is white then I'm a baboon. Worst of all was Faux Karen's galling mistreatment of our precious English language. Now, I recognize that "liaison" is a difficult word to pronounce correctly, being a relatively recent import from that wacky French language. The final syllable may be nasally absorbed in Gallic fashion, but that sort of performance is usually reserved for the truly snooty. The rest of us try to be satisfied with something on the order of "lee-AY-zn," with the final syllable partially swallowed in muted, guilty acknowledgement of our inability to handle it properly. But this girl — sorry, woman — had mangled the word so that it came out sounding as follows: "LIE-us-on." Uggh. And those hideous declarative statements posed in interrogative fashion! You know how I feel about those. My skin crawled. My scalp tingled. My palms itched. My girlfriend applauded.

"I think that's a very important issue," Gregory lied. "Maybe the campus organizing committee should be in charge of that."

He was shouted down by cries of "No! Separate committee!" He buckled immediately. He really wasn't much of a leader, old Gregory. He may have been a terror on the bike paths, but faced with any verbal opposition he tended to retreat like General Custer at Little Big Horn. Actually, I'm not sure if Custer even had a chance to retreat, surrounded as he was, but I find the Indian metaphor irresistible.

Gregory strove to save face with a rapid-fire succession of command activities: setting the next meeting time, designating committee meeting zones within the room, distributing a phone list which had been photocopied during the meeting — an impressive little technological coup — and adjourning the meeting to a round of half-hearted applause.

The floor of the room quickly transformed into a flurry of confused, chatty commotion. The event now seemed like some misbegotten offspring of a political party convention and a high school reunion. Purposeful politicos who had sat still for the better part of two hours were now ready for some action. Friends greeted friends, strangers struck up pointless, nervous conversations, and committees met like mad. Gregory dashed from one group to the next, desperately fearful of losing control.

I was ready for some action myself. I turned to Karen to see if this dog had earned his bone.

"Time to go," I said.

"Wait," she said, "I have to go to a committee meeting. You can't just sit through the general meeting and not go to a committee meeting."

"Yes, I can."

"Well, I can't." She clambered down from the window sill.

"Karen," I said, pulling my keys out of my pocket, "I've been patient. I've been a good boy — you know how I hate all this political bullshit. It's been almost two hours. It's time to go. In ten minutes I shall turn this key, rev Great White's engine several times, curse, restart it, and head for home. With or without you."

"Oh, come on," Karen pleaded, "be a little more patient." She leaned forward and whispered, "Don't worry, just wait for me and I'll take good care of Great White's engine."

I ask you: what could I do? The temptress had spoken. The siren

26

had sung. I was in thrall. I was in for a penny, in for a pound. I was in for a long night.

Karen wandered off in search of the committee that best matched her biorhythms. I stayed on my sill, safe and secure, observing the wreckage and trying to avoid eye contact with overzealous purveyors of volunteer guilt.

Some minutes later Karen returned, with Gregory in tow.

"Him," Karen said, pointing at me.

I winced. What deviltry was afoot?

"Hey, guy," Gregory said, speaking directly at me without introduction, "she said you're a good writer. The media committee is kind of fucking up. Could you help them out?"

I gave Karen what I hoped was a devastating, withering look.

"I would prefer not to," I said. This was meant to be both a passive, polite, but firm refusal, as well as a witty reference to Melville's "Bartleby the Scrivener."

Gregory leapt cleanly over both meanings like a track hurdler in prime form. "The media committee's in the corner, over there, near the trash can."

"I see," I said. I sat patiently, hoping that, having asked what he came to ask, Gregory would now depart. None of us moved.

"Come on, Ronnie," Karen said, "they need somebody who's really smart, and good with words. Please? Come on. Please please pretty please?"

Ah, shit.

The media committee consisted of two drab, innocuous youngsters of muted intelligence. I could see on first inspection why they had ended up near the trash can. Gregory introduced me to Alex and Marianne, and departed. The dynamic duo gazed at me listlessly.

"What are we doing?" I asked.

"What?" Alex asked.

"What's our mission, our goal?"

"Mission?" Alex asked.

"This is the media committee, is that right?"

"Yeah," Alex said.

"Is there a particular task this committee ought to be performing?"

"A press release," Marianne blurted out.

"Ah! O.K., a press release," I said. "Let's get started."

"We kinda already did," Marianne said. She produced a ragged, smudged sheet of flimsy paper embedded with absurd, inscrutable little chicken scrawls of tiny, old-fashioned type. Along the margins, like a surveyor's markings at a busy intersection, could be seen pencilled corrections, arrows, and circles. The whole thing appeared to be — and was in fact — a carbon copy of an original typed on a manual typewriter with fading ribbon which had been replaced in mid-paragraph. The incompetence was staggering.

"This is what you've done so far?" I asked, just to be certain.

"Yeah," Alex said. It was to be his last contribution to the conversation. At least he went out on a high note.

I read the draft press release. I present it to you now as it was then, without emendation or alteration of any sort. I saved it for posterity, and lo! posterity is upon me.

```
TO: Whoever it may consern
FROM: The E. Club The Enviromentalist Club

     This press release is about the Enviro is to enform
you that we don't like have taken a position against
the Dearpark Meadow project. There are many reasons
for our position which we have taken, which would be
to many numerus to mention. Let's just say fxx For
starters In the first place, p;utonium is a very
badidea. 2. There are dead native indians buried in
the ground their. 3. THe enviroment of the world is
in danger, and we cant just let it go away. We have
to protect it the enviroment.
```

"That's as far as we've gotten," Marianne said.

"It's a start," I said, careful not to specify of what sort. The real outrage of the whole matter was that these dimwits youngsters had been admitted to a reasonably competitive public university. Two earnest young applicants had been denied admission so that room could be made for Alex and Marianne. One could only wonder what utter dolts the other two applicants must have been.

"Listen," I said, "maybe we should try to type this on a computer. It might be easier to edit."

Alex looked as though I had shot his collie. He put a reassuring hand on his trusty, rusty Smith-Corona manual typewriter, manufactured circa 1955, half obscured under a pile of scratch paper. Why the man owned a manual typewriter and brought it to meetings with him was a mystery I did not have the energy to unravel.

"I've got a PowerBook," I said.

"What?" Marianne asked, doing her best Alex impression.

"A portable computer. In the trunk of my car. I'll go get it." I dashed off before opposing viewpoints could be raised, pausing to give Karen another dirty look. She beamed back from the comfort of her agitated little committee, clearly pleased with the progress of her machinations against me.

The evening had grown chilly, and the fresh, cool air was bracing. The night sky bloomed with thousands of unexpected stars. I took a deep long drink of oxygen. My head clearing, I was moved to a sudden resolve not to let myself grow too angry with a couple of kids whose great crime in life was a gift for turgid prose. They were probably science majors who faked their way through the world of words, much as I had faked my way through their peculiar universe of vectors, variables and cellular mitosis.

I grabbed the PowerBook out of Great White's secret trunk compartment. The computer was a gift from my parents, a tool to ease my way through college, and it had indeed served me in good stead in my studies. Since graduation, however, I had not had much occasion to use it.

Early in my endless post-graduation job search I had concocted a wondrously attractive, fabulously false resumé using the desktop design program. If only the content of the resumé had been any kind of match for its form, I might be a wealthy man today.

Once in a rare while, when a stray thought which seemed worthy of being recorded passed my way, I pulled the computer out. On the whole, however, I took it on faith that if a thought was worth recording, my brain would make the effort automatically.

For a brief interlude I used the PowerBook to indulge a passing fancy of writing short stories. At times I even found merit in my work. But the concentration required, the mental discipline, was far too great for my meager fortitude. Once, on an obscure whim, I showed Karen a few of my stories. I had shared them with no one else, not even my sister Eva. Karen loved them. She clucked on and on about them like a mother hen.

Strangely, it was her reaction that more than anything caused me to stop writing. This puzzles me, because one might expect that my fragile writing ego could not have sustained negative feedback, but it was the very opposite which destroyed my will to continue. Odd.

Still, I lugged the computer with me wherever I roamed, armed against the possibility of a word processing emergency — which was exactly what I now faced.

I had a rule against using the computer in a public place. Not because I feared theft, but because there are none so repulsive as the pretentious little goblins who carry their conspicuous little laptops into every coffee shop, typing a pathetic few words every few minutes and peering about to see who might have noticed.

If I'm ever that desperate for attention, stab me in the eyeball with a toothpick.

I had strongly resolved never to commit the social crime of flagrant display of personal technology, a felony subject to a fine up to $10,000 or public ridicule, whichever is worse. The press release, however, seemed like an appropriate public use. I did not feel I was countermanding my code by pulling out the PowerBook.

These opinions regarding computer use I do not flaunt casually. I have earned them the hard way. I've paid a due or two. I spent the entire summer after my junior year staring down a computer, stuck like a fly in amber in a horrific mind-numbing condition known colloquially as "employment". At my side stood the silent sentinels which were my essential resource: reference books listing the nation's banks, A-Z. Before me, a small screen impatiently, incessantly prompted me to enter, in turn, the name, address, phone, assets, and president of every bank in the country. The presidents, incidentally, were all men, as were my co-workers. This monogendered office roster created a stale, listlessly macho environment. We tried our best to swagger with clerkish abandon, but there's not much point being macho when there ain't no babes around to macho at.

Every day I arrived late and tired, ate my morning muffin, drank the first of seven or eight coffees, read the paper, shot the proverbial shit with my cubicle-mates, ever pushing the edges of propriety and promptness and delaying the onset of the daily drudgery. But New Mexico or North Dakota always beckoned, their banks eager to be entered into the master memory banks of my computer.

I confess to you now two things: first, that after working on New York for an entire month, I deleted all of its files, through a series of blunders so intricate I wonder if it may not have been an act of subconscious sabotage. Second, I report with a buoyant burst of self-esteem that my supervisor once confided to me that the company could have easily bought all of the bank information on disk, but hiring me to enter the information by hand was just a slight margin cheaper.

I slammed Great White's trunk and trotted back to the Student Center. In the distance I caught a momentary silhouette of Alex, shuffling away from the building with his typewriter case under one arm. I did not know him very well at all, but it seemed to me that I read a sad resignation in his body language, as though the humiliation he had just experienced at my hands was nothing new to him.

The sight gave me pause. Had I been too unkind? Was I truly so different from him? We both lugged useless mechanical writing devices around with us, hoping against hope to wrest the grail of human emotion from the fortified castle of language.

Enough morbid stargazing, I told myself. You've got work to do. You hold a position of chief responsibility for the creation of a proper press release for an organization to which you don't belong, in conjunction with a group of people you actively dislike, on behalf of a cause for which you care nothing.

I gazed at the heavens and heaved a heavy sigh, wondering why I was bothering with the whole ordeal. And then, as though hearing a distant strain of a heavenly Beethoven symphony, perhaps the incomparable Ninth, I was calmed by the inspirational memory of nine little words which might yet become our organizational anthem:

"In the first place, p;utonium is a very badidea."

Back inside, I powered up and sat down to render our little missive into passable English. Marianne leaned over my shoulder, muttering, shifting about, chewing her fingernails and spitting them out. When a particularly long one landed on the screen, my patience bottomed out.

"Listen," I said, "could you do me a favor? Find out from Gregory where we can output and fax this from."

"Fax? Why do we have to use a fax? We could just send them all letters."

"Yes, we could," I admitted. "We could also hand-deliver clay tablets that have been impressed by stylus with cuneiform hieroglyphics and then baked in a mud oven for three days. I suppose it's a matter of making the best use of available technology."

Marianne's face was a blank. I became strongly convinced I was having a conversation with myself.

"Please," I asked nicely, "could you just ask Gregory where we can find a fax?"

She trotted off obediently. I finished off the press release, leaving blank a few spots where I was unsure of the factual details. Presently Marianne returned with Gregory.

"Hey," he said, "a PowerBook. Cool."

He read the press release off the screen.

"Wow," he said, "that's great." He filled in the factual blanks, dictating with irritating confidence. I entered the changes, popped a "— 30 —" at the end of the page, and we were done.

"What's that '30' for?" Gregory asked.

"It's the standard journalistic notation used to inform the reader that he has reached the end of the press release."

"He or she," Gregory responded in an automatic absent-minded correction. I grit my teeth.

"Wow," he repeated. "Where did you learn all that?"

"Not sure," I said. The truth was, I had probably learned it when Mom worked as an editorial free-lancer, but I didn't have the energy to go into the necessary detail.

"I thought it was common knowledge," I said. "Have you got access to a fax?"

"Oh, yeah, easy money. There's one in the E. Club office upstairs."

"Good," I said. "Now, we're going to need to know fax numbers for all the media outlets. Marianne, can you find a phone book, call them all and find out their fax numbers?"

"No need, guy," Gregory said. "We're compatible. There's a Mac in the E. Club office upstairs, with a fax/modem. All the media numbers are programmed in."

"Great! That's perfect," I enthused, and I don't enthuse often. The job had just been reduced from what might have been several hours' work to a few minutes at the most.

I said, "If you've got a floppy up there I'll just copy this over and send it out."

"Cool," Gregory said, and tossed me the keys. "Room 204."

"Wait," Marianne said, trotting after me like a faithful puppy, "I don't get it."

I was now in an expansive mood. We went up to the E. Club office and I slowly and patiently demonstrated the mysterious process of digital communication through the miracle of fiber-optics.

" ... and that's all there is to it," I said, concluding the demonstration.

"Rob," my charming little sidekick said, "where did you learn how to do all that?"

"It's Ron. I don't keep track of the source of everything I learn. Maybe I was born with the knowledge. Where did you learn all the things you know, Marianne?"

Dumb question.

"How do you know they got it?" she asked.

"Remember the message which read 'fax completed'?"

"Yeah," she said slowly, the wheels of cogitation spinning mightily in her brain, "but that just says it was sent. It doesn't say they got it."

I paused. "No, it doesn't. But it's self-evident. They got it."

"But how do you know?"

I sighed. "Your question mystifies me, Marianne. It goes to the heart of epistemology, of existentialism: how do we know anything has occurred which we have not directly experienced? How do I know there is a Bulgaria? How can I be sure that the Ohlone Indians existed? I've never met any. The answer is, I take it on faith. The fax has been received."

"But how do you know for sure?"

I groaned inwardly. "If you want confirmation, feel free to call all the media outlets and ask if they've received any faxes lately from obscure student groups with unclear agendas." Before she could digest this possibility, I shot down the stairs, hoping to shake her.

This business of asking "How do you know?" is a popular sport. It was a big favorite of Karen's. She posed it as a challenge to any assertion I ever made. If I could not track down the source of my information, that was clear evidence that I did not know whereof I spoke. It was a galling little habit which tended to inhibit the free exchange of ideas — my ideas, most specifically.

I found Karen and we were finally able to drive a wooden stake through the heart of that meeting of the undead.

On the way to Karen's house we talked about the meeting and the Deerpark plan. Karen found the meeting exciting and the project horrifying. I found the meeting alternately boring, irritating, and insufferable. On Deerpark I was neutral.

"But it's such a huge project," Karen said, "how can you not be against it? It's going to be bigger than any four colleges, combined."

"How do you know?" I asked with feigned innocence.

"Because — oh, no, I'm not falling for that one!"

We both laughed.

Karen elaborated on her theme of excessive growth, and threw in some new, damning information, including additional evidence she had garnered concerning the plutonium processing facility and the Indian burial ground.

"Alright, alright" I said throwing my hands up, sending Great White into a mild fishtail spin, "it's a bad idea. It's a sucky project. It should never have been proposed. Millions of people will suffer severely if it is built. Happy?"

"Whoo-weee!!" Karen hollered.

I raised an eyebrow as we rounded the last corner for Karen's home.

"I think this is historical," Karen said.

"What is?"

"I think this is the first argument between us I've ever won."

"Shit," I scoffed, "this doesn't count. This isn't really an argument."

"Yes, it is."

"No, it isn't."

"Yes, it is."

"No, it isn't."

"Yes, it *is*, Ronnie. Listen to us!"

"No, it *isn't*, Sherpa. Don't listen to us!"

Karen laughed and clapped her hands like a child.

"I'm so glad you came tonight and helped out and everything. You know," she said playfully, "sometimes I think that, despite everything, I might really like you."

"Why would you?" I asked, suddenly verbalizing a question that had been troubling my overactive paranoia for some time. I parked and turned to face her as Great White's engine began to tick his song of arrival.

I said, "I'm not much of a catch, you know. I have neither money nor ambition. I'm not the handsomest feller in town. I'm surly, insensitive, condescending, politically incorrect and crude."

"True," she said thoughtfully, "but you make me laugh."

We went inside, hands clasped in quiet contemplation. She lit up her room with dozens of candles and put on some Marvin Gaye, and we played cards. I cheated and lost. Karen laughed, and then, slowly, patiently and passionately, she made good on her 100% guarantee.

In the candlelight, the red wing of Karen's butterfly tattoo glowed like a delicious apple picked at its ripest. I tasted the forbidden fruit with the delight of a dusty field worker at a harvest festival. It was a juicy apple, sweet and succulent as late summer, with a strong and heady scent of blossom.

Many hours, perhaps days or weeks later I found myself again, floating on her bed, thinking only that if I died right then, it would be alright with me. Life would get no better.

Chapter 5

Karen woke me with a cup of the coffee she knew I needed, and spread the morning newspaper open in front of my sleepy eyes.

"Wake up to a bright new world, sweetie," she said. "You're famous."

The press release had been picked up. It had landed on the front page, as the core of an article on the Deerpark project.

"Goddamn," I said, "we got lucky."

"We, is it now?" Karen smiled. Her hair, wet from the shower, was turbaned in an orange towel piled high on her head. A second orange towel was wrapped around her body like a sarong, knotted off directly above her sternum with a loose, insouciant twist that barely kept things together. She stepped over to the dresser. I lay on my back, watching the contours of the towel conform to her succulent posterior as she bent over to search through her underwear drawer. She stood back up, and as she turned, the towel fell from her body in a loose, carefree crumpling; and I swear to you by all that is holy that despite the early hour, despite my fatigue, despite the wear and tear of the night before, despite the coarse emotional shell behind which I hide; I swear to you that the sight of her then was as close to a religious experience as I have ever had.

She sensed it. She stepped to the bed and loosened her turban so that her hair cascaded across her breasts, framing them flawlessly, without intention. She was an irresistible living incarnation of Botticelli's Venus, smelling of organic shampoo. She crawled onto the bed, smiling, and peeled the covers off my naked body. She smiled softly at the sight, grazed her right breast across my exceedingly dry lips, and leaned over to form a cradle with the infinite wisdom of her loving hands.

"You're beautiful," she whispered. "You made me happy last night."

"Unnnhh," I noted.

"But I've got to go to school."

"Nnnnnhh," I moaned. "Stay."

"Jonathan's leaving in five minutes." Jonathan was apparently some form of housemate. "He's going up to campus and I have to catch a ride. I have to go to European History. I've already missed it twice."

I reached out a mute hand to caress whatever was within reach.

"Poor sweetie," Karen said, petting me one last, lingering time. "Five minutes just isn't enough time."

"Fuck European History," I managed to croak.

"I think the Ohlone would agree with you there," she said, and swung quickly away from the bed and into her clothes.

Painfully and regretfully, I banished the hope of a morning dalliance from my mind.

"Pick you up after school?" I asked.

"Sorry, I can't. Tonight I've got a section, then I'm in the library until late."

"Tomorrow?"

"I can't. I've got two Deerpark meetings. Plus petitioning. And the day after that is that press conference kind of thing, and then another night meeting. You wouldn't want to come along for any of it, would you?"

"Pass," I said.

"Well, I'm not sure when we can get together, Ronnie. I'm just kinda busy right now." She shoved a few books into her backpack and slung it on her shoulder. The weight of the strap tugged at her blouse and pulled it gently off her round, sweet and freckled shoulder.

"I yearn for thee," I said.

"I'll call you," she said. "Congratulations on the article. Bye." She gave me a quick kiss on the forehead and was gone.

Shit. I hated being left behind in her house. I could hear one thousand and one housemates scurrying about, just beyond the bedroom door, spying on me. I decided to try to wait them out. Was it too much to hope that they might all have some place they needed to go mornings?

Karen's awful, creaky, drafty converted Victorian house was a horrible crowded hippie airport, new flights constantly arriving and departing. Snide leftist political cartoons were plastered all over the refrigerator, the walls, the bathroom, even the ceiling. Cultural artifacts from bygone decades were on display everywhere in a self-conscious display of fake regression to a fantasy childhood that never could have existed. The display was meant as evidence of the aloof, sardonic adulthood of the decorators, but instead blared their insecurity and arrested adolescent development.

In one single, giant living room, over, around, and between dilapidated couches and frayed easy chairs, the museum of kitsch was on display: Sesame Street puppets, lava lamps, cereal box toys, bean bag chairs, Sonny and Cher album covers, fast food tray liners, Barbie dolls, coloring books, 50's posters extolling the virtues of chemicals, period pieces culled from periodicals instructing house-wives in the finer points of properly pleasing hubby on his arrival home from a hard day's work. Everything was so unhip, it was hip. Every day brought new mementos and several pounds of the finest Snide, fresh from the fish market.

"Check this out, this is so cool. I used to have the whole Kiss collection. Kiss rules."

I tire so of witnessing people beat up on the 70's for cheap laughs. I am aware that the 70's have now earned their rightful turn in the pantheon of decades past as a time to be mocked and laughed at with the aloof campy irony which characterizes American cultural nostalgia. But when I was a young'un I lived the 70's, and there was no irony. It was the only decade available to us at the time, and there was nothing ironic about it.

Plenty of things were goofy, sure. And everyone mocked what everyone else was wearing, doing or saying, which after all is one of the great privileges of membership in the human race. But when we laughed at the music or styles it was not with the aloof security of mocking it from two decades later, because we were secretly afraid that we were Wrong; we quivered in daily fear that what everyone else was wearing was truly cool, and that we were secretly, desperately and irreparably uncool.

But the current sport of mocking the 70's, or any decade now safely behind us, from the lofty perspective of distant years later does not impress me, because it carries no risks. It's like an octogenarian mocking the fashions of an eighth-grader.

"Oh, I love this Charlie's Angels thing! Let's make like a little diorama of the three of them."

"Look what I just got. Pat Boone's 'Greatest Hits'. I model my life after him. I'm serious."

The gutless punks. Nothing in that house was displayed on its own merits. No one was willing to put something up and run the horrible risk of saying: *I like this*. The entire house was one massive, failed attempt at irony.

I hated it the first moment I laid bored eyes on it. But I was the New Guy, I was trespassing, I tried to be good. I said hello when introduced, which was seldom. I laughed at banal remarks, I pretended to be amused by collages of Bazooka Joe cartoons, but as soon as I could, I fled to Karen's room, with its entirely different strain of unconventional interior decorating.

Karen's sensibility was deep spiritual hippie, punctuated with touching little reminders of the tenderly spoiled teenager she had been not so long before. A large golden paisely fabric was tacked to the ceiling, billowing gently down in swooping folds, suggesting a sultana's harem. The floor was covered with Japanese tatami mats. On the large bed lay thousands of pillows, Snoopy-and-Woodstock sheets, a unicorn bedspread, and several stuffed animals. Among them were a yellow bear, a brown dog, and a greenish furball which defied identification. The animals were loyal little subjects, battered by long, docile years of hugging companionship, support and love for their insecure queen.

Moving away from the bed east to west could be found a window hung with gauze drapery, which permitted a filtered sunshine. Dozens of refracting crystals hanging on beaded chains twinkled in the morning sun with irritating iridescence. Further west came a decent stereo system, hundreds of bootlegged Grateful Dead tapes and some reasonable music, a shelf of high school yearbooks and cutesy childhood photo albums alongside Noam Chomsky screeds, novels detailing the suffering of oppressed black women, and some Goddess poetry. May you never have the ill fortune to encounter the latter. In the far corner of the room were a highly conventional dresser, mirror and closet. The centerpiece of the room was a bizarre personal shrine of some sort, an intricate construction consisting of totems charged with deep spiritual meaning, ringed with incense and candles.

I tried to go back to sleep, but the house was too active and the sunlight too bright. After a while I abandoned the pretense, sat up, and drank the cold coffee. Then I read the Deerpark article. The editorial bias was clearly in favor of the project, but the writer had incorporated my exact phrasing several times, which I had to admit brought a little thrill to what had by now become a morning decidedly devoid of thrills.

A sudden lull in the noises outside the bedroom door sent me hopping into my clothes, hoping for a window of time to escape the premises. I clicked the door to Karen's room closed, and made my move.

"Hey, Rod. Good morning."

Damn. Spotted by a Couch Hippie. He gazed vacantly at the shoes and newspaper in my hand and the sheepish look on my face.

"Morning," I muttered, "it's Ron."

"Who's he?" asked a hostile female voice from the kitchen. "Are you with Tony?"

"No," I told the kitchen, "I'm, uh, I'm with Karen." I leapt for the door.

"Is he paying any rent?" Kitchen demanded, "or at least utilities? Because I swear to God ... "

I gave Couch Hippie a brief nod and shut the door behind me. Then, a minor miracle: on the very first attempt at ignition, Great White sprang into action like a magnificent thoroughbred. It was going to be a good day.

First order of business: back to my hole for a shave and shower. I drove home, climbed the stairs with shoes and newspaper still in hand, and unlocked the door. There on the couch, asleep, lay my sister Eva.

It was going to be a very good day.

I slipped into the bathroom, shaved and showered, trying not to make noise. When I got out she was still asleep. I ate breakfast and read the entire paper, keeping an eye on Eva as she hovered near consciousness. She groaned once during the international news, ignored the sports page, turned over for the editorial pages, and yawned mightily at the job listings. With a fist curled under her chin she looked exactly the way she did when she was seven and had the upper bunk.

"Evie," I whispered.

She awoke and smiled a tired little smile, without opening her eyes. She yawned and said, "I snuck in, Little Guy."

I tisked. "Such lax security. And to think what I tip that doorman every morning."

"I could have stolen everything you own, you know. But then I'd have no room left in my glove compartment."

"And then where would you put your gloves?" I wondered.

"I'd be the laughingstock of the debutante ball."

She opened her eyes, focussed, and found me.

"Come here," she said. I came over and sat on the couch with her. She was wearing an oversized T-shirt of mine that made her look like a little kid. She hugged me for ten seconds and flopped back down on the couch.

"Little Guy ... " she yawned contentedly.

"Why so tired?" I asked.

"Where were you all night?" she asked.

"What glove compartment? You don't have a car, do you?"

"Duh," she said. "It was a joke."

"Did you hitchhike? You better not have hitchhiked, Eva."

"Is Great White still alive?"

"Alive and well. What's the plan?"

Eva always had a plan.

"There is a plan," she said, "and I could tell you what it is, but then I'd have to kill you."

I laughed. "Damn, it's great to see you, Eva."

"When do I get to meet your girlfriend?"

"What makes you think I have one?"

"You were out all night."

"Maybe I work the graveyard shift."

"You're smiling before noon."

"Maybe it's because of your radiant presence."

"Maybe it's because you're getting laid. Nice to know somebody is. What's her name?"

"Karen Anne Bellamy."

"Same middle name as me."

"Yeah," I said, "you and half the girls in America. Anne, Marie, or Lynne: the only three middle names for girls officially sanctioned by the federal government."

"You practice safe sex?" she asked.

"Oh, please."

"You want a lecture?"

"You want me to throw up? Mind your own business."

"You are my own business. Don't die."

"I'll do my best. Don't hitchhike."

Suddenly Eva laughed. "Well, I guess there's no point calling Mom and Dad. We've become them."

I laughed too. "Why can't evveybuddy just go metric?" I wondered, in my father's voice. "Izzat so hard? Evveybuddy should just go metric."

"You're so very right, Abe, dearest. Sweden utilizes the metric system, of course. But you're so very right to bemoan its absence in the States."

"Hunh," I said, frowning. "Do you really think she's that obsequious?"

"Tsscch," Eva sneered, "she's his little slave girl."

"Never noticed."

"Fuck. Open your eyes next time. She'd bind her feet if she thought that's what he wanted."

"Nah. That's bullshit. Nobody tells her what to do."

"Shit, Ronnie! Nobody has to. She does it on her own. He never says a word about what he wants, he just pouts and acts disappointed if she gets it wrong. He's got her totally manipulated with that passive-aggressive little act."

"Huh. Never noticed."

"Well, notice."

She stomped off to the bathroom. Water ran. After a few minutes she yelled "towel!", and stuck her hand out the door. I gave her my wet gray towel. It was the only one I had. A moment later she came out, wrapped in it. She searched through her pack for some clothes and headed back to the steamy bathroom.

I considered the fact that this represented the second time that morning that a woman had paraded before me in a towel. It's not every fella who can boast such a record. Ah, but what a difference a towel can make.

Inside the orange towel had been Karen's perfect jewel of a body which rendered me asthmatic just thinking about it, and her largely inert mind, which made me shrug just thinking about it.

Inside the gray towel was my sister's gift of a mind, which made me grin excitedly just to think about it, and her dumpy body, which made me yawn if I ever thought about it.

Which I didn't. She's my sister, for Christ's sake. I don't give a shit what she looks like in a towel. And neither, from what I could gather, did anyone else. I thought about that as she sat on the couch, lacing up her Doc Marten boots. I wondered why she had come all the way from Oregon without calling first.

"So," I said, "how's your love life?"

"Bad question."

"Bummer. What about —

" — don't even mention him. Look, I don't want to talk about it, alright? Drop it."

"Alright, alright."

"I left, O.K.?" she said quickly. I noticed she was breathing hard. "I mean Eugene," she said. "I mean for good. I moved out of my place and put all my stuff in a storage locker. Heather's going to send it to me as soon as I figure out a permanent plan. Meanwhile I thought I might, you know, crash here for a little while."

"Oh, yeah, Eva. Long as you want."

"Cool," she nodded. "Listen," she said, brightening up, "what I want to know is, how did you end up being such the little Romeo, you and your little Karen Anne Blow-me?"

"Bellamy."

"Below-me, that's what I said. Is it the real thing?"

"Hell, no."

"Mn. And what, pray tell, are the weaknesses of the relationship?"

"One half of the participants are brain-dead. I am not in that half."

"Hunh. Strengths of the relationship?"

"Duh," I said.

"What does that mean?"

"What do you think, Eva? It's not her ability to read a topographical map. We do what we do, and when we're done doing it, there's not much left to do."

"Huh," Eva said skeptically, "I don't buy it."

"You don't?"

"Nope. I think there's more to the story. It's ten in the morning and I've never seen you so cheerful in my life. Either you're on something, which you're not, or you're in deeper than you think."

"Thank you for that penetrating insight. It's of great value to me, based as it is on such lengthy research of the matter."

"Oh, come on, Ronnie. You're flying high as a kite. I tease you about her name and you get all touchy. You're in deeper than you think."

"You already said that."

"When do I get to meet her?"

"You already asked that."

Eva sighed, defeated. She pulled a compact mirror out of her purse and checked her face. No makeup, puffy bags under her eyes, her damp blonde hair streaked with a fading black dye job. She smiled weakly at me, knowing we both had the same thought.

"Perfection," she said. "I'm a goddess."

"So I'm in the newspaper today," I said, tossing it at her.

"Shit, you're not selling Great White, are you?"

"No, it's not a classified. Besides, who the hell would buy Great White?"

"So what is it?"

"A press release that I wrote got picked up in the lead article."

"What? Get the fuck out of here!"

"My house. You get the fuck out of here."

"Good one, Ronnie," she sighed. "What press release?"

I explained the meeting as best I could, given that I did not understand it myself. I pointed out the specific words in the article that had originated in my pen, or PowerBook.

She was amazed. "Since when are you the big politico?"

"I told you, I'm not. I hate that shit. It's just that no one could handle a simple press release. Ya want a job done right —

" — ya do it yourself," Eva said, completing our dad's saying. "Damn," she said. "Good for you, Ronnie."

"It's no big deal."

"I think it's cool. Now, what about some lunch?"

"Lunch? It's ten-thirty in the A.M."

"Well, I want to eat a large green salad with some cherry tomatoes and parmesan cheese and big fat croutons and ranch dressing slathered all over it. Whatever meal that qualifies as, let's go get it."

"I just ate breakfast."

"So? Some host you are. You could come and watch me eat."

"There's a thrill."

"Damn, Ronnie, no sense of hospitality. I can't believe I accepted that invitation you sent."

I laughed. "What invitation?"

Eva was quite serious. "James Dean," she said.

"Oh, that, right," I said, remembering the postcard. "God, that was six years ago."

"Does that mean it no longer applies? Because I can —"

" — no, no, stay, it's cool," I said.

We eyed each other. The room was suddenly full of wary tension. Moods move fastest among those who know each other best.

"I'd love to watch you eat," I said.

We went to brunch. Eva got her salad. I had a burger, so that Eva wouldn't feel too uncomfortable as the only one eating.

"Hey," Eva asked, making serious headway into her giant salad, "what do you do for money anyway? Shouldn't you be broke?"

This question neatly encapsulated an entire season of employment frustration for me. It's lovely the way close relatives can cut right to the desiccated heart of a sensitive matter.

"Yes," I said, "I should be broke, if there were any justice. I've been temping on the railroad, all the livelong day."

At the time I had a temp job so unremarkable and dreary I have since forgotten it was. I have erased the memory from my hard drive. I'm sure I have a backup floppy disk with the information somewhere around here. Wait. Hold on a minute. Sorry the place is such a mess. Ummm ...

"Temping?" Eva snorted. "Why don't you get a real job?"

"Oh, my God!" I said, smacking my forehead. "That's — that's brilliant! You genius! What do you think I've been doing for the last six months, playing shuffleboard? There's nothing out there."

In my own personal epic quest for the perfect job I faced the twin-headed mutant snake: What I wanted I couldn't get; what I could get I didn't want. For every job I was interested in, I was only one of many thousands of applicants, each seemingly more qualified than I. And the truth is, I didn't really want to end up working in a pointless, rat-trap, 9-5 (which is really 8-5) white-collar McJob. The only thing worse than looking for a good job is working a bad one. I had already spent three of my college summers in dark, dank offices where the coffee tastes like styrofoam. I knew exactly what to fear.

"Hey," Eva said, sipping her Diet Coke, "you know a little about computers, don't you?"

"Emphasis on 'little'," I said.

"What about the Web?" Eva asked. "You should get some Internet job, make money that way."

I smirked. "Heaven forfend," I said. "My own sister, conned by all the hype."

"You should do it. There's gold in them thar hills, junior."

"Did you know," I asked her, "that merely by uttering the words 'World Wide Wait' you can make more money than you ever dreamed of? Just say 'html' three times, click your heels, and you'll be back in Kansas."

Somehow, this failed to amuse her.

"Fine," she said, spearing a cheery cherry tomato with a hostile fork. "Don't look for a job. I'll live through the night."

"I've been looking," I said. "I just haven't been finding."

I brought her up to the slow speed of my trivial travails. The process of looking for a job is so humiliating and painful it makes having one's teeth drilled without the benefit of Novocaine seem an appealing alternative.

All that long employment season I had spent in endless interviews, continually astonished at the capacity of small-minded functionaries in pointless, dead-end jobs to condescend to young job applicants.

Interview after interview, these automatons all followed the same set routine, programmed into them by their designers, who consulted with leading expert Isaac Asimov when constructing their robots. Very lifelike, very commendable.

The androids all asked the exact same questions, each no doubt thinking himself the first guy to put on a pressed white business shirt and bland tie and inquire, "Why do you want to work here?" with that charming, insincere baritone.

The interviews repeated themselves with such alarming and mind-numbing frequency that I was in danger of losing all sense of perspective. More than once I found my attention wandering, despite the intense focus of the microscope upon me. There were times when I no longer knew which job I was applying for, nor which asinine flunky from which faceless company sat there in judgment of all my wrongs.

The endless parade took its toll. I became less and less able to keep a straight face, nor a civil tongue in my mouth.

One question that always got me was this zinger: "How much would you like to make?" I never knew what to do with that one. Do I go low? Do I go high? How much is low, how far is high? And what the hell kind of question is that, anyway? How much do I want to make? A million fucking dollars an hour, not a penny less.

I could not say that, of course. And yet, given that it was a foregone conclusion that I was absolutely, unquestionably not going to get the job, I often found myself yearning for some simple shortcut through the process. Why couldn't I open the interview with a burst of candor?

"I want money. You have money. To get some of your money, I'm willing to suffer the indignity of whatever menial drudgery you may assign me. I'm even willing to spend time in your unutterably dull presence to get it."

A simple shortcut: Go directly to Jail. Do not pass Go, do not collect $200.

Here are some snippets of actual conversations from the Interview Period. Was I excessively flip? You be the judge:

Law Firm Flunky: What would you say is your greatest weakness?
Ronnie: I respond with hostility to stupid questions.

Janitorial Firm Flunky: Why do you want to work as a custodial apprentice?
Ronnie: I want to better myself and the world around me.

Computer Sales Flunky: Where do you want to be in ten years?
Ronnie: In a karaoke bar in Ho Chi Minh City.

O.K., alright. I was a smartass. It is a registered personality trademark. But these people, these questions! What would you have done? How do people do it? How do the toiling millions keep their heads afloat, swimming through rivers of humiliation every day, all over the world?

I hold a Bachelor of Arts degree from a major university, fully accredited, home to two Nobel Prize winners, and what's more, winner of three straight Division III tennis championships. In an earlier era that would have meant something. I would have been handed my diploma and marched straight into a fine job with a fine salary and married a fine girl of fine breeding. I would have been Dick Van Dyke, and Mary Tyler Moore would have instantly materialized for me.

Well, that was the 50's — or at least the TV version, the only one I know, the only one that exists. No such luck at this end of the century, bubba. It's a bleak landscape out here in the unemployed heartland.

Eva nodded like a hobby horse throughout my troubled tale. She knew the story well. She related her own highly abridged version of the same miseries.

'What'd you expect?" she asked, a significant sliver of lettuce wedged in an incisor. "Jobs are jobs. They suck by definition. If it was fun, they'd call it a hobby. They offer money because it's unpleasant."

I sighed and pushed my plate away from my bloated belly. "Ain't it a great time to be alive?" I asked.

Eva considered the matter. "Are we slackers, do you suppose?" she wondered. "I've always wanted to be a slacker. I think I'm a bit too old. I'm sort of generationally cuspish. I think I might have slacked for a little while in Portland after I graduated."

I nodded. "Portland's supposed to be a good place to slack."

"The whole Northwest, really, is prime slacking country."

"What about California?" I asked. "We slack here."

"Nah, not really," Eva said. "You're slacker wannabes."

"Now, wait a minute," I said, growing indignant, "I think we slack as much as anyone."

"You said yourself you've got a job. You call that slacking?"

"A temp job. And I'm bored a lot. More than bored — I have ennui."

"Big deal. Everyone's got ennui. Ennui's passe. Do you have *Weltschmerz*?"

"What the hell is that?"

"World-weariness."

"Oh, yeah, I've got that big time. I've got extra if you need some. Plus, I have no idea what I'm doing with my life."

Eva seemed impressed. "No idea?"

"Not a clue."

"Hmm," she said. "You might qualify for a slacking apprenticeship with that."

We laughed grimly with the shared bond of an accurate but unpleasant insight. And we laughed not just for ourselves, but on behalf of an entire generation of comrades born in the 70's who've been so thoroughly and comprehensively mislabeled and misunderstood by morons in the media.

Listen, you want to know what this mystery generation of ours is all about? Slackers, is that our *nom de guerre*? "Generation X", is that the *au courant* label? How about Baby Boomer Afterbirth? That's my nominee. Whatever. Call us what you will, we're just too damned bored to really care.

Doesn't our inexplicable, frightening nihilism just fascinate you? I certainly hope so. Gosh, I hope we make an entertaining oddity for you amateur sociologists.

Gee, what makes them youngsters tick? Quick, somebody fetch an anthropologist. Is it the computers? These kids seem awful good at them. No, grandpa, it ain't the computers. No, grandma, it ain't the haircuts. It ain't the drugs, it ain't the beer, it ain't that awful music, it ain't the piercings and it ain't the tattoos. It ain't even the bad grammar.

Because if you want to generalize — and merely to converse about the concept of generations we must do so — then let's be honest. None of our wacky cultural traits differentiates us in the least from previous generations of ungrateful, disaffected white middle-class whiners. Both Gatsby and Kerouac would recognize us in one drunken glance. We abuse certain substances, we excel at the most modern technologies, we indulge in wanderlust, we revel in ennui, we suffer *Weltschmerz*, we have sex and transmit disease, and we derive our most intense pleasure from shocking our predecessors with the latest outrageous behavior. Nothing novel there. Textbook youth culture.

I do have a degree in history, you know. And although I didn't pay much attention and nearly failed six separate courses from sheer lack of effort, any schmoe who's heard of Marx knows it's always the conditions of employment that best define a given society or subset thereof.

What distinguishes the Afterbirth Generation is our absolute, universal inability to imagine ourselves comfortably smothered in the corporate bosom. We spend years at college chasing some elusive greased pig of a career that will be fun, interesting, meaningful, easy but challenging, part time, with high pay and higher prestige. Plus benefits. There are, of course, no such jobs, and in the end the main function of our meager education has been to learn enough to know what we don't want, leaving us paralyzed by the illusion of choice.

Yes, choice, for cultural oppression has been lifted away! Hooray! We new young'uns need not marry immediately, as was the expectation not so very long ago. We need not work in Daddy's office. We need not feel bound by geography. We need not tether ourselves to one company for life. Women are free to pursue employment over child care. Men are free to pursue child care over employment.

Yeah, that happens a lot.

Yes, ours is the first generation free to choose the future. And nobody has the slightest fucking idea what to choose.

By delicious irony, those of us who are sufficiently organized to fill out an application and can actually stomach the idea of toiling away at some pointless endeavor can't get a job anyway. Ha ha ha. And if by some accident, by some glitch in God's Plan they do get an actual long-term job which devolves into a Career, well then, they're no longer in the club. They get booted unceremoniously right out of the treehouse.

The true-blue, card-carrying members of this generation survive on a long series of menial jobs and loans from parents, without any plan, hating whatever we're doing only one micron less than the specter of a lifetime climbing a corporate ladder which is now missing half its rungs anyway.

Rules and regulations, meetings and memos, ties and tights. Who needs it? That's no fun. Somebody make it fun, fun, fun! We grew up in a world of easy entertainment. Boredom is our greatest fear. Another day at the same job? Change the channel.

There is a precedent. Our older cousins, the mythical Sixties Hippies, rebelled for a few minutes against the idea of entering the regimented work force. But they had long, drawn-out ideological theories and fairly cool music to back them up. We don't get caught up in all those annoying abstractions. We're too dumb anyway. We couldn't tell you the difference between hegemony and a hedgehog.

But we do know enough to recognize hypocrisy. We watched them hippie folk get haircuts and proceed to betray every single principle they supposedly had. Now they run the world and wouldn't venture out in public without a double-breasted suit and double-barreled Volvo. Our generation makes no pretense of any ideological rationale. We're lazy and bored, and if the world isn't presented to us on a gilded platter we bawl with the incoherence of one million babies the day the pacifier factory blows up in a toxic industrial accident.

Oh, we feel the guilt. Have no worries on that score. The Protestant work ethic, the Catholic guilt, we get it all; sometimes it seems like the schisms of the Reformation never arrived on American shores. We young folk carry these burdens.

Our mercurial mettle is tested. We steel ourselves against a heavy, leaden pressure to go for the gold; to seek the silver lining in every cloud. To grab the brass ring, whatever the hell that is. I used to ride plenty of carousels when I was a wee feller. Never saw one goddamn brass ring. But I know I'm supposed to be reaching for it.

And it's your fault, all you older types. You sold us a bill of goods.

You hired the barkers who convinced us there was a snake oil that could remove worry, conflict, boredom and hard work; and leave a late-model car, a suburban dwelling and cable TV in their place. You led us to believe that instant gratification was our birthright — and now you want us to get a job? Damn. That's not fair. That there's child abuse, that's what that is. And let me add that a special place in intergenerational hell is reserved for all you damn billions of Baby-Gloomers, always clogging up the airwaves and the highways and byways of pop culture with your dominant, homogenized, self-important iconography.

I blame you all. You handed us the telescope. All our nervous, disaffected little lives you told us this gadget was all we required to see the stars. But we can't figure out how the damn thing works. It hasn't even got a remote control, for God's sake. So we keep looking back at the long century through the wrong end, trying to make sense of the blurry figures in the phantasmagoric, miniaturized distance.

Eventually Eva and I, heaving our tiny wills against the immense weight of millenial history and generational responsibility, finished our goddamned brunch.

We clambered back into Great White, smoked some exceptional weed Eva had brought with her, and dashed off to Its Beach, one of the more popular spots in town for locals. A peculiar name, "Its". It has always inspired in me a vague grammatical unease. Tourists know nothing about the place. They go to the cheesy main beaches and annoy one another, which is just fine with the locals.

Neither one of us had a bathing suit, so we lay on the sand in our clothes. We made an amusing spectacle, surrounded by legitimate beachgoers in more suitable attire, with their busloads of the various accoutrements of maritime leisure. We watched bold body surfers dash into the freezing cold water. We watched families unpack lunches sufficient to feed small armies. We watched hot-shot frisbee players hit innocent sunbathers with rifle tosses, apologize, and hit them again.

Eva and I couldn't stop giggling. We laughed at everything we saw, but especially at ourselves, stretched out in black clothes on a sunny day, flying higher than the sea gulls wheeling overhead. After a while Eva took off her blouse and tried to pass off her blue bra as a bathing suit. At that point I suggested we move over to what might be called the Counterculture Cove, a smaller and hipper subdivision of Its Beach.

The cove is home to every previously cataloged species of hippie and more. Eva and I giggled like mad at everything there. We listened as an endless chain of bad drummers came and went through a drum circle, never changing the same dumb beat. We watched free hippie children run naked and dirty through great mounds of beached kelp and thick clouds of sand fleas. We watched hacky-sack players kick their idiotic little bags of beans, stoop to pick them up, kick them again, stoop to pick them up, repeating the entertainment for hours. We gaped at tattooed couples engaged in very suggestive massage.

Given the environment, Eva's bra was not an especially risky maneuver. Karen usually went topless whenever we went to the cove. Karen also insisted that I massage sunblock lotion into her soft, salty body, warm and pliant in the California sun. This charming little beach custom of hers was clearly calculated to drive me straight out of my little mind. Even the memory was jarring.

Eva's blue bra was quite enough for me. She kept complaining about the heat, and debating whether her underwear could pass as bathing suit bottoms. I made her keep her pants on. She whined about the restriction, but I managed to distract her with the amusing sight of a troop of mellow rasta freaks communing with vicious-looking rottweiliers. Eva loves dogs. In another life she might have made a good hippie.

Its is the only beach in Santa Cruz where dogs are permitted to roam leashless. Wild packs of the beasts chased sticks, tennis balls and each other up and down the length of the beach, frequently wheeling just in time to send a spray of sand our way. Sometimes a small pack of mutts would bowl right over us. I got irritated, but Eva couldn't stop laughing. The sun and the pot were really doing a number on her.

Without warning, some hippies struck up a conversation with us. I would have sent them on their hairy, merry way, but Eva was in a jolly mood and we were soon surrounded. In short order some joints materialized and were passed around. After a few minutes it occurred to me to tell Eva I thought she had smoked enough already, but there was an unexpected breakdown in communications between my brain and my mouth, and instead I ran to the freezing ocean water to test a very important physics theory, a breakthrough in the field of wave mechanics, which I have since forgotten.

Hours later, mildly sunburned and coming down nicely, we headed back into town. I called up my friends Benny and Hal. Surprise, they weren't doing anything. Eva treated us all to a fancy steak dinner on her credit card, gave Hal advice on his haircut, argued with Benny about gratuitous use of the Internet, fell in love with the waiter, changed her mind, and fell fast asleep in Great White on the way home.

When we arrived at my place the absence of motion nudged her to the brink of consciousness. I glanced at her fatigued features, lit only by the orange glow of a streetlamp, and for a moment she seemed a stranger. Her eyes shot open and stared into mine, but her mind was still asleep. For an instant she put up both her hands as if to ward me away, and uttered a choked cry, her features contorted with fear and confusion.

Then she awoke fully, her face embracing clarity.

She smiled tiredly. "Long day, Little Guy."

"Long day," I agreed.

Chapter 6

Eva slept on the unpleasant couch, snoring with that familiar, feeble, failing chainsaw gurgle I knew from childhood. I lay in the darkened bedroom considering matters. Spending time with Benny and Hal had induced in me a certain bemused melancholy. There had been a time, not so very long before, when we boys had all lived together. Certain circumstances had conspired to remove me from their company. Circumstances weighing approximately 118 pounds in sandals.

Six months earlier, there had been four of us living in post-collegiate bachelor guy squalor in an apartment that would have been flattered to be called dingy. We ate in an alcove in the kitchen, and when I say alcove I mean the tiniest of nooks, decrepit and ill-equipped. The table was a slab of unfinished wood, bolted to the wall and cornflaked into submission. Strange scavenged chairs were arrayed around the table like a dysfunctional family: one drummer's stool, one lawn chair, one legitimate kitchen chair, and a bar stool. If we four residents happened to be sitting at the alcove at the same time, two of us would float at a very low altitude, our eyes barely above the height of the table, our heads bobbing like hungry children at Thanksgiving. One head would hover at the right height, and the last one would tower above the others like Wilt Chamberlain, who in my childhood was, and therefore shall always remain, the greatest basketball player ever.

Our attention to hygiene would have won no awards from home decor and etiquette guru Martha Stewart. Dirty dishes piled up in a massive unbalanced ziggurat in the sink until there were no clean ones to be found. For weeks at a time each of us would simply snatch the few plates and forks he needed from the cesspool and give them an obligatory rinse, waiting for the other residents to crack. Eventually the weak-willed sucker would buckle, and be forced to spend a few hours soaking, scratching and harassing the dishes back to their virginal form, and the cycle would begin anew.

Sweep the floor? We didn't even own a broom. In the late hours of the evening when all decent cockroaches have died or gone to bed for the night, a squadron of renegade roaches would race over from their ghetto under the sink and dash past booted stompings in a mad rush to supply reinforcements to their embattled garrison, which was fighting madly to push the refrigerator over from below.

Perhaps you've heard the term New Car Smell, a pleasant plasticky aroma that wafts up from the vehicle with an unmistakable ersatz freshness. Apparently it's an actual fragrance used by car salesmen, sprayed into the car to lure unsuspecting consumers. Fake new. In many ways, a very handy pocket metaphor for American culture.

But I digress. Our apartment had the opposite problem — Old Car Smell. Something like a 1921 Model T. that's been sitting between the family garden and the corn field on an isolated Iowa farm, collecting leaves and discarded garbage, a vehicular coffin which still boasts the rotting carcass of a leprous opossum who met her Maker twenty years ago chewing on some loose wires.

Carl, the apartment's obligatory computer programmer, dwelt in one bedroom, and it was an island of order within the chaos. An elegant futon graced the far wall, shapely pillows dancing lightly upon it. Unhip airbrushed Nagle posters of anorexic grey women postured glassily down on everything.

The other three of us were barracked in the second bedroom. We wrestled with our fatigued mattresses, trying to keep them straight on the floor, where they were strewn about on a socky, jeansed shag carpet of golden tint and dubious ancestry.

I remember a lot of violence to the laundry process in that apartment. We took revenge on resistant trash bags full of filthy clothes by scalding them at the laundromat three blocks away; two blocks too many for my weak and weary arms. I have always been a devotée of the boil-and-burn school of laundry, according to which stain removal, separation by colors and folding are strictly for sissies. Lose a button, you've lost the shirt. I acknowledge that this policy has left me with a diminishing wardrobe consisting of shrunken, wrinkled clothes, all graying towards one another over time, but once a month they're damn clean.

Let me describe the boys as best I can within the limitations of my strictly second-rate long-term memory. Last and least was Carl Davies, the neat one, whom you've already met. He was strictly a classified-ad respondent, not a friend nor even an amiable acquaintance. We suffered him because he paid the rent. Why he suffered us is a mystery utterly beyond my ken.

Benny was an artist. He looked like one and he smelled like one. He did not, however, have the talent to be one. Poor, misunderstood, intellectually gifted Benny was deeply and helplessly untalented, and a mess, too. Peculiar patches of paint found their way onto every surface in his wardrobe, and uncertain scraps of canvas seemed to follow him around like critics. Yet Benny was deeply wise in his own self-indulgent, pedantic, beard-scratching way, and he was and is the most well-read person I have ever known.

Hal was loud, large, and funny in an unassuming way. He slept an average of eleven hours a night without apology. He spent most of his waking hours plucking idly at a beaten-up bass guitar. He could not afford an amplifier, an obstacle he sorely lamented, but one which Benny and I secretly celebrated. If only the bass had been missing its strings, we would have considered the arrangement perfect.

Hal was Benny's closest friend, even though he teased him mercilessly. More than once I witnessed him inflicting examples of Benny's minimalist abstracts and multimedia collages on innocent observers, displaying the works with extravagant, sarcastic flourishes. For those who could only scratch their heads in befuddlement at the incomprehensible constructions, Hal would unleash his favorite mockery of Benny: "He's an artist — you wouldn't understand."

Benny was grimy and learned, Hal was round and relaxed. They had almost nothing in common, and they were virtually inseparable.

Benny and I originally met during my third year at UC Santa Cruz, the institution of higher learning which, by bucking the trend of its rival institutions and charitably accepting my thoroughly unremarkable application, originally lured me to this sunny seaside city from my home town of Camarillo, CA.

From the first day of the fall term Benny's path crossed mine constantly, in classes, food establishments, the library. He and I were both doing our best to project hostile post-adolescent misanthropic tendencies to the excessively cheery world that surrounded us. For months we did our sullen damndest not to become friends, but fate would not be denied. Lord knows I tried to keep my head down and my mouth shut, but I ran into the man so often, the project of avoiding him became too much of an effort in itself.

I can't remember what exactly put our trains on the same track. I do remember that a good part of the first week I got to know Benny we spent sandblasting through some work of Hegel's that had been assigned us. I was completely mystified by good ol' Hegel. His writing, thinking, and philosophy were as thoroughly impenetrable to me as a lead safe. That first week Benny not only cracked the safe for me and gave me a Hegel crash-course, but got so wrapped up in the excitement of explaining it all that he ended up writing two essays, one for him and one for me. I was a little hesitant about turning Benny's essay in as my own, not for any reasons of guilt, since I have always been an accomplished and satisfied cheater, but because I wondered if this fast-talking maniac Benny really knew what he was talking about. As it happened, the paper nearly blew the teacher into the next county, and my friendship with Benny never looked back.

Soon thereafter Benny introduced me to Hal, an old high school buddy and his only friend. They were fellow refugees from the great agricultural inland empire of California. Their home town was a dusty, superheated, overfertilized hitchin' post by the name of Tulare or Modesto or Fresno or some such. Hal accepted me into their exclusive little friendship club with the cheerful nonchalance of a captain of a pickup softball team on a lazy Sunday afternoon: sure, why not? What's one more? Need a mitt?

The wet cement on the driveway of our friendship solidified for good on Graduation Day, 1992. As juniors, we were poised in grim anticipation of enduring a repeat performance of the ceremonial torture a year later. We were there on a reconnaissance mission, and in hopes of access to the free champagne and appetizers at the reception that followed. We stood perched on an observation deck high above and away from the stage, feeling infinitely superior to, and yet secretly envious of the massed participants. They looked goofy and uncomfortable, but at least they were escaping. This betrayal merited vengeful ridicule.

"Observe," Benny said, "the mortarboard and dark gown, a throwback to Oxford and Cambridge, where this stuff was the everyday uniform. Gowns were worn for convenience, not for show, certainly not for formality. In these United States gowns are never owned, only rented, and meant to convey ceremonial dignity. What manner of dignity can be rented for a day? Gentlemen, we see before us a vast display of ignorance in a putative celebration of the triumph of knowledge. Nothing could better illustrate the inferiority complex which the American academic establishment has always held vis-a-vis its Old World roots."

"Roger that," Hal said.

Earnest speeches began to filter through the feedback shrieks of the cheap microphone. We grimaced.

"If no one says, 'today is the first day of the rest of your life,' I want my money back," Hal said.

"I see before me today the leaders of tomorrow," I countered.

"Most of all," Hal said, "I want to thank my parents."

"We did it, you guys, we really, really did it!!" I offered.

"Ouch," Hal said, "good one."

"Have you ever noticed," Benny mused, "that these saccharine valedictorians tend to be students on whom one has never before set eyes? Do they spend all four years hiding in a dungeon, preparing their graduation speeches?"

"Possibly," I said, "but you spend all your time in a dungeon, preparing your anti-graduation speeches."

"Well," Benny said, miffed, "we can leave, if you prefer."

"I just need to hear the term 'melting pot' one more time," Hal confessed. "Then we can go."

"Diversity is our strength," I said. "Let's see if they're popping the champagne yet. Maybe we can get drunk early and beat the crowd."

They had, and we did.

That summer I got a job in San Francisco, but I stayed in touch with Benny and Hal. When our senior year began we hooked up early and often. From then on, being the three of us was mostly what the three of us did.

After our own graduation the next year, which was an exact replica of the previous year's ceremony, we each realized with a sentiment somewhere between casual anxiety and a nervous breakdown that we had no real post-collegiate plans. Benny developed a theory that one ought to graduate either as a rock or as a feather. In this model, a rock has a good job or law school lined up directly after graduation; a feather travels through India and meditates. The plans are considered equally sensible, and no moral superiority is ascribed to either. The goal of the graduate is to be the rock or the feather truly and with conviction, and not heave between the two extremes towing the busload of guilt that comes from having lofty goals but no working game plan.

A fine little theory. If the extremes are rock and feather, all three of us were wet cardboard. We were unwilling to forge ahead onto sterile, forbidding career paths, but neither were we about to go seeking inner harmony and dysentery in Nepal.

Chapter 7

I dreamt that Eva and Karen were playing outfield for the Cubs. Chasing a hard liner to left, they became entangled in the ivy that covers the outfield wall at Wrigley Field, but they seemed to enjoy the moment. It was an opportunity to chat. Steve Garvey hit the next ball far over their heads, a monster home run that soared over the bleachers and landed on Waveland Avenue. Unimpressed, Karen and Eva kept looking for the ball in the ivy and gossiping.

As soon as I was awake I knew that Karen and Eva were talking in the kitchen in my apartment, that it was late morning, and that Steve Garvey had retired a long time ago. I wondered if Karen had bicycled or taken the bus over. I wondered what she and Eva were talking about. I strongly suspected it was me.

"Morning, ladies," I said. "I see you've met."

"Good morning," they chorused. It had been three days since I had last seen Karen, and I was pleased she had come; but I wasn't sure if excessive display of affection would make Eva uncomfortable. I compromised by kissing them each on the cheek.

"How'd you get here?" I asked Karen.

"I called, but you were asleep, so Eva picked me up."

I looked at Eva, confused.

"I took Great White," she said. "Hope you don't mind. I put the keys back in your pants."

I was nonplussed. "Great White started?"

"After a while."

"There's no gas," I remembered.

"We put a couple bucks in," Karen said, laughing. Eva joined her. "What's so funny?"

"Nothing," Karen said.

"Just the gas station — some guy," Eva said, and they burst into a fresh round of giggles.

I had nothing to add to this, so I told them my dream.

Karen was fascinated. "How in the world do you know the name of the street that's behind some stadium in Chicago?" she marveled.

"How do I know, Karen? Do we really —"

" — Dad," Eva said, nodding. "Big into sports. He really influenced Ronnie."

"What?" I demanded. "You're claiming Dad and I watched sporting events together?"

"It was their little male bonding thing," Eva said to Karen. Karen nodded appreciatively.

"Oh, bullshit," I said. "I never bonded a single sports bond with Dad or anyone else."

"Man, you don't remember anything," Eva said, shaking her head. "When you were a little kid you used to follow him around and he used to teach you sports. You worshipped him."

"Ah, bullshit," I said. "This is defamation of character. I could sue."

"Please don't," Eva said. "Ours is an overly litigious society."

"Oh, that reminds me," Karen said, brightening up, "did you hear we're going to sue over Deerpark?"

We hadn't. Without encouragement, Karen proceeded to fill us in on everything she had learned in the previous 72 hours concerning the Deerpark saga. A lawsuit had been launched. Protests were proceeding. Sit-ins were scheduled. Civil was being disobeyed. Meetings were going on at all times, in all places. We learned the names of evil administrators brandishing menacing blueprints. We learned the names of heroic students circulating brave petitions. I felt as though I was watching a soap opera I had never seen before, whose characters were unimportant to me, in a plot destined never to end. I spent many a teenage afternoon in just such a stupor, the waves of electromagnetic ennui emanating from the television so powerful they stifled me in a straightjacket, rendering me catatonic.

It was apparent that Karen had become a Deerpark-head. She had signed up for countless hours of petitioning, she had spoken to dozens of faculty members, she had lobbied campus organizations for support. More than anything else she had debated strategy with her fellow trouble-makers. Sue now, or sue later? Forge alliances with like-minded organizations, or go it alone? Continue to operate on group consensus basis, or create a formal leadership structure? Lobby the administration with respectful restraint, or shut down the fucking school? These questions consumed her.

With all of these distractions, Karen and I had not seen one another for three long days and nights. Would we never again have intimate relations? This question consumed me.

The truth was, Eva was crowding me, she had nothing to do, and she was on the brink of broke. Eva had always had a plan before this visit. What was it now? Should she move on to visit her friend in Santa Fe? Should she stay in town? Should she try to find a job? Should she find a place of her own? These questions consumed her.

Karen sneezed once, twice, a third time, and then a fourth blast so powerful it shook her half out of her chair and into Eva's arms. That seemed to settle the matter.

"I've godd to gedd oudda here," Karen said with a snuffly accent. She hàd long accused my innocent apartment of exacerbating her allergies, one of the many reasons why we rarely spent time there together. I felt no particular need to defend my personal palace from unwarranted defamation by a woman who, after all, voluntarily lit noxious incense in her own bedroom.

Great White swam off like a porpoise without purpose. All three of us sat on the front bench seat, like the 20-14-6 combination to my high school locker.

What we unlocked, I cannot guess.

I drove. Karen sat in the middle, her hand on my thigh and her head blocking the rear-view mirror. Eva gazed out the passenger window with an aura of deep distraction.

Eva wanted to be dropped off downtown. She claimed she had business, but it wasn't anything I knew about. I asked her what it was, how long she'd be gone and whether I should pick her up, but she brushed off my questions like picking lint off her shirt. At the first red light she hopped out and walked away without looking back.

Honk. Honk. Green light.

Great White took one last glance at Eva, shrugged, coughed and barrelled off.

"Where are we going now?" Karen wanted to know.

"Your place?" I suggested.

Karen frowned, a full-face frown, and suddenly I felt like a dirty old man, a politician caught in a trenchcoat outside a peep show.

She had misunderstood me. As it happened, at that particular moment, in that isolated crater of time, I was no slave to libidinous monomania. I was content to keep my pants on. The truth was that I had missed Karen's cheerful ways, not just her peerless body. I wanted to relax a few hours in her company. I had missed it. I wanted to hear her laugh with abandon at my driest jokes; I wanted to watch her string beads with her quick, childlike fingers; I wanted to brush her hair, thick and fresh like harvested wheat; and, yes, if her insatiable demands had to be met, I was willing to capitulate and copulate.

"I have to go up to school," Karen said. "I've got a meeting. Could you drop me off?"

"Christ, Karen, what did you call me up for if you didn't have any time to spend together?"

"I did have time. We had a nice morning together."

"Sitting in the kitchen, sneezing with my sister? You call that a nice morning together?"

"Yes, I do. I like your sister."

"You do?"

"Yeah, I think she's great."

"Well," I said. "Well."

I dropped Karen off outside some classroom inside of which, I have no doubt, absurd academic arguments about arcane and immaterial concerns were being advanced with grave sincerity by earnest undergraduates who had not done the required reading.

As I drove away, Great White pointed out in his rearview mirror that Karen had stopped walking. She stood under a tree, talking to it. GW and I stopped, squinting. Surely she couldn't be talking to a tree. Well, not so very surely. She — ah. A squirrel. She had stopped to talk to a squirrel. It stared down at her, nervous, confused and inarticulate, wondering what in the world to make of this hippie chick.

Squirrel, I hear ya.

My memory claims it was exactly 7:15 on a Wednesday evening five months earlier when my apartment mate Carl Davies, who never had a date, had a date.

Benny, Hal and I were watching bad T.V., because there is no other kind. We eyed Carl's nervous preparations with hostile, transparent envy poorly masked by cruel jokes muttered just under his threshold of hearing.

Karen Bellamy, whom Carl had met in his capacity as computer science lab tutor, showed up earlier than expected. She stood at the entrance, smiling tentatively, a mountain bike grazing faithfully at her side.

Carl was standing by the stove, a surprised look in his eye and an unfinished bowl of oatmeal in his hand. Carl was an oatmeal addict. The fiend could not have consumed more oats if a horse trainer had strapped a feed bag on him. His evening agenda with Karen no doubt included a pricy dinner at some showy restaurant, but without his dose of oatmeal he felt less secure, less sure of his decisions and emotions in a puzzling and unpredictable world. He had clearly hoped to finish the oatmeal and rinse his mouth out before her arrival, and his keen disappointment was readily apparent.

Karen stood in the doorway with an uncertain expression, and I certainly didn't do anything to make anyone feel more comfortable by chasing noisily after a particularly massive and frenzied cockroach. I knew the insect personally — I'd seen and chased him before, to no avail. He was so massive, so imperial and so magnificently disgusting there was no mistaking him for any other of his kind. He was the Moby Dick to my Captain Ahab. I dashed after him and stomped three times in rapid succession. There was a voluble crunch, and I believe I let out a Tarzan-like howl of primeval glee. The blood-lust of the kill swelled in my primeval loins, as Edgar Rice Burroughs might have put it. All that remained was a juicy stain at Karen's feet.

The skirmish afforded me my first look at Karen close up. I didn't think too much of her at the time. I took in her sandals, unshaven legs, Indonesian skirt, Guatemalan blouse, friendship bracelets and long, naturally curled hair at a glance, and pronounced her hippie scum. Her charming figure was of obligatory, predatory interest, and there was no denying the casual beauty of her features. But the aesthetic sensibility and the expression she wore made me think "dingbat" immediately, and I wrote her off.

Carl liked her plenty from the first, however, and the emotion was apparently reciprocal, because she was soon a regularly recurring shadow passing hurriedly between the front door and Carl's bedroom.

It was only weeks later, emerging from the bathroom and brushing up against her intriguingly spongy ass as we passed in the hallway, that I grew actively aware of Karen.

The weeks that followed are fuzzy in my memory, but at some point there was a party somewhere. I know that Hal and Benny were out of town together, on a pilgrimage to their families in their inland home town. Had Hal and Benny been at home where they belonged, I never would have gone to a party. The trouble with parties is that there are always people there.

Like all parties since the dawn of hi-fi, this one featured a mockery of music braying at vehement volume. I drank watery beer and glowered. It was a fairly low-key bacchanal, as bacchanals go. Of vomiting there was little, and excessive public displays of personal affection were reasonably well reigned in. What little conversation I endured through the pulsating beat did not, I fear, lead me very far down the Buddha's sevenfold path to enlightenment, but I did join an animated kitchen discussion on the relative merits of pot-bellied pigs as pets, a subject concerning which I know nothing. Subsequently a small group of strangers began a private, intimate conversation right beside me, gossiping viciously about all the friends they hated in common.

When I finally managed my escape I returned to the living room, drank some beer from an abandoned plastic cup, and surveyed the remains of the party. It was a typical too-many-chips-and-not-enough-salsa affair. A keg of Miller. A pulsating strobe light carefully timed to induce seizures in epileptics. And, after a time, nothing to do but dance with my housemate's quasi-girlfriend, Karen.

Dance we did. In increasingly intimate fashion. While the hip-hop boomed and the walls sweated, Karen and I hovered near enough to exhale our hormones on each other.

Seven or eight doomed courtships had at least taught me age-appropriate gyrational dance techniques and what I nervously deduced was fairly competent love-making, but fidelity and honesty had cleverly eluded me by disguising themselves as commitment.

I was certainly curious about Karen's spongy ass and the rest of what I now, belatedly, recognized was a sensuous presence of unearthly magnitude. Thoughts of mischief popped into my head like overnight mushrooms. I was cheerfully willing to forgive myself for invading Carl's territory. I rationalized to myself the uncertainty of his and Karen's — *relationship*, to employ the local vernacular. If he truly cared for her, he'd have been dancing with her, the putz. His whereabouts were unknown.

Gazing at Karen's form as we orbited one another like earth and moon, I was stunned that Carl could have abandoned her for even one gossamer dance. For rare and complete beauty was hers that evening, hers to give or withhold. She knew it, and she chose to give it to me. I was awash in lustglow.

And yet, hippie she had always been, hippie she remained. Every cell in my mind and heart was imprinted with a deep and abiding distrust and dislike of her breed. I felt as though I was being offered a rare but mischievous gift, and I did not know if I should open it or wait until Christmas. I danced to stall for time.

Karen danced with astonishing grace, not at all like a whacked-out hippie spinner, but like the refugee from years of ballet classes she was. With carefree control, her mesmerizing body floated over the landscape like an endangered eagle, her eyes remaining fixed on me, and she was not afraid to hold the gaze, inch for inch, measure for measure.

I was a weakened 19th-century colonial territory. Faced with the might of her British imperial majesty, I was alternately enchanted and frightened, bellicose and acquiescent. But before long, the hard truth became clear: my petty internal struggles were irrelevant. My sovereignty had evaporated before the heat of Karen's sun that never set.

So there we were one hour later in my bedroom back at the apartment, enthusiastically engaged in intimacies when — you guessed it — Carl sitcom-barged in, sleepy-eyed but suddenly not so very sleepy.

I moved into Karen's house on the first of the month and it was an impossible situation by the third. We were as well suited to living together as Newt Gingrich and Hillary Clinton. We quarreled incessantly from the first. Culture, politics, art, religion: the world was pleasantly full of contentious and controversial subjects about which we could disagree in style.

Our lifestyles were utterly incompatible. I tend to stay up quite late. For the first several hours of the morning I am a shade less irritable than a walrus with hemorrhoids. Karen woke with the sun most mornings, cheerful as a blue jay, equally loud, and twice as annoying.

I lived on burgers and fries; Karen was a vegetarian. Indeed, for a time she was something termed, if I have this right, a "vegan." Please ask me no questions.

I wore serviceable black boots; Karen wore Birkenstock sandals or went barefoot. I read Dostoevsky and Faulkner; Karen read women's fashion magazines, and moved her lips when she read.

Perhaps you find her choice of reading material out of character, but I'll let you in on a dirty little secret: all women, no matter how liberated, no matter how hip, no matter how outwardly scornful of the dictates of French fashion, are secretly mesmerized by thick, glossy women's magazines; despite the noxious, obnoxious scented perfume advertisement inserts that serve only to make the reader sneeze.

The planter for our seedling relationship could hardly have been less nurturing. Karen's creepy commune of campy kitschmongers was hardly a match for good old Hal, Benny, macaroni-and-cheese dinners and our ancient black and white T.V. with its inconsistent vertical hold.

"Hi ,guy, here's a pen," Karen said one afternoon shortly after her return from school. "Sign right here, line seven."

I looked up from my book as she sat beside me on the bed. "What is this?" I asked.

"PETA petition. You can put my house as your address."

"Payta?"

"People for the Ethical Treatment of Animals."

"What's it for?"

"It asks the state to stop all testing conducted on animals. Here, sign, I'm going to see who else is home. I'm supposed to get one hundred signatures."

"Sorry," I said, "I'm afraid you can't have mine. I am religiously — no, I am secularly opposed to signing petitions."

"Don't be immature. Just sign it, Ronnie."

"Just give it a rest, Karen. You think anyone really cares about your petty petition? All you people running around politicking like you have any kind of impact on reality truly amuse. I hate to tell you this, but people who have power aren't going to give it up just because some touchie-feelie Santa Cruz troublemakers sign some piece of paper."

"I hate to tell you this," Karen said, one fist on her hip, "but just because certain people are in government doesn't mean they really have power. That's what you don't understand. The only reason they have any power at all is because people give it to them, or because we don't take it away from them. All power derives from the people."

"Thank you, Thomas Jefferson, for that penetrating insight. Listen, there are only two kinds of power: force and wealth. You people haven't got either one."

"We have democracy."

Poor, poor Karen. Her naiveté was so adorable I had to restrain myself from laughing out loud.

"Sorry to burst your bubble, baby, but democracy doesn't mean shit. It doesn't work. It never has, it doesn't now, and it never will. You really think we live in a democracy?"

"No, of course not, and please stop calling me 'baby'. You think I don't know how messed up things are in America, Ronnie? But that's the whole point. That's why we have to get involved, to make it work better, to create democracy with our actions."

"It's pointless, Karen. It's never going to get you anywhere. You might win one small fight once in a while, but that's just because they need to throw you a bone every now and then to make sure you're happy little doggies. But there'll never be true democracy. It goes against man's nature. Ours is a competitive, selfish species. The history of man is the history of war and greed, pure and simple."

Karen's lungs heaved a deep sigh. She shook her head in quiet frustration and desperation, and went off to recruit less enlightened residents of the house to sign the petition.

By the time she came back I had marshalled several new points to shore up my case, but she just looked at me quizzically — and this is the most peculiar aspect of the whole episode — and wanted to know if I wanted to go see the sunset.

"That volcano that erupted is going to make some beautiful sunsets," she said, "because of all the dust it threw into the air."

"Did anyone else sign the petition?" I asked.

Karen frowned. "Why do you ask? Just to get in another fight?"

"Well, yep. Pretty much," I said. "To further debate the issue, I would prefer to phrase it."

"Listen, I'm heading to the knoll to check out the sunset. Coming?"

"No, going," I said. "Definitely going. I've seen sunsets. I need a burger. You need anything?"

"I need peace," she said, and walked off into the sunset.

Allow me to summarize: Karen and I got along like a mouthful of toothpaste and orange juice.

Chapter 8

Deep in those desperate days, I went back on a secret foray to the old apartment one afternoon when Carl was at work. I wanted to see the boys and hear their counsel, such as it was. They were the best I had. Truly useful advice is available only from those two sisters from Iowa who have monopolized the advice racket for fifty years.

Benny had found an old computer monitor and keyboard and had taken it apart, strewing the pieces across the room. It was an art project of some sort. Poster board, a doll's head, sequins and several bottles of Elmer's glue were also involved. Hal lay on the couch, eating a TV dinner for breakfast at lunchtime and reading a very old *Rolling Stone*. Pearl Jam was on the cover. Hal and I shared an obsession with Pearl Jam worthy of the most adoring teeny-bopper.

"Find anyone to replace me?" I asked, watching Benny toy with his project.

"As if anyone ever could," Benny said, his voice dripping sarcasm, his hands dripping glue.

"We figured we'd clean up around here a bit before we brought anyone over," Hal said. "Sometime in the autumn of 2017 we hope to have the place all *primo*. Hey, how long were you planning on sticking around for? I was thinking of getting a nap in."

"Not much longer," I said. "Thanks for making me feel so delightfully welcome. Anyway, I gotta clear out before Meathead comes back."

"You know," Hal said, "Meathead's really not that bad. The other day he shared a fantastic oatmeal-jello recipe with me. We're bonding, I tell you. You really should give him a chance, Shorenstein."

Benny took a deep breath and launched into one of his endless sentences: "Ronald doesn't really dislike our friend Carl to the extent he pretends; actually, he feels overwhelming guilt for stealing the man's girlfriend, but is too much of a coward to acknowledge and face that guilt, so he externalizes it onto Carl, thereby distracting from the real issues at hand, and indulging in a little blaming of the victim in the process."

"Bingo," I said, with genuine admiration.

"So what does the future hold for the happy young couple?" Hal asked me.

"I don't know, boys, truly I don't. My log is at a jam. To outward appearance, things would seem to be going as well as might be expected. But the truth is, the woman drives me absolutely up the fucking wall."

"What seems to be the problem?" Benny asked.

I hesitated, suddenly unsure about confiding in Benny. Not because I didn't trust him, but because I couldn't imagine that he had ever been near a woman. Still, the man hoards a wealth of insight about a great many subjects about which he cannot possibly have first-hand knowledge.

"Where do I start? She's a nut," I said. "She's — a child. A flower child. She's a fully accredited cadet in the space program. She sings to her plants. She hugs everyone she knows every time she sees them. She massages strangers. She dances if the sunrise inspires her. Right smack in the middle of her bedroom sits an incense- eagle feather- Bob Marley shrine with candles, sage and a rusted-out green Buddha."

"What does she sing?" Hal wondered.

"What?"

"To her plants. What does she sing to them?"

"'Puff the Magic Dragon,'" I said.

"Ouch!!" Hal said, "that smarts."

Benny nodded. "This is very serious. 'Puff the Magic Dragon'? Boy, you weren't kidding, were you?"

"No, damn it. I'm at my rope's end, I tell you."

"What to do, what to do?" Benny muttered.

"And?" Hal asked. Coming from him this could only mean one thing.

"That's just it," I said. "It's unbelievable."

"What is?" Benny demanded.

"The sex," Hal explained patiently.

"Magnifique," I said. "Incroyable. La creme de la creme. Nonpareil."

"Me amo Miguel," Hal added, nodding appreciatively. "In vino veritas. Perestroika."

"Ich bin ein Berliner," Benny threw in. "L'état c'est moi. Gung hay fat choy."

"Eine Kleine Nachtmusik," I said, "and let's just leave it at that."

Hal gave me an emphatic high-five.

"Whew," Benny said. "I can see we have our work cut out for us."

"What work?" Hal said.

"Extricating Ronald from this dilemma, moron."

"What dilemma?" Hal wanted to know.

"Weren't you listening?" Benny said, exasperated. "The poor man is dating Puff the Magic Dragon."

"The poor man is getting laid," Hal said. "Big time. Right, Shorenstein?"

"Big time," I confirmed.

"So, what's the problem?" Hal shrugged, wiping gravy from his mouth with his sleeve. "Someday you'll wanna settle down, maybe breed some puppies. When that happens you'll want someone you can, you know, discuss Proust with, if that's what swells your lymph nodes. Whoever Proust is. Meanwhile, you're a swinging bachelor guy, a free agent on the talent market. Enjoy it while you've got it. You're carefree, you're young, she's younger. Have fun. God bless."

"God bless the child," I said, reflectively.

"Exactly," Hal said. "No worries, mate."

"Many worries, mate," Benny insisted. "Ronald is poised on the horns of an excruciating dilemma, square in the middle of a duality. His mind is telling him one thing, but his heart the opposite."

"Not quite his heart," Hal corrected him laconically. "A little south of that."

"Hegel would dissect the matter as follows," Benny said. "Thesis: your body is pleased with the status quo. Antithesis: your mind begs you to flee at the earliest possible moment."

"Synthesis," Hal interrupted, "stop thinking so much."

"Synthesis," Benny continued with a glare in Hal's direction, "seek inner harmony."

"Inner harmony? Jesus H. Christ," I said, "you sound like Karen now. Wanna do my tarot? Inner harmony, my left nut."

"Amen," said Hal. "No New Age crap from you, Benny."

"New Age? New Age??" Benny cried, horrified. In his agitation he knocked over a box of golden sequins from his art project. A good many of them landed on the legs of his jeans, upon which he had been wiping his gluey hands. The result was a look not unlike an Olympic ice skater's, or Tina Turner at her flashiest. I thought it suited Benny, somehow.

"I'm not talking New Age," he insisted, picking futilely at his clothes. "This is Old Age. This is time-tested wisdom. Inner harmony is a basic tenet of all Eastern philosophies. From the time — "

" — oh, for God's sake," Hal growled, "just give him your useless advice and get it over with."

"Time, then," Benny said, "time and distance. Remember those two elements. You have not known the young woman in question more than a month, yet you spend the great majority of your waking and sleeping hours in her no doubt exalted company. It's no wonder you're confused. I have a simple motto for you to memorize: when getting together with someone, do it slowly; when breaking up, do it quickly."

"What the hell are you doing walking around with a motto like that?" Hal wondered. "It's not like you'd ever have use for it."

"It's an utterly sensible plan," Benny said, ignoring him. "And it's so easy to remember. It's astonishing how many people do the exact opposite. Remember: getting together, do it slowly. You've been moving too fast. Move out of her house immediately. Once out, you will be able to think more clearly. Make no decisions regarding your romantic future for the next month or two. If you decide after that time to break up, do it quickly. End of sermon."

Damn that Benny. Damn that sequined little bookworm. He was right, as usual. Great White and I kissed the boys a fond farewell and rumbled over to Karen's house. I gathered up all my belongings and left her a long, confusing note, full of ill-founded hostility and misplaced maudlinisms. Later I returned to tear it up, but the light was on in her window, and Great White slunk away sheepishly before I could stop him.

He and I headed out to face the grave gray world. I knew I was up against a generally unacknowledged reality of American life: the rental market is actually quite hard to crack. The town I call my home ranks as one of the most difficult and expensive housing markets anywhere. Even if one has the money, anything remotely desirable is highly competitive. One has to prove oneself worthy of the exalted privilege of shelling out ungodly sums of rent through a humiliating process of applications and interviews horrifyingly reminiscent of the Great Job Search. I was not yet ready to crank up the rusty engine of charm and face Phase Two of The Inquisition, so I slept in Great White's belly that night and the next. An educational experience, that. What I learned: it is both cold and illegal to sleep in one's car in Santa Cruz, California.

It is difficult to conceive of a more humiliating, absurd, and — dare I say it — fascist law. What damage was I doing others? Had I stayed awake, parked by the side of the road, reading a road map or flossing my teeth, I would have been innocent of any wrongdoing. The simple loss of consciousness was an inexcusable and offensive harm to society's best interests. I felt as though I had been caught asleep while standing guard in the army. For the second time in a month I was rousted by cops with flashlights, but this time I was alone, and in a very bad mood.

The cop said, "I need you to move along, kid."

"You don't *need* me to," I snarled, "you'd *like* me too. I despise the substitution of the phrase 'I need you to' in place of 'please'. Commit another breach of grammatical etiquette around me and you'll sorely regret it, you lazy, corrupt, donut-eating pig. You want to take me in? Why don't you just try it, fat boy?"

Well, not quite. What I actually said was this: "Yes, sir."

All other options exhausted, I rented an apartment in Swan Lake Apts., a notoriously sleazy apartment complex, home to the lowest dregs of society: pushers, pimps and Amway sales representatives. It was the one place in the entire county where I could be certain my application would be accepted as long as I had the money, in cash, up front, which I did — barely.

If the residents of Swan Lake had been anyone but the marginal dregs of society, that tenement would have been condemned years ago. My apartment was the absolute cheapest little hovel this side of Rwanda. A dwarf would have found it cramped. By comparison, my former apartment was the Palace at Versailles, making either Benny or Hal — or Carl, I suppose — the modern reincarnation of Louis XIV, the Sun King.

Safe in my new rat hole I contemplated my newfound solitude. Was life truly better in my new digs than in Karen's bed? Was Benny right? Was living together with Karen in close quarters a curse, as he claimed, or was it a blessing, as it now seemed? Was it the only thing that kept Karen and me together, or was it the cause of all our misery? At times during the long sleepless days and nights in my new purgatory, I convinced myself finally and utterly that our romantic enterprise was utterly hopeless. Our interests were utterly divergent, and there was no evidence they would ever grow much closer. While they remained apart, there was not much sense in our remaining together. A decision seemed to be making itself. Time to end it.

And yet, and yet. There were the astrophysics to consider. The law of gravity states that all bodies attract one another according to mass. We do not just fall to the earth. We pull it closer, and it pulls us. Everything which surrounds us — birch trees and buckles, mosques and missiles, U-Haul trucks and kindergarten swings, all pull at us and at the earth, all the time. We do not sense the pull of these smaller objects because the pull of the earth is so very overwhelming, its mass so very much greater, that all other mini-gravities are cancelled out.

But if two small bodies found themselves out in deepest space, far from the gravitational pull of the earth or the sun or any cosmic mass, would they not, naturally and inevitably, fall toward each other?

I called Karen a few days later. She was happy to chat, as always. No mention was made by either party of my dramatic departure from her dreaded domicile. We talked of one thing and another, but mostly she wanted to know if I had seen the purple and yellow flowers blooming in the ivy along West Cliff. I had not. Would I like to?

And so the months tripped over themselves. I could not follow Benny's dictum, because I was never sure if I was getting together with Karen or breaking up with her. Things developed as things generally do, absent of drama. At no point did Karen and I throw heavy dishes across a seething kitchen with a ferocious sense of dramatic climax. Neither did we stand hand in hand, humble, well-dressed and abashed before a preacher, reciting outdated wedding vows.

We never even spoke about such outcomes. We chitter-chattered. We caught some flicks. We dined at diners, as diners will. We bickered like children. We shuttled our needy bodies between our two hopeless homes like animals in heat, letting the coil of mortality unwind itself as it chose.

And then Eva came to town.

Chapter 9

"Wait, he's just coming in," Eva said into the phone upon my return from dropping Karen off into the waiting paws of her friend Sam the Talking Squirrel. "Hold on."

Eva tossed the receiver at me. I held my hand over the mouthpiece. "Who is it?" I asked.

She shrugged. "Some guy. He didn't say."

"Is it about a job?"

"Ronnie," Eva said, the gears of anger mode swiftly meshing and engaging, "he didn't say. You need me to hang up on him for you? Grow up and talk to people."

I glared at her. Very poor call screening. She glared back.

"Hello," I told the phone.

"Hey, man," came the unceremonious greeting, "it's Gregory Thompson, from the Environmental Club. How you be?"

I invested a very pissed-off look at Eva. She returned it with accrued compound interest in the form of a lethal, malignant sneer, then turned away.

"I be fine," I grunted into the phone.

"Hey, we need your help."

"Yeah?"

"Hey, remember that press release you did?"

"Only too well."

"Well, hey, listen, that was the only time we ever got any media coverage."

How very surprising.

"Since then," Gregory continued, "we've kinda been treading water. We've got a big event coming up and we're asking everyone who really cares about Deerpark to come help out."

The effrontery. How the hell did I get on the list of those who really cared about Deerpark? I often find myself on inexplicable lists. I continually receive catalogs targeted at the electronics consumer, despite never having purchased anything more technical than batteries. I'm also very popular with the makers of outdoor apparel. No matter how often I change my address, the gortex parka people track me down. Maybe that's how I got on Gregory's list, by virtue of some marketing mixup or credit company snafu.

"Anyway," Gregory said, without divulging his sources, "you're the one guy I can count on to deal with this shit right. Is there any way you could come up here around five? Karen's around, and said you'd come up, and we sure need you. I mean, you're the man."

There being no job interviews scheduled, my choices of afternoon entertainment seemed to have been defined for me: circle warily around the apartment with Eva like a pair of caged rare white Bengal tigers, with neither Siegfried nor Roy to tame us; or be sucked back into the vortex of sophomoric shenanigans perpetrated by a group of dropout aspirants and future panhandlers who for some odd reason looked to me as their scribe and savior.

I have this weakness: I'm a sucker for sycophants. Sue me. No, don't. Eva claims ours is an overly litigious society.

The little twerps had their sit-in going on in the large lobby of the campus library. Don't ask me why. Maybe they felt the need to be near reference material and the rigid comforts of the Dewey decimal system.

The tall glass walls of the library lobby were fogged up with the humidity of the fifty or so creatures flopped about in various positions of offensive comfort within the cavernous greenhouse. Some were sleeping on mattresses and sleeping bags they had brought into the building. Some were ladling out bowls of a horrid gray vegetarian porridge slop, and little conferences of great consequence were going on in every little corner. The lobby was noisy with echoes and smelled like a boxer's armpit.

Words were everywhere. Butcher-paper banners were festooned high on the walls, proclaiming, "Tell UC Regents where to GO!" and "No Nukes in Deerpark" and "E. Club Gen. MTg Daily 12"

Tables were piled high with literature. Background information on the project, on the University of California, on the Ohlone Indians, fought for space with poorly copied handouts detailing the history of the protest to date, obscure Communist Party journals, and hastily scrawled personal messages on the order of, "Patti, meet us here @4 unless you're already gone, JB & CC."

From this chaos I was expected to distill order. A great big protest was scheduled for the next day. It was to be the grandaddy of all protests of the entire week, perhaps the month, and the E. Club needed big press coverage. To do the job right, they were bringing out the big guns: viz., me.

"Excuse me, would you like some information about the Deerpark project?"

Never make eye contact with a beggar, leafleter or petitioner. Once human eye has met human eye, hope for escape is severely diminished. I demurred and pressed on, searching for the nerve center of the operation. I scanned the lobby, but Karen was nowhere to be found.

I did find the fabled Gregory, but he was in no shape to chat. He was, in fact, stretched out on a bench, pale, pained and bloodied. Blood-soaked bandages adhered to his legs, arms and face in what I initially assumed was some macabre protest costume.

The truth was more pedestrian. Gregory had been speeding down the bike path when a pedestrian had appeared out of nowhere and Gregory, ever the nonviolent sort, had avoided collision by swerving and flying headlong into a gravelly grave.

Hyperbole. He was still alive, but the moans issuing forth from his prostrate form would have aroused the pity of even the most petrified heart. I confess I was largely unmoved.

Gregory was surrounded by ten or fifteen nervous, solicitous followers. Their leader, the issuer of all instructions, the inspiration and the guiding light, had just been rendered a moaning wretch. It was a jolt to the whole group, a blow of both great gravity and subtle nuance difficult to convey. Think of it this way: the group was Marie Antoinette's body, heavily scented and inert; the accident on the bikepath was a guillotine; and Gregory was Marie's severed head, bloodied and useless, falling with a thud into a bucket originally meant to hold the finest red Bordeaux.

"Ron Shorenstein?"

Yipes! Who? I whirled and —

Shit, spotted. Fred Miles, history professor. My advisor. Probably the only teacher on campus who would remember me. We faced off near the library entrance, he shuffling papers, I shuffling my feet. I kept a wary ATM distance.

"Hello, Fred," I admitted. All UCSC professors go by their first names. No Dr. Miles, no Professor Miles, No Mr. Miles for them. Here on the avant garde West Coast the educators reject academia's nominal formalism while heartily embracing its income, security, and petty departmental authoritarianism.

"I thought we'd graduated you, Ron."

"I've uh, returned to the proverbial scene of the proverbial crime, as it were," I said. The well-educated intimidate me. It pains me to hear myself straining to sound erudite in their presence. I usually come off sounding like a badly written high-school paper. Don't think I'm unaware of that. The memory makes me grimace with embarrassment.

"Are you involved in the Deerpark protests?" Fred asked.

"No, not. I mean, I'm not a participator — participant."

"Too bad," Fred said, "we could use more of an alumni presence."

"Oh, I — sympathize," I hastened to add. "I'm kind of a fellow traveler, as it were."

"Very good," Fred said. "Maybe I'll see you at the rally tomorrow."

"Maybe," I said.

Maybe, maybe not. Two phrases of exact equal value. I smiled at Fred with my yellowed teeth of uncertainty.

He said, "They've asked me to say a few words."

"Really? Oh, good. Very good. Very good for you. A — uh — a propitious outcome, as it were."

"That remains to be seen," Fred laughed. "I'm not tenured yet."

The deeper meaning of this joke escaped me, but Fred seemed to find it rock-solid material. I laughed along with a clueless, edgy, false hilarity. Did the man have nowhere better to be, nothing more important to do on the gigantic campus than intimidate alumni?

Suddenly sirens sounded. They grew louder. Sharp-witted as ever, I took this to mean they were getting nearer, and sure enough bustling paramedics in tight-fitting blue uniforms were soon chopping with machetes through the hippie forest to find Gregory. As the crowd parted to let the paramedics through, I was left exposed, and Gregory spotted me.

"Hey, man," he called out in a strained voice. I checked behind me to see if, merciful God willing, Gregory might be calling to Fred Miles. No such luck. The good professor had flown the coop at the first sign of authorities. He probably grows pot in his backyard and finds anything resembling a cop disconcerting.

"Yeah, you, Karen's boyfriend," Gregory groaned, motioning me closer. I approached him just as the paramedics came running up. There ensued a peculiar triangular conversation: the paramedics trying to determine Gregory's medical status; Gregory trying to explain what he wanted from me; and self trying to determine the quickest escape route.

"Can you tell us your name?" the paramedics asked.

"Gregory Thompson. What's your name again?"

"I'm Dave and this is Jack."

"No, you," pointing at me.

"Ron Shorenstein."

"Who are you?" the paramedics demanded.

"Passer-by," I said.

"Please clear the area."

"He's my friend," Gregory said, greatly exaggerating. "I need to talk to him. Come here, Ross, take this." He held up a sheaf of paper.

"It's Ron. I have to clear the area," I pointed out cheerfully.

"Can you stretch your toes?" Dave asked.

"Sure," I said, honestly confused.

"Not you," Dave said, "you, Thompson."

Thompson stretched his toes, and screamed in pain.

"OK," Jack said, "we've got fractured right tibia, multiple abrasions. Pulse and BP OK." Dave nodded in agreement with the diagnosis. They began setting the leg in a splint.

"Do you have any pain in your head?"

Like you wouldn't believe, buddy.

"No, not at all," Gregory said, the pain and delerium readily evident in his voice. "I'm fine, I don't need an ambulance."

"Why don't you relax and let us figure that out, O.K.?"

I started backing away from the unpleasant scene.

"Oh, man, I need your help!" Gregory moaned.

"We're going to take you to the hospital," Dave said, squatting attentively. "They'll fix you up there."

"No, him. I don't need your help, I need him. Ross, come here."

I came back closer. I felt like a yo-yo on Gregory's bedside string.

"I asked you to clear the area," Dave said.

I held my arms spread-eagle, palms to the sky with the universal expression meaning: what can I do?

Unfortunately, Gregory was just the sort of schmuck who prepares answers for such questions. As they strapped him onto the gurney, he handed me his sheaf of paper and started talking very quickly in a low voice. It felt very much as though he was trying to convey his dying wishes before they shipped him off to the funny farm.

As I danced in and out of the way of the efficient boys in blue, Gregory confided the sad fact that he did not really trust any of his campus colleagues. They were good-hearted, but none had the intelligence, the charisma to replace Gregory the Great, who apparently conceived of himself as the second coming of John F. Kennedy.

That's where I came in. As they loaded him into the ambulance, it finally dawned on me that what Gregory had given me was his speech for the rally the next day. A darker dawn followed: he was asking me to deliver it in his stead.

"O.K., back off," the paramedics said to me.

"Will I be out of the hospital and walking around by noon tomorrow?" Gregory asked the paramedics.

"Sorry kid, not a chance. You'll need to rest."

"Then please, Ross," Gregory pleaded, "take the speech. I'm going to be in the hospital. You're the only one I know who can do it."

This was really getting to be too much. Gregory's little act was dripping with sufficient sappy melodrama to rival one of those annoying, excessively reserved British films in which the upper-class Victorian heroine must choose between the passionate pauper and the wealthy, well-meaning but insufferably dull fiancé.

I knew Gregory's act was bullshit, but listen: the sheaf of paper I now held in my hands was actually splattered with blood. The man was screaming in agony whenever his leg was bumped. The paramedics were cranking up the sirens and the lights, and the crowd was staring at me. They could tell that Gregory had issued a deathbed request, but they were unsure what it was, or whether I was going to accept. Shit. You try to refuse under those circumstances.

"Promise you'll do it?" Gregory called out in his most pathetic voice.

The crowd waited.

Aah, shit.

"I'll get it done," I said.

Christ. How do I get myself into these messes? I immediately determined to find someone to do it for me, and fast.

As the ambulance rolled away and the crowd dispersed, Karen came skipping up the path. She spotted me and gave me an impromptu all-body hug.

"I was just thinking of you," I said, trying not to touch her back with the bloodstained paper.

"Good thoughts, I hope."

"Nope," I said. "As a matter of fact they were sucky thoughts."

"Oh, what?" Karen pouted. "Are you still upset about this morning?"

"No, I'm upset about tomorrow."

I filled her in on the circumstances of Gregory's dramatic departure.

"Poor Gregory," she said. Tears formed on her corneas so rapidly it was like alchemy.

"Yeah, poor Gregory," I said, "he left me in charge."

"Oh, that's so exciting," Karen gushed, her eyes sparkling with joy. Suddenly, she was no longer upset for Gregory. Karen would make a great mourner. She shot through the stages of denial, acceptance, anger, and reconciliation in approximately seven seconds, and moved on to the next emotional project.

"Oh, this is great," she said. "You get to give the big speech!"

"Karen, this is insane. I know nothing about Deerpark and I care even less. You should be giving this speech."

"Oh, no," she said firmly, "I couldn't. I get stage fright. You'll be great, I can just see it. Besides, you promised Gregory."

"And suppose I withdraw the promise?"

"Then you're an Indian giver," Karen said, teasing me loudly.

As it happened, this comment was overheard by none other than our resident Indian, John Lone Pine, who was sitting cross-legged on a mattress just behind us, drinking malt liquor and reading an economics text book.

"Offensive term," he said, in that quiet voice of his.

"Oh, God," Karen said, clapping one hand over her mouth in mortification. "I'm so sorry, JLP, I didn't mean to — I'm sorry, you're totally right, I can't —"

"— it's cool," JLP said.

You know me: ordinarily his aloof holier-than-thou attitude would have inspired in me a rich desire to defenestrate him through the library's plate glass windows, but it gave me such great pleasure to watch Karen squirm for once like a worm on the hook of political correctness that I almost felt like thanking the self-righteous punk.

We stood there feeling nice and awkward for a few moments. Finally JLP glanced around furtively, and then pulled out a couple of little green bottles of Mickey's Big Mouth from a reserve hidden inside his sleeping bag. He offered one to each of us. We sat down and joined him.

Chapter 10

"A toast," John Lone Pine offered, holding his bottle aloft, "to alcohol: the single greatest enemy facing the Native American people today."

"Cheers," I said, admiring the man's dry delivery.

Karen grinned uncertainly, touched her bottle to his and to mine, and drank a delicate sip.

"Did you hear Gregory had to go to the hospital?" she asked JLP.

"I saw," he nodded. "Heavy drama."

I liked his choice of words. Evidently someone other than me saw through Gregory's thespian mask.

"I missed it," Karen lamented. "Did you hear that Ronnie is going to give his speech instead?"

"Unconfirmed rumor," I said.

"He asked you to, didn't he?" JLP said.

"Yeah," I admitted.

"And you said you'd do it, didn't you?"

I sighed.

"Yes, but my word isn't any good. I'm an inveterate liar."

JLP drank to that. He had an easy-going style about him. I studied him for a little while through the jade green bottle, compelled by an unnameable curiosity. At length I felt a question coalescing in my mind, and then I felt myself restricting it. And that infuriated me. There I sat, mildly subsumed with a reasonable desire to learn more of the world around me, but I was restricting myself as surely as if someone had clamped a hand over my mouth. By the rules of the game, I wasn't supposed to ask the simple question that was on my mind.

That's what bothers me most about these political correctness freaks: the way the tentacles of their thought-control squids can invade my own mind, strangling my thoughts, causing me to censor myself before I've even started to speak.

But like a great scarred sperm whale, I fought off the attack of the giant squid, blurting out my question with a blast of my cetacean blowhole.

"So," I asked JLP, "what's it like being an Indian?"

Karen gaped with horror at the question. "I'm sorry," she said, "he's not —"

" — no, it's cool," JLP said. "I like people who ask direct questions.

Most people tiptoe too much, you know?"

As he spoke I stretched out my cramped right leg and my booted foot thudded to the floor. The echo concussed in the library lobby chamber.

"I'm not very good at tiptoeing," I said.

"Think of us Injuns as mascots," JLP said. "You know, like the Washington Redskins."

"Yeah, right," I said, "or the Atlanta Braves."

"Or the Cleveland Indians. That buck-toothed grinning clown from Cleveland should tell you just about every useful thing you need to know about the Native American experience."

I consider myself something of a connoisseur of sarcasm, and as such my appreciation for JLP's delivery was growing by leaps. No bounds yet, just leaps.

"Well, I for one have learned a lot," I said. "Here I thought all Indians did with their spare time was scalp people."

"Ronnie!" Karen reproached me.

"No, that's one stereotype I like," JLP said. "Makes people think we're scarier than we are."

"How scary are you?" I asked.

"Not too."

I took another gulp. In the back of my mind floated the fearful fact that I had been issued a field commission to deliver a speech the next day, and I had yet to find the proper spud to whom I could toss the hot potato. Karen had already refused. JLP seemed a leading contender. Best to keep him talking, thought I, let him think we're the fastest of friends.

"Seriously," I said, "what's it like being an Indian? I'm really interested."

Karen flinched visibly at the lie. JLP took it at face value. He was quiet for a little while, his features reflecting the contortions of the mind's thought processes.

"I'm not a woman," JLP said. I found this a puzzling and largely unnecessary remark. Fortunately there was more to the thought: "and I don't want to speak for women." To Karen he said, "Stop me if I'm getting it wrong."

She nodded.

"I'm lost," I said, "what are we talking about?"

"You asked what it's like being an Indian. I'm trying to tell you. It's the way women talk about being raped. Violently raped. You have everything taken from you: your life, your dignity."

He looked at Karen for approval. She gave an understanding nod of mutual suffering.

"And the worst of it," JLP said, "is no one believes you. And then you're blamed for your own failures. The native peoples of this land are blamed for our own genocide by the few who remember that it occurred."

I had a brief vision of JLP in a tuxedo, his long hair flowing behind him, a supermodel at his side, as he accepted the Oscar for Best Performance In a Tear-Jerking Lecture. His green cummerbund matched the supermodel's skimpy, sequined miniskirt.

"Did you grow up on a reservation?" I asked.

"No," he said, "I grew up in Oakland."

"What kind of Indian are you?" I asked.

"The angry kind."

"No," asshole, "I guess I meant, what tribe are you from?"

"Cheyenne and Crow. One quarter each, on my father's side."

"Oh," I said, "so you're not — I guess I thought you were one of these Ohlone Indians."

"I'm not," JLP said, "but I've been trying to learn more about them."

"Maybe I'll do the same," I said, not meaning a word of it. "How would you recommend starting?"

JLP shrugged and pointed laconically to the doors behind me. "We're living in a library here. You could look up 'Ohlone'."

"Here," Karen said, reaching into her bag, "you should read this. I just finished it. They're selling more copies at the lit. table if you want your own."

JLP nodded his approval. "That's the best book to start with," he said.

Karen handed the book to me: *The Ohlone Way*, by Malcolm Margolin. The cover depicted an artist's pen and ink rendition of an Ohlone tribesman. He was a squat, hairy guy pulling his boat out to the bay, presumably to do some fishing, and this is the peculiar thing: in that instant when I first looked at the picture I was reminded so deeply of my father that I literally shivered. It was not a physical likeness. The Indian had long hair, features something like an Eskimo's, and was tattooed and naked, but the expression on his face as he headed out to fish was pure Abe Shorenstein.

I remember it was early and late. Early in the morning, late in life, too late in my adolescence for some sudden reconciliation. But Dad had decided that he and I needed to go fishing together, his penance for sins unconfessed. The whole horrible, clumsily staged event felt derived from a third-rate Hollywood psychobabble melodrama. I desperately wanted to avoid the saccharine enterprise, but Mom tricked me into going by slipping guilt pills into my orange juice when I wasn't looking.

Dad woke me up early, as though to make up for lost time. We drove to the Santa Monica pier, where we joined a group of five or six other dysfunctional family fragments heading out to sea on a fishing boat that doubled as a floating surrogate therapy session. Each little fragment had its own special aura of resentment and choked anger, and all hope for reconciliation was invested in the time-tested, mystical powers of fish-murder to serve as catharsis. The stench of our malignant doubts and destructive miscommunications was as prevalent in the air that cold morning as dead flounder on the third day.

If you've never baited fish, you've missed nothing. Get the hook through the eye, kid, right through the eye, there you go, don't be bashful. Christ. I hooked, I tossed my line in the water, I caught absolutely nothing. I did manage to not get seasick. Not much of an accomplishment, I suppose: absence of nausea, more a lack of failure than an achievement, but it nevertheless merited glowing praise from my proud father and the grizzled seawise captain. Considering that most of the crew were auditioning for roles in a Dramamine commercial, I let myself bask in the glow of pointless praise.

Dad, who was raised "with a reel in one hand and a rifle in the other," caught the prize of the day. Just as we were heading back to the pier he landed a small sand shark, approximately twice the length of my skateboard, my new one with the wide polyurethane wheels and the bitchin' trucks. The captain took a Polaroid of the shark, insisting that I hold one end of the tail and Dad the other. He was a piece of work, that captain. He undoubtedly had an MFCC license framed in his quarters below decks somewhere.

In the photo we looked like a couple of idiot Laplanders displaying our grotesque kill, grinning and squinting at the first camera ever to arrive on our shores. The shark was largely inedible, and the other fish Dad caught were too small to do anything but stink up the house. By midnight the neighborhood cats were fighting over the scraps in the garbage can. So the only souvenir of the day was the photo. Mom framed it and displayed it over the fireplace, which itself was strictly ornamental, a Southern California imitation fireplace with no chimney.

The odd, distant look on the Ohlone Indian's face on the cover of the book was copied directly from Dad's expression in the framed shark photo. Maybe the Ohlone gentleman also had a son who shared no interests with him; maybe he had a couple of children who baffled him, who spoke too quickly for him to follow along, who grew ever more impatient with his tiresome sayings and unsolicited advice the older they got. Maybe he was overwhelmed by the peculiar burdens of patrimony. Maybe that's why there was such a resemblance. Do I know?

I shivered. At the first glimpse of that pre-Columbian doppelganger I shivered. Within moments an eeriness seemed to descend upon me, a nameless dread or anticipation or foreboding.

JLP sensed it. Cheerful Karen had no idea anything was amiss, but something seemed to pass between JLP and me; some unspoken acknowledgement of the potency of obscure and ancient talismans to seize and freeze the confused mind and the aching heart,

One of us may have nodded, and that was all, but at that moment his status was elevated from meddlesome college kid to something else, something more respectable or empathetic. I can't say for certain. We finished our bottles off and by tacit agreement started on two more.

"JLP," I said, "you're not going to give that speech for me, are you?"

"Nope. I'm already speaking tomorrow."

"Then you could say my part."

"So could you."

I swallowed a disconsolate mouthful of suds. "Damn. This is ridiculous. Do you really think I should give this speech?"

"No," JLP said, "I think Gregory should."

"Oh, God," Karen said suddenly, "we should visit him, in the hospital."

"Pass," I said.

"Yeah, pass," JLP echoed.

"Oh, damn," I said, "I just remembered. The whole reason I came up here in the first place was to write a press release for Gregory. Now he goes and gets shot behind enemy lines. What am I supposed to do now?"

Karen and JLP gave me an identical look. Their body language, translated into modern English, said: "Quit whining."

What the hell, press releases were my bailiwick. Might as well get it over with. I stood up and surveyed the terrain. A few dozen hippies were coagulated into little clots, organizing one thing and another. Braving the elements, I asked the nearest coterie for information regarding the following day's event. I was directed towards another group, which chased me off to the public information desk. My quest was evolving into a fun little hybrid between a treasure hunt and a visit to the DMV.

The information desk was a card table with the words "Prop of S.C. City Parks and Rec Do Not Remove" stenciled on one of the legs. A stack of red flyers was fluttering up against the weight of a large rock that had been set atop them. A lesser mortal might have given up right then, thinking the journey at a dead end. But not I. My research skills sharp as ever, I pulled out one of the flyers and read it. It yielded all the information I needed to issue the press release. Next I needed to find the keys to the Environmental Club office and its computer.

I could bore you with the painful details of this prolonged search and rescue mission, but I will charitably resist the temptation. I leave it to you to imagine my happy state of mind after two hours of this sort of chasing around.

I returned to sit with JLP and Karen, who did not appear to have moved. In fact, they seemed to be having a grand old time, yukking it up and reminiscing about their old Vaudeville days together.

"Hey, there's a protest tomorrow," I pointed out, irritated. "Am I the only one pulling his weight around here? Aren't you supposed to go to some crucial meeting or other?" I asked Karen.

"Been there, done that," she said sweetly.

"What about you?" I asked JLP.

"Native American issues committee. Nobody but me showed up."

"They're intimidated," Karen said, "because JLP knows way more than they do about Ohlone history and everything."

I sat in fulminating silence for a moment or two, working on a new malt liquor. "Time out," I said to JLP, "I thought you said you weren't an Ohlone Indian. You're some mix of — Sioux and something, right?"

"Crow and Cheyenne."

"Whatever. Plains Indians, right? So what makes you such an expert on extinct coastal tribes?"

"I read," he said. "Us Injuns can do that."

"Really?" I muttered grumpily. I was getting a little tired of him yelling at me in that soft, even voice of his. "Oh, tell me more, JLP," I begged, "please do. Your people, they are so fascinating to me. Are they all condescending little alcoholics?"

"Not all," JLP said slowly. "Most, though. Do all your people shirk responsibility by masking it with nasty sarcasm?"

"Damn straight," I said, laughing in spite of myself, "and damn proud of it. Say it now and say it loud, I'm a smartass and I'm proud."

JLP laughed. "Another toast: to heritage and pride."

We drank up.

One thing led, as things do, to another. Quantum physicists claim that time is a much more mysterious mechanism than we have imagined. Effect can actually precede cause, they tell us. I dispute this. In my experience I have found time to be largely a linear proposition, and on the whole I feel no worse off for the arrangement. Cause: I got pretty damn toasted on malt liquor. Effect: I decided to stay the night with Karen on a mattress on the library floor, two mattresses over from JLP.

Our neighbors in between were a pair of highly serious, ascetic and disapproving young lesbians, who clearly found my malt-liquor-inspired belching contest with JLP an affront of a magnitude very near that of sexual harassment. They appealed to Karen for assistance with severe sisterly stares, but she was busy buzzing about the bustling library hive in search of psychedelic mushrooms for sale.

Negotiations completed, she purloined ten hard-won dollars from my wallet, solicited an equal amount from JLP, and the three of us headed out to the great redwood forest to trip.

Mushrooms are a big favorite with the UCSC crowd. I daresay they are the drug of choice. They are natural, even organic, cheap and readily available. They grow wild in the woods, for God's sake. There is a piece of student lore, no doubt apocryphal, which posits the existence of a variety of mushroom which grows in fresh cow shit. One need only locate the proper mound of steaming cow shit, and the psychedelics are abundant, free, and ripe for the picking.

They also taste like cow shit. The taste was so awful I joined Karen and JLP in downing some of the bland vegetarian slop on offer at the library feed table in order to steady my stomach before swallowing my mushrooms.

We got the giggles, and bad. Before long I felt a giddy euphoria so compelling even a jealous Old Testament God could not have wrenched it from my tenacious grip. Mushrooms provide a trip which is less harsh than LSD, more — dare I say it — more natural. The hallucinations do not have the overwhelmingly vivid, intrusive and often frightening quality of acid. With mushrooms the world comes alive. That may well be the best way of describing the experience. The moon was full that night, which seems to happen periodically, and the visual hallucinations were as fantastic as any I have ever experienced. Lines and shapes changed and shifted beautifully, even magically. The trees glowed with a corona of rainbow colors, as though the spectrum of visible light had been separated by a gigantic, unseen prism. I sat for a time and watched with absolute clarity as a pile of pebbles moved back and forth in a dry ditch. The sight of the pebbles moving and the certain knowledge that they could not actually be moving coexisted peacefully in my amused brain.

We capered about the woods, giggling about this and that, pursuing one or another mission of the sort which seems of vital importance when under the influence of mind-altering chemicals, but in the light of day can readily be identified as the behavior of *Chaeropithecus Africanus*, the African giant baboon.

Primates were, in fact, a recurring theme that evening. Deep in the dark woods JLP decided he had to climb a tree, and the three of us lit into our best impressions of monkey chatter. I can tell you without fear of boasting that I have mastered a chimpanzee impression that is nothing short of miraculous. Karen was working on peculiar low grunts she had learned from renting *Gorillas in the Mist*. JLP turned out to be an agile little gibbon, and he made his way up a tree without killing himself, which in retrospect is little short of amazing, considering that we were all still drunk on malt liquor.

I think the drunkenness introduced a hostile and unpleasant undertone into the mushroom experience, which generally consists more of giggles and fears than of malice or aggression. At the base of the tree Karen and I got in a peculiar little argument which I blame largely on the cheap crap we had been drinking.

"You know why baboons have red butts?" I inquired, squeezing hers.

"Don't!" she squealed.

"It's an invitation," I explained. "The female gets inflamed and red when she's in heat, and then she points her ass at the male that's supposed to fuck her. It gives him a nice easy target."

"That's not true."

"Is true. Makes things easier, don't you think? Human beings should have that arrangement. It would take a lot of the confusion out of the dating scene. Although," I added philosophically, "you and I never needed that, did we, Sherpa?" I fondled her ass again. It seemed, in fact, to be inflamed and glowing red.

"Knock it off!" she said, smacking my hand.

"Be my baboon," I said. "Come on, Karen, be my baboon under the moon."

"I'm not a baboon," she said peevishly, "I'm a gorilla. A gorilla could beat up a baboon easy."

"JLP!" I yelled up into the tree, "don't you wish women had big red butts like baboons so they could signal the men when they're ready for action?"

"... could sure use it," Karen muttered.

"What?" I demanded. "What the fuck did you just say?"

"Nothing."

"No, you said something about my sister."

"Stop," Karen whined, "you're making everything all squishy. Ugly. I don't like it."

"Don't you say shit about her," I said. "Ever."

"Baboooon!" JLP yelled out. "Baboooooon!"

Karen and I started laughing so hard we forgot our argument. It was not until days later that I remembered it.

"Baboooon!" JLP yelled. It's a very funny word.

"Shhhh!" I yelled back, giggling like a Japanese schoolgirl, "the cops."

"Baboooooon!" He sang: "And the big baboon/one night in June/he married them/and very soon/they went upon their abadaba honeymoon!" This turned out not to be hallucinatory gibbering, but an actual song. Actually, it may have been both; I was not present during the composition process. JLP yelled down that it was a hit from some 50's musical. Once he started singing it there was no stopping him. Mr. J. L. Pine may have presented a quiet and measured countenance to the outside world when sober, but inside him Debbie Reynolds was struggling to emerge. That night she gave her finest performance since "Singin' in the Rain," which was Evie's favorite album when she was eight. Mom had purchased it in Sweden. It played an integral part in her Americanization process. I was not allowed to use the record player, but Evie was. She used to play that record over and over and we'd sing it together.

After a serenade that seemed hours long, Karen and I started pleading with JLP to come down, but he grew a bit fearful and in the end I had to climb up and get him. I remember that climb with great clarity.

From the moment I first hoisted my body into the lowest bole of the tree, I began to experience the most powerful sense of déja vu. It was an uncanny, almost supernatural sensation. I'm not sure if déja vu is the right term. It almost felt as though it was both memory and premonition, as though I was remembering, with great prolonged clarity, something important I was going to do in the future.

"JLP," I called out, "are you there?"

His silhouette, seen from below in the gathering moonshine, seemed to be frozen and glowing, like a dimmed computer screen stuck in system failure. He sat motionless with a species of paralytic paranoia, one arm extended before him. I clambered up and took an awkward seat at his side on a wide, gnarled branch of what was in all likelihood an oak tree. It stood thick, mighty, and alone on a elevated, dignified hillock. It was no doubt the solemnity of its isolation which made JLP climb it in the first place.

Below us stretched the forest, undulating like a giant carpet, some scattered lights twinkling cheerily, and the ocean miles below. Despite the darkness, I could see individual trees at great distance with great clarity, which rendered me wildly euphoric. The trunk of a redwood tree is a thick, dusty pillar of distinctive scent, of rare beauty and strength, but it has a soft, permeable bark, the outer layer of which can be shredded by the human hand. I could smell the rust-brown bark of every tree, and feel on my face the great green canopy of leaves and twigs and glorious oxygenated photosynthesis. There was a tactile joy in every perception.

JLP glanced at me once, like a nervous, humble rodent, and looked away. His hand was still outstretched, reaching towards a broad sweep of moonlit forest, pointing.

"Look," he said, "the trees!"

I gazed in the direction of his accusatory forefinger. Across the ravine, into the hills and human habitations, one by one, the trees were disappearing.

"Oh, Christ!" I said, suddenly obscenely frightened. "What do we do?" My voice was a strangled whisper and there was an element of fear in every word I spoke.

"We can't stop it," JLP said. "Don't you think they tried?"

When I stared at them directly, the redwood giants stood with majestic, steadfast serenity, unmoved by the ravages of fire or flood, of time or mortal danger. But those trees that hovered in the periphery of my vision kept disappearing, so that at every moment I turned my head, trying to witness the uprooting as it occurred.

We watched, petrified, as a mighty, unseen force slowly, steadily, plucked every living tree from the heart of the great redwood forest, yanking them into horrible oblivion with a fearsome and alien force, unstoppable, incomprehensible and disdainful. The cataclysm seemed to be striking both directly below us in the wide, shallow valley in which the university lights twinkled, and at the far edges of the forest, in the mystical distance beyond known lands.

The pace of the destruction was enormous, astonishing and brutal. The entire forest was being decimated, leaving behind a scorched and naked earth. There was a great tearing noise that shattered the sky. Small creatures ran scurrying from under brush, hopping madly for any shelter. Frightened, elemental birds departed their accustomed perches and flew off in great, silent flocks into the endless west, and were gone. Only the ocean, glistening far below us, seemed unmoved by armageddon.

Breathing heavily with nervous rage, I had to tear my eyes away from the carnage. I peered down into the gloom at the base of the tree to check on Karen. She was staring at her hand, fascinated, and seemed content to continue doing so until the new millennium rang in.

JLP was shivering. "I can't move," he cried piteously.

I put an uncomfortable arm around him. "You can, you can," I said. "It's just bad tripping, JLP. Close your eyes. It will end. Just wait. It'll be over. It will end. It's just a trip. It will end." I kept repeating that calming mantra, which Eva had pioneered in our experimental years.

We sat there for what seemed a century or two. By common reckoning, I imagine it was close to an hour. I comforted JLP, avoided looking at the forest, and stared at Karen below me. Her head shrank, swelled, and shrank again.

An eon or so later, JLP came around. I looked out into the forest and saw that the trees had returned.

"I feel sick," JLP said.

"So do I," I said, "let's climb down."

His knuckles were white and red with grasping tension as he moved down the tree. He was breathing so hard I spent a minute mentally reviewing CPR procedures, which I have never really learned.

Eventually we landed.

"Everything is beautiful," Karen said, but then again she always said that.

"You can touch ... " JLP said, breathing hard and sweating, " ... you can touch ... touch the past tonight."

I nodded, because it seemed true.

"You know ... you know how old this tree is?" he asked. We all patted it, as though to comfort it.

"This tree was here before them," JLP said.

"Them?"

"The missionaries. This tree was here when only animals and native human beings walked here. This same fog wrapped itself around them."

"Oooh," Karen shivered, "creepy."

"No, it's not, it's not," JLP said. "Not creepy. It's ... good. It's like, even if they're all gone, even if we can't see them or hear them or talk to them, we're living in the same world as them, so that makes them still alive. It's the same place, the same conditions, right? All around me, just as it was hundreds of years ago. That makes me one of them. That makes you one of them."

That was a very disturbing image. The powerful sense of déja vu returned to haunt me. Everything moved as though in a dream, but a dream strange and foreign to me. It felt more as though I was a shadowy figure in someone else's dream.

"In the tree," JLP said, "I felt like I was going to fall."

"Me too," I said.

"But not onto the ground," JLP said. "Like I was balanced on the brink. Check it out: there was this Ohlone song, the only one that was ever written down, called *Dancing on the Brink of the World*. But that's just the title. Nobody knows what the words were, because they were never written down. Except I just figured out what it was all about.

"Between past and future, JLP said. "Between life and death. See, between morning and night, between land and ocean, between this world and the next, there is a brink, and we are all poised on the brink of the world."

"I feel sick," I said.

"Uggh, God, me too," JLP said.

For the next half hour, with great solidarity, we vomited like brethren.

Chapter 11

I awoke with a headache you wouldn't believe if I gave it to you. My body stunk, my mind was gray, my belly was angry and hungry, and my speech was due in three hours.

I went to the library men's room. Quite a few of my furry library campground companions were performing their morning ablutions; washing, shaving and even shampooing in the sinks. I contented myself with the bare necessities. I dried my face with a brown paper towel which was quite charming in many ways but utterly lacked absorbency, a deficiency one rarely finds in the best towe¹s.

Above the toilet paper dispenser were inscribed the following words of wisdom in felt-tip marker:

UCSC diplomas: take one

Also on display upon the yellow tile wall were the following:

What has a thousand teeth and holds back a monster? My zipper.
Ha ha ha that's not funny.
The Pope smokes dope
O-Chem sucks.
You suck dicks fag!
Pele's real name is Edson Nascimento Arantes
Dante is in Milton's Hell and Milton is in Dante's.

I just thought you might need to know.

I sat down in a quiet carrel in a corner of the library to familiarize myself with my inherited text. I do not know what exactly I had imagined was contained in the sheaf of paper Gregory had thrust my way. By way of content I suppose I had expected a stirring revolutionary manifesto, sensible yet outraged: the Magna Charta meets the Port Huron Statement, with a heart. The form I expected was something on the order of five pages, double spaced, one-inch margins, key words in bold face.

Surprise, Shorenstein!

The exact contents of the speech, as scrawled in pen in Gregory's hand, are listed below. The blood of Our Fearless Leader had splattered on the page as he was carried away by the boys in blue. It had dried and formed an intricate Rorschach blot that I interpreted either as Gregory, with an afro, sliced in two by a nice sharp machete; or his bicycle, crushed into scrap metal by a giant gavel.

Blot aside, the less compelling part of the page read as follows:

Introduce self.
Who we are. petitions. ~~skit?~~
Links with other uc.
Thanx admin/faculty/staff
Bkgrnd on Drprk: regents/ ac. senate/ prjct hstory.
Size!
Deer/Park explain magic of name
Global enviro link — deforestation
Ohlone remains. Sacred.
Smoking gun
Do cheer 4x
Demands
Remind mtg.
Thanx

I was stunned by the sparsity. Surely there was more. I certainly could not stand before a crowd of hippies — even before a crowd of normal people — and recite those meager marginalia. I leafed hastily through the rest of the paperwork, hoping against hope that the real speech was buried somewhere inside. But the packet merely consisted of supporting materials: newspaper articles, bureaucratic documents, maps, and many pages of signed petitions.

My head sank lower and lower as I made my way through the pointless pages. I remember quite clearly that after I mined the last page to be certain it did not contain some hidden nugget of oratory, my tired forehead slumped down and smacked directly onto the carrel desk, producing a loud, hollow wooden thud. You may reproduce that sound, now, in the comfort of your own home, if you'd like. Take a large bath towel. Roll it up and wet it thoroughly. Now, with a relaxed motion, slap the towel on the bathroom floor. Take care not to snap your wrist. We're not looking to produce a sharp, gunshot sound. What we're after is the wet thud of despair, the sound made by an anguished, hung-over derelict realizing at last the magnitude of the responsibility he has accepted, the absolute certainty that he cannot escape it, and the bleak knowledge that he is about to look like a clueless buffoon in front of hundreds of people.

Oddly, my first thought after sensation returned to my dull skull was vast relief that the skit had been scratched from Gregory's list. I tried to imagine what the plot might have been, and in doing so broke into a semblance of a smile for the first time that morning. It was no doubt the sort of amateur guerilla political theater that makes vaudeville seem subtle in comparison. The idea of Gregory Thompson, the self-righteous causemeister, hamming it up in a skit sounded as appealing as Dr. Ruth Westheimer doing the Charleston in a leotard.

Goddamn Gregory, thought I. Hope your leg hurts like hell. Hope it's fractured, infected and gangrenous. Hope you have to spend six months in the hospital piling up astronomical medical bills.

No, I won't sign your goddamn cast.

The son of a bitch had abandoned me with a scratch outline. Surely I could be absolved of my speechifying responsibilities now.

I ran the scenario through my head quickly: I could run to Karen, to JLP, to the yahoos in charge, explain the problem, hand off the absurd skeletal notes, and beam back to the dimensional plane you and I customarily inhabit.

This fantasy lasted a happy few minutes, but I could visualize the results: I would plead and whine, they would insist and whine, and we'd repeat the same arguments from the night before to no particular avail. My mind was like a gerbil on a Habitrail, quickly running in a very small circle and getting nowhere. *I don't wanna — but you gotta; I don't wanna — but you gotta.* The rhythm was rather hypnotic, almost as steady as the passage of the minutes as the fateful hour approached. I grabbed the keys to Great White, fairly certain he had already eaten a nice sourdough parking ticket for breakfast. Maybe I would just make my break, perhaps troll down the hill before anyone could see me.

But I stopped in my tracks. There was another factor at work. I had given my word. I'm certain you'll find this hard to believe, but when I give my word, I take pride in it. That's why I almost never give it. It takes coercion. I don't know where I got this particular streak of obstinate moral code, because Lord knows it does not mesh with my generally unreliable and shifty character, but the fact is, I never betray such confidences. My word is my bond. My exact words to Gregory had been, "I'll do my best."

Damn.

I put the keys to Great White back in my pocket and jumped up from the carrel. I needed help. I needed fast and thorough research assistance. Did I rummage through microfiche? Did I ask a librarian for help? Did I search the library's Web computer, perhaps under http://hippie.speech@rightnow.goddammit.com?

Jiminy Christmas, what do you take me for, a rank amateur? I didn't get a Bachelor of goddamn Arts degree by playing computer games or gossiping with librarians.

I found the pay phone and used the finely honed skills that got me through college. Benny answered on the seventh ring.

"Christ," I said, "I thought you were never going to pick up."

"Good morning to you too, Ronald."

"Listen, no bullshit, I need help. Fast."

I detailed my litany of woes. Over the phone I could almost see Benny's eyes glaze out of focus in that meditative pose that means his mind's conductor is tapping the baton on the music stand.

"Well, Cicero," Benny said, "I hate to do it, but I'm going to have to invoke a cliché here."

"I hope it's 'break a leg'. That seems to be the hot ticket out of this mess."

"No, it's 'be yourself.'"

"Oh, Christ, Benny. I'm serious here. I need help in the next hour. Quit fucking around."

"I'm quite serious. Be yourself."

"Hal was right," I fumed, "you really are turning New Age, you know that? What's next? Don't tell me: everything you needed to know about Venus and Mars you learned in your twelve-step program. Shit. Remember when you nailed that calculus thing for me? That was useful. That was help. Those were the days. Who's Cicero?"

"Greek orator. Now shut up and listen. When I say be yourself, I mean it in practical terms. I mean, behave as you ordinarily do. You don't ordinarily read prepared remarks when you say something. Don't do it now. It's phony. You don't ordinarily speak to crowds of people, but you do speak to individuals. Speak to the crowd as though you were talking to one person. In fact, pick one or two people out and pretend you're conversing with them. Not Karen, though. Then say exactly what you just told me."

"What did I say?"

"You said you hate this political stuff, but you got dragged into giving this speech, and the truth is you do think it's a stupid project. That's great material. Just be honest."

"Be honest? Should I tell them I think they're a hateful bunch of troublemaking punks?"

"Sure."

"What? I was kidding."

"No, say that if the fancy strikes you. You could soften it a bit, but I like it. It adds authenticity. You know how these protests go. People are used to having true believers lecture them in pious tones. It will be quite refreshing to hear from someone who doesn't want to be there, but feels as though he must. In fact, I'm rather sorry I'll be missing it. It should be fun."

"Do it for me."

"Not a fucking chance in hell. I mean that in the nicest possible way."

"I'll pay you. Mm — no — I'll work for you."

"I don't have a job."

"I'll clean the —"

"Stop, Ronald, you can't buy your way out of political responsibility." He paused. "Actually, it was common in the nineteenth century for wealthy landowners to buy dispensations freeing them from military service."

"This isn't going to work, you know. I'm royally screwed."

"Oh, kill the self-pity act. I told you, it's going to work just fine. Do I mislead you so exceptionally often that you can't trust me?"

"Not at all," I said, "there's nothing exceptional about it."

Actually, I couldn't decide what would be worse, a teeming, hostile mob with pitchforks, or an embarrassing, intimate, small gathering; a circle of enemies. At minimum, I knew I could count on the fifty permanent residents of the library lobby.

An assortment of freaks began milling about a good half hour before the protest was to begin. A television van with a very tall antenna pulled into position. A guy I recognized from the local news started interviewing the crowd for local color. He was wearing a suit jacket and tie, but below the waist, the formality receded to a pair of threadbare jeans. I never realized they could get away with that.

My headache, lonely for company, manufactured a stomach ache from the butterflies fluttering in my intestines. Karen came over to give me a pep talk, like a fight manager in a boxer's corner, but I told her, in what I like to think were fairly diplomatic tones, to get lost. I needed to think and review my notes, such as they were.

Jessica Carothers, on whom I had never before laid eyes, was in charge of introducing speakers. Apropos of absolutely nothing, I might mention that Ms. Carothers packed a tremendous set of knockers. Not obscenely massive, mind you, but of decent size, and shapely in the extreme; and displayed to very good effect in a white blouse trimmed with tasteful lace.

Jessica found me as I was scouting the early arrivals.

"You're Gregory's friend," she stated.

"Not really. Think of me as his understudy."

"Whatever. You're on fourth. First I do a basic intro, then Fred

Miles, then JLP, then you. How long are you going to go? Don't make it more than fifteen minutes."

I smirked. "I think I can restrict myself to that. Who else is speaking?"

She showed me the list. There were ten or fifteen names, only four of which I recognized: Fred Miles, Gregory Thompson, John Lone Pine, and M'Bopape, the self-righteous snot with the ungodly schnoz. His last name turned out to be Katzenberger. Just imagine: M'Bopape Katzenberger. What a ridiculous name. Reprehensible. I pity the stonecutter who will have to carve that guy's tombstone. Someday it will stand a silent sentinel in massive pink granite between Ruth Feldman, Beloved Mother We Will Miss You; and Baby Grossman, He Was Too Pure For This World.

"Listen," I said to Jessica, "I'm not really very good at this. The truth is that Gregory asked me to go on instead of him, but — "

" — Yeah, Karen warned me you were going to try to weasel out of it. Forget it."

"But it does look like you've got a lot of speakers, and they'll probably repeat everything I was going to say."

"Yeah, but they're for, like, factual stuff. They said you were supposed to be funny, or whatever. So I can't really cut you out. Personally, I don't like comedians, but it's not my call. Remember, you're on fourth, right after JLP. Be funny, or whatever it is you do," she said.

She scurried off to find the other speakers. Be funny, indeed. She was a coarse and unpleasant person who, I'm forced to say, did not inspire comedy. The view as she walked away was shapeless and uninviting, thereby offering further evidence of the unnerving, melancholy possibility that maybe even owning the finest breasts in the kingdom is never really enough.

I heaved a nervous sigh.

Be funny. Be honest. Be yourself. Be all that you can be, cause we need you, in the Army. Catchy tune, that; although I've always found it both puzzling and macabre that the military forces advertise on television for volunteer killers.

The protest started, as all UCSC events do, fifteen minutes late. The needle on the nervous meter was zooming dangerously into the red zone.

Jessica started things off with a bang, invoking the immortal refrain: "Testing, 1-2-3. Testing. Check. Check." The microphone shrieked at the cliché.

The proper acoustical adjustments were made. Jessica urged the crowd to huddle closer. There was a momentary shuffling about, which quickly subsided. Jessica made some cheerless prefatory remarks. She warned us not to block the library's emergency exits, thanked some obscure volunteers, instructed us where to find the sign-up table, urged us to register to vote, and outlined the afternoon's proceedings.

Jessica received the same general level of interest and sustained attention from the crowd as a stewardess does from the passengers when demonstrating the emergency evacuation procedure.

Situated as I was within the crowd I could feel the early excitement sapping from them as pus from an infected wound. Having an immediate and personal interest in the subject, I asked myself: why exactly is she losing the crowd? Well, she's less entertaining than a pet lizard, of course. But why exactly is that?

Delivery. It's a highly underrated talent. Jessica's material was garbage, but a fella like, say, Mario Cuomo could have transformed it into the next Gettysburg Address simply with stage presence. Mel Blanc, who served as the voice of Bugs Bunny, Daffy Duck and their many colleagues, and was the most underappreciated comedian of the century, could have rendered Jessica's remarks maniacal, stealthy, ironic, farcical, outrageous, or even interesting.

Jessica was strident, and spoke too quickly. Her voice was too high-pitched, and her nervousness was annoying and embarrassing. What else? Her sentences tended to start quickly and then wander, stranded like the Children of Israel in the desert for forty years, with no clue where the Promised Land might be located. A crowd straining to hear a weak microphone at a boring rally needs its information fed to it in short and snappy bites of sound.

Mercifully, she concluded her remarks. She introduced renowned Professor of American History Frederick Miles — Fred to you and me — who, we learned, had long been a supporter of student causes, from his days as an anti-war activist in the Sixties, through his participation in campus anti-apartheid agitation, to his current opposition to the Deerpark development.

I was more nervous than I care to admit. Saliva was in short supply. I barely listened to what Fred had to say, concentrating instead on my newfound role as oratory critic, the self-appointed captain of the debate team.

Fred was much sharper than Jessica, I'll give him that. Big professor, punk student, it's the least one might expect. He knew what he wanted to say and he spoke in complete sentences. Unfortunately, he was didactic and condescending, and he had the embarrassing habit of punching the air whenever he felt he had made a critical point. And he rarely gave the crowd anything to cheer about, anything to participate in. At first he lectured us concerning the importance of understanding the class struggle in every venture we undertook, including the present one. This produced glazed eyes and some scattered yawning. Mostly he regaled us with irrelevant, misty-eyed reminiscing from the good ol' anti-war days.

" ... because the Establishment didn't take us seriously until we *made* them stop the Machine, and that's what you have to do, because the machines of war are never going to be stilled until *we the people* still them. Now is the time for that action. The danger is as present now as it was during the War. In fact, it is far (air-punch), far (air-punch), far (air-punch) greater! We face the real possibility of a thermonuclear holocaust which would destroy our planet. The potential calamity of is so astounding, we have difficulty even imagining it, much less organizing ourselves to action. And yet, by inaction we are complicit! (Air-punch) The Deerpark proposal is intended to manufacture those same weapons right here in our very backyard. As a singer by the name of Bob Dylan once said, 'And you tell me over and over again, my friend, you don't believe, we're on the eve of destruction.'"

I felt a brief, unexpected stab of subconscious unity with the assembly as we all groaned inwardly simultaneously: Dylan! Dear God, this dinosaur is actually quoting from Bob Dylan for our benefit. Christ, Fred, if you can't get a decade, maybe you can rent, or lease with an option to buy. Dylan! What next? Were we all going to have to sing "We Shall Overcome"? Was Fred going to hand out daisies? Was he going to paint our faces with peace and yin-yang symbols? How about a couple thousand rounds of "Hare Krishna"? Tambourines for everyone! Let's play Earth-ball! It'll be a great day when the Air Force has to hold a bake sale and schools get all the money they need! War is not healthy for children and other living things! Tune in, turn on, drop out!

Drop dead.

JLP was up next. God, he was awful. He lit sage. He actually took a clump of sage, the herb, and lit it, waving it to the four winds and muttering something about ritual purification or some such mumbo-jumbo. It took him several minutes to light the sage properly, and after that it seemed forever before he started speaking.

He lost the crowd quickly. The initial goodwill he received through the absurd merit of not being white lasted until somewhere in the middle of his third sentence. He spoke so quietly, only those of us in the front rows heard anything at all. He mumbled, and he often repeated words, phrases, even whole sentences. He paused for long stretches, and just when he seemed done he began anew. The poor miserable son of a bitch was more than a little hung over, but my guess is that even sober as the Sisters of Mercy he wasn't much of a speaker.

Conclusions began filtering into my nervous system. Don't mumble. Don't be boring. Don't lecture. Short sentences. Give the crowd something to do. Make sure they can hear you. No sage.

JLP finished whatever the hell he was talking about. I watched him walk away, quiet, studious and boring, and thought about the night before. What had happened to the guy who yelled "baboon" at the top of his lungs? Were the intoxicative and hallucinatory chemicals really the sole explanation for this transformation in his personality?

The next words I remember hearing were, "... Ronald Shovelstein!"

There was scattered, marginally hopeful applause as I stepped to the front and was handed the microphone. I remember well my first thought: *holy shit, there's thousands of the little bastards.*

"It's Shorenstein, not Shovelstein," were my first words, and the sound took me by surprise. It's a strange thing to hear one's voice projected at great volume into a sea of silence.

I improvised on a quick thought: "Shovelstein must be the name of the Deerpark developer." This got a big laugh. They were suckers for any remark vaguely critical of Deerpark. I scratched my head.

Be funny. Be yourself. Engage the crowd.

"So what do you think of this Deerpark thing, anyway?" I asked loudly and clearly.

A huge roar of boos, hisses and laughter broke out. That gave me a brief moment to look the mob over. The faces I saw were grinning, and gazing expectantly at me, waiting for the next one-liner.

How can I explain what happened next?

There must be something at which you excel, something which feels utterly comfortable to you. It doesn't have to be anything important for you to understand my point. Perhaps it's the smooth way you shuffle cards, or the way you fold large bedsheets into perfect squares without assistance, or the way you twist your long hair into a braid and tie it off without thinking about it. Think of some skill you have perfected that is second nature to you, a skill you can't remember being unable to perform.

As I gripped the microphone, the gods air-mailed me a moment of pure clarity, and I realized that I was completely at home in front of this large crowd. It sent an odd thrill of insight up from the base of my spine, a feeling that was somehow both transformative and utterly relaxing.

Survey after survey shows that public speaking is among the top five fears for most adults. But a papal dispensation has seemingly been granted me; I am exempt from this fear. Maybe it's because of the thousands of hours I spent watching performers on T.V. Maybe it's a skill I inherited from my mother, the linguist. Maybe it's pure chance. Maybe I learned something from Benny's morning instructions, or from observing the speakers directly preceding me. Maybe I was too hung over to care. The important thing is, I felt a wave of pure confidence at that moment. I completely abandoned my notes and spoke as Benny advised: as though speaking to one person, to a friend.

"So, plutonium," I said to the crowd, "good idea, huh? Do me a favor and yell out if you think it's a good idea."

Silence.

"That's odd, can't hear you. Please scream at the top of your lungs if you think it's a solid idea to have the world's most toxic substance floating around the campus."

Silence, expectant silence.

"Alright," I said, "let's try this another way. If you think Deerpark and its plutonium are a bad idea, please make a noise like a chattering monkey."

A howl of noise went up and rattled the library windows.

"Stop!" I yelled out when I thought they'd had enough fun. "I distinctly heard some of you doing chimpanzees, perhaps a few orangutans, and I believe there was a fearsome silverback gorilla over here somewhere. Listen to me, people! Those are apes. I told you to make a noise like a monkey. Monkeys have tails, apes do not. File that knowledge away. Knowledge is important, and that's why you need to listen to the speakers today, to gain the knowledge, the information, the details concerning the Deerpark proposal and your strategy for opposing it."

Long, respectful applause, and lots of nodding.

"So, listen, I'm an imposter," I said. I was getting really comfortable now, walking into the crowd a bit, making eye contact, making sure I faced each side in turn.

"I was not supposed to speak to you today. I know almost nothing about Deerpark. I'm not an activist. In fact, I hate politics. I'm appalled that all you people are out here today when you could be in class, sleeping. I think you're a hateful bunch of troublemaking punks."

Loud cheers of ironic self-congratulations.

"So you're wondering why I'm talking to you. Same here. What can I say? I was in the wrong place at the wrong time. I was asked to speak by Gregory Thompson, Chair of the Environmental Club, the man who has done so much hard work organizing on the Deerpark issue. Cheer now."

People will do almost anything someone with a microphone tells them to.

"Unfortunately, Gregory had an accident and was unable to speak to you today. Before he was so rudely interrupted, he only had a chance to jot down a brief outline of what he was going to say. Let me read it to you. Each of you can write down the outline, and then improvise your own speech to fit. Hell, that's what I'm doing."

I read Gregory's outline to them:

Introduce self.
Who we are. petitions. ~~skit?~~
Links with other uc.
Thanx admin/faculty/staff
Bkgrnd on Drprk: regents/ ac. senate/ prjct hstory.
Size!
Deer/Park explain magic of name
Global enviro link — deforestation
Ohlone remains. Sacred.
<u>Smoking gun</u>
Do cheer 4x
Demands
Remind mtg.
Thanx

"O.K., so here we go. 'Introduce self': Did that. 'Who we are.' A bunch of monkeys and apes and troublemaking punks. 'Petitions.' May I have a volunteer from the audience, please?"

An eager young pony-tail jumped up.

"What's you name, son?"

"Jeremy."

"Have we ever met before this very moment, Jeremy?"

"No."

"And let's hope we never do again. Here," I said, handing him a stack of paper. "These are all the petitions. They're probably signed by millions of angry, well-informed students who hate the Deerpark thing. Make copies for yourself first, so you can have the phone numbers of eligible young women whose politics you share. Frankly, you look like you can use all the help you can get. Next, go to the office of the most important person on campus and hand these over. Demand whatever the petition demands. Don't give in, ever, no matter what, unless you think you ought to. Steal a pen before you leave the office."

Jeremy dashed off with the petitions and a goofy grin.

"O.K.," I continued, "back to Gregory's list. 'Links with other uc.' This is one of nine or ten campuses of the University of California. They are linked. Who cares? Next: 'thanks admin/faculty/staff'. Screw admin/faculty/staff."

Lots of cheering and a small frown from Fred Miles.

"Next: 'Background on Deerpark': it used to be a meadow, then it was a burial ground, now it's going to be a big building full of Homer Simpson types handling plutonium. Next: 'Size!' Big. Next: Magic of the Deer/Park name.' My educated friend Benny informs me this is a reference to the Buddha, who received enlightenment at a place called Deerpark. Whoopee. Moving along. Next: 'Global enviro link — deforestation.' O.K., trees are being cut down elsewhere. If we cut down trees here, we'll have fewer trees on the whole planet and we won't be able to breathe. We like to breathe. Next: 'Ohlone remains — sacred.' Speaks for itself. Next: 'smoking gun.' I have no idea what this is. Sounds like spy stuff. Sounds like old Gregory has seen one too many Oliver Stone movies. Next: 'Do cheer 4x.' Hip-Hip —"

"Hooray!!"

"O.K., pretend we did it three more times. Nobody tell Gregory we shortchanged him. Next: 'Demands.' Let's see: how about everyone yell out the first demand that comes into your head, and Jessica, our MC, will write them all down. Go!"

Chaos and bedlam. Through the noise Jessica gave me a look so dirty it made the whole day worthwhile.

"O.K., shut up, people. Back to Gregory's list. 'Remind Mtg.' You see the banner to my left announcing time and place. You may attend or not as you choose. There will be heavy discussion, free food and an orgy. Wear condoms. Last item is 'thanx,' I think we can all figure that one out, but I do want to add one last thing of my own. I've been flippant and sarcastic about much of this stuff. Those few of you unlucky enough to know me well, know that's just the way I am. Those who don't know me, count your blessings. But I will say this: I went to school here for four years and I've never been able to figure this whole student thing out. You're both the consumer and the product. You pay the money and they, the administration and teachers, tell you what to do. It seems to me that since you pay them all, the least the ungrateful bastards could do is listen when you tell them you don't want them destroying your home or desecrating graves in order to construct a radioactive monument to bolster their fragile egos. Alright. I'm through with you."

Standing ovation, I kid you not. I was as shocked as anyone. I floated over to the speakers' hideaway, not completely certain what had just transpired. Fred Miles gave me a big, chummy thumping on the back like a football coach on Super Bowl Sunday.

"O.K.," Jessica said, back at the microphone, reading from notes, "that was, um, Ron Shovelstein, but, uh, I just wanted to announce that we, the Environmental Club, would like to give our apologies to anyone who might have been offended by anything he might have said, or whatever. I know I was, but we just wanted to say that he's not affiliated with the Environmental Club in any way, so, um, O.K.. Next up ... "

I didn't stick around long enough to find out who was next up. I began making my way through the crowd blocking the library doors. I was pressed upon with congratulatory remarks and presumptuous pats on the back which I found embarrassing and uncomfortable. Suddenly someone in that crazed hippie mob grabbed me forcibly. I wheeled around to register my anger and disgust with the guy. At first I saw no one, but when I let my focus drop a half foot lower down, I realized it was Karen. She slipped her hand into my coat pocket and pulled me closer. I stopped and leaned down into her familiar face.

"Hi Sherpa," I said. "You're certainly short today."

"Funny Ronnie," she said delightedly. She gave me a manic public kiss.

She was flushed with excitement. She stood on barefoot tiptoe and whispered something so lewd in my ear I blush to repeat it. Let's just say it was an invitation, or more like a demand, delivered in graphic detail, with a devilish grin. A half hour later we were in her bed, and a half hour after that we fell into a deep, exhausted sleep, sinful, unrepentant and carefree.

Chapter 12

— and then I'm back home and the phone rings and I know, somehow, that it's the cops. They've been following me all summer, kicking me and Great White off the streets, monitoring my campus activities, the troublemaking speechifying and the drugs. They've been building themselves a thick dossier.

But it's not the cops. It's the hospital.

The heart stops beating or speeds up like timpani, I can't tell which.

"Hello? This is Dominican Hospital Emergency Room calling in regard to Ms. Eva Shorenstein."

And then I — huuhhhhh, stomach sinking sinking into itself, mind contracting, voice hoarse, thoughts are pain sudden pain. Please, please speed up, time. Move past me now, leap ahead over this awful wall and deposit me on the other side. Take me with you with you I'm breathing and speaking and I'm staring at the actual sweep of the second hand on the wall clock. Just before each painted black stripe it pauses, waiting for approval from eternity, and then gives a little jump ahead to the next stripe. In between the jumps I can hear the voice at the other end, but the words are strange sour slices of bell peppers and onions and I can't find the kebab to skewer them all together into some kind of meaning.

"Whay?" I ask, caught between two questions.

"We retrieved Ms. Shorenstein's phone number from her purse. Are you a friend of hers?"

"Uh, uh ... brother." Itchy suddenly I'm itchy everywhere and I can't think, I can't scratch, and I "she's my brother, no .. I'm ... "

"I'm sorry, did you say you were Eva Shorenstein's brother?"

"Was? I am her brother. Wait wait, what is it, what happened?"

"Mr. Shorenstein —" and the molasses honey slow time is strange because I can see hear smell so clearly like on mushrooms and I can sense every nuance of the voice and I know, I know why they're stalling and I —

"— oh, fuck, oh, fuck, oh she's dead! Oh Christ I can't —"

"No, sir, that's not —"

" — believe it, oh, shit, Eva, why —"

"Stop!! Excuse me, sir, please listen! She's not dead, sir! Listen to me! She's not dead!"

"Oh. Ohhhh."

"She's being held for observation in Intensive Care. Would you like to visit her?"

"Intensive Care?"

"Yes. She's had a severe — a severe trauma, but she's in good care and there's a good chance of full recovery."

Ohhhh .... and now I'm writing down information and the second hand on the clock is still ticking away, bouncing from one second to the next, much slower than my heart moves from one thought to the next. I guess that makes sense because my pulse must be over sixty a minute especially now, especially out here in the cold parking lot, damn it's cold tonight, I can see the breath that was just inside my guts fogging the air like a semi-truck exhaling into a heartless winter. Is it winter or what? Because I'm shivering like a homeless drunk and here I go.

Great White starts up without any kidding around. Guess everyone tries to be on their best behavior during a crisis.

Man, he says, you sure went ballistic on the phone. Never thought you'd turn into such a gibbering monkey in a crisis.

Just drive, I tell him, just drive, and no fucking stalling out. I need you now, GW.

He pulls onto the highway with a reassuring rumble, and I think how good it is to have a friend at a time like this and then it occurs to my exceedingly dull mind that it might be even better to have an animate friend, I mean GW is animate, he's nothing if not animate when things are going well, it's really his *raison d'etre* when you think about it, I guess the word I'm looking for is sentient I wonder what the etymology of that word is, and yes I know I'm avoiding thinking about, thinking about, yes, but that's alright, I'll avoid what I want to, it's my brain, my sentience, my sentence my semblance ... wonder if I should wake Karen no it's too late and it's not her sister. Should I call Mom and Dad? Not until I know what ... I'll call Karen from the hospital.

Intensive Care. Where do I go? Follow me please. Why do they have to wear white shoes? Round the corner, past the curtains and Room 317 peach walls and —

"Evie."

A big white bed and a small little body and tubes and wires and machines chirping and I certainly know that face. It feels like I'm being asked to identify the body but that's not what's going on here. And I ask what, what, and the nurse says something about sleeping pills and pumping, pumping, pumping her poor stomach and I don't want to hear that, I don't want to listen. And I don't know what I expected had happened, but I'm not sure I'm really surprised, no, it makes sense somehow.

"Evie," I say again. She turns her head and her open eyes glaze and gaze at me.

"Ronnie," she whispers, and she sounds so tired, like the fatigue of ten thousand people packed in one little voice.

I kiss her forehead because it looks so wide and white and empty and lonely.

She whispers, "What a fuckup, huh?"

For failing? Or for trying? I'm not sure which one she means, but I don't want to ask, I don't want to talk about that.

"Ronnie?" a cracked whisper, "Could you get me something to drink? They won't give me anything, Ronnie. I'm not supposed to put anything into my stomach. But I'm so thirsty. Could you get me a Diet Coke?"

I jump into the hall and find a machine and feed it a dollar bill but it doesn't want to swallow it so I have to force the money down its throat like feeding with a tube and then only regular Coke is available.

"They were out of diet," I say.

Eva drinks like an oasis and I watch. We sit for five minutes without speaking, and then, at the exact same moment, we both start talking; and that's funny but we don't really laugh.

Eva doesn't look at me and says, "You want to know why, don't you, Ronnie? You want to know why I tried to kill myself."

I hate that sound and I can't speak.

"Oh, just ask," she says. "Just ask."

"O.K., then, why?" I ask, breathing hard.

"None of your fucking business," she says, and breaks into a rippling dry little chuckle, a vestige of her feisty self.

"Oh, fuck you," I say, relieved and teasing and, if I stop to think about it, angry as hell.

"Ronnie, I do love you," she says. "I guess."

"Me too," I say. My throat gets very hoarse and I say: "Are you going to do it again?

"I don't know, Little Guy," she whispers, "I honestly don't."

"Will you tell me when you — when you feel it coming on?"

"Can't promise that."

"What can you promise?"

She thinks for a good long while, and her eyes softly close and I get scared and wonder if I should call the nurse or maybe she's just sleeping and —

"Not you," Eva says, "I can promise it's not about you. Never was. You're a good baby brother."

"I can't —" and I don't know what to say.

"Can't what?"

"Can't ... can't figure out how you got here."

"Ambulance," she says. "Rescue 911. Like on TV."

"But who called?"

"I did."

And then I see the picture, and Eva is lying on the floor of my apartment, dying, one hand holding an empty bottle of pills and the other stretching full length to a phone that seems a half world away, and meanwhile I'm yukking it up with a bunch of hippies and soiling Karen's sheets, and maybe if I had been home and —

"I gotta call Karen," I say.

"You do that," Eva says, "you call Karen."

The next day is a blur but at some point Karen comes and we all sit up and talk about nothing. A case worker comes and goes and talks to Eva privately and then to me and shows me a schedule of some sort and gives me a map somewhere and I sign something and Eva is tired and I'm tired, and Karen's chattering starts to drive me up the wall, and I start wondering what matters. What really matters now?

And how did things ever get this way?

Chapter 13

There are no childhood memories which do not include Eva in some capacity. Evie and I were best buddies. We played together, laughed together, schemed together. She was a giggly blonde co-conspirator, two years older, with a protective streak. Evie drew the comic books and I wrote the copy. Evie built the fort and I scavenged the furniture. Evie claimed responsibility when I broke the car window with a fierce smash of an old gray tennis ball. Evie held my hand when we crossed the street, even when there was no traffic, because you can never be too safe.

When I was seven Evie decided we were going to own pet fish. She had seen a wondrous aquarium in a bank lobby and became entranced. She whipped me into a frenzy of fish mania. Mom caught the fever and took us to the pet store where we were permitted to splurge on an aquarium, fish food, a filter, little blue pebbles and a tiny brass diver with a bubble helmet. And fish. Lots of brightly colored little fellers, fireball orange, dynamic blue, forest green and exotic black with a dramatic streak of fuchsia. And as a complement, the obligatory guppies, drab, colorless, ubiquitous and utterly uninteresting, the civil servants of the fish world.

Only the guppies survived. The dramatically colorful fishies died with shocking regularity. We tried everything, we consulted with the pet store, we bought more, but there was an ancient Phoenician oceanic curse upon them. Every morning we would find another fish floating as though on a funeral bier cast upon the waters.

The guppies took no notice of all this. They thrived. They swam and ate and grew, and were content. One became pregnant, and through her translucent belly we watched the fascinating developments with breathless anticipation. When the little ones came, we were ready. We had learned that mother guppies and their offspring must be separated at birth, lest the mother eat them. After the serial suicides of the more colorful fish, this guppy tradition did not overly upset us. It did seem eccentric, but at least this time we could prevent death. Forewarned, we bought and prepared the appropriate netting. And here was life, life at last! Dozens of the little suckers swam out and about like miniature, translucent proto-beings. They were healthy and we were happy.

Except for one small baby guppy. This poor creature came into the world swimming in circles. It did not eat, it did not respond to changes of light, temperature or current. It simply swam in a tight little circle, endlessly chasing its ever-elusive tail, bumping into obstacles and bouncing off them without a break in the action. We caught the little autistic in the net, thinking to distract it, but when we returned it to the waters it resumed its monomania with renewed zeal. For two days Evie and I watched it, fascinated and horrified, expecting at any moment that it would abandon its foolish, suicidal course, perhaps tire of its dizzying ways and rest for a moment in the caverns of the little underwater castle which its siblings had already explored and approved.

Fifty-two hours after birth, the little misfit began to tire. Evie called me excitedly. We peered at it, wondering, hoping, whispering. The circle it described began to widen, as if it could no longer keep up the concentration necessary to maintain its preferred tight loop. As it widened its course, it appeared for long moments as though it was actually swimming in a straight line. But it was only a wider curve, and moments later the little guppy paused, exhausted and starved, corrected its course once, and died.

I cannot tell you how many times I have thought of that little guppy over the years. Throughout my childhood, the image of that fish would come to me at the most unexpected, inopportune and peculiar times.

I tried in vain to understand that guppy. Why had it come out so wrong? What were its tiny thoughts as it steered its hopeless course? Why was it born at all? Did it suffer? What is it like to devote oneself so utterly to a cause?

Maybe it experienced pleasure in the completion of its circles, the satisfaction of doing well that which it had been born to do. Sometimes I convinced myself of that.

The life of a standard guppy, after all, consists of not much more than swimming in circles, with nothing much to aspire to, no lofty goals, no honor, no beauty. In fact, Evie and I abandoned the aquarium project soon after, as soon as we realized that fish are utterly, irremediably boring.

Except for the little circler. In some way, hadn't it lived as well as any guppy ever? It had taken the essence of guppyhood, of fishtank life, and condensed it into a manic spark of bizarre achievement. Our little guppy lived life to the fullest and died when there was nothing more left to prove.

At least, that's what Evie said in her eulogy. She posthumously dubbed the fish Janis, after Janis Joplin, and gave her an honored burial in the back yard.

That damned fish was on my mind as I paced the hallway beside Eva's hospital bed. I wanted to tell the story to Karen, who was curled up in a chair, softly singing nothing in particular to no one in particular. I wanted to ask Eva if she remembered that fish, but she seemed asleep and I'm not sure I could have conjured up the nerve to mention it.

How did I get to be so afraid of speaking to Eva as though she might be my sister?

For the first eight or ten years of existence Evie and I were inseparable. Then the gender and age gaps grew too significant and we parted ways.

Eva transformed into a teenager straight from Central Casting. She was high-strung and temperamental and so easy to tease it was barely worth the effort. At the age of thirteen, like clockwork, she became cynical, pouty and rebellious. She remained that way until she headed off for college.

But in the two years just prior to her departure, when boyfriends had used her and girlfriends had manipulated her so gravely she was willing to admit me back into the sanctity of her messy bedroom and the maelstrom of her life, we had a re-bonding of sorts. She taught me to smoke pot, complained about every one of her friends, and instructed me concerning the correct music to listen to: Elvis Costello, the B-52's, the Talking Heads.

I must say, we smoked a lot of pot. We were not the only ones. I recall reading a newspaper poll at the time indicating that 60% of all teenagers reported using marijuana. This poll I found laughably naive. At our junior high and high school the percentage of those experimenting with recreational drugs easily crested 90% and more likely approached 100%, a demographic consisting of both boys and girls, skinny and fat, A-students and dropouts, rich and poor, with braces and without, and of every goddamn ethnicity God saw fit to create.

Duty compels me to add that Eva and I tried most other drugs within reach, with the exception of opiates. I suppose neither one of us will ever be elected to higher office or confirmed as Supreme Court justices. For we inhaled. We certainly inhaled.

A partial list of illegal substances we ingested includes cocaine, barbituates, speed, LSD, amphetamines, and even PCP once, accidentally. And of course alcohol and nicotine. For a time Eva was charmed by and addicted to clove cigarettes, but I found their smell nauseating and considered them a trendy affectation.

There was a sweetness to the way Eva introduced each ne   drug to me. She would research the effects, how long they might last, how addictive the substance was, and what particular dangers to avoid. Whenever I tried something new, she would stay by my side for the entire trip, sober, maternal, calming, and delightedly curious. Possibly because of her careful guidance, I found none of the drugs particularly compelling and discontinued most of them after a few tries.

There were exceptions. Marijuana has always stuck around like the little brother I never had, always eager to play, but usually a dull disappointment whenever I bother. Cocaine dragged out far too long — more than a year — and was the toughest to kick. But on the whole I avoided disaster, largely because of Eva's guidance. She was a responsible little Timothy Leary, leading me with care and attention through an important rite of passage into modern American adulthood.

And why did we do all of this? Why did we ingest and inhale substances we knew well were poison? For the precise and utterly compelling reason that we had nothing better to do.

Drugs cost money, of course. Eva and I got jobs at the same family restaurant, she waiting tables and I bussing them. It was a large establishment located off a freeway exit, where most finer American dining takes place. It had absolutely nothing to recommend it beyond reasonable tips and a break room where one could get stoned. Sister and brother working together was the source of endless hilarity for our clever fellow workers, but Mom thought it was character-forming, and was happy to transport us there and back.

And so, for a time Eva and I felonized in a private partnership, returning for a time to the partnership in giddiness of our lost childhood years.

Then, with incredible swiftness and awful headlong irreversibility, the Eva Era ended. She openly and traitorously declared her desire to leave us in order to attend some schlocky institute of higher learning.

Hell, I knew the decision was coming. She was a smart kid and a superior student despite a stunning lack of academic interests. For some pathological reason she always did her homework. Despite the distractions of assorted melodramas with ill-suited suitors and a head clouded with chemicals, Eva rarely missed class and always did her homework. These two unheard-of habits easily vaulted her among the elite of the disaster that is the California public school system.

Eva earned the pick of almost any university she deigned to attend.

I suppose I ought to have been better prepared for her departure. I knew better than anyone how badly she wanted to go. For years she had confided to me her disgust with the oppressive melancholy of characterless Camarillo and her dream of one day escaping the asylum. I understood the impulse, and strongly shared it. And yet the unreal possibility of her imminent departure was so very odd and disturbing, even a touch frantic.

For months I moved about with a fidgety nervousness bordering on paranoia. Cocaine may have played a role in this turbulence. I constantly felt on edge. There is a moment, when one first realizes that one's wallet is missing, when the heart skips an adrenalized beat. I felt that way at all times. I was getting cut off from the known world in a frightening, novel way. It was an odd sort of novelty, because my life would remain the same. Eva was, after all, the one leaving for new and unknown surroundings. But I was the one with the jitters.

Eva chose the U. of Oregon, where her best friend Heather had blazed a trail, like Lewis and Clark before her. Mom and Dad drove Eva all the way up to Eugene, and she settled in so comfortably she didn't even call me for a week.

And in that hateful house I sat for a long, disembodied weekend, consoling the television on our mutual loss.

Chapter 14

When Karen and I brought Eva home after nearly two days in the hospital she went straight to my bed and fell asleep immediately. Karen sat up with me until I could barely breathe from exhaustion. Finally I crawled over to the couch and Karen threw a good warm blanket over my exhausted soul. I was so tired I never even heard her leave.

Construction guys working across the way woke me up early the next morning, yelling and blasting away with machinery. The stereos in their tough-guy pickup trucks reverberated in full volume, tuned to bad classic rock radio stations hosted by awful, cheery morning drive-time DJ's.

I groaned like a third-century Christian martyr, feeling like my old hostile self.

Want to make a million dollars? Invent quiet construction equipment. Want to do the world a great favor? Assassinate all the morning DJ's.

I stretched, turned over and yawned. I was unaccountably sore. I tried to go back to sleep, but thought came. I tried to remember the night before in its fullness, and with sudden anxiety I leapt off the couch to look in on Eva.

The door to my room was ajar. I thought I could hear soft, steady breathing, but I wanted to be sure. I pushed the door open a bit more, and then I saw her.

She was sleeping quietly, angelic and serene, with one arm over Eva's shoulder.

Karen.

She had stayed the night, sleeping at Eva's side.

And if, at the moment of my death, a memory comes unbidden across the empty years to ferry me across the dark threshold, it may well be that lyrical instant when my eyes understood Karen's freckled arm and her familiar hair, fanned protectively all over Eva's sleeping form.

For one blessed moment, the cynical, doubting, fearful voice that patrols my mind like secret police was silenced. I did not think, I did not analyze, and I did not act clever. I felt. An oceanic sense of gratitude buckled my knees, knowing that my burden of fear and worry was taken up and shared and relieved.

I went in and lay down quietly beside sweet Karen. She stirred, sensing my weight on the mattress. Without speaking, nor even waking up, she hooked her ankle around my calf, pulling me closer.

I would have wept had I known how.

Chapter 15

A peculiar, foreign and fleeting constellation of counterintuitive conditions, this shapeless bale of cotton you humans call emotion.

The way you contort your face in that way, showing your teeth — that's an expression of mirth, or pleasure, isn't it? Those furrowed eyebrows — is that anger? Strange. Implausible. Unfamiliar.

And yet, I believe there was a time, many moons ago, when I may have actually been able to identify these sensations with some accuracy . But now I feel as though I were a witness in some confusing cerebral police lineup.

I'm sorry, officer, I am looking them over, but nothing seems familiar. Can Number 4 turn sideways, please? No, I think that one's jealousy. Possibly anger. I'm not certain. The glass is fogged up, these witnesses are surly, and it's difficult to distinguish one from another. My memory is fading. I'm fairly sure Number 1 is sloth, boredom or alienation. Is that right? As for the rest — well, jeez, it's just that the crime occurred so long ago. Childhood? Yes, I believe I had one. What was it like? Hard to say. Hey, uh, should I call my lawyer? I mean, is this important?

O.K. I'm sorry. I'll try to remember, officer. Can I have some coffee? A bear claw? Yes, please. Might jar my memory. Cinnamon. Thanks. Hmmmm.

Earlier.

Earlier there was a different me.

I see a giant, puckered hand, wrinkled from the bath, reaching to wipe my spittled, gurgling chin. Dad.

I feel hair, blonde in a great cascade, tickling my face like itchy grass after an endless tumble down a sunny hill. Mom.

I hear: "Stay up here. Mom and Dad said to stay up here. You'll get a big surprise." Eva. And downstairs, the sounds of merriment. My third or fourth birthday party.

The house was a living thing, but stupid, like a manatee. Kindly, large, and dumb; it meant well but it could never be elegant. There was too much linoleum and fuzzy wallpaper, and green shag carpeting ubiquitously underfoot like moss on the tundra in spring.

The neighbors deserved the name only because they lived nearby, not because they did any of the things the neighbors on TV did. The neighborhood kids never played together. We stayed inside and avoided each other at school. The neighborhood grandmothers never baked apple pies for us. I'm not certain there were any grandmothers.

Only young families in Camarillo, California. Some lower-middle class, some upper-middle class, perhaps some middle-middle class, if there is such a thing. Camarillo is a bedroom community at the far outskirts of the great State of Los Angeles. Camarillo's sole claim to fame is a large state nuthouse that really slaps it on the map. We locals had no cause to go near the imposing loony bin. It afforded us a few giggle fits when we were quite young, but thereafter we ignored the massive, mysterious structure and the ghostly vehicles conveying unknown souls on unimaginable pilgrimages.

Think of walls. If you're trying to imagine that hazy Southern California suburb, think of cinder-block walls, eight feet high, pink and tan and faceless, running along the sidewalk for miles. Walking the half mile to elementary school, the only creatures I ever encountered were the dogs that appeared and disappeared at the top of the wall with vicious snarls of territoriality.

Of parents I had two, one of each gender, in accordance with traditional custom. The female was born in a village somewhere near Stockholm, Sweden. She moved here when she was twenty, I believe. She met Dad at a brick-laying festival.

I am not making that up. I couldn't possibly, if I had to.

How does a heavy, hairy Jewish guy born on D-Day, 1945 in Olympia, Washington find his way to a brick-laying festival in Saginaw, Michigan in 1966, just in time to meet a tall, thin blonde woman from a poor Swedish village? How does such a meeting impact the barely functional emotional disposition of a son unborn and unimagined?

There are answers, but those are facts, designed to confuse us. They don't answer the fundamental question of fate: why am I here? Sure, I know I'm not the first guy in history to pose the problem. But my concern is genuine, I assure you. I worry about these things. I stay up nights, tossing and turning, turning and tossing.

As I lay there beside Karen, her scented, inert form shielding me from Eva's snoring, I threw memory back in time, toying with it, operating under the dubious Freudian notion that parents and childhood are the most formative forces in the character development of the adult human.

My parents were married in 1968, the Summer of Love. Or was that 1967? Who knows? My parents had real lives to lead. Dad started going to college. He was doing alright, too, studying economics or something. Maybe business administration. He always had a head for numbers. But when Mom got pregnant with Eva they decided to move to California for a reason which remains clouded to this day — not just to me but to them as well. Dad had to stop going to school. He got a good job in construction instead, which is what he does to this day. Now he's the contractor. The boss.

"Basic needs," he says. "There aren't too many of them. You gotta have food and water. You gotta be the right temperature, not too hot, not too cold. And you gotta have shelter. That's why I like construction. It fills peoples' basic needs."

Gotta fill basic needs. One of Dad's millions of mottos. *Ya don't vote, ya can't complain* was a big favorite, used to countermand all complaining. I'm not sure he ever actually voted.

Grease for peace, that was another. In high school he used to hang out with these five guys who called themselves the Diablos. They weren't really hoods, as I understand it, but people thought they were, and that's what counts. They rode motorcycles, of course, and wore leather jackets. In fact, I remember a brown bomber jacket Dad still wore when I was a kid. The zipper didn't zip, the sleeves were ragged, and the brown had turned to white at the edges, but man, I loved that fucking thing. It astonishes me to think how much I used to love that jacket.

Because Dad was not really a leather jacket kind of guy. Not when I met him. He was a wake-up-at-six-in-the-morning-and-go-to-work kind of guy. He was a listen-to-talk-radio-in-the-car-while-chain-smoking kind of guy. He was a burn-the-burgers-at-the-barbecue kind of guy. A Cubs fan, if you will.

What I want to know is, how did that happen? How does a Diablo end up wrestling with lawn furniture and worrying about his prostate? What trauma, what catastrophe can initiate such a bizarre transformation? Was it Mom? Was it the kids? Or was the middle-aged golfer present somehow, residing in a nascent form, deep inside the teenage Diablo? Or maybe the Diablo never left. Maybe the Diablo is still there, struggling to emerge from within that pot belly, ready at any moment to hit the road on a Harley.

Maybe not.

I suppose Mom was more of a risk-taker, more willing to throw proverbial caution to the proverbial wind. She was the only one from her village ever to leave, much less move to the United States.

More than once she hustled our family into the car with no particular destination in mind, and we'd take off for a weekend of camping. We would hike up dusty Sierra mountain trails, Dad plodding along like the Tortoise, Mom racing like the Hare, we kids stumbling along like kids.

I just remembered something else, something I have not thought about in years. I'm not certain what importance it holds. Once or twice a trip Mom would climb on a rock or an outcropping or a precarious perch dangerously near the cliff edge. She would shade her eyes with her hand, ignore Dad's measured warnings to "get the hell down from there, for chrissakes Sonya," and gaze headlong into obscurity. I could never see her face at those moments, nor read her body language, so I cannot report if she was squinting or smiling, whether she was full of bravura or apprehension, whether she was moved by regret or despair or euphoria. At length she would jump back down with a light step, and the incident would pass uneasily.

But those were brief moments of mystery. All told, those moments likely added up to half an hour in the life of a woman who was always the model of predictability. I mention it only because I dreamt about that very scene the other night. In my dream Mom stood at the edge of a cliff, arms spread in a gesture that looked like a shrug but that I somehow interpreted as a flapping of wings in preparation for a leap into the abyss. I rushed to her side and pulled her to safety but it was not her, it was another person, someone I knew but could not recognize. Someone important to me, someone I have spent a good deal of time with and know very well. I often dream of people I know but somehow can't place. I find it a peculiar and disturbing sensation, one which often stays with me for hours or even days after the dream.

But make no mistake about moments of mystery. Mom's primary identity was as the responsible caretaker, the homework helper, the one who dabbed that mysterious, cabalistic purple liquid on my knees when I scraped them.

Mom mommed. She cooked, she cleaned, she went to teacher-parent conferences, she carpooled us to Little League and the like. She engaged in all the expected mom-type activities, but it seems to me that her foreign origins made her even more energetic in pursuit of the American Dream than her peers were. New converts, as we know, are always the most zealous sheep in the flock.

In Sweden there was nothing but herring and failing socialism, or so the story goes. Sonya came here with a clear vision of suburban American familial bliss, and saw it through without a hitch. Congratulations are in order, I suppose. Drinks all around.

What else can I tell you about my origins? Looking for some repressed memories? Sorry, can't help you. You want me to tell you that Dad beat me mercilessly, or that Mom molested me? Would you like a crazed grandparent to abduct me?

Nope. No high drama in the Shorenstein family. Our ship of state moved along on an even keel in temperate waters. The weather which governed our temperaments was usually fair, although there was always a chance of partial cloudiness throughout the late afternoon with choppy waves offshore, and perhaps a small craft advisory.

And so we come to this question: what of me and my own elusive identity? Can my life be understood only as a reflection of my family? Wasn't I remarkable in any way of my own? Did I excel at anything? Was I nuts in some fascinating adolescent way? Did I display an early but marked tendency toward greatness of any sort?

No, no and nope.

Once upon a time I was a decent child, obsessed with dinosaurs, skateboards and hobbits. I then became an indecent teenager, obsessed with sex with a monomania so common to that age as to be absolutely pedestrian — a handy piece of perspective I gained only later, of course.

I learned things in school and forgot them on the way home. I read a great deal of poorly written science fiction. I had friends, I grew bored with them, I met others. I watched endless acres of T.V. I was singularly and unconscionably boring.

O.K., false modesty aside: there were perturbations in my seemingly monolithic mediocrity. For three straight years I led the local Little League in both on-base percentage and steals. In sixth grade I wrote a report on snakes which was sent on to some regional essay competition and received a silver ribbon; highly placed sources tell me that the kid who won the gold was sleeping with the judges.

I have always excelled in English classes without serious effort. I have always read busloads of books and sunned myself in the soothing syllables of speech.

But that's really not much to go on, is it? A mouthful of words is not much help in warding off the hot tar of depression when the summer heat melts the sweltering street. An armada of aphorisms could never for a moment help me delay nor even comprehend the hideous looming coda of mortality.

With an eye toward full accuracy, I report that for as long as I can remember I have always felt myself an outsider, never truly belonging in the social world. I am reasonably sure that this was not nearly as apparent to others as it was to me. Only Eva could guess at my true nature, but I can't say I recall her trying. I could always pass as a plainclothesed pedestrian on this planet, but I have never felt secure in the act. It always seemed to me that other people, other kids, knew something I didn't.

Were they perfect little poppets, and I the Frankenstein monster?

No, there was never perfection of any sort in Camarillo, California. Perhaps they were just more comfortable than I with their own inadequacies. But at least they had genuine inadequacies. Mine felt fake to me. I was a posturing pre- and post-pubescent. I could never be like Eva. She was either maniacally cheerful or smokily hostile, but when she was down, she was down in a real way, with gusto.

Up or down I always felt like I was pretending, looking at myself from the outside in, capable of proper reactions but without true motivation, able to throw a tantrum but incapable of feeling the hot rage that is alleged to accompany it.

No, that can't truly be the full story either. I don't believe I was a complete automaton. I'm certain there were many times when I laughed and cried and even jumped for mindless joy. Some of those moments I even remember. Surely I did not emerge from the womb verbal, analytic, and morose. Perhaps I spent my early years in a wordless bliss I cannot remember because I cannot name it.

It was a childhood, a prolonged period of time, but in trying to rebuild it, the structures of my memory collapse into generalizations and ineffectual stabs at a global analysis destined to elude me. In retrospect, it seems as though those years took no time at all. A few days stick out, and no more. Yet I know that while it was happening, it took the amount of time that time takes. Days were as long as they are. Nothing flew by. In fact everything went far too slowly.

But I can't stop it from collapsing, in the way objects on the ocean's horizon appear condensed from a distance. The fears and tragedies of my little landscape obscured the unimaginable future. I was a tiny rowboat bobbing in the turbulent wake of the Titanic, straining to catch a glimpse of the icy waters ahead.

And through it all I sailed alone. When I was at my lowest, falling, falling, falling inward, Eva was not there to catch me.

My early teenage years were a time of deep, dark mental anguish; a hormonally driven, intellectually modulated miasma. I came to doubt and even negate all the old moral structures and codes of authority of my familiar if not necessarily rose-tinted childhood.

It was an ugly time. My timid body had been hijacked, seized with unimagined, uncontrollable urges, forcing me to commit acts of awful ecstasy with alarming, frenzied frequency.

My mind observed the horrific display, detached and disgusted. I knelt in repentant humiliation before the altar of my own self-loathing. Listlessly mortified, angrily dispassionate, I searched desperately for a refuge from my own self. Hot shame and cold suicide coursed past one another like icy lava in the muddled grey passageways of my utterly confused brain.

I knew the words. I could name my problems, identify my perils, but I could not summon the authentic, passionate emotions I knew lay hidden behind the scenes, waiting like a faithful but useless theatrical understudy.

I knew what depression was, but not what to do about it. An inevitable pattern developed. The cycle would begin the moment I grew depressed, which occurred daily. I would then turn a morose and bitter inner eye at my own depression, observing it, examining it, dissecting it, searching for its cause. Rational analysis, the only tool available to me, dictated that there had to be some external stimulus which could explain my depression.

With the overdramatic nihilism which is the badge of honor of any good teenager, I sought refuge in blame. I blamed others — parents, teachers, friends, parents, siblings, parents again, and again. I blamed circumstances: the futility of existence in a world where war, plague and poverty have always been the norm; I blamed the disturbing, absurd array of pointless career paths I saw laid out before me like one thousand dead-end roads; and most of all I blamed all the schoolgirls who passed inches from my tantalized, tortured talons, but seemed to have no idea they orbited the same sun as I, even as I yearned with all my burning, lunatic, deadened soul for the merest brush with their maddeningly developing succulence.

All these things I blamed, and more. And yet self-honesty, a commodity of which I have always had a preciously small reserve, and self-hatred, of which I have a bountiful surplus, teamed to force me into a difficult admission: external causes were not the problem. I was. I alone, wandering like a lost and choking coal miner in the caverns of my own mind, was responsible for my own depression. This realization, far from empowering me, served only to depress me further, a depression which I would in turn analyze, dissect and inevitably fall further into. *Cogito ergo cogito*: I think, therefore I think.

It was a brutal downward spiral from which there seemed no hope of escape. The absurd effort of actually waking up and going to school, of sitting still through stifling science slide shows, of cheerfully greeting overbearing grandparents at overstuffed Thanksgivings, was an insufferable, Herculean masquerade.

Without Eva's miraculous return to my life before leaving for college; without drugs, music, and books; without an unexpected and unmerited physical maturation which mysteriously rendered me passably attractive to a peculiar, eclectic little subset of the female universe; and without my climactic exodus to college, I might still be a permanent resident of the darkened land of my adolescence.

I have never felt as though I truly left. I do live here, now, in my version of the real world, a somewhat sunnier place, where in time I have come to accept with skepticism the theoretical possibility of a condition known as happiness.

I do live here, but I'm on a visitor's visa. I haven't decided yet whether to apply for permanent status. I might risk having my childhood citizenship from the Land of Cynic permanently revoked.

I tell ya, it's rough being an immigrant in this country.

Chapter 16

The phone must have been ringing for several minutes, but we lacked the energy to move. We three logs lay in our bog immobile and irritable, silently cursing the clattering late morning phone and wishing a lead safe might fall on it and possibly impair its functionality. The curses worked, but only temporarily. The ringing stopped for a full minute, and then started again. Finally Karen ran out to the kitchen to pick it up.

She left a colossal chasm in the middle of the bed. From the far edge, nine thousand miles away, Eva stared back at me with a piercing listlessness.

"Totally," Karen said to the phone.

I had to look away from Eva's eyes. My gaze fell on her pale, pudgy hand.

"Where'd you get that ring?" my voice croaked. "Never saw it before."

Eva didn't answer for what seemed a minute. At length, with great effort, she asked, "Who cares?"

"No, I completely agree," Karen said in the kitchen. "It's just that right now isn't great. I can't ..."

I tried again. "You want something to eat?" I asked Eva.

Several decades later she shook her head and made a noise of negation. It was barely audible. She shook her head from a horizontal position. It seemed less an indication of negative response and more as though she was bashing her head into the pillow in the softest despair of futility.

"I'll try," Karen said.

She came back to the bedroom. She pulled jeans on, and had almost finished buttoning them when she realized they were mine. She kicked them off and began searching through a pile of clothing at the base of the bed for her own pants.

"Who was on the phone?" I asked.

"Jessica Carothers. I guess I have to get going," she said, casting Eva an odd, shy, dimpled smile with raised eyebrows and tentative shrug.

"Need a ride?" I asked.

"Don't go," Eva whispered. She had not changed the direction of her gaze. It was impossible to tell if she was talking to me, to Karen, or to some unknown or imagined third party.

The phone rang again. Karen was hopping into the correct pants, so I got up to answer it.

"Hello?"

"Hey." Hal.

"Hey," I agreed, "what's up?"

"Zachary's?"

"Mm. Kinda busy here."

"Doing what?"

"What?"

"What are you doing that's —"

" — nothing. I mean I'm not sure what I'm doing."

"So what about — "

"O.K., O.K. When?"

"Ten minutes."

"Cool."

I scratched back to the bedroom, feeling exceedingly guilty for leaving, and buttoned up my own pants.

Then Karen spoke. "If it's alright, Eva asked if I could stay a little while with her."

I stopped at the top button and stared at the two of them. Karen was wearing her Buddha smile. Eva was still gazing at the same distant horizon. It was hard to believe she had spoken at all. She was glassy-eyed, despondent and inert. I felt a nervous pity, an uncertain, guilt-driven motivation to entertain her, to make her laugh, to get her out of her funk somehow. In the space of three long heartbeats I realized, with a sickened sense of defeat, that I could think of no way to help her. I was way out of my league.

"Of course, absolutely," I said to Karen, or to Eva, or to both. "Stay as long as you want. Only thing is, I just told Hal I'd go to lunch with him."

"O.K.," Karen said. "Bring back something."

"Like what?"

"Like anything. This house needs nourishment."

"Where you been?" Hal asked.

I slid into the booth across from him. That was the moment I first realized that Hal was an early devotee of male pattern baldness.

"Busy as hell," I said.

"Same here," Hal said, "except for the part about being busy."

"Where's Benny?"

"Art."

I smirked. The waitress came by and we ordered without looking at the menus.

"Heard you gave a speech," Hal said.

"Don't believe everything you hear."

"Heard you kicked ass."

"Really? Bullshit. Who said?"

"I don't know," Hal said, shrugging. "Grapevine, you know. People talk. Tongues waggle. Loose lips, sinking ships. You're a big celebrity now."

"Don't believe the hype."

"Mr. Big Shot Political Leader," he said in mocking tones.

"Shit," I said. "Leader. Feh. I'm no leader. A leader ain't nothin' but ... nothin' but ..."

I couldn't think of the ending. It was a failed takeoff on the adolescent classic *A Hero Ain't Nothin' But A Sandwich*, which I have never read.

"A metric quart," Hal said.

"Say what?"

"A liter ain't nothin' but a metric quart. That's the line you're looking for."

"Oh," I said. "Thanks."

"No problemo."

The waitress brought our breakfasts. Hal leaned his head forward.

"Behind you," he said. "In the green sweater."

I turned casually. A typical Hal blonde bombshell.

"Too skinny," I said, "I like a little meat on the bones."

He shook his head in disbelief.

"Oh, man, walking in right now — wait, don't look yet — O.K., now."

I looked, turned back, and shrugged.

"Man," he said, "what are you, a eunuch?"

"Show me something impressive, I'll be impressed."

"I know what your problem is," he said. "You're married."

"I am? Damn, I missed the ceremony. Good cake?"

"You know what I mean. Karen's got you by the huevos rancheros."

In my mind's eye I saw Karen's arm as she lay in my bed, sheltering Eva from the noise of a chaotic world. I shrugged at Hal and sopped up the last of my egg with the last of my toast.

"Look," Hal said, "just because you've eaten doesn't mean you can't look at the menu."

"Is that meant as a metaphor or as timely restaurant advice?"

"You know what I mean. Jes 'cause yer courtin' a gal don't mean y'all can't go to the hoedown."

I laughed. "Where do you get this stuff? 'Hee-Haw'?"

"Television made me what I am," he said, quoting the Talking Heads, as he often did. "Listen, I'll put it in Shorenstein English for you: it is no betrayal of your romantic relationship to acknowledge that there is an unusual array of absolutely stunning young women in the building today."

"Fine," I said, "I so acknowledge."

"You don't sound like you mean it."

"Listen, I'll tell you what. You're the one who's so hot to trot. You're single, why don't you go talk to one of them?"

"They're taken."

"How do you know? I don't see any guys with them."

"Trust me. Anyone that good-looking is with someone. If she isn't, there's obviously something wrong with her."

"You know what your problem is?" I said. "You have a defeatist attitude."

"Yeah, well, I get defeated a lot."

I found that a very depressing remark. No grand examples of Hal's defeats jumped into my mind, but somehow the accuracy of the analysis resonated like the body of a cello in full vibrato. Hal lived life like a man floating on his back in the ocean; utterly relaxed, lifting his head only for the biggest waves. He was lazy, unmotivated and unreliable. I had always found that reassuring and considered him constitutionally calm, complacent and carefree. But maybe the truth was that he was beaten down. By what? By whom?

"How's Eva?" Hal asked.

"What? Oh, she's ... uh, she's alright. Why do you need to know?"

"No reason. Just making conversation."

I crumpled my napkin onto the plate. "Listen," I said, "I actually have to head out. Maybe we can hang later."

"Don't tell me," he snorted, "another peace protest with your hippie buddies?"

"They're not my buddies, asshole."

"Oooh, touchy, touchy," Hal said. "Crab city. I was just making a joke."

"I've heard jokes," I said, "I've even made some. I know what they're like. That ain't it."

"Peace, man," Hal said, his fingers flashing the peace sign.

I shook my head, pissed off. "Look, if you must know, it's not even a peace protest. It's a debate over land-use policy."

"*We are the world,*" Hal began to sing, swaying his arms over his head, "*we are the children.*"

I had to laugh. "Screw you," I said gently.

"Ah," Hal said, "you say that now. But will you mouth off when I tell you what I have arranged for you out of the goodness of my own heart? I think not."

"Arranged?" I scoffed. "What have you arranged? Your mama's funeral?"

"Wow," he said, rolling his eyes, "now that is some humbling comedy. Jesus, you could be headlining in Vegas with that material. What wit! You could get easily get a job writing Bazooka Joe comics."

"Hey, at least I'm looking for jobs. I have career goals, buddy boy. I'm going places."

Hal laughed at me.

"Hey," I said, "don't laugh. I can enter the workforce any time I please. I got an eddication. I got skills. Listen and tell me this doesn't sound professional: 'Would you like fresh ground pepper with that?'"

"Very convincing. Do you want to hear what I arranged or not?"

"Alright, O.K. What'd you arrange?"

"Only Pearl Jam, Friday night at the Greek Amphitheater, and you and I are stage crew."

"What? Bullshit!"

"My hand to God."

"Pearl Jam?!?"

"I shit you not. And — are you sitting down? — we're invited to a party with the talent after the gig." He slobbered a huge, dopey, self-satisfied grin.

"Ooooh la-la," I said, "'talent', 'gig': you've really got the lingo down, don't you? Did anyone ever tell you how astonishingly *in* you are?"

I was trying to play it cool, but in truth Hal had engineered a major miracle. He and I had been trying for at least a solid year to see Pearl Jam. Three times we had tried to buy tickets, but they had sold out in the first fifteen minutes. To work the stage, to meet the band, to go to a party — well, you know the lure of celebrity. This was as big as big got in our little world. Hal knew it and just kept snickering.

"O.K., you're fucking amazing,' I admitted, "how'd you do it?"

"I know a guy who knows a guy, yadda yadda, not important. Point is, are you interested?"

"Am I interested? Is the Pope interested?"

I knew Hal did have some odd connections as a fallout from a failed garage band he had once been in. Accurately speaking, Hal had failed; the band had gone on to some minor success.

I was impressed with his coup, but I would never want to be accused of contributing to the swelling of Hal's head. "So," I asked, "how'd you manage something like that without ever getting off the couch?"

He sucked his teeth with a sort of inverted whistle and shook his head. "Now, Shorenstein, my boy, that is not what I call a constructive attitude. Would you prefer —"

" — no, no! Sorry, I'm very sorry if I've offended you in any way, and count me in, and what do I have to do, when do I show up?"

"Ah," Hal smiled. "Appreciation. I'd forgotten what it sounded like."

"I appreciate you. I really appreciate you, ever so much."

"I feel appreciated. Ever so much."

"Listen, I really do have to get going, but let me know when and where and what," I said, standing and tossing my crumpled napkin in his general direction.

"You're the man," Hal said.

"No, you're the man," I corrected him.

"No, you're the man."

"Oh, no," I insisted, "you're absolutely and positively the man."

"How could I possibly be the man if you're the man?"

"Alright," I conceded, "I'm the man."

Remembering Karen's request, Great White stopped off at the supermarket on the way home. He made me buy an enormous amount of groceries. I loaded GW up with huge, overstuffed brown bags full of a dazzling assortment of foodstuffs, most of which had never seen the inside of my kitchen: fresh fruit, leaf and root vegetables, a variety of high quality breads and cheeses, sandwich meats, a whole chicken, flour, rice, crackers, milk, butter, eggs, salt, mayonnaise, tea, pancake mix; and some items that had been seen before, but not recently: pop-tarts, cookies, ice cream, soda.

I spent $112.73. Why banks award credit cards to any university freshperson applicant, no matter how irresponsible or unemployed we may be or become, is a complete mystery. Someday a few hundred of us will default on our debts at the same exact instant, and the whole electronic credit card empire will collapse like the savings and loans before them. You heard it here first. And I might add with all due humility that you would be well served to heed my warnings, for I have extensive experience in the hurly-burly world of international finance.

The summer following my collegiate sophomore year I was sentenced to hard time as a security guard, imprisoned for eight endless hours, five days a week, in a tiny bulletproof glass booth buried deep in the bowels of a bank in the Financial District in San Francisco. I was not permitted to read, listen to music, watch television, use the telephone, compose intricate legal appeals to the governor, or engage in any other activity which might distract me from the critically important role for which I was being so handsomely compensated.

For vast expanses of time I had nothing to do but stare straight ahead and listen to my brain cells atrophy. Before me stretched an empty hallway. On the left side of the hallway, halfway down, was one thick glass door. On the right, across the hall, was another. Once or twice an hour a guy in a suit would appear outside one door or the other. Then the real drama would begin.

If I recognized the guy in the suit, I was authorized to push the Green Button. If recognition eluded me, I was authorized to push the Red Button. There were only four guys, and only one suit as far as I could tell, so it is with great regret that I report that recognition was never a problem, and I was never called upon to push the Red Button. I often wondered what blaring alarms, what phalanx of police the Red Button would summon. At times during the lengthy reveries that characterized my incarceration, I was more than a little suspicious that the Red Button was not even hooked up. At other times I actively plotted to disconnect it myself, just to see what might happen. It is a fearsome a thing to be locked up with only one's mind for company.

The Green Button activated each of the doors. Once I pushed the button, the suit could then go through the door and proceed into the hallway. Once in the hallway, the suit would nod to me curtly, and cross over to the opposite door. My pushing the Green Button once more would open the next door. But it was not as simple as that, nosirree. This was a high class, high tech, high stress outfit.

Now came the trickiest part of the operation, a moment of delicate, precision timing. Try to follow along. The vital detail was this: until the door that had just been traversed clicked shut, no force on earth could open the other door. For strictly dramatic purposes, the two doors were wired so that they could never be open simultaneously. The suit would cross to the locked door, yank on the handle, but the other door behind him would still be yawning to its slow, pneumatic closure. The suit would tug on the handle again, twice, and then look up at me in my unlaundered white security guard shirt in my bulletproof glass booth, and motion to me impatiently: push the button, moron! I want to go through this door, is that so hard for you to understand? Where do we get these people?

At first I tried to signal back a pantomime explanation of the complex interrelationship between the doors, to name the condition which rendered me temporarily unable to push the Green Button with any effectiveness. But the suits never understood this little detail, and before long I began to take a certain perverse pleasure in their discomfort.

For they were mine. Whatever mysterious position they held at the bank, whatever lofty title might have been theirs, whatever Third World countries they might have owned via foreign aid loan programs gone berserk, once in the hallway they were mine to toy with as I pleased. If I chose not to push the Green Button a second time, they would be forced to live there until the end of eternity, or until the next shift came on, whichever was greater.

On the other hand, the suits easily had the power to fire me, assuming it occurred to them that I was a human employee and not just a poorly oiled cog in the money machine. So I did not delay very long in pushing the Green Button. That Green Button was my bread and butter, indeed it was my specialty, my pride and joy, my *raison d'etre*. The game became to push the limits of patience, to delay pushing the Green Button just long enough to irk, but not enough to truly annoy. A delicate art, one I took great pride in perfecting as the long summer dragged on. One of the essential tricks was neither to make direct eye contact with the suit, nor to look away, but to gaze with an inscrutable Mona Lisa smile into the distance, as though the mysteries of the gods of beauty and anger might lie just behind them, at the far end of that long hall.

The summer after the security guard job, I accepted the data entry job requiring me to type the name of every bank, thrift, or failing savings and loan in America. This new job I accepted with a giddiness in my heart, gaily contrasting its novelties with the security guard minimalism. I would be permitted to speak to others, to engage in tactile activity, even to photocopy on occasion! My senses were positively flooded with external stimuli. Where would it all end? Was there no limit to the reckless hedonism of data entry?

Ah, youth.

Chapter 17

I lugged the grocery bags up the stairs like Odysseus arriving home. Eva had showered and dressed and was sitting on the couch in a patch of sunlight, cradling a cup of coffee. Her golden hair was drying misshapen and brittle, like the pages of an unusual little novel which has fallen into the bath and then been set on the radiator. She looked up when I came in, and smiled softly.

"Hey, Little Guy," she said quietly, "get anything good?"

My heart soared to see her so. I beamed back a goofy smile.

"Much to munch, much to munch," I said in a jolly manner we both knew was falsely offhand. I started loading the refrigerator, needing only to shove a few beers aside to establish all the room necessary. I glanced at Eva from time to time as I stocked the larder. She watched my movements with an expression alternating between disinterest and irritation. Several times my mouth opened as if to speak, and then closed. Eva scrutinized my peculiar performance, frowned, and drank her coffee.

There was so much to say, but the conditions of our reality severely limited conversation. The crux of our problem, simply stated: I spoke Japanese solely, and Eva was fluent only in Urdu. We desperately needed a translator.

A short little hippie chick, a cute curiosity who really had no business being in my corner of the cosmos, nor in Eva's, stepped into the living room, rubbing skin lotion into her arms; her beautiful, loving, capable arms that had borne Eva's cold, deadened spirit from the mattress of gloom and cleansed her with a hot shower and warm kindness. I wanted to take those lotioned arms and caress them, to press my unworthy lips against them again and again in expression of a gratitude that has no language.

Karen surveyed the groceries and pronounced them worthy, tactfully withholding comment about the odious presence of meat. She and I made a meal together, like an old married couple. I had eaten, but I wanted to help. I made potato salad for later. Karen made a vegetable and rice dish and got Eva to sit down at the table to eat.

I watched Eva wolf the food down with gusto and began to wonder how Karen did it. She was something of a marvel. Nothing she said was particularly innovative; I could have thought of any of it, and better. "Lunch, Eva," was the clever announcement she used to lure Eva to the table. Simple enough, on the face of it. And yet I knew with a fair degree of certainty that had I uttered the same phrase, I would have managed to annoy or upset Eva, or myself, or both. Karen had a direct but gentle bedside manner that almost made me want to contract typhus so I could enjoy her ministrations. Throughout the meal she made cheerful, pointless conversation and somehow induced the edgy, morose Shorensteins to join in. Every now and again Karen uttered a quiet syllable in Eva's direction, or touched her arm in some special way, the hidden meaning of which I could not decipher, but I could not miss its effect. Eva continued to brighten up, even forgetting for long moments her own resolve to be the hard granite against which we were supposed to chip away with our soft flint.

Karen wiped her mouth with a brand new paper towel and got up to do the dishes.

"I can do those," Eva said quietly, as though confessing an embarrassing secret.

"Super," Karen said. With her eyes she steered me into the bedroom, a development I had not anticipated. I was trying to decide if I was up for it when I realized she just wanted a private conversation.

We lay on the bed but left the door open, so that Eva would not think we were hiding something from her, which we were.

"Listen," Karen whispered, "I've got a problem."

"What is it?" I asked, nervous. Lately the problems in my life had escalated with an alarming severity.

"Well, you know Jessica Carothers called."

"Oh, her?" I asked, relieved.

"She needs me up there. Gregory's still out of action and everything, and there's a big — a thing against the developers or whatever. I didn't understand exactly."

"Some dubious Deerpark drama," I said, rolling my eyes.

"Yeah. But the thing is — Eva."

From the kitchen came the sounds of dishes being washed slowly and methodically.

Karen pitched her voice even lower, "Eva asked if I could stick around, you know, kinda hang out while she's still recovering. She needs someone, you know. She doesn't want to be left alone right now."

"She doesn't?" I was having trouble with the idea that Eva had asked anyone for anything, ever. In twenty-five years I had never once known Eva to ask for help.

"No," Karen said, "it would really be a bad idea for her to be alone right now. That's why she asked me to hang around, to do stuff with her." Karen pursed her lips with uncertainty. "But, listen, if you don't want me to hang around too much, I totally understand. I can check out or stick around, whatever you think. I don't want to get in your way. But I'm worried about her. I'm real worried about her."

I studied Karen's bright eyes, glistening with apprehension, and I could tell she had no idea what I was thinking.

"Karen," I said, "I think you are an absolutely lovely young woman."

A great smile of sudden joy burst over her features and she kissed me with great gravity. When we came up for air she wore a bittersweet smile.

"Ronnie," she said, pulling my earlobes softly, so that I had difficulty hearing what she said next, "do you know that's the first time you've ever said anything nice about how I look?"

"Is it? I don't think so. I must have said something."

"No," she said.

"Are you sure?"

"Positive," she said.

"Well," I swallowed, "Karen Anne Bellamy, let me say that I think — and I could be wrong — but I think you're wondrously beautiful."

She beamed at me like a full moon.

In the kitchen, the dishes were rinsing and stacking themselves with quiet lethargy.

"Listen, Karen," I said, "I — you — your offer to stay at Eva's side. Of course it's cool. I'm just a little ... overwhelmed. But you can stay here as long as you want. Screw Deerpark."

She frowned. "I can't do that. I gave Jessica my word I'd help out. And it matters to me, O.K.? I know you don't understand that, but it does."

Had there been an ounce of guile in Karen's avowedly beautiful body, I would have suspected her of manipulating what happened next. As it was, it seemed the most natural development conceivable.

"Well," Ronnie Shorenstein said, of my own volition, "I'll just have to go up there for you."

"Really? What, really?" Karen said, stunned almost to the point of alarm. "Up to campus?"

"Yeah," I said, "I'll do whatever you were going to do for Jessica. Why are you so surprised? Think I can't handle it?"

"No, no, I think you'd be great. It's just that you've only said about a jillion times how much you hate all that political stuff."

"I do," I said, "I do indeed."

Before expressing my next thought, I hesitated long and inhaled mightily, like a diver filling his lungs.

I'm not much of a swimmer in the pool of human emotion. I swallow chlorine and call it drinking. I restrict myself to wading in the shallow end, the kiddie pool. The beckoning, menacing black lines at the depths extend for the length of the pool, seemingly indicating the natural progression expected of me, but I have never found it easy to swim out into the adult end, where my fearful toes stretch through fathoms and never reach the comfort of a solid foundation. And my bathing suit never really fits right.

"Yeah," I said, holding the wall with one hand as I swam toward the deep end, where Karen was calmly treading water. "It's true. I do hate all that political stuff, but I ... well, I care about my sister even more."

Karen touched my cheek with a small, warm hand and kissed my forehead.

I had known Karen for quite a few months and spent considerable time in her earnest company, but only in the last few days had some very important conclusions begun to penetrate my waterplugged ears.

Karen was a very capable swimmer. She was, in fact, the lifeguard.

Chapter 18

"Hey," Eva called out, "you two lovebirds want some ice cream or what?"

"Yeah!" Karen yelled out. "A big ol' bowl for me!" She gave me a sudden glare.

"Oh, me too," I called out. "Thanks."

We came back out to the kitchen to eat it. Inspired by the convivial glow which frozen confections suffused with chocolate tended to awaken in her, Karen decided to display for our inspection a letter she had been carrying around for the previous few days. It had the tattered and worn look of paper that has been folded and unfolded many times. It was inscribed upon the official parchment of Her Royal Highness, the Vice-Chancellor for Student Affairs at UCSC. It was addressed to Karen personally, but apparently all of the leading Deerpark troublemakers had received a facsimile thereof. It was couched in bureaucratic mumbo-jumbo, but the subtext was clear as a cupcake: any more of this protest shit and we bounce your ass out on the front lawn.

"Can they do that?" Eva asked.

"Not for protesting *per se*," Karen said, with the first proper application of Latin I had ever heard issue forth from her bountiful lips, "but I've kinda been letting my classes slide. You know how that goes." She looked glum.

"But they wouldn't be harassing you if you weren't on their political shit list," I said. "I should know, I used to be a permanent dweller on the academic probation cliff. Nobody ever cared. As long as Mom and Dad paid up."

"And then guilted you about it," Eva added. That was actually untrue, but was impressive as the purest expression of the psychological phenomenon of projection I had ever witnessed.

"I really don't want to get kicked out of school," Karen said, finishing her ice cream and licking the bowl out with that exquisite tongue. Tendrils of her hair became flecked with mint-'n-chip. "But I'm way behind in *Women and the Law*, and I haven't even bought the books for *Dev Dep Dom Lat Am*."

"For what?" Eva and I chorused.

"*Development, Dependency and Domination in Latin America*. I think. I just haven't had the time, you know? And now ... "

She didn't finish the thought. The implication was painfully clear to all three of us: now she would have to devote all her time to Eva's rehabilitation.

Eva looked for a long moment at Karen. I wondered if she was feeling guilty and obliged to dismiss Karen as her nurse. Instead, Eva said quietly, "I know a bit about women and the law."

"Do you?" Karen asked.

"Yeah, a little something," Eva said, "and I've taken a look at Latin America, too."

A rush of pure joyous hilarity swept over me. What Karen didn't know that I did: in her soft-spoken understatement, Eva was exactly like one of those quiet, peaceful martial arts guys in the movies; like Billy Jack, or that Chinese guy played by a white actor.

They're all the same: they would never harm a soul, but a few times a show they're forced by circumstances to set aside their meditative ways for the good of humanity. "There's gonna be trouble, kid," the barkeep says. "Better get on your way. Just let them take the girl and stay out of it. These boys play for keeps." And then, in a quiet voice, without an ounce of bragging, Billy Jack says, "Oh, I can take care of myself pretty good," and you just know he's about to kick the living shit out of a couple dozen outlaws.

And that was the voice that Eva used to say she knew a little something about women and the law. Amid the tide pools of her fears and anguish, this was a dry rugged rock of confidence. I've never felt such swelling pride at the sight of a rock.

Listen to me: Eva was pre-law as an undergraduate, top of her class, you understand? She nailed the LSAT, finished in the 99th percentile, O.K., buddy? Without studying, you understand. She didn't need to. She never completed her law school applications, but both Yale and Boalt wrote *her*, inviting her to apply. How had they heard of her? Oh, just a little article she and her teacher had published in *Law Review* entitled "Women in the Judiciary: Toward Formulating a Systematic Problematization".

"Maybe I could take a look-see at your assignments," Eva said, "I might be able to lend a hand."

"Oh, no, that's O.K.," Karen said, "there's just so much to do, and I haven't even been to class in forever. What I was really thinking was to talk to the teachers about maybe getting incompletes and finishing up over the break, or the summer. Or something."

She looked at me for help. I shook my head, smiling slowly. Eva was so goddamn bright, it hurt. So why had she ... ?

Enough of that. It hurt to think about that.

I indulged myself instead in an inarticulable joy and pride at Eva's complete competence. Maybe she couldn't handle the pain of a planet that spins far too speedily; maybe she had tailored her own private, customized hell, but even in her lethargic convalescent state she could write a college term paper far superior to anything that illiterate punk Benny could manage on his best day. Poor, sweet Karen had no idea what an asset she now had on her side.

"The papers have to be really long," Karen said, worried. "Like ten or twenty pages."

"Yeah, well," Eva shrugged, "I think we can find the time."

The more I thought about the letter Karen had received, the angrier I grew. I drove up to campus in a fulminating boil. Those anonymous administrators with their scaly hides had actually threatened Karen's educational future because she had dared to leaflet her peers. It was a move straight out of the J. Edgar Hoover textbook.

By the time I left the apartment, Eva had reviewed Karen's assignments and was casually, professionally lecturing her on Sandinistas, manifest destiny and liberation theology. Eva's voice still carried that fatigued, indifferent breath of the morning, but the afternoon had added a note of competence, clarity, and very faint amusement that only I could detect. Karen cheerfully took notes and kept praising the breadth of Eva's knowledge. She uttered a "wow" or "how do you know that?" every now and then, either out of honest admiration, or for Eva's therapeutic benefit, I couldn't tell. But there was no doubt in my mind: the symbiosis was working.

Dad often says this: "The Italians have got themselves a saying, Ronnie, and it's a good one: *uno mano lavo de nada; duo mani lava de face*. You know what that means?"

I should write Dear Abby or Miss Manners for some advice, because this is an etiquette dilemma I've often faced, and frankly, I'm stumped. Should I tell Dad I do know what his saying means, or keep lying and let him repeat himself until I'm moved to patricide? You see, the fact is that after more than twenty years of suffering his mangled Italian, it just so happens I know exactly what it means, or what he claims it means: *one hand washes nothing; two hands wash the face.*

One hand: Eva. Two hands: Eva and Karen. Together they were going to cleanse every pore.

Everything was coming together, need matching need. The uncertain, ephemeral hope of redemption and salvation fluttered in the air like an injured dove.

Karen and Eva gave me identical little smiles as I left, and I knew exactly what they were wondering: will he hold up his end of the bargain? As the hypothenuse in this odd little triangle of dependence, I was certain the question on their minds was: will Ronnie really help with Deerpark, or is he just bluffing?

Would I help with Deerpark? You better fucking believe I would help with Deerpark. Too much was riding on it. The time for monkey business in the woods had long passed. GW and I shot up to campus like Arnold Schwarzenegger in his Humvee.

"Don't stop for red lights," I barked at GW, who rarely did. "They've messed with the wrong hippie chick this time, buddy boy. Now it's personal. They've got me on their bad side. I'm going to make those money-grubbing executive developer administrator sons of whores wish the doctor had never spanked my little red ass in the delivery room. They don't intimidate me, those assholes. I'm a veteran of their wars. I know what the Red Button does, I know what the Green Button does, and I'm in a very nasty mood."

GW didn't say a word. He didn't have to. We understood each other. His silence spoke volumes. It was time to get down to business.

"I know it's not Shovelstein," Jessica Carothers said as I bounded into library HQ. "It's Shorenstein, right? The famous 'outside agitator.' But I forget your first name."

"Ron," I said, "what do you mean by 'famous outside agitator'?"

She displayed a newspaper article covering the rally of earlier in the week. It was quite a story. Apparently both the local and state news media had picked it up. In all the excitement with Eva, I had missed it. There on the front page sat a grainy photo featuring my own gorgeous mug. I was identified in the caption as "Students protesting Deerpark proposal cheer remarks by Mr. Shorenstein, an outside agitator." The article copy made extensive reference to my speech and my outside agitation. Hunh. I hadn't realized my agitation was so evident to outsiders.

So this was celebrity. A sour taste, really. A citrus of gorgeous orange peel but bitter grapefruit flavor. A disappointing and elusive Holy Grail for which we Americans are cursed to quest for all eternity. Apparently I, me, myself was, for some obscure reason, considered newsworthy or entertaining. What an amusing crock. I never realized how desperate the news media are for even the most remotely entertaining stories.

"Everybody said you were great," Jessica admitted.

"Really?"

"Oh, yeah. People have been coming to meetings more. A lot of them have been asking about you."

This tidbit of information gave me pause. Maybe I had underestimated the little punks.

"What gives with this 'outside agitator' moniker?" I asked Jessica.

"The reporters didn't know what else to call you." She squinted. "They asked me. I didn't really know what to tell them. What are you, anyway?"

Swallowing a hundred sarcasms, I said, "I'm an alumnus. And I'm — well, I'm here to help. Karen Bellamy asked me to. I ... she said to tell you I'm ... kinda taking her place for a little while."

Jessica bit her lip for a moment of thought. "O.K., cool. Tell you what. Why don't you go by the front entrance and hand these out to everybody that comes by?"

And may God have mercy, I went to hand these out. It was some meeting announcement, and for two of the longest, most painful hours of my young life I did my level best. I truly tried. But the grand young lords of the feudal demesne did not want to have the meeting announced to them by some lowly serf.

I've never felt so humiliated in my life. Is it so fucking hard to take a free piece of paper from my hand? Would it kill you to read a few words, college kid?

Most of the young nobility completely ignored me. Some glared as they approached and pointedly said "no," although I had not said a word. Some took the leaflets and tossed them in the trash five feet later, or even let them drop at my feet. Miserable haughty bastards. God forbid someone should slow them down one iota as they headed back to their dormitories to waste their parents' hard-earned money on pizza and beer.

It's your goddamned university, not mine, and it's about to come down around your ears, idiots. But don't let me interrupt your precious gems of conversation about the coolest bands and the hottest Web sites. Oh, no, so sorry, wouldn't want the real world to intrude on you. Oh, hey, sure, you're gonna be mixing plutonium fallout into your amino-acid smart drinks in a few months, but why let that derail your schedule? You're busy, you're important, I can see that. You've got places to vandalize, people to abuse. Go, go, go!

But beware: snotnose punks, I know you for what you are. Tattoo yourself all you will, dress yourself like some grunge-retro Seattle band, pierce your fleshiest protrusions. I see you. I got my X-ray specs on. I know you unmasked. You are yuppie larvae. In five years a suit and tie will conceal those tattoos of youthful indiscretion and you'll inquire with great sincerity why I would like to work for General Consolidated. You'll demand that I push the Green Button faster, faster, ever faster. You'll be busy, so very busy with the critical matter of how to phrase that e-mail announcing the company's downsizing, and then there's that costly upgrade of your dashboard-mounted stereo equalizer, and your Friday nights at the fern bar where you'll laugh as loudly as you can, because you're so miserably lonely.

Don't blink! No time! No time to read the paper, no time to watch the news, no time to vote, no time to take a leaflet from the hands of a fellow human being and read it as though you might actually live in this world of ours. No time to be anything but an uninformed, irresponsible dolt. No time to do anything of consequence but keep your head down and rush swiftly to a painful death without being bothered. Let someone else run things. Because it's not your problem, really, you know? You don't need the hassle. You don't need the grief. You've got your own life to worry about and, hey, that's rough enough, am I right? You've earned that chardonnay. Have another. You've earned that raise. Have another. You deserve it. You're downright special.

Selfish pricks.

I wanted, oh how I yearned to toss the rest of the leaflets in the trash myself, and head to an environment more supportive of my special needs. A dark, empty bar with cheap beer and a pinball machine that doesn't tilt easily would have fit the bill nicely.

But I could not go. I was the hypothenuse. Without three sides there can be no triangle. A case of elementary Euclidean geometry.

Without the fragile support struts, the whole fragile biplane of our little family triumvirate was going to plummet to a crash landing and explode with a spectacular fireball.

I stayed out there for two hours until I finally handed out every single one of those goldenrod tickets to my own public humiliation. And how good a boy was I? Shit. I reported back to Jessica C. for more duties. Somewhere out there is a Congressional Medal of Honor with my name on't.

"How did it go?" she asked.

"Like taking candy from a baby," I said.

"Or giving candy to a baby," she said cheerfully. "That's just as easy, you know."

These fucking hippies. Someone get me a high-powered rifle with a laser scope.

"Hey, my man!"

Oh, good God. Gregory Thompson, teetering on aluminum crutches, hobbling with cast-bound leg in my direction with a grin like army buddies reuniting on the desolate field of Iwo Jima after the battle.

I ask you: how egregiously have I sinned? Did I slaughter innocent children in some previous life? Was I Genghis Khan's favorite executioner? What else could I have done to deserve this obnoxious chumminess from a man I had presumed knocked out for the duration? I sat helplessly trapped, wondering if the leg injury had ruined Gregory's chances of being accepted into the Peace Corps. Not that I had inside information of his interest in that foreign service program. It just seemed the likeliest career choice. What else does one do with a lousy education and boundless energy to meddle in the lives of others? It pained me to know that somewhere in deepest Africa, thousands of starving Zaireans were desperately yearning for Gregory's arrival so he could lecture them on the havoc that digging a well would surely wreak on their fragile ecosystem.

"Hey, man, great speech! Hey, thanks a million and one for pinch-hitting for me." He motioned to his leg. "Got all patched up. Hey, I heard you knocked 'em dead!"

"Not quite. Some still live," I lamented.

"Hey, hey, what's wrong?" Gregory said in a voice dripping with enough sympathetic consolation to reduce Oprah Winfrey to a face full of tears.

"Nothing of consequence. I was just leafletting the front —"

" — oh, yeah," Gregory said, "I hear ya. Bet they didn't want anything to do with you."

"Not a goddamned thing."

"Well, you know how it goes."

"No, I don't. How does it go?"

"Hey," Gregory frowned, "you haven't done much organizing, have you?"

"Not much," I admitted.

"Yeah, well, it's rough," my new best buddy said chummily. "The thing to do is keep reminding yourself why you're out there, what the big picture is, you know?"

Good questions: why was I out there? What was the big picture? How big was it? What did it portray? Whom was I attempting to kid? And was there any real hope that the aluminum in Gregory's crutches might attract lightning?

"Well, there's no substitute for real organizing," Gregory pontificated from behind an invisible lectern. "You can analyze all you want to about why this movement or that revolution failed. We could argue ideology all day long."

Christ, I hope not.

"I've sat through endless hours of bullshit theory in politics classes," Gregory confessed. "Never learned anything useful. You learn more in five minutes on the streets. The only thing that ever changes anything politically is face-to-face, grassroots organizing."

"You may well be right," I said. The remark was intended to serve as a conversational dead-end, a flat yellow metal diamond reading "Not a Through Street." Gregory never saw the sign. Maybe he never got his driver's license. Maybe that's why he rode a bike around — when he could keep from flying over the handlebars.

"I am right," bicycle-boy said. "You know what your problem is?"

How does one respond to this particular inquiry? Yes? No? Oh, please tell me? It's a son-of-a-bitch of a question, plenty rude, intimidating as hell, and impossible to answer without admitting guilt. I had nailed Karen with it plenty of times. The poor girl never knew how to manage it.

Karen. Yes, well; Karen. There it is. Eat your oat bran, Ronnie. Swallow your pride, remember the big picture. Because while you're idly wondering if a banana peel placed in front of Gregory's crutches would be excessively cruel, Karen is in your apartment, massaging the feet of the only woman you have ever —

"I give up," I said to Gregory, "what's my problem?"

"You're operating blind out there. You're not up on the background. You need the 411."

I blinked caustically. "411 is Directory Assistance," I said with all the vinegar in my pantry. "Do you mean information?"

"That's what I mean. The thing is, there's all this stuff about Deerpark that needs studying so we can argue with the admin about the facts and stuff. I've been trying to get to it forever. I've just got so much to organize," he boasted. "There's never enough time to read."

With this contention I do not agree.

"So I was hoping," Gregory pleaded, "maybe you could read this stuff for me, maybe kind of summarize it for me. Or, wait, if you want, we could switch: maybe you could do some of the organizing stuff and I'll do —"

"— I'll do the reading," I said hurriedly.

Well, why not? I mean, reading I know. Reading I can do. Ask me to leaflet and you've got worries. Ask me to read and you've got a chance. I took up Gregory's challenge like a grim and prim English noble accepting a duel. I found a good bench out of the stream of traffic and sat down to read everything. I read environmental reports. I read student manifestos. I read minutes from obscure committee meetings. I read economic projection studies. I read correspondence exchanged between people I had never met.

I read shaky seismic reports, traffic and circulation studies that went nowhere, water table assessments flooded with extraneous information, and cryptic political cartoons.

And I read *The Ohlone Way*. Karen and JLP had told me to, and it was prominent on Gregory's syllabus as well. And I wanted to find out why the guy on the cover reminded me of my progenitor, Abe Shorenstein.

I went into my reading thinking: O.K., Indians, American history, I know the drill: they'll smoke some peace pipes, ride their pinto ponies around some conestoga wagons, give a few war whoops, herd some buffalo off a cliff, eat some pemmican, call their wives "squaws" and their babies "papooses". Next they'll get the shit kicked out of them by the white folk who speak with forked tongue. Treaties will be violated, redskins will be shuffled off to reservations. Then they'll suffer the utter shame of having to appear in John Wayne movies; with the final, irremediable humiliation of being portrayed by low-rent white actors wearing wigs and warpaint.

But it didn't happen that way; at least not according to the bearded pundit archaeologo-anthropolo-professoro types. Not in California. Not in our Golden State. Not on our lovely Central Coast.

Yes, indeed, I read my book. So here's my book report. Wanna know how many Ohlone are alive today? Zip. None. Zero, rhymes with hero. And although I do happen to know everything and am shocked by nothing, I must admit I find that a pretty damned low number.

I was a history major, you know. Says so on my diploma. So I can never figure out why people read mystery and horror novels. You want gore, read history. This Ohlone story was a classic of the genre. I got a good kick out of it. Good summer reading. Three-and-a-half stars.

In 17-something-or-other the first Spanish missionaries arrived in Santa Cruz. There were no bars or movie houses in Santa Cruz at the time, so they entertained themselves by enslaving and killing Injuns. The Spaniards didn't think of it that way, of course. They were saving the souls of lost heathens. They were administering the salve of salvation for the wounds of 250,000 doomed sinners in California alone. God's work, that's what it was. Cuttin' down the weeds to clear a path to Heaven. A love song from the enlightened to the heathen.

Junipero Serra was the Father in charge of all California missions, and a weirder, more sadistic bastard you won't run into in a monthful of Mondays. He used to whip himself on the altar with zealous self-recrimination, dumbfounding the locals, who thought him loco. Two hundred years later the Catholic Church has nearly beatified ol' Junipero. The guy's only a couple miracles shy of sainthood. Even better, he's got a stretch of freeway between Palo Alto and San Francisco named just for him. Now, there's an honor. Me, I'd kill for an off-ramp, and he's got half of the 280, from the Stanford Linear Accelerator to the goofy giant statue of Junipero himself, pointing into the distance like it's someone else's fault.

Yes, indeed, fault; and we're not speaking seismically. What do I mean by fault? Well, you know me. I'm not much of one for politics, and if I start getting all sentimental and self-righteous about it, just slap me upside the head a couple of times. I'll wake up.

But the way I see it, in certain historical conflicts it's just not all that challenging to figure out who occupied the moral high ground. Give it a shot.

We are now floating high above a fateful encounter. In one corner we see a group of Spaniards, both men of the cloth and military types, exploring parts unknown on the western coast of a strange new continent. In the opposite corner we see an indigenous people who have been hanging around this particular marshland on this particular inlet of this peaceful bay for about 17,000 years, picking their collective noses.

Zoom in on your basic ignorant, half-naked Stone-Age Ohlone schmuck living in some pathetic backwards village right between what is now the 7-11 on Mission and Emily's Muffins at Laurel. Up comes a troop of soldiers. They're wearing sturdy leather and shiny armor, their heads are crowned with silver Conquistador helmets and they're riding big ol' horses that snort like the gathering thunder.

Stone-Age Charlie Ohlone can't believe his eyes. He thinks he's seeing some new kind of god, and it's early in the season for that sort of thing. So he trots out of his hut along with all his village buddies. He genuflects and grunts a little, and after a while it becomes apparent that he's offering the new gods some food, some drink and a place to stay, maybe his wife for the night, who knows? Nice guys, Ohlones. Very hospitable, from what the Spanish chroniclers tell us.

And do the Spaniards say, "Hey, thanks for the acorn bread, you're a real sight for sore eyes, we've been traveling forever. Tell us about your charming local customs"?

Guess again. The Spaniards take this friendly Ohlone sucker and a few of his grubby buddies and pack them off to the freshly built military compound and tell them they can't leave until they've become good Christian missionary slaves. And the Ohlone troglodyte hasn't got a fucking clue what the Spaniards are talking about: "Jesus Christos, Madre de Dios, baptism, communion, blasphemy, clothing, agriculture? Stop already, you're giving me a headache. I'm heading back to the village. Maybe I'll rustle up the medicine man. He can cure what ails me. He's got that mojo working overtime. I'm outta here."

And the Spaniards say, "Oh, yes, ha, ha, but you can't really leave the compound, not until you've been baptized and accepted Christ as your personal savior and helped build the walls of the fort, because without local labor we're screwed." So Charlie sits down and scratches his head about this for a while. But eventually day turns to night and this Ohlone feller gets hungry for some wild grass porridge or some such pre-Columbian crap. He walks out the hastily erected compound gate. And then boom! A fateful musket pops, and that's one dead Injun with his face in the most fertile dirt in the world. And the poor sucker never got baptized. He's winging his way halfway to Hell by now, you gotta figure.

Next day his little brother comes a-callin', to find out whatever happened to Charlie, and the game starts over. But by this time the family's wising up a bit. So Little Brother crosses himself before the missionaries and hollers out, "Woah, yeah! Christ, my Savior, hallelujah and amen! Praise be! I once was lost but now I'm found, amazing grace, how sweet the sound."

And Junipero says, "Good, good, my son. Now go and get the rest of your family, because really we didn't come all the way here, across a mighty ocean and through perils unimaginable, just for your soul. No offense, but when we come into town, we come for everybody's soul. And, by the way, we need someone to work the soil, because time's up with this hunter-gatherer bullshit. I mean, it was quaint while it lasted, but this here's the eighteenth century, buddy. Progress is our friend, and get that bone out of your nose. Get with the program. Were setting up shop. We've got plans, boy-o. Imagine this valley with nice long, tall rows of wheat and corn, stretching into the distance. Sheep grazing on all that lovely grass no one's using. Missions all over the place, with bells ringing constantly. Ah, can't you just see it? Can't you just hear them bells ringing in the Judgment Day?"

So Little Brother gets sent as an emissary back to the village to try to explain to the gang how things stand. And a few of them lick their fingers, stick them in the air, and decide the wind is definitely blowing in the Spaniards' direction this century. Yes, indeedy, it's just a really good millennium for colonialism. No point fighting fate. So they pack up a few odds and ends, who knows, maybe an elk toothpick or a pet muskrat, and head off to the plantation.

But some of the hardcore beatnik Ohlone insist on doing things their own way. They've got their own problems, what with fish to throttle and deer to worship and a moon festival or whatever to dance about.

But the Spaniards have food. And they have impressive organizing skills. They read, they write, they do long division. And let's not forget they've got muskets. A shitload of muskets. In other words, they're very persuasive people. By and by, the Spaniards herd nearly all the locals into the compounds.

In a few short years things are going beautifully. The Ohlone villages, the culture, even the language have been, well, shot to hell, if you'll pardon the expression. The locals are starting to speak Spanish better than Junipero's headmaster back on the Iberian Peninsula. Ohlone are getting baptized so fast, even God can barely keep track of who's a heathen anymore.

The lack of gratitude is appalling. The missionaries didn't come to town, after all, because of the bitchin' surf. No, they came to bestow the loving gift of life, eternal life. And does anyone so much as mutter a "thank you"?

But then problems, problems, always problems when you're trying to destroy a civilization. See, there's too many of them natives, and it's really hard to organize a bureaucracy around these illiterate boors. The whole thing is just too chaotic. It's an imperialist's worst nightmare. There's all kinds of dissent, and lone wolf types running off to the woods like savages, and to top it all off the lads just won't work the fields. They don't understand the meaning of hard work. It's starting to eat up all the Spaniards' free time just oppressing the multitudes.

But then the Spaniards catch a lucky break! Imported diseases ravage the compounds, destroying eighty per cent of the locals, who have no immunities built up. Whew! There's a dicey management problem solved.

Within sixty years, the experiment was over, having run critically short of test subjects. The Spaniards went back home. They had to prepare for the 1992 Summer Olympic Games in Barcelona. And did you catch those opening ceremonies? Powerful stuff. Some archer fired the burning torch up from the field to the very top of the stands, where it passed just over the wide bowl of fuel and lit the eternal flame. The stands were packed, billions of people were watching. An inch to the right or left and we're talking massive explosion, international diplomatic disaster, maybe World War III. No wonder the missionaries couldn't afford to dawdle in California.

After they left, a new breed of animal moved into town, the animal that forced the Spaniards out. Dangerous, unpredictable and avaricious; a hunter by day and night. The Yanqui.

Under the new regime the remaining straggler Ohlones became known as Diggers. No one really knows why. Probably because they dug, but let's not jump to any archaeolinguistic conclusions. After the arrival of the Yanqui Americans, Ohlone history seems to transform from a mildly appealing sort of noble tragedy to a shabby, poorly written trash western. In the Old West town of Santa Cruz, which means Holy Cross, it was good fun for gold miners to get likkered up and gun down some Diggers.

Every once in a while some Old West do-gooder would hear the call of a little voice; an atrophied, atavistic trace of imaginative empathy. They would work day and night, sometimes even on into the next day to make life better for Diggers. But really you can't help these people, and they're so dirty and unsanitary, and not very bright. They don't want to be helped, that's the problem.

Well, you know the story. Americans kept doing what we do best: moving in, tearing up the land, talking too loudly, eating too much, kicking ass and taking names. The law essentially permitted white folk to abuse and even kill Diggers, as long as they filled out the proper paperwork. It's important to keep good records.

Around the beginning of the 20th Century — the best and brightest century of them all — the Ohlone wound down; like a radio that keeps playing for a little while after the plug has been pulled.

So here's a fun riddle. You can play along at home. Get out your crayons, if you like.

Q: What do you call the complete annihilation of an entire race?
A: Genocide!

Gee, that was fun.

Genocide, pure and simple. Sugar me no coats, that's the word for it. The obliteration of an entire race in less than 150 years. People, culture, tradition, language, customs: destroyed.

And down at the United Nations, they can't agree on what color drapes to order. They can't enforce a single treaty, they bicker like children, and they can't get a budget together. Even the most basic resolutions are vetoed by some shithole country with some private agenda.

But not genocide. Genocide is the only thing that the U.N. has ever agreed is worthy of its universal condemnation.

And you know me, this political bullshit doesn't wrinkle my prune too much. I'm kinda like the United Nations myself. Whole lotta talk, lots of opinions, no energy. But I'm also willing to go dangling out on a moral limb here and condemn genocide. I mean, it's not exactly a borderline call.

But damn, there's a lot of good stuff on T.V. this week. Believe me, I know. I checked the listings. There's a Twilight Zone marathon, two great woman-in-jeopardy movies on the Lifetime channel, and then Letterman's got Cindy Crawford on. You can't beat that with a stick.

So why should I care? And it's not just me, you know. I didn't just rip apathy out of the pages of an obscure, archaic dictionary. If it were a fashion, all my neighbors would already be wearing it.

Watch as the yuppie guy down the block considers the genocide question for a moment, and says: "You know, honey, it sure would be great to get away for the weekend, get away from the kids. We haven't been to Tahoe in ages. I forget, do we take the 280 to get up there?"

Observe the plumber downing his lager lunch as he ponders the implications of colonialism and cultural oppression, and declares: "Lord-a-mercy, but I do get a lot of mail every day, and they all want a piece of me, and the government wants the biggest piece of all. And nobody cares about the little guy any more. My momma always said that if you work hard and play by the rules, you can be anything you want to. But now, hell, I just don't know if she was right. I mean, you work all your life and all they do is shit all over you. You can't fight City Hall. Buncha bureaucrats. What do they know about a working man? Huh? Whassat? Indians?"

Yeah, that's us. We're the kids next door. We're busy and we're bored, we're angry and we're tired, and who really gives a shit about some dead Indians?

Genocide, shmenocide; we've got malls to build.

And what makes our little crumb of the universe so unusual anyway? Every piddling pothole on this piteous planet is a place somebody killed somebody else to get.

I've got my own headaches. I can't find a goddamn job, my sister is evidently several sandwiches shy of a picnic, and my girlfriend could walk out on me any day. How do I know she won't? She betrayed my predecessor's faith with a carefree infidelity. Why should I be immune? She's a shotgun of affection that shoots the whole world. I just happen to be in the crosshairs at the moment. That's what's on my mind. That's what troubles my sleep, not some paleontological puzzle for the ethically challenged.

But, see, the nagging little thing is this: when you stroll down Pacific Avenue in Santa Cruz, California, you're stomping through a graveyard.

And when you buy that great dress you've been watching for weeks to see if it would go on sale at your favorite Monterey boutique, and finally it did, and you feel a surge of victorious pride in your own patience; well, you know. I mean, I hate to keep bringing it up, but that dress store is located right smack in the middle of the village, where ritual religious dancing was the hot thing for 20,000 years after the last Ice Age.

Nice dress, though. Looks great on you. You really should be a model. No, really, I'm serious, you could easily be a model. Hey, are you doing anything after work?

Oh, did I mention that they had to bulldoze the burial ground and dig up busted femurs and decayed eye sockets to make room for those lovely sunflower-print dresses? Tell me, when you rub the rayon between your delicate fingers to test the fabric, can you feel the sheer violence, the bloodbath that occurred right there, within a long tee drive off the infamous 18th hole at Pebble Beach?

How many hours of psychotherapy are you gonna need to efface that kind of guilt?

Oh, I know. You didn't do it. You've got an iron alibi. You were booked solid. You're in the clear. Your conscience is unburdened. You weren't even alive then. Me, neither.

Well, somebody did it.

Ah, yes, but is it fair to blame us for violence committed by our forebears, most of whom weren't even in the country, let alone the neighborhood at the time? Isn't there a statute of limitations on ancestral crimes? Do Germans who were born after World War II bear any responsibility for the Holocaust?

What are you asking me for? How should I know? What am I, your ethicist?

Chapter 19

Friends, you may remember that I worked at a restaurant when I was in high school. Eva worked there too, in the elite waitress position. We lowly busboys were required to purchase ugly functional black work shoes. I found this a great injustice. I was obligated to spend my own money in order to perform the duties assigned me. In my innocence, I had previously conceived of a job as an arrangement whereby money would flow in my direction, and not the other way around.

By happy fortune, I discovered a pair of work shoes of my size sitting unclaimed atop the locker assigned me. I asked around, but no one knew to whom the phantom shoes belonged. And so I claimed them as my own. They were fairly new, but already worn in all the wrong places. They were quite painful at first, especially since my busboy duties involved a good deal of running from one place to another. In fact, my duties seemed to consist of little else.

For a while those shoes changed the way I walked. They were pitched at an angle that leaned me forward, making me hustle far more than is my natural inclination. The effect was so profound that it impacted my basic gait. Even in other shoes, in my schoolday yellow Converse high-tops, I began to walk as though I had somewhere to go.

Some months later it devolved that the ugly black work shoes had belonged to an employee who had died in a motorcycle crash. He had plowed his Yamaha into a brick wall at eighty mph. I was hired to fill the opening created by his absence. In short, I was wearing a dead man's shoes.

Word got around. Others at work found it spooky. He had worked there only briefly before dying, and none of the employees had known him very well. But they considered me quite odd, even macabre to continue wearing the shoes once I knew their ghastly past.

Eva found my behavior sacrilegious. She strove mightily to persuade me to stop wearing the shoes. She even offered to drive me to the grave site so that we might return the shoes to their rightful owner in some ceremonial fashion. I might add parenthetically that Eva was always keen on a visit to the cemetery. She liked the quiet, the grass and the trees, the drama of death, and the opportunity to smoke pot unmolested by any living soul.

I maintained my position. I refused to give up the shoes. These boots were made for walkin', I argued, not for some maudlin ritual sacrifice. I had come to love those shoes. By now they fit my feet better than any shoe I had ever worn. And I had earned that fit with hard work. Eva was disgusted by my indifference to tragedy. I argued that it was a waste of money to throw away perfectly good shoes. She offered to buy me new ones, an extraordinary offer really, but likely indicative of a pathological new obsession of some sort on her part. I refused. I never told her the real reason. I was too embarrassed to do so.

I had decided in my secret heart that it was an homage of sorts to wear the man's shoes. It felt right. I knew he would want me too. I did not just think so. I knew, because I knew him intimately. He had been a fast mover, an energetic guy. He would not have wanted his shoes to sit idly on his gravestone, among the flowers and flags, confusing elderly mourners on their lonely pilgrimages to conversations with spouses long gone. He would have wanted me to wear those shoes down to the soles. I felt awkward in the certainty of this knowledge, like a medium at a seance; the only one at the table capable of interpreting the message coded in the tapping.

The Great Shoe Debate ended in rather unglamorous fashion, without really resolving any moral issues. I was fired — a fate I richly deserved. I needed the shoes no more.

Before I leave this topic entirely I have to get something off my chest that's been a great burden to me, lo these many years. I have to confess that on my last shift I didn't clean the fryers. I'm sorry, but they were always disgusting, filthy grease pits, impossible to clean well, and on my last shift I threw caution to the wind and risked a bad recommendation just to avoid the fryers.

The proper procedure was to dump the rancid used grease into a large barrel which sat bubbling with satanic malice, brooding malevolently in a corner of the storeroom. A yellowish froth crowned the scum and oozed through the lid and over the barrel's sides. Every few months the accumulated grease was dumped into a toxic truck that hauled it away to a destination so grotesque I shudder to imagine it. It made me sick just to walk near the grease barrel. It was a loathsome presence. Dr. Frankenstein could have brought it to life with a couple of rusty electrodes. It was so foul and putrid I once offered to get inside the barrel, head completely under, if every employee would put up ten bucks to watch. Hey, listen: I was young. I needed the money. I'm not proud.

But I digress. On my final night of work I left the fryers for the morning boys to curse about, removed my name tag one last time like a retiring football great, and set the dead man shoes back on top of the locker for someone else to use.

I was thinking about those shoes when a pair of worn-out sneakers shuffled up to me across the library floor.

"JLP," I said, "long time no see."

"Long time," he agreed. "You come back to save the day again?"

"Say what?"

"You know exactly what I mean. Why don't you just fuck off?"

I squinted at the guy, mystified. It's not so very rare for people to tell me to fuck off, but when they do I usually know why.

"What crawled up your ass and died?" I asked JLP.

"Like you don't know?"

"Exactly like that."

"Man, you and your fancy speeches. Who the fuck you think you are? Another white man come to save the day? Thanks for nothing."

"What is your major malfunction?" I asked. "I thought we were solid, you and me."

He squinted. "Yeah, so did I. Then you had to go and steal the fucking show."

I declare for the record that I had to pause and think about what show he meant. It took a few seconds, but slowly a gear turned, a tumbler whirred, and somewhere in my brain a conclusion formed. Jumpin' JLP was pissed off because my outside agitator speech was well received, and his sage-waving act was treated like the Gong Show reject it was.

"Hey, I'm sorry if I bothered you. I was just trying to fill in for Gregory. I thought we were all in this together."

"Yeah, right," bitter-boy said. "The team's all on the field together, and I'm the mascot, is that it?"

"Hey, listen," I said, "did I do something to you? Did I shoot your grandmother? Because the last time I checked, I was the guy that hauled your ass out of a tree because you were too scared to move. So I don't know what exactly your problem is, but I'm just trying to help out."

"Are you?"

"Damn right."

"And you help out by taking over everybody's cause for them?"

"I don't know. I help out however people ask me to."

"Bullshit. You help out however makes you look good. You don't earn it."

I really should have just stayed clear of the self-righteous snotnosed punk. It was absurd. There I was, a being composed purely of good intentions and golden sunlight, getting harangued by a refugee from the Land of the Terminally Ungrateful.

I should have just pissed on his shoes. But I felt badly about how things had turned out. The truth was that he was a decent JLP. I had even liked him some, in the happy days before he started calling me an asshole to my face. Was it my fault he was a shitty public speaker? Was it my fault the Indians were wiped out? Because if we ignore distractions, that was really the essence of our little drama. Indians had died, and JLP was making me feel like it was all my fault.

Alright, alright, I'll use the word: I felt guilty, O.K.? Guilty, guilty, guilty. And sorry for the guy. I suppose I do have some vestigial human emotions. In a few generations, natural selection will wipe those sentiments clear out of my descendents' DNA. With proper genetic management, regret and compassion will disappear, unused and unneeded, like my tailbone. But for now I'm cursed, possessed by a tiny little creature residing within me; a flimsy ectoplasm which, if magnified one-thousand-fold, might be called a conscience.

"Well, the thing is," I said meekly, "I am trying to earn it." Yecch. I sounded like a whiny little pimply-faced punk. "I've been reading up, like you suggested." I held up my reading for his perusal.

JLP's face was a textbook study in emotional transition. Slowly, cautiously, he went from anger to confusion to contrition to curiosity.

"Did you really read that book?"

"Really did."

He looked at me as a proud father might. Then he unzipped his backpack and uttered a very characteristic phrase.

"You want a brewski?"

I joined him. We drank silently for a moment, eyeing each other carefully. Then JLP grinned.

"Hey," he said, "sorry."

"No problem," I lied.

"So tell me,' he said, scooting closer, "what'd you think about that book?"

"It made me think about my shoes."

This puzzled him a great deal. I had to laugh at the expression on his face.

"Sorry," I said, "it's an inside joke, and I'm the only guy on the inside."

It took me a while to tell my shoe tale. Night had fallen on the protestor compound, and it felt a bit as though JLP and I were seated around a Boy Scout campfire, as I told the famous scary ghost story of the dead man's shoes and the graveyard at midnight. Which is pretty silly, because we were talking about a pair of sweaty work shoes left on top of a locker in a family restaurant in southern California.

"But what's the point?" JLP asked.

"Well, this is what I was thinking when you walked up: those shoes are kind of like the Ohlone. Or maybe that guy who wiped out on his motorcycle was. Because he was gone before I ever appeared on the scene."

"But you wore his shoes, so you, like, inherited his legacy?" JLP said, catching on.

"Exactly. I walked in his shoes after he was dead, so I absorbed a part of him. In the same way, people living in Santa Cruz must absorb something of what the Ohlone were like, just by living here. Just by walking around in the same place, breathing the same air, swimming in the same ocean, or whatever."

JLP thought about this for a little while. In fact, he studied the matter for an entire beer. Which really wasn't that long in his case.

After a while, he said, "Bullshit".

"Bullshit?"

"Bullshit. I think you just read one book and now you think you know what it's like to be a Native American in this country. But you don't know shit, actually. First of all, it's not even the same air or the same ocean; if you'd paid attention, it says in the first chapter that even the natural environment was way different two hundred years ago, before it was destroyed by the Europeans. Second of all, you show me some signs of people in Santa Cruz supposedly absorbing what the Ohlone were like. You show me one example of somebody who breathes the same air as them and suddenly has a clue what they were like. Third of all, it's insulting to imply that you can take a whole culture, a whole people, and absorb it somehow, by breathing the air. It's not a perfume. And most important, the Ohlone aren't all dead. So they don't need you representing for them."

Wow. Coming from taciturn JLP this was a major oration. I was beginning to feel like his private little whipping boy.

"Wait a minute," I said. "Weren't you the one who said that breathing the same fog as the Indians made us all like them, kept them still alive?"

"When did I say that?"

"When you climbed down off that tree."

"Oh," JLP scoffed, "you mean when I was on shrooms? Shit, stuff you say when you're tripping doesn't count. God, you've got a lot to learn."

"Oh, why don't you educate me?" I asked, in jest. JLP, unfortunately, took the remark at face value. And for the next hour, he proceeded to spin an endless socioethnic sob story involving reservations, treaty violations, and Russell Means, whoever he is. I wasn't paying particularly close attention, I'll admit that. In fact JLP and I were pretty toasted on malt liquor once again, and then of course we must account for the fact that the lecturer was not renowned for superb public speaking. My attention wandered. Perhaps I ought to have made an outline. I, II, III, A.B.C., just as they taught us in high school, just as I have never used once in my life. Outlines are a diabolical plot by small minds to shrink other minds down to their size.

I suppose I remember the gist of things. As the rap singer teaches us: *it's like this and like this and like this and like that / it's like this and like this and like this and like that.*

What follow are JLP's thoughts on the state of affairs in modern Native American life. Edited, annotated and indexed by Ronald J. Shorenstein. The J is for Johann, named for my mother's father. He was a fisherman in Sweden, a devout man who read the Bible to his children every evening. Christ, imagine what a bore he must have been. Might have even rivaled JLP.

Go to South Dakota today. What did you see while you were there? Indians, that's what. They've got thousands of them out there, doing their workaday thing. There are thousands more of them on reservations that make up half of the entire state. Then you've got your Hopi in Arizona, working their village goat thing from the top of a mesa isolated high above the canyon floor. Mohawks build all the high-rise buildings in New York. They've got some rite of passage thing about heights. Go check out New Mexico. Here we find Taos Pueblo, the oldest continually inhabited building in North America. Indians crawling all over the place, selling crappy bread and warm soda to sucker tourists like the singing von Shorensteins on a hot day in the summer of 1976. Long story.

Now, I ask you — because JLP asked me — what do all these Indians have in common? They're alive, that's what. Oh sure, settler white folk slaughtered who knows how many of the poor bastards back in the day, but there's some left standing, contrary to popular opinion. A million or more.

And I mean, maybe it's not my call, in fact JLP insisted that it's not, but I think maybe the lucky ones died. The ones that are left? They're some of the poorest sons of bitches on the planet. The U.S gummint cleverly gave them measly little scraps of the shittiest land on the continent for the reservations, so they can't grow a damn thing. They can't build industry there either. They need a couple bucks, so maybe they sell out their rights to some mining company to come in and rip out all the magnesium. Take a wild guess who makes the money: the mineral company or the tribe? Oooh, good guess.

Then you got your casino schemes. Lots of places it's illegal to gamble, but not on reservations, because they've got some weird quasi-sovereign status. So in comes Bally's and offers to build a casino. You know, way off at the edge of the reservation where it meets the road, out of the way, where nobody will notice the glaring multicolored fifty-foot neon Indian in a headdress. It won't even remotely interfere with all that authentic back-to-the-old-ways Indian crap on the reservation.

Not that anybody lives that mumbo-jumbo primeval lifestyle lately anyway, according to JLP. As far as I can tell, Indian culture today is based on a different set of traditional values: alcohol and pickup-trucks. Forget pinto ponies and Apache appaloosas. Indians like their vehicular transport much more sturdy these days. Nobody buys pickup trucks, jeeps and big American cars like Indians.

Think about that. Ever wonder how it would feel to be a Cherokee and buy a Jeep Cherokee? My money is on pretty fucking stupid.

I mean, picture swinging your hulking honky frame into the tiny driver's seat of the sporty new GM Anglo-Saxon Teasipper Snob 400: leather bucket seats, five speed manual transmission, available in white only. Don't that motor just purr?

Although the truth is, if you're talking about an Indian rich enough to buy a car, you're talking richie rich. Most Indians couldn't shoot an arrow high enough to even graze the poverty line. And who do you suppose spends all that money in the casinos: fat tourists in fat RV's or skinny losers from the local tribe pouring their profits back down the same sinkhole? Correct answer: both.

But hey, everybody's got to make a living, except college kids. So most of your Indians do the urban-blend thing like JLP's family, or go scraping by on food stamps and sweatshop jobs. Indians are so goddamn poor they aspire to be black and unemployed. Then there's drugs, and busted families, and welfare — bing, bang, boom, and you know the way that song goes. Coda.

There do exist a number of sell-out assholes, people to whom JLP wouldn't give the time of day, who like to give the tribe a bad name by running curio shops by the side of the road; selling fake plastic war bonnets and baby moccasins and cowboy-and-injun dioramas and cheap crappy kachinka dolls and bullshit turquoise jewelry. Turquoise, turquoise, they're always making with the damn turquoise. What's that all about anyway? That and dream-catchers, which are phony catgut and feather dealies that hang from the ceiling and catch dreams for the sucker tourist who buys them and immediately sticks them in the attic.

I don't know, maybe it's not my place to judge — and frankly I don't really give a shit — but do I detect an unpleasant scent here? Sniff. Snuff. Maybe it's that delicate aroma of rotting carcass wafting up from the corpse of indigenous cultures past.

And who's an Indian these days, anyway? Most of these sideshow souvenir Indians are mixed-blood by now. Few speak the old language, eat traditional food or engage in any indigenous activity except when a powwow comes around, for old times' sake and a couple of laughs. And then these caricature Indians go and sell off little memorabilia of their mythical culture to the descendents of the very same people who killed their ancestors. Well, wash my mouth out with dishwater if that kind of commerce isn't a steaming pile of horseshit.

Allow me to rephrase delicately: you don't see too many Jews selling miniature plastic menorahs to passing Germans outside the gates of Auschwitz, do you?

O.K., so I was growing a bit angry. I have a temper, you know. I'm entitled. I may not shove the beast raging within me on public display very often, in fact it rarely even makes private appearances, but that makes it no less tangible an entity.

I hadn't had solid food since breakfast. I had a headache from that cheap brew JLP had forced on me. I had been rejected by snobby sophomores, condescended to by gregarious Gregory, and harangued by the suddenly circumlocutory JLP. Keep that context in mind.

Alright, so I said something offensive to JLP. There, you happy? I've confessed. The truth is, I don't even remember what it was. It just slipped out, just a few choice words selected practically at random. I've been complimented from a very young age for my sizable vocabulary. Can I help it if a few nasty adjectives leak out every now and then?

I believe I may have compared the condition of Indians begging the U.S. government for handouts to a dog awaiting the master's bone. Either that, or I might have made some jocular reference to Christopher Columbus. Touchy subject for JLP, ol' Columbus. Tres touchy. If memory serves, I said Columbus did the Indians a favor by bringing them civilization and real culture. I didn't even mean it. I said it strictly in the spirit of offending JLP.

I might add in my own defense that JLP was a tremendously easy guy to offend. Such people practically invite the attack. You've walked past dogs who can smell your fear, and snarl to enhance it. I am that dog. I like to utter the forbidden when in the company of the touchy. A good third of my time with Miss Karen was dominated by this delicate dynamic.

Yeah, well. No one ever accused me of excessive kindness.

"I knew it," JLP said, livid. "I just fucking knew it." He glared at me and gathered his belongings toward him like a kid taking his ball and going home. "I said you just didn't get it, and I tried to explain it to you, but you didn't get it at all. You know what your problem is?"

Uh —

"You haven't got a soul. I used to think that all living things possessed a soul, especially human beings. But not you, man. You're just empty inside, so you try to tear everybody else down with you. You have no people, no roots in the earth, and no soul. Why don't you just fuck off?"

I didn't alert him to the fact that he had extended the same invitation earlier in the evening, and then effectively withdrawn it, the little hypocrite. I was too caught up in his theatrical performance.

"I'm through talking to you," he concluded, slinging his backpack to his shoulder. "Period. I tried to be nice to you, but you don't listen. You just insult my people, and I can't stand for that. I'm outta here."

Oh, bravo! A standing ovation on the balcony, and bouquets of roses tossed on the stage. Such a tragic, moving, dramatic performance. Someone award the boy his Tony, and let's cut to commercial.

Chapter 20

The sole pay phone in the library lobby had finally freed itself from Gregory's sweaty chokehold. I punched in my own home number and held the disgustingly warm receiver a resentful distance from Gregory's energetic germs.

"Hi there?" Karen answered.

"Me," I said.

"Hi, me! How's it going? Did you organize the press thing? Is it going to be a big deal?"

"Uh, yeah. Massive. Listen, more on that in a moment. First, is Eva in the room with you right now? Just answer yes or no, so she can't tell what you're talking about."

"Yes."

"O.K.," I said softly. "Is she — is she more like she was last night or like she was this morning?"

"Um, no?"

"O.K. Sorry," I whispered. "Let's do it this way. If she's more —"

"Tell him I'm fine," came a remote, tired voice in the dim background.

"Eva says she's fine," Karen said. There was a muffled exchange. Karen added, "and she says for you to stop being ..." There was another muffled pause, followed by: "oversolicitous. Stop being so oversolicitous. What's that mean?"

"It means mind my own business." My shut eyes and the bridge of my nose suddenly needed deep and desperate rubbing. "Fine," I said. "Forget it. Is it kosher to ask how you are, Sherpa?"

"Good. We're totally breezing through those papers I have to write. Why didn't you ever say how smart Eva was?"

"You never asked."

"Well, anyway, we got a lot done today. I can totally see the light from the tunnel, or whatever. Do you know who the first woman to argue a case before the Supreme Court was?"

"No, but I have a feeling you're going to tell me."

"Not if you don't want to hear," she said in an injured tone.

"Christ," I sighed, "don't tell me I've offended you. I just offended JLP so horribly he took off for good. Told me to go fuck myself, as it happens."

"Oh, God! What'd you say this time?"

"I don't know, I just — it's not really important. Listen, Karen, I'm getting off track here. I called for two reasons. The first is this: what exactly were you going to do up here? I mean, if I'm substituting for you, what do I need to do? Can't believe I never even asked. So far all I've done is hand out some leaflets, read a bunch of materials, and had JLP lecture me. What now? I'd like to come home now, but am I done? What would you have been doing here?"

"What needs doing?"

"I don't know. That's why I'm asking you."

"I have no idea. I can't tell from here. Ask Gregory. Just ask him what needs doing."

I groaned. Turn the other cheek, Jesus of Nazareth urged us. I have never been strong enough in spirit to follow this teaching, but at that moment I came as close as I ever have: I transferred the phone receiver from one ear to the other.

"Ronnie, don't make noises," Karen said. "Do what I told you to, O.K? Gregory will clue you in."

I sighed an assent.

"I hope you can get home tonight," Karen said.

"What? Of course I can get home, Great White willing."

"Not necessarily, Ronnie. These things take a lot of time to plan. You could be there all night. You might have to sleep in the library again."

"Oh, shit. You're kidding."

"I'm not saying for sure. But it's a definite possibility, from my experience."

"Oh, Christ," I moaned. "This is really getting out of hand. I am a martyr, Karen. I hope you appreciate that. I truly suffer. I am a lamb sacrificed on the Deerpark altar."

"You are a lamb," she agreed.

"Ahhh, Christ," I said, sighing with convincing despair. "Jesus H. Christ Almighty. O.K., alright, listen. Here's a joke: Jesus walks into a motel, slaps down three nails, and says: 'put me up for the night.'"

"That's not funny," she said, laughing.

"Oh, I hope I didn't offend you, or any of your people. I seem to have found the knack for doing so." I ran my hand through my unshampooed hair. "Hoo boy, what an evening this is turning out to be. Alright, I gotta get going."

"Wait, what was the other reason you called?"

"What? Oh, I forget. Nothing major. I was just ... I was probably going to tell you that I missed you, or something smarmy along those lines."

"But now you're not going to?"

"Didn't I just do so?"

"Doesn't count."

I heaved one last sigh. "It's as close as I can get right now, Sherpa."

"I miss you too, Ronnie."

"Glad you asked," Gregory said. "Everyone's been flaking on me lately. M'Bopape promised me he would — well, never mind. Good thing you're here." He gave a self-satisfied smirk. "Guess that reading really inspired you."

"Guess so," I replied laconically.

"Cool. So cool. See, this is my theory: student politics is fifty-fifty. It's only fifty per cent about getting done whatever it is you want to get done. The other fifty per cent is about learning, which is supposedly why we're here, right?"

"I'm not a student," I observed.

"Oh. Right." He seemed nonplussed for a moment. "Well, you can still learn stuff, right? Learning is a lifelong process. I mean, doesn't reading that stuff give you a much better appreciation for the historical struggle of Native Americans? Plus I noticed you really exchanging ideas with JLP, weren't you? I think that's so cool."

"We exchanged ideas," I agreed. "What needs doing?" I repeated myself.

"O.K. Here's the deal. We're going to completely block both entrances to campus."

"What? Why?"

"To protest the University's involvement with the Deerpark development."

I thought about this for a moment. "How is blocking the entrances going to help?"

"It will draw people's attention to the problem. The media are gonna be there in full force. What you can do is join Cass and Bruiser Bob and go around to the East Side colleges. They're gonna go around to every dorm room and just get the word out. I'm glad you're here, we're way short of people. After that maybe you could come back and do a West Side circle before midnight."

"Hold on," I said, setting the Bruiser Bob issue aside for the moment, "isn't this just going to get people mad at you?"

"All you do is knock on their door and tell them — "

" — no, I mean tomorrow. If you block the only two entrances to campus, how are people going to get on and off campus? There's probably ten thousand people who come up here every day. Going to classes, working up here, whatever. Commuting to the fact factory."

"I know! Just think of the visibility. It would take us twenty protests all over campus to get that kind of visibility."

"But won't this interfere with people's lives?"

"It's going to interfere a whole lot more with their lives when there's a nuclear reactor built on campus. Man, the problem is you're too politically active. You're an insider."

Explosive internal guffaw.

"What you don't understand," Gregory kindly explained, "is that most people don't even know about Deerpark, even after all this time. They don't get it yet, and time is running out. We have to do something to wake them up. If we inconvenience a few people along the way, hey, that's life. Maybe they'll learn something. More than they ever would by going up to some theory class. This is real life, man! That's how you learn. We're going to have a teach-in going on at both entrances, so people can figure out what *time* it is, you know what I'm saying?"

I ignored the unbearable hipness of this phrasing, and pressed my point. "You can't just block their access. It's illegal."

"Of course. We're all planning on getting arrested if it comes to that."

"This is a really bad idea." I could actually feel it in my adrenal glands. "I've driven up to campus plenty of times. If anyone was blocking my way I'm absolutely certain I wouldn't thank them for educating me. I'd be pissed off for the huge fucking traffic jam they caused. You'll create so many enemies in one day, the administration will be doing backflips of joy."

A wisp of doubt, like stray pollen, grazed Gregory's nose. He looked uncertain for a few moments, as though he might sneeze.

"You think the admin will be happy with this?"

"Of course," I said emphatically. It was obviously a thought that caused him great concern. "Listen to me," I said. "I'll tell you right now what the headline in the paper the day after tomorrow will be: 'Students Arrested at UCSC Blockade'. Subhead: 'Key Services Forced to Turn Back'. Pull-quote number one: 'Chancellor says: "We must maintain free access for all."' Pull-quote number two: 'Maybe things did get out of hand,' Gregory Thompson, student leader.'"

"No, mine would say, 'We are protesting to express our outrage at the proposal for a plutonium processing facility on an ancient Native American burial ground.'

"Wrong. That kind of thing would be buried in paragraph forty-two, if it even got in. That's substance. Nobody gives a shit about substance when there's a protest to report. It's all about the arrests, and about the administration restoring law and order. By the time anyone reading the paper gets to the point of why you protested, they'll already think you're lunatic troublemakers."

"You're wrong! If we just get a chance to tell our side of the story, just a few points even, I think there's a lot of decent people in Santa Cruz who would be shocked to learn what's going on up here."

"They'll never get the chance. Haven't you been following the coverage you've been getting? The media are going to make you look as shitty as possible, because they're on the administration's side. Always have been, always will be. Responsible adults vs. crazy kids. It's a classic. On TV they'll show the most extreme thing that anyone says or does. By the time they get done with you, you'll seem like an insane mob who almost killed the poor brave cops."

"Yeah, but ..." Gregory pouted. "It's not like we're doing this just for the media spin."

"Why else?"

"To educate people."

"You can do that other ways. Circulate a petition. Write letters to the editor."

"We have been. Nothing gets published."

"Uh-huh, and you think that same paper that doesn't publish your letters will report the news the way you want them to?"

The protest pontiff appeared peeved.

"Listen," I said, "you're already going door-to-door making announcements, you could educate them that way instead. And you wouldn't piss off half the campus by blocking their access to education. Some people actually take school seriously, you know. Or so I hear. They can't afford to miss classes."

He folded his arms. "Even if you were right, we've already sent the press releases out. People are planning on being there. The ACSDM already voted to do this. I can't just cancel it."

"Acts dumb?"

"ACSDM. Ad-hoc Committee to Save Deerpark Meadow. It's the umbrella organization for all opponents of the development, including environmentalists, students of color organizations, faculty, student government, women's —"

"Alright, I get it," I said. "How many people are in this group?"

"Well, hundreds. The ACSDM represents —"

" — no, I mean how many people actually run the show?"

"Well, there is an executive committee which is empowered to make emergency decisions, although ideally they would consult the constituent groups and arrive at a consensus."

"Greg," I called him, just to bug him, "I'd say you're looking at an emergency. How many people are in the core group?"

"Active members? Well, let's say four."

"Four?"

"Usually, of course, there are more."

"You one of these four?"

"Yes."

"How long would it take you to contact all the other three?"

"Oh, they're all here," he said, motioning to the library lobby.

"Easy money," I said. "Go round them up. It's emergency meeting time."

He looked at me with grave doubt on his ugly mug.

"You're about to piss off half the campus, thrill the administration, and send the media into a feeding frenzy," I said. "If you go ahead with your plan, by this time next week they'll be splitting atoms on Deerpark Meadow, bulldozing Ohlone bones into dust, and absolutely no one will remember your name."

That got him right in the crotch. He hobbled off on his crutches to assemble the war council.

Jessica Carothers I had already met. Carmen Hernandez I met that night. Sean Flaherty I wish I had never met. I knew that after spending eleven minutes in the man's company.

There may be places in the world where the incidence of insanity is higher than in Santa Cruz, CA. I don't dispute that. This town's stock in trade, however, our coin of the realm, our delectable house specialty is the borderline wacko. I'm referring to the type of personality with whom one can readily interact for ten minutes and enjoy pleasant, reasoned conversation on any manner of subjects — and then blamm! When that eleventh minute hits, these characters are suddenly compelled to explain, patiently and quietly, that our entire fascist, capitalist military-industrial complex in fact answers directly to the Trilateral Commission, which is secretly linked with the Federal Reserve Bank, which is utterly beholden to the CIA, which is essentially synonymous with the Mafia, which assassinated both Kennedy brothers, who knowingly suppressed vital data on alien visitations with the aid of the FBI, which is why computers can't be trusted, alternative energy should be free to all, and drugs should be legalized. See you in Roswell.

Perhaps you are familiar with the series of pictures anthropologists and museums favor to demonstrate the evolution of Homo Sapiens. We start with a little ape, little more than a walking tree shrew. Over the ages, depicted in the course of six drawings, the little fella gradually gets taller, stands up, sheds hair, enrolls in night school and gets a job. Sean Flaherty was strictly a Figure #2, late Pleistocene. The sloping jaw, the receding forehead, they were all there.

For the first ten fine minutes of our little protest powwow things proceeded apace. Our little team of five, which would have made one of the worst basketball squads of all time, began our conversation with a detailed review of the plan to date. We all agreed this was a necessary step before considering my proposed changes. Gregory did most of the talking. I did most of the disagreeing. Jessica Carothers appeared to be taking notes. Carmen Hernandez appeared to be too nervous to speak. Sean Flaherty appeared to be an Earthling. He offered a few helpful remarks and asked several useful questions.

We were reviewing the media plan when Dr. Jekyll turned into Mr. Hyde. We never should have mentioned the media. These Santa Cruz conspiracy theory loonies abhor the media. Without warning, this Flaherty fella launched into some incomprehensible diatribe about networks and Noam Chomsky and cable company monopolies and closed-circuit TV's in his very own house.

Now, I know you think me a miserable misanthrope, an uptight judgmental jerk with no patience for original expression. I respect that opinion. It is not without merit. Let me guess, you're thinking I misjudged Mr. Flaherty. I should have displayed a little patience. Perhaps if I had paused to truly listen, I might have understood his brilliant, certainly eccentric, but nevertheless highly valuable discourse. If only I were a little more humane. If only I weren't so insecure in my own sense of self, I wouldn't need to compete constantly and blame others for my own shortcomings. Gee, thanks for straightening me out. I appreciate it. Sure do. Honestly. Here's your check, doctor, can I get up off the couch now?

Ha! I'll tell you how nuts this joker was. He had succeeded in transforming three of the world's most excessively patient process freaks into an instant junta. I was still blinking in confusion when Gregory, Jessica and even Carmen jumped all over the sullen psychopath. I almost felt sorry for the guy. Clearly, the other members of the Fab Five were fully familiar with the man's meandering monologues. As soon his mental clock gonged the fateful eleventh minute, they were all over him like a cheap suit. Before I knew what was going on, before I got a chance to defend my crackpot comrade, before he got a fair chance to prove irrefutably that absolutely anything can be made out of hemp, they had hustled him off to execute some obscure, unnecessary task.

My jaw dropped in admiration as he slunk away. I would not have thought Gregory and his ilk capable of such nicely manipulative and aggressive tactics. There was hope yet.

When I had first demanded the emergency meeting, I had no clear idea of my own agenda. I was quite certain that the plan in place was a bad one, but I had nothing to offer in its stead. As Gregory finished reviewing the protest particulars, an idea came to me. A damned good idea.

Ah, I tell ya, there's nothing like it. Scientists tell us we only use five per cent of our cranial capacity. How they prove such a dubious claim I'm not sure. Still, I don't believe I even hit that low water mark on an ordinary Ronnie day. But if you give a hundred monkeys a hundred typewriters and leave them alone for eternity, one of them might compose a classic. In other words, the law of averages was on my side that night.

"Hold on," I said. "Gregory, repeat what you just said."

"White armbands will symbolize a sympathizer who is not protesting?"

"No, right before that."

"Cops," Jessica said, reading from her notes, "Dangerous? Defensive tactics."

"Oh, right," Gregory said, "I was saying we need to make sure no one breaks ranks. If the cops come to us —"

" — stop!" I said. "That's it! Listen, I've got a great idea. Forget blocking the base of campus. I say we let them come to us. Wait! There was something in that material you gave me to read that I just remembered. Where is that stuff about county regulations? This is good, this is good. Hold on a second. Here it is. O.K., tell me what you think of —"

Oh, it was coming to me now. Protest strategy was flowing through my mind like extra virgin olive oil from an immaculate Italian urn. Such a smooth moment, and so unlike me. I think I may have been channeling Abbie Hoffman. It was like taking dictation straight from his yippified soul.

And they bought it. They stopped for a minute and listened to reason. They sent speedy runners into the Stygian night to announce the cancellation of the blockade plan. We four spent the rest of the evening planning, arguing, amending. The basic shape of the infamous events about which you've no doubt read came together that very night.

And yes, if the North Koreans came to torture me, I would have to confess under great duress that each of the other attendees present at that midnight mass impressed me with their thinking a few times. If you tell anyone I said that, I'll flat-out deny it.

I called Karen as soon as I had a spare moment, and explained the new plan. She got it immediately, and was as excited as I had hoped she'd be. We reviewed Eva's status: no change. We reviewed Karen's status: pleased with her paper, happy with Eva, very happy with me. We reviewed my status: we agreed there was no time for me to come home, and that I would sleep on campus again. I hung up with a rushed expression of affection, because there was a good deal to plan and not much time.

I want to tell you what happened later that night, because I'm not absolutely certain it did happen, and my thought is that perhaps by telling it I can reify it, I can actualize it and place it in the proper beaker for chemical analysis.

This was the setting: I was sitting on a bench under quiet lamplight just inside the library doors. I was studying certain sections of the county civil code when Jessica Carothers materialized. Abruptly she kneeled before me, jeansed knees on the pebbled concrete floor. She slid a bit to my right, and leaned forward to peer at my notes upside down. This graceful pose set both of her legendary breasts poised lightly on my left knee like a tray of dessert, thereby exposing them almost entirely to full, luscious view. And as if this were not enough, at that moment she scratched at one shoulder, tugging tank top and brassiere to the edge of the rounded precipice, affording an even better view of her celebrated cleavage and setting in motion a marvelous series of mammary tremors.

As I've said, I do not know for certain that the encounter transpired precisely as described. It was late, and dark. I do know she came by and spoke with me in close quarters. I can't recall what she said. Probably some inane platitude about the glorious struggle. I do know for certain that she did not utter with breathy voice any of the following: neither "see anything you like?", nor "let me know if there's anything I can get you", nor "I really love the way you leaflet, big boy."

What I do know is that in the past, when faced with such seductive ambiguity, I would most certainly have pressed the point. I might have pulled a strand of her hair away from her face, letting the back of my hand slowly stroke the nape of her neck with a faux absent-mindedness, circling the conversation around some utterly irrelevant, prosaic distraction, subtly shifting physical position in preparation for sudden contact, all seemingly without intent. There have been times, believe it or not, when such strategies have worked for

167

me. Courtship is a ritual based on carefully contrived yet easily deciphered deceit.

But this time I did not take up what may have been a direct offer, damned tempting though it was, and I suppose you know why. Simply put, Jessica and I were not alone. Without knowingly having chosen to do so, I had brought someone else under the lamplight with me; someone who was beyond deceit and duplicity; someone who seemed to decipher my innermost desires before I could resolve to confess them; someone who asked nearly nothing of me, and to whom I was increasingly prepared to give almost everything.

Chapter 21

"Shit, I don't know," Gregory said, scared, exhaling nervous bursts of late morning fog. "This was all his idea. What do we do now, Ronnie?"

Good question. Seventy-five college kids — or seventy four plus one Outside Agitator — seem like a thick burlap sack of strength and resistance in the middle of a night spent in the velvet forest. But in the morning light, with cops in well-ironed uniforms approaching like a phalanx of latter-day Roman centurions, ideas that seem to glow in the middle of the night become like the moon in daylight: visible, but irrelevant.

My plan was simple: occupy Deerpark. My reasoning was intuitive: Why go to the base of campus and harass bus drivers when we could force the administration to deal with us by occupying the very land in dispute?

On the basis of sketchy thinking of this sort, I had endured an exceptionally uncomfortable night in a sleeping bag flung atop a matted bed of sticky redwood leaves, followed by a horrid forest breakfast of granola and soy milk. During the night Gregory, Inc. had assembled a clan of true believers to establish a solid, if illegal presence on Deerpark Meadow.

The important thing, I felt, was to control the conditions. Protesting in the library foyer accomplished precisely zilch. It was not an act that shone the fierce spotlight of confrontation and resistance. It was the dim bulb of cooptation and coexistence. The demihuman denizens of the library lobby lived there according to the administration's rules, through the godfather's loving beneficence. For God's sake, the Chancellor had even discreetly arranged for the protesting mobs to borrow a key to the library to use the bathrooms at night, as long as they promised to be very good little revolutionaries and put the toilet seat back down when they were done.

Ah, but in the forest we made the rules — or so I initially conceived of matters. During the midnight *hegira* from the library lobby we hauled the entire encampment on the backs of a caravan of camels imported from the Sahara for the occasion. Everything from banners, tables, sleeping bags, mattresses, and food fixin's, down to the last poorly articulated photocopy was smuggled in the midnight hour to destination Deerpark.

Instead of moping about in the cavernous lobby of a bastion of research, we had reclaimed the people's land — or so I initially conceived of matters. Instead of bustling between busses at some blockheaded blockade at the base of campus, we had seized the territory that had long belonged to the indigenous people away from the mighty powers of capitalist hegemony and colonial oppression. In honor of the tribes that had once dwelt there we had become our own tribe, sleeping and waking on the very same land, breathing the same musty redwood air, warring against the same enemy. Don't you find that a much more compelling protest, symbologically speaking? Thanks. Thought of it myself.

One small catch. Occupying this particular meadow constituted, technically speaking, an act of criminal trespass. Deerpark Meadow was encircled with a long chain-link fence, a massive ugly necklace fastened at the neck with a forbidding, heavily locked gate. Somehow, however, in the process of moving from the library to the meadow, the lock had illegally broken itself and the gate had opened to let us in. Equally mysterious was the kryptonite lock that had newly formed at the gate now that we were inside. It was the sort of lock one might use to secure a bicycle.

And now the constabulary was trudging up the dusty service road to evict the new tenants. And I know I'm supposed to be a tough male type of guy with testosterone coursing through my cursing veins like an intravenous tidal gush. And I've watched enough savvy criminal TV to know I'm supposed to act all cavalier and crack wise in the presence of the Donut-Eaters. But the truth is that they were big, they carried guns, and they scared the shit out of me.

Lord have mercy, I sure do hate a man in a uniform.

At the front of the invaders' parade strode two women. The shorter of the two was dressed in standard issue Santa Cruz adult hippie wear: jeans, a white cotton T-shirt with a multi-colored Indonesian vest. The taller woman wore a business suit with massive shoulder pads, standing wide as a football player. She had clearly changed out of heeled shoes and into Reeboks for the forest trek.

The sight sent me spinning onto an irrelevant déja vu track back to my days as an employee in San Francisco's financial district, where every lunch hour thousands of women emerge from high-rise buildings in magenta, ruby or sunflower business suits and stocking legs shod with cheap sneakers. God, I used to love that lunch hour. A veritable buffet for the eyeballs. I adored the way they would balance their little take-out salads and frozen yogurts on cautious laps, striving mightily to lift reprehensible utensils to lipsticked lips without soiling blouses nor letting skirts hike too high up the thigh.

Lord have mercy, I sure do love a woman in a uniform.

The delegation had arrived at the gates of destiny.

"Good morning," Shoulder Pads called out pleasantly. "I'm Barbara Meyers, Vice-Chancellor for Student Affairs. Your presence on this land is illegal."

Our tribe was silent, except for a few childish snickers, inspired no doubt by the double entendre implied in the phrase "student affairs".

Ms. Meyers stood for a moment gazing at us expectantly. We were either unyielding with the fierce determination born of revolutionary solidarity, or too stupid and disorganized to say anything. The net effect was the same.

Indonesian Vest nudged Student Affairs. She spoke in an urgent whisper for a few moments. Presently she was granted permission to step forward.

She smiled. "Hello, Gregory," she called out.

"Hi, Ann," he admitted sheepishly.

"Are you the spokesman for the group today, Gregory?"

"Uh, no, no," Gregory said. "We don't have a hierarchical leadership structure. I'm not empowered to negotiate anything."

"O.K., then let's not negotiate anything. Mind if we chat instead? How's your leg?"

So now we knew the cop strategy. Ann was obviously Good Cop, Meyers was Bad Cop, and the real cops were just following orders.

Gregory gave Ann a sickly, sweaty smile. He had been hobbling round on his crutches all night long and the morning sun had not defrosted a certain sickly pallor from his flesh. Forests and meadows were never made for crutches. He kept sinking into soft grass and losing his balance, or bumping into logs and yelping in forlorn pain. Even I almost felt sorry for the wretch.

"I'm O.K.," Gregory lied with false bravado. "How are you, Ann? Yeeouch!!"

This last remark was delivered with great gusto as Gregory attempted to step forward to greet Ann, lost his footing, and slid back on his ass onto a clump of weeds. Laughter broke out among the cops until Meyers turned around and glared them into submission.

Ann said kindly, "Do you need a doctor, Gregory? We can fetch one. You wouldn't have to turn yourself in or anything, of course."

"I'm O.K.," he insisted. "How are you?"

"Just fine."

"How're things at Student Activities?" Gregory asked.

"Pretty slow lately," she smiled. "I finally got around to color-coding the calendar the way you suggested."

Well, this was getting to be one mighty silly mass arrest. I looked around to see how my comrades were reacting to this cozy conversation. They seemed every bit as puzzled as I.

"So," Ann asked nicely, "just out of curiosity: did you folks want to stay for a while and get a photo opp, or were you thinking more along the lines of getting arrested?"

This cavalier woman made us very nervous. Someone retrieved Gregory and a hasty meeting of the tribe was convened a good distance away from the gates. There followed a rapid-fire argument about who could speak for whom and whether we should craft a formal response, and how to respond if we were charged headlong by rhinos in cop outfits.

"Who is this Ann woman?" some no-name demanded of Gregory.

"Ann Capriati-Mentzinger, Student Activities Coordinator."

"How come you and her are such good friends?"

"We're not. I just know her from booking rooms and stuff. She's cool."

"Oh, great, so she's cool. Is that supposed to help? What are we supposed to do now?"

"I don't know," Gregory admitted. He looked like death warmed over on a low flame for twenty minutes, allowed to cool and served with seasonal greens. "Ask him," he said, pointing at me. "This was his big idea."

Hoo boy. I just love that sort of thing. I think I'll name my first child Gregory. Maybe my second one too. Boy or girl, doesn't matter.

"O.K.," I said, taking up the burden of this beloved generation of mine, "let me ask everybody a question. This isn't a formal vote," I hastened to add, knowing what sorts of trouble such a bourgeois suggestion could lead to. "Let's call it a straw poll. It's not binding. It's just to get an idea of what everybody's thinking. How many people want to just present our demands and try to get out of here without getting arrested?"

Approximately half of seventy-five. Call it thirty-seven and a half.

"How many think we should force them to arrest us?"

Approximately twenty hands, forcing me to conclude that abstention was coming in a close third.

"O.K.," I said, with a voice like a toe in ice-cold river water, "how many people would object if someone went to talk to them, presented our demands, and tried to see how much we can get — without getting arrested? We would compromise nothing, we wouldn't have to end the occupation, everyone could still get arrested. It's just to hear what they're prepared to do."

Many calls to rephrase the question. Prolonged bickering on picayune points of process. I won't bore you. Eventually they wised up and agreed to my strategy, which was utterly obvious in the first place. Twenty more minutes before they could in good conscience conceive of delegating a spokesperson, ten more until that spokesperson transmogrified into a spokesman; ergo, me.

And what was the enemy doing all this while? Picture cops and sundry administrators, their numbers now growing, all leaning or sitting against redwood trees, some picking their teeth with meadow grass. Positively pastoral. Moo.

"Ms. Meyers!" I called out.

"Yes," she stepped forward. She was the only person in all of Deerpark Meadow who had neither leaned nor sat on anything, fearing a blemish of her yellow skirt suit.

"We have some proposals for your consideration," I said.

"Hi, what's your name?" Ann Capriati-Mentzinger asked pleasantly, without getting up from her seat on a log. She did everything pleasantly. In fact, for a forty-year-old woman she was ... well, anyway.

"Carl Davies," I said.

This response I had prepared some time in the night in anticipation of just such a confrontation. It was an easy choice. I had stolen the man's girlfriend. Might as well steal the rest of his identity.

I had things I was supposed to say. I consulted some notes I had scribbled moments earlier, jotted in the margins of some obscure leaflet about pathetic political prisoners in Burma or Myanmar or some such Asian backwater. Actually, I think those two may be the same country. Why would they have two names for the same place? I have no idea. Why were they political prisoners? I have no idea. How did the leaflet come into my hands? I have no idea. How did I feel proclaiming our manifesto as though I were some latter-day Che Guevara? I have an idea. Like an ass, that's how I felt.

"I'm speaking on behalf of the Ad-hoc Committee to Save Deerpark Meadow. We are here, as I suppose you have guessed, to protest the University of California's development project planned for Deerpark Meadow."

"Yes," Meyers said, "we had in fact guessed that."

"Well, good. Right. Thank you. Please be informed that this is intended to be a non-violent confrontation," I said.

"Thank you for the information. We share that intention."

I looked behind me. Apparently the supporting cast had no speaking role at that point in the script.

"O.K.," intrepid Ronnie-Carl continued, "Uh, so: our first question is to formally ask whether the University is prepared to stop all plans to develop Deerpark."

Meyers just laughed. Ann and the cops joined in. So did I. I couldn't help it. It was infectious. It was a merry moment.

"Okey-dokey," I said, still grinning, "I will take that as a formal 'no'".

"It is exactly that," Meyers said.

"Seeing as you have refused our first demand, we would like to know if the University is willing to make full disclosure of the use of, um — fissionable substances in the Deerpark development."

"Oh, come on," Meyers said. "Haven't we been over this?"

"What gives, Gregory?" Ann asked.

"I'm not spokesman!" Gregory yelled out.

"For the record," Meyers said, "the University does not now, nor has it ever had plans for the use on Deerpark Meadow of what you call 'fissionable substances', by which I take it you mean radioactive material. Moreover, this is a public university. All research activity is fully disclosed."

"Oh," I said, because it was the cleverest thing that came to mind.

"What about Livermore Labs and DOD research?" M'Bopape yelled out. "That's not disclosed."

"I am not familiar with, nor responsible for, the management principles of Lawrence Livermore Labs," Meyers said reasonably. "However, it is UC policy that all research done by UC employees under grants from the Department of Defense is unclassified."

There was an angry buzz behind me. M'Bopape said, fairly distinctly, "Bullshit."

Meyers looked sunny in her yellow outfit. "Now that I've answered some of your 'demands', as you phrase it, I'd like to make a request of my own. You are in this area illegally. Please acknowledge for me formally that you recognize that I have given you a warning that you may be arrested for trespassing, as well as reprimanded for a variety of violations of campus regulations, including a gathering that does not conform with the time, place and manner restrictions."

"I so acknowledge," I said.

With that, every pair of shoulders in the meadow, from Meyers' in her shoulder pads to stocky coppy shoulders to Gregory's crutch-swollen shoulders, gave a collective shrug.

I beamed back to the mothership for more instructions. Meyers began conferring with Head Cop. Large bolt-cutters materialized like manna from cop heaven.

174

I received my marching orders from Protest Central and headed back to the gate.

"Please be advised," I said, "that we intend to occupy this land until the University changes its plans."

"I see," Meyers said. "Please be advised that we intend to arrest and remove every one of you from the premises, beginning immediately."

There was a tense silence. Mysterious command conversations began to shoot through the ether. The cops started squawking on walkie-talkies and Gregory began whispering with fierce determination on, of all things, a cellular phone he had brought into the wild with him. He was a big one for roughing it, old Gregory.

I watched things happen with a dull, glazed interest, having absolutely no idea what history might be demanding of me at that moment.

Ann the adult hippie moved forward. She leaned on the chain-link fence, hooking her fingers in the gaps and pulling playfully. She motioned me towards her with a subtle gesture of her head. I walked up and dug for lint in my jeans pockets. Ann spoke in a low voice, so that only I could hear her. "You know," she said, "occupying a meadow is nuts. I was at Columbia in '68 when we took over the administration building. We could lock doors and keep the cops on a narrow approach. This set-up is strategically miserable. You're surrounded and isolated. I mean, we could starve you out in about two hours."

"Not likely," I said, bluffing. "We've arranged supply lines throughout the woods. Even now, our supporters are watching this confrontation from strategic hidden locations."

She laughed. "You're a funny one, Carl. Good sense of drama. Next you'll tell me you're having your food airlifted in, like the Berlin Wall in — what was that, 1963?"

"'62, I think. And we may well have paratroopers standing by. You have no evidence to the contrary."

"Are you sure you're a student?" she asked. "I feel like I know you from somewhere else. Davis, is that your last name?"

"Davies," I said. "What was the Columbia thing about? Vietnam?"

"Yeah. The War, of course, always the War. Plus we didn't want them to build some gym." She smiled. "I can't for the life of me remember why. Why do you suppose we cared if they built a gym?"

"I can't imagine."

"It seemed to matter then. It sure doesn't matter to me now." She paused to let the obvious implications of this remark sink in. "Listen, would you do me a great big favor, Carl," she asked nicely, "and call this off before someone gets hurt? I'd really appreciate it."

"It's not mine to call off."

She sighed pensively. "Thought you'd say that. You know, I think that one of the great disservices of the Sixties was that they gave succeeding generations of students the impression that the only valid form of political expression is a protest."

"Maybe," I said. "But you're in no position to complain. You helped create the monster. You can't blame an attack dog for attacking. It's the master's fault."

She looked at me quizzically. "You sure you're a student? You sure don't seem like one."

"You sure you're an administrator? You sure don't seem like one."

A large cop walked up behind Ann. "Pardon me," he said, in a tone so polite the Queen of England would have raged with jealousy. "I'll just be a sec," he said apologetically. He examined the fence, gate and lock for a moment. Then he extended his hand wordlessly, like a surgeon requesting a clamp. An under-cop produced the bolt-cutters. Head Cop worked quickly, cutting a nice efficient hole around the kryptonite lock which was their only barrier. In five seconds he had the gate swinging wide to the wind.

Wordlessly, the tribe began backing away from the gate, up the hill to the top of the meadow where the fence perimeter ended all possibilities.

Chapter 22

There are only two sanctioned groups in this country whose skulls the cops can bash in without much fear of retribution: your basic inner city minority type hoodlums; and protesting leftist students with felonious hair.

We had no way of knowing what, if anything, was on the minds of the militia. Bloodlust was the best guess. In retrospect, I suspect that the collective pig psyche was a sloppy mixture of three emotions: hostility, fear and trepidation. Hostility: their basic condition and a reflex response to uppity beatniks. Fear: yes, even cops are afraid of physical confrontation. Trepidation: I do believe that some of them wanted to avoid conflict altogether. The last thing they needed was some latter-day reenactment of the bloody confrontation between the authorities and the American Indian Movement at Wounded Knee in 1973, which itself was a bloody reenactment.

So far the confrontation at Deerpark had been more like a zen meditation retreat than a riot. But things were about to change.

We never would have had any worries if the opposing team had consisted strictly of UCSC cops. Santa Cruz campus cops listen to Donovan on the cop radio, grow organic snap-peas in their spare time and meditate on the job. The only times I've ever had contact with them were when they helped me jump Great White's battery. This they had done several times, always cheerful as magpies and helpful as kindergarten teachers. Nice guys. UCSC: it's a cushy gig for a pig. I mean, they actually wear shorts while on duty. The most trouble they ever encounter is when some hippie freaks out on drugs and gets lost in the woods. That's why the cops have a search dog, a German shepherd who is easily the most vicious guy on the whole squad.

But somebody, somewhere high up, had ordered cops to come down from UC Berkeley that fateful Deerpark day, and that threw an entirely different wrench into the monkey. Consider this SAT-style analogy: Berkeley cops :: UCSC cops, as methamphetamines :: herbal tea.

The Berkeley Cop is an atavism, a throwback, a testimony to the legacies of an earlier era. Apparently they had some disputes of a highly charged nature up at the Berkeley campus in the sixties. I forget what it was about. I wasn't even born yet. Eventually, by Darwinian natural selection, the weak cops were weeded out and only the strong survived. The nasty, brutish cops who were happy to smack some heads in were the ones who stuck around.

These days, as I understand it, cops who fail in nearby jurisdictions have the Berkeley campus as a haven of last resort, a sort of French Foreign Legion for the Rodney King set. The scumbags who get kicked off the Berkeley or Richmond city police or Alameda County Sheriff Dept. for bad attitude, for repeated disciplinary problems, for violent tendencies, all end up at Cal.

That's another thing that bothers me (and there's a brand new topic for you). The University of California has ten or so branch campuses, UC This and UC That, spread across the face of the great Golden State like academic zits. One of them, and only one, the very first one, is called "Cal." It's pretty damned egotistical, if you ask me. If they're Cal, what's that make this campus, a mere hour down the same California coastline? UC goddamn Mexico?

At any rate, for weeks rumor had been traveling up and down the Gregory grapevine that Cal-Berkeley-Gestapo cops were being brought in to end the Deerpark nonsense. It was this rumor which in large measure precipitated the move to block the campus, which I had aborted. Now I was definitely starting to wonder if that was such a good idea. At the base of campus, the whole world would have been watching. Here in the woods they could have buried our bodies beside the bones of the Ohlone dead and no one would have missed us.

During the long foggy night we had found the site where the Indian bones had been unearthed. It was marked off with stakes and had all the appearances of an archaeological dig: a small sand pit and some tools, and not much for a lay observer to recognize. In the dead of night, some of the hippie kids had formed a circle around the dig and performed some cheesy improvised sacred ritual.

As the cops moved in, my mind wandered in a poorly timed reverie to the human being whose spirit had once animated the bones which were now in such dispute. What would he — and it was a he, that much had been established — what would he have thought about the great dispute over his grave site? We knew so little about the guy, and yet we were pretending with such gusto that we were defending his remains from violation by the forces of evil. What a crock.

Who the hell knows if we were on the side of justice? I mean, would this guy have felt honored or disgraced? Would he have felt solidarity with the students? Would he have had the slightest fucking clue what was going on? Would he have cared the least little bit? Would he have considered us all completely certifiable? Would he have considered us all some kind of albino bears, or spirits from the sky?

Would he have wondered why we didn't praise the spirit of our food before we ate it? Would he have been distressed that we failed to purify ourselves in the sweat lodge before battle? Would he have wondered why we insulted the Great Spirit by failing to touch our foreheads with our thumbnails whenever we spoke about parsley? Would he have wondered why we let the women speak? Was he a perfectly typical Ohlone whose remains could teach us a great deal about his people, or was he some loser outcast no one ever took seriously? And how did he die, anyway? Why did he die?

Our foes moved through the gate with the arrogance of a film-maker taking over a shooting location. The bastard Berkeley cops were easy to spot. Several features distinguished them. They had just arrived. Their uniforms were clean. They wore Cal blue, not UCSC khaki. Oh, and they were outfitted with riot gear from helmet to steel toe — complete with billy clubs, plastic shields and sidearms. They moved through the gate and lined up in front of the local cops, forming a wall with their shields. I believe this is referred to in law enforcement terminology, without irony, as a defensive posture.

Man, oh man, may God have mercy on your soul if you're ever in a position to see cops from the nasty side of their wall of shields. I wiped my face with a stray sleeve and it was damp with clotted sweat. I could smell my own fear. My palms were sticky and my stomach clenched itself like the poorly formed fist of a third-rate boxer.

Despite our proximity, the head Berkeley cop pulled out a mega-phone and barked the following: "Attention, students. You have been warned to leave this area. This is your last warning. You have one minute."

Didn't even wish us a nice day. Fascist pig.

Suddenly M'Bopape yelled out, "Civil disobedience!" in a drill sergeant's voice. "Sit down! Form circles! Link arms!"

Arrghh! A manic game of Simon Says, played for very high stakes. You put your left foot in, you put your left out, you put your right foot in, and you try not to get shot.

Confusion reigned. Dust rose. M'Bopape's followers, a small but significant group, all did as he had instructed. A few other kids sat in a circle, but they seemed too embarrassed to link arms. Some people crouched, unwilling to commit utterly to civil disobedience, but clearly sympathetic to the idea. The rest of us remained standing and blinking owlishly. Gregory hobbled and howled into his cell-phone.

"Hey, Gregory," I yelled, pissed off, "what are you doing? Ordering pizza?"

He put his hand over the phone mouthpiece. "Don't you fuck with me, Ron! I've got shit to take care of! If you hadn't messed with the plan — what?" he yelled back into the phone.

I walked away from him and paced around the perimeter of the group, because it seemed the most productive thing to do. I tore my hand through my hair. The truth is that on top of a condition approximating panic, I also felt no small amount of guilt for the way matters had escalated. I stopped on a small hillock and addressed the children of Israel.

"Hey," I yelled out, "doesn't anybody want to get out of here now? These cops want blood. We could leave now and try again later, when we're better prepared. Anybody with me?"

All I got for this snippet of oratory were hostile stares. Frustrated and feeling cowardly, I turned my frightened gaze downhill.

Confusion reigned among the authorities as well. Ann Capriati-Mentzinger was engaged in a major shouting match with the head Berkeley cop. Even if stray words had not floated up the hill, the nature of the disagreement was intuitively apparent. She was trying to prevent violence before it happened; he was trying to determine whether the chain of command mandated that he actually listen to this annoying woman. He clearly was not the sort of person who relished meddlesome intrusion into his riot management technique, especially not from hippie women. His posture, his expression, and his mustache made that abundantly clear.

Finally he grabbed one of her gesturing arms by the wrist. He seemed perfectly content to twist it right off. But she too had backup. Meyers, who after all was nominally in charge of the whole operation, came to Ann's rescue. Meyers practically knocked the whole domino line of cops over as she rushed up to the head honcho cop. Ann got her hand back double quick.

As they stood and argued, we all heard the sound of dirt and asphalt grinding under tires. Odd. What sort of vehicle could be barrelling up the lousy little service road? It was a peculiar sound to hear deep in the forest, a deep engine rumble with a distinctive macho cough. A very distinctive cough.

Great White!

And behind him, a procession of other vehicles, bicyclists, a sudden mob of student sympathizers and observers, chanting slogans and carrying supportive signs. And who do you suppose was driving Great White?

Wrong. Guess again.

It was good ol' Hal gunning GW up the hill with a nonchalant smirk that neatly encapsulated his opinion of protests and dramatic rescues. Beside him, her pretty forelocks bobbing to the chants and the excitement, sat — well you've already guessed that one. And beside her — did you guess the presence of a sullen, aloof young woman with puffy complexion and nothing better to do than watch her brother get the shit kicked out of him?

Neither did I. I stared at the procession, trying to figure out what the hell was going on.

Which was precisely what the authorities were trying to determine. Their tactical situation had just gotten very much worse. First they had trapped us in a fenced compound, but now they found themselves trapped in between two hostile forces, with no clear escape route. Bad strategy. Very poor piggery, to tell you the truth.

Hal stopped the car as close to the gate as he could get it. It occurred to me that the car was registered in my name and I could wind up in water even hotter than the stuff boiling all around me, but I was glad as hell to see the gang anyway.

Eva, Karen and Hal stepped out. Two of the three had apparently shared a bottle of an unusual henna which gave their hair a nice eggplant tint in the late morning sun. Hal surveyed the scene for a sardonic moment. Then he pulled an entire wrapped egg salad sandwich out of his shirt pocket and began to munch at it. If the sandwich stood more than fifty yards away from me, how do I know it was egg salad? Hey, I used to sleep on the same floor as Hal. I know these things. Egg salad is the mortar fortifying his emotional pyramid.

The cops oscillated between turning to watch the new developments and keeping an eye on the original troublemakers. A thrill of renewed energy rushed through the top-of-the-hill gang. Gregory finally got off the phone. Things got pretty quiet. I exhaled for the first time in a month.

And then a truly unexpected thing happened. Eva — yes, Eva Shorenstein, recently released from intensive care, you remember Eva — climbed up on Great White's hood and stood facing the cops. She held a legal pad in her left hand. Her eyes were dark sunglasses and she shone in the dazzling sun like a Valkyrie in singing armor.

"My name is Eva Shorenstein," she yelled out. "I am acting as legal advisor to the Ad-Hoc Committee to Save Deerpark Meadow. We are here to monitor the behavior of law enforcement officials. Please be advised that this is at present an unlawful arrest. You may not proceed unless you charge the alleged offenders with a particular civil or criminal violation. You must also extend full Miranda rights to each of them. We intend to monitor these procedures. We are also recording these activities with a video camera in order to be certain that all procedures have been followed correctly, and in particular that any physical confrontation is limited to that amount necessary to transport bodies engaged in passive civil disobedience. Any activity in excess of that limit will be noted in our report.

"Moreover, it has come to our attention that the University's development activities on Deerpark Meadow are themselves patently illegal. I read to you from the Santa Cruz County Code, Section 16.40.080, entitled 'PROHIBITIONS.' Paragraph (a) reads, in part, as follows: 'It shall be unlawful for any person knowingly to disturb, or cause to be disturbed or to excavate, or cause to be excavated, any Native American cultural site ...'

"Given these complications, we suggest that the two parties convene a mediation to attempt to resolve this dispute before it escalates unnecessarily. We propose a meeting between two representatives from the Ad-Hoc Committee and two representatives of the University, to take place as soon as all law enforcement officials have left the area. You have five minutes to respond."

Oh, the pride, the joyous fucking pride of it all! Have you got a sister that cool? Goddamn right you don't. Standing up there on GW's hood like some avenging angel and reading the riot act *to the cops*! And two days earlier she couldn't even lift her eyelashes to filter out the dirt of the world. So you'll forgive me if a little pride trickles into the narrative, because on top of Eva's performance there was the fact that I, me, Ronnie, had personally unearthed that particular statute in the County Code, thank you very much. The one thing that baffled me was how in the world Eva knew —

Cell phone! So that's who Gregory had been talking to all morning. Now it was all falling into place. While I was marching around trying to round up cowards and sellouts, he had called out the cavalry, and not a moment too soon. He had probably been in constant contact with Karen, who had no doubt marshalled the backup protestors. It was obvious now. Who else could have gotten all those people to the middle of the forest on such short notice? Only someone with extensive protest connections, someone who was such an insider she should by all rights have been literally on the inside of the fence perimeter. She was only on the outside for a peculiar historical reason. And that particular historical reason had just jumped on my car and given a rousing speech based on statute information she had gotten from Gregory only moments earlier, and spun a legal manifesto which would have left superlawyer Alan Dershowitz stunned and speechless. Whoowee!!

Please forgive me for dwelling on the euphoria of the moment. I only do so because it lasted so very briefly.

Chapter 23

The thing about a standoff is, it lasts forever. The two lines of antagonists stood there for at least forty-five minutes, trading uncertainties. The atmosphere had become both more tense and more relaxed. More tense because — well, obviously. More relaxed because after a while it seemed fairly evident that nothing much was going to happen any time soon. Eva's dire warnings had hit the authorities below the belt, a knee shot right to the litigles.

From what we could determine, two factions seemed to be asserting themselves. They were embodied by the two chief councilors pleading their respective cases before Her Imperial Majesty, the Most High Lady Vice-Chancellor for Student Affairs, Ms. Barbara Meyers. Head Cop was the War Minister, urging a swift strike against the peasantry. Ann was the Royal Astrologer, counseling patience and a parley with the Enemy.

The Queen's throne seemed more than a bit shaken, but all the while the pawn cops kept brandishing their billy clubs with steady fortitude. Those of us on the hill settled in for what appeared to be a long siege.

Suddenly the ground beneath us began to tremble!! I lost my footing and there was a great wrenching noise as the earth split in two right in front — nah, just kidding. You think we have earthquakes constantly in California, don't you?

What actually happened next, not too surprisingly, was that I got hungry. I tried to make my way toward Karen, Eva, Hal, Great White and the egg salad sandwich, but the cops were having none of it. They let me know I was not to descend very far down the hill. Apparently the uniformed rank and file had been enjoined from actually speaking with us, but when we approached too close they would instead tap their billy clubs against their shields like lethal little woodpeckers. Subtle message.

Karen waved to me across fifty yards and mouthed something. I shook my head, unable to read her meaning. She held her hand to her mouth, as though that might help amplify her silent expression. She stretched every syllable slowly across her face with exaggerated motions and threw in some very expressive eyebrow action. She seemed to be uttering something like: "Irony! Hell of a view! Big awful! Hell of a view!" I tried to crack the code, but I wasn't wearing my decoder ring. I didn't have a clue what she was trying to say. Not a new problem for us.

Eva slid back into GW's front seat, slumped with exhaustion, and let her sunglasses speak for her. Hal wandered around enjoying himself hugely. He surveyed with dopey amusement the tribal encampment we had constructed, then watched the second wave of protestors try feebly to organize themselves, and finally listened in on some cop conversations. I could tell exactly what he was thinking. I would have thought the same, had I the luxury of being on the outside as he was. Once he glanced up at me and shook his head with a smirk. I shrugged. Not much else to say.

And then an actual event occurred right before my eyes. Usually events occur in our absence, and we must rely upon the press or the kindness of strangers to filter the facts for us. This time I was there, and although my brain was certainly not reacting with customary speed, my eyes were clear and I remember what I saw.

I know you read that the students attacked the cops. I know you read that Lieutenant Angelo "Lou" Costello was set on by a pack of wild beasts of the forest, who overwhelmed him and viciously broke his leg with an unknown heavy object.

I'm here to tell you that's bullshit.

The cops just moved forward. That much I remember with complete clarity. We never stood a chance. How this putz Costello broke his leg I have no idea, but we certainly didn't break it for him. His poor innocent shin was probably attacked by someone's excessively hard head.

It was astonishing how quickly things happened. I happened to be looking in Karen's direction when the action began. At that moment thousands of crickets stopped chirping. I had not even noticed them, but their sudden silence was jolting.

One of the first things the police did was knock out the camcorder. A skinny, greasy cop just grabbed the camera right out of some film student's hands and smashed it on a rock. As soon as he had done that he ran over to GW and snatched Eva's legal pad out of her hands. She barely had time to look up.

Meanwhile the main line of cops was marching straight up the hill. We were trapped. My heart rate shot up with simple animal fear and my jaw began to tremble. All I could see or hear was the sound of trudging, marching steps and the cloud of redwood dust that rose behind them.

Among us were a few young guys who were not with anyone, who had only joined the protest the night before as a sort of sleep-over camp for hipster college kids. These guys suddenly decided, without saying a word, to hop the fence behind us and dash off into the forest. A few cops rushed forward to stop them, but a command came down the line to keep formation. The rest of us barely moved. Girls began to scream for no reason but fear, the best reason of all.

Things began to move in crisis time. I stood motionless and frozen. Crisis time is an adrenalized distortion in which one focuses on minor images and sounds and experiences them in astonishing detail, every action and heartbeat occurring in extreme slow motion; while the grand-scale events for which the moment will later be remembered occur so quickly one never sees them at all.

I watched for what seemed a half-hour as a cop stepped up to M'Bopape, who was seated cross-legged with seven other kids in a circle of linked arms. The cop lifted his billy club high to the sky with a flourish like a conductor twirling his baton before the first downbeat. The sun glinted dully off his scratched plastic shield, and I noticed it had a bullet-sized hole in the upper right-hand corner.

The club came down in a great arc. M'Bopape's arms were linked with those of his seated neighbors, pinning them back. As the club reached full height, M'Bopape jerked his right arm up as though asking a question in a social movements class. The blow hit him full force on the elbow, just above his face. His arm buckled and the club struck a glancing blow to his forehead.

Blood on the face has a particularly frightening quality. We know human beings from their eyes, from their mouths, from their faces. M'Bopape's face running with a torrent of blood looked broken, smashed, violated.

We started fighting back. There were two students for every cop, and although they were armed and we were not, we had sudden animal rage on our side.

I fought. Without pausing, without thinking, like a child in wild panic I rushed against the line of cops, slamming my shoulder into one and knocking him into another. Both fell off balance, their jackboots clotted with the thick mud of the pastoral meadow. Another cop grabbed my arm to twist it behind my back. It hurt like hell, but I managed to tear it out of his grasp. Beside me the rest of the wild tribe was throwing itself at the cops, trying to land a punch or a kick or simply overwhelm them with the lunatic frenzy of animal hatred.

The cops' disciplined line of formation began to sag, lose shape, and finally retreat down the hill. A roar primeval in origin blasted through my throat. We jeered and laughed for a gleeful moment, and then gathered ourselves to defend against the next attack.

186

M'Bopape lay sprawled on the forest floor, groaning and wiping his eyes with his hands. Two girls leaning over him tried to pull his arms away from his face. He fought them off initially, blinded and confused. After a brief struggle, they convinced him to relax. One of the girls took her sweatshirt and tried to wipe his face off. Blood was still running freely, but I could see it was from a cut above his eye, and it did not appear serious.

Suddenly the cops charged again. I turned to prepare myself, and then my face slammed into the soft green grass of Deerpark Meadow. The next thing I felt was a heavy buzz, a melding of the screams of protestors and an angry swarm in my head. My mouth was full of the acid taste of my own bile and my eyes burned with horrifying pain. I lost time and place and choked on my own misery.

After a time I sensed that my shirt and sweater were bunched up at the throat. Then I felt my body swimming in a helpless backstroke. The heels of my boots dragged at the forest as though to protest my departure. I could feel redwood twigs and oak branches resisting my progress.

My stunned senses processed this information very slowly, so that I must have travelled at least thirty feet before I turned my head to see why I was moving, and by what means.

Through eyes cloudy with pain and tears, I made out the general shape of Hal, my friend Hal, pulling me by the scruff of my neck across the forest floor. Behind him, running towards us, was Karen, my sweet friend Karen.

Chapter 24

I had always imagined tear gas as a relatively benign substance that somehow induced crying; but delicate tears, the kind shed when one is overwhelmed with the pathos of a particularly poignant operatic aria.

Well, opera it ain't. The shit makes you blind. It makes you nauseous and weak, it makes your eyes vomit and your stomach retch. It's hard to believe they let cops use the stuff. Then again, the police are the only sector of our society sanctioned to carry lethal weapons and abuse their power as they see fit, so there you go.

I'm sorry. I don't mean to preach. I don't know where you stand on law enforcement issues. Perhaps you consider the police our protectors. Perhaps you think they carry out a dangerous and thankless job on our behalf. Perhaps you've even uttered the phrase "putting their lives on the line every day." Perhaps you maintain your defense of the boys in blue in spite of all the bad press they've been getting lately. Perhaps you've used the term "bad apple" to describe what you consider to be isolated instances of abuse on a force consisting mostly of stout-hearted defenders of the public good. Perhaps you're full of shit.

Deerpark Meadow was a war zone. Most of the students were on the ground, coughing and retching. Many had been clubbed and were bleeding. Their bodies were strewn about as though a grenade had exploded at the doll store. The cops in their gas masks looked like midwives of the apocalypse. Smoke rose from the field as though from ten thousand sweat lodges.

My field of vision was suddenly filled with Karen's large, kind, familiar face, smiling at me with a drop of uncertainty hidden in an ocean of maternal concern. She wiped my face with a hem of her skirt and kissed my brow.

Then we were in the belly of the beast; the only beast in the world with enough loyalty to its master to have braved it onto that hellish battleground.

Great White.

He and Hal shot down the hill in reverse until the first turnaround, spun matters around, and gunned it down the road and off campus. Eva sat in front, trying to hold on and look cool doing it. I lay in back, my head in Karen's lap. She brushed the hair off my forehead and applied consoling noises and caresses.

With the air rushing in through the car window I revived some of my senses. I sat up, fighting hard against gravity and the pull of a hard left turn.

"He's going to be fine," Karen announced to the others.

"Where are we going?" I asked.

"Downhill fast," Hal said.

I tasted the air, and it was good. The sun was shining, tall trees glimmered, and I could not have chosen better company. But a part of me wanted to go back to Deerpark Meadow. I am, goddamn it, the son of a Diablo. We don't run. Dad always said, "Never turn your back on your man. If you ever get in a fight, land the first punch." He also said, "The best defense is a good offense," and "The bigger they are, the harder they fall."

Nice sayings. Very catchy. I wonder if Dad and his little leather jacket tough guy Diablo buddies ever got tear-gassed. I wonder if they ever got cracked on the skull with a billy club.

We had fought back. We had even managed to do some damage to the cops; and if we broke Officer Costello's leg, my condolences to his sow. But as they say in elementary school: they started it. The cops could have pulled M'Bopape and his fellow civil disobedients off the ground gently. They could have lifted them to a waiting cop car; but instead they just went into a feeding frenzy. They were not "provoked," as they later claimed. They were not "responding with appropriate force to a hazardous situation". I watched as they started bashing heads in. I know, and I will maintain to my dying day, that they used the legitimacy of the badge as a cover for nothing more than a glorified street-fight, for which they had all the preparation, equipment and weapons and we had none.

You know how I feel about M'Bopape. He always was and likely always will be an annoying hippie freak with a self-righteous streak and a disastrous beak. You know I have never gone bowling with the man, nor shared a chocolate malted from a diner seat opposite him. But I will say this: the man took his nonviolence seriously. When the cops came up the hill he held his little group steadfast. And the only time he raised his hand was in self-defense. So don't try to sell me any of this "provoked" bullshit.

A disturbing truth in the whole mess was that the mellow UCSC cops prevented none of the worst from happening. For the most part they did not bash in any skulls, but neither did they try to prevent skulls from being bashed. They stood silently at the rear, and in that silence they were complicit. They may not have lobbed any tear gas bombs, but they had gas masks, and that certainly positioned them squarely on one side of the conflict and not the other.

The students who had arrived in the second wave with Karen turned out to be largely useless. When the mayhem began, they stood around, unsure how to help. They did yell some creative obscenities, but for the most part they were like younger versions of the UCSC cops — all show, no action.

"There's something I want to know," I said.

"Oh, God, me too," Karen said, in a voice bursting with cooped-up energy. "Can you believe it? They could have killed you! God, I never would have thought they would have used tear gas in the middle of the woods. What are they, crazy? What about the fire hazard? And what happened to the negotiations? All they had to do was just talk to us, but instead — oh, my God, did you see what happened to M'Bopape? Is he alright?"

"Yeah," I said, "it looked a lot worse than it was."

"Are they going to arrest everyone?"

"Yes," Eva spoke.

"Oh, my God," Karen said. "How long can you go to jail for for trespassing?"

"That's not the big deal," Hal said. "Resisting arrest. That's the killer."

"I wouldn't worry," Eva said, and it was the weary Eva again. "They'll issue tickets. With that many arrests, everyone will just post a tiny bail and get released on their own recognizance. Eventually the judge will throw all the cases out. They don't need a county jail full of first-time offenders who pose no real threat to anyone."

This turned out to be an amazingly accurate prognostication.

"There's still something I want to know," I said.

"What?" Karen asked.

"Halcyon, where'd you get keys to Great White?"

Hal glanced at me in the rear-view mirror and grinned sheepishly. "I always had a copy," he said. "I used to sneak out with GW when you lived with us. I thought you knew."

I didn't know. But it clarified something for me.

"Is that why he was always so low on gas?"

Hal shrugged. "Where's a guy like me supposed to come up with gas money? What am I, Bill Gates? Sorry, buddy."

"S'alright," I said, amused. it was very hard to be angry with Hal, especially when he had just hauled my eggs out of the frying pan. I thought about his confession for a minute. "Wait a second," I said, "let me ask you this: did you intentionally name him 'Great White' from the beginning because you wanted me to think he guzzled more gas than he actually does?"

Hal looked at me, and we both knew how absurd a question that was.

Great White was Great White. It was his name, it was his destiny.

We went back to my apartment. Karen made twenty rapid-fire phone calls to find out where Deerpark matters stood, but could find out nothing. After seven calls to Gregory's cell-phone went unanswered she gave up. I went to the bathroom and cleaned myself up. Eva went to the bedroom and took a nap. Karen and Hal played cards. I believe Karen won nine of ten hands of gin rummy. That's my gal. Should have played for money. I made a late lunch and read the same newspaper that had been sitting there since Eva's arrival in town. The news had not changed, but I had forgotten enough to make it interesting. It was amusing to read the original Deerpark article in the light of recent events.

Later Eva woke up and there evolved an unspoken consensus to do something to change the dreary cycle of protests and tear gas and airless apartments. We went downtown, checked out the bookshop for a while, then browsed through CD's at the record store. It was somehow massively comforting to know that despite all the mayhem in our lives, somewhere on this planet, bad guitar bands were still making millions of dollars thanks mostly to their hair. Hal and I checked out the Pearl Jam albums, all of which we owned. There is something reaffirming about reviewing one's own collection at a book or record store.

At the last minute we decided to catch a buddy-cop movie. It was an entertainment choice redolent of irony. I don't want to spoil it for you, but I have to tell you this amazing plot twist: at the beginning of the flick, the male cop and his new female partner hate each other. But by the end, they fall in love!

Those wacky Hollywood screenwriters. What will they come up with next?

Given the day's events, I found it rather peculiar to sit in that audience and root for the cops. I'd never really noticed before just how much the audience eats up the violence. Positively devours it like a midnight snack. Yum, yum, yum. The macho star cop had this charming habit of twisting the necks of the mobster thugs to kill them, and the audience cheered louder every time he did it. It made a crackling sound, and that was a cool thing, a funny thing, a catchy thing that made the guys sitting directly behind me laugh and yell, "Yeah!"

I sat there feeling sick to my stomach. It was either from too much popcorn with butter flavoring, or from the growing certainty that our species has not evolved much from the law of the jungle. Hunt or be hunted. Kill or be killed.

It was probably the popcorn.

After the movie we went to a cafe to postpone going home for a while longer. This particular cafe was one of the finest living examples of the Santa Cruz miserably-incompetent-lazy-bad-attitude-bad-service cafe. Because hippie students have an endless supply of their parents' money to burn, and an endless thirst to be seen drinking coffee, there are dozens of such establishments, each boasting hipper decor than the next and a haughtier attitude toward customers. One of the distinguishing features of such establishments is that it is absolutely imperative for the employees to have much more interest in one another than in the customers. A request for service is an imposition, a highly inappropriate interruption to the employee conversations, which are continually in progress. They will argue for ten minutes over the music selection while the line extends out the door, onto the porch of the old Victorian house in which the cafe resides, down the steps and onto the sidewalk.

Another curiosity of these eccentric eateries is that a customer can order the same items night after night and pay a different amount each time. Fixed prices are just another form of the oppression of labor, you insensitive creep.

But most important for the self-respect of any such establishment is that the employees must have complete immunity to the concept of hustle. To expect a prompt response when standing in line is very bourgeois, even — dare I say it — traditional. It implies that you believe the employees are there to serve whatever you want whenever you want it. I hope for your sake you can handle the guilt of such an assumption, fascist. If you want a table, you'd best be prepared to clear it yourself. You want the worker to wipe the table? What are they, your slaves?

If you want a refill on your coffee, plan on a good half hour. And woe onto your mortal soul if you get caught in line behind a customer who happens to be a friend of an employee. These frequent encounters bring slow employee activity to a complete and grinding halt while they get caught up on all the gossip, leaning shamelessly on the counter and yapping away.

The perverse thing is, Hal and I actually liked the place, because there were always dozens of amusing hippies to observe. Karen adored it, because it was just so — well, you know. Eva had no opinion.

That night the place was busy, but not too crowded. I had feared the place might be swarming with Deerpark enthusiasts and analysts, but no one bothered us. Maybe they were all in jail, offenders and sympathizers alike. Nah, I couldn't be that lucky.

The walls were adorned with an art show, a set of charcoal drawings of the interior of the cafe itself — a cup, a table, a conversing clique. I regret to report that nowhere was there a picture of an employee dashing from one table to another. On the whole I found the art well-executed, but objectionably self-referential, cutesy and precious. I asked Hal what he thought.

"I may not know art, " he declared, "but I know what I like. This is art."

Within a few short hours, Hal was permitted to purchase some chocolate biscotti and a large coffee. I got biscotti too and tea to settle my stomach. Eva got nothing. Karen got chai. Chai is this spiced — oh, never mind. It's a hot beverage so hippie you'd have to smell it to understand. We had finally managed to push two small tables together to seat all four of us when in walked Benny like a punch line to a forgotten joke.

He had that faraway look in his eye and was startled to see us. He pulled up a chair and muttered a generalized greeting.

"Hey, Benny," I said. "What are you working on?"

"Oh," he said, as though coming up for air, "working on? Well, writing. Hack writing. Yes. Lately I've been haunted by this postmodern satire on Dante's 'Divine Comedy' I'm tentatively calling the 'Divine Infomercial'. It's about the media commodification of the spiritual, as viewed through a deconstructionist lens."

"Deconstruction," Eva snorted. "What a joke. It's indistinguishable from relativism."

This remark launched them into a ten minute argument which lapsed only momentarily into English. Hal, Karen and I watched like dogs trying to snatch home runs out of the air from first, second and third base, respectively.

"Hey, Karen!" came a sudden rush of hippie flesh.

"Oh, my God, Louise!" Karen said, hugging her. The hug lasted a while, but that's the way hippie hugs are. They are generally accompanied by an expression of absolute ecstasy on each face. This hug was no exception.

I had no idea who Louise was, nor how Karen knew her. But since Karen knew just about everyone, especially in hippie hangouts, I wasn't too surprised. Nor was it unusual that we were not introduced. Hippies aren't big into formalism, as you may have noticed. They consider all conversation to be an ongoing public domain, created especially for them to interrupt, hug through, and move past.

With Karen and Louise gabbing away on one side and Benny and Eva discoursing on the other, Hal and I leaned in for a private chat.

"So, Shorenstein," he said, "what's the best way to stop a hippie from getting his hands on your money?"

"What?"

"Hide it underneath the soap."

I usually reward that one with a few chuckles.

I shot back with: "What did the Deadhead say when they took his pot away?"

"I give up."

"'Hey, wait — this music *sucks*!'"

Hal laughed with that bearlike moan of his. "So what the hell were you doing up there? What the hell's gotten into you?"

I shrugged. "I don't know, Halbert. It all just kind of got out of hand." I sipped the dregs of my tea. "At first it was just one meeting, you know? Then it was a protest, and I kept telling myself I could stop any time, and now —"

" — Dammit, man, you've got a problem, can't you see that? I'm telling you this as a friend. You've got to get a hold of yourself!"

"I know, I know. I've signed up for a wonderful twelve-step program. They're very supportive, but I — I just can't help myself. You've got to help me! I'm at my rope's end."

He shook his head, amused.

"Hey," I said, as guys will when trying to convey heavy emotion, "thanks for saving my ass."

"Hey," Hal said, "No problem."

We stared at the table for a while.

"So," Hal said, brightening up, "call up Oliver Stone. I solved the Kennedy assassination."

"You did?"

"Yeah. It was a suicide."

"Good God," I said, "that's brilliant."

"It's right there on the Zapruder film. I can't believe I never saw it before. You know who you can spot on the grassy knoll, in the background?"

"Who?"

"A young Jack Kevorkian. Coincidence?"

"I don't think so."

We laughed like the children we are.

Louise's voice suddenly grew louder. "You know what your problem is?" she asked Karen.

"What?"

"Too much Mars, not enough Moon."

That one gave Hal and me the outright giggles. We turned our heads to avoid eye contact with Karen, who was nodding vigorously. On the other side Benny and Eva were still going at it.

Benny said, "It's an historical moment for our generation, and we fail to appreciate it. That's what troubles me. Do you see what I mean?"

"Sure," Eva said. "It's nothing new. It's 'The Grand Inquisitor' all over again. You have no faith in the moral courage of your peers."

"No," Benny said, "I'm talking about the era, not the people. That's what's unusual: a moment, frozen in time. The twentieth century is now like some huge whale, and we are barnacles clinging to the underside of that whale, that engorged leviathan which does not acknowledge our presence and moves whichever way it pleases without concerning itself with us."

That sounded fairly pointless, so Hal and I returned to our biscotti and our conversation. It seemed to reside precisely halfway between the other two conversations both geographically and in intellectual content. I was content merely to see Eva out in public, even if she had to suffer Benny's opaque philosophical meanderings.

Hal asked, "Do you think Great White can make it all the way to Berkeley and back Friday night? Because I know a guy who's also going. We might be able to swing a ride, depending on when you want to head back."

"What are we talking about? Topic, please."

"The Pearl Jam show, Shorenstein. Duh."

"Oh, shit, that's right!" I said, growing excited. "That's Friday night?"

"Yeah."

"Hell, we can squeeze a few extra miles out of GW. He's big on Pearl Jam. He's got all their albums."

We laughed and munched on biscotti crumbs for a quiet minute. Without warning, I felt an unusual sensation wash over me: I felt good. I was content with my little world. It was an unfamiliar condition, especially given the damnable difficulties of the preceding week. I could still taste tear gas on my tongue, but for some reason I felt positively chipper. Go figure.

Bemused, I watched morose Eva and pedantic Benny chase each other down obscure philosophical alleyways. I watched blissful

Karen weave a strand of jasmine stolen from the table displays into Louise's hair. Then sturdy Hal began to lick his plate for the last crumbs of biscotti chocolate, and I joined him at my plate; and it occurred to me then that we might represent the very best that our generation had to offer. It was not an entirely mournful thought.

We were a motley collection of stupes, certainly. But we were conducting ourselves as we thought best under difficult circumstances, trying to find our way through a forest, a dark primeval forest of deep confusion.

Consider this forest; consider the Sequoias which previous generations have planted in our way: every day complex streams of information jet through the ether, impossible to comprehend. Every day power and wealth aggregate in unimaginable ways on distant golf courses. Every day the life of a solitary individual like our buddy Hal becomes less and less important. There are more than five billion people on the planet, and every day millions of them die of hunger in vicious obscurity. How are we supposed to make sense of that information? Where are the moral scales on which to weigh that sort of colossal injustice?

In previous eras, we might have relied upon some authority to sort it all out. Remember that old time religion? In the Old Testament, God used to converse directly with common folk. Boy, one conversation like that would certainly make faith a lot easier for ol' Ronnie Shorenstein. I'd be on my knees genuflecting before you could say "Sodom and Gomorrah". But God has gotten out of the habit of making small talk in the last several thousand years.

So the Church took over His dirty work, teaching the rules of the obedience game to those openmouthed puddinheads we call ancestors. After a while, folks got tired of the same Church, so they invented some new ones, and new kinds. But chuckleheaded obeisance to authority remained a constant. In an earlier generation, each of us in that cafe would have been brainwashed by the Church or Marx or Gandhi or some other charlatan into accepting some absurd universe where everyone is kind and no one gets hurt and shit doesn't stink.

But as the 20th century falls into the lap of the 21st, those structures of authority have collapsed. We young disaffected middle-class white punks on dope have no church, we have no traditional families, no set moral code, no mantras, no nothin'. By all rights, we ought to wander about like street dogs, beaten into complete submission. But we do not, because we have learned to erect our own structures on the ruins of the old ones, and I for one feel pride in that.

Isn't it better to make one's own way than to have the way previously paved, polished and prepared?

Friends and acquaintances, popular culture and solitary insights, useless technologies and useful gossip, advice columns and marketing schemes, chance meetings and odd jobs: these are the raw materials from which we smelt a new iron.

"Hey, Hal," I said, emerging from reverie, "what do you want to be when you grow up?"

In response, he sang a miserable falsetto ditty: "I'd like to be a cow in Switz-er-land/where the grass is always green/I'd like to be a cow in Switz-er-land/ where the bulls are not so mean!"

For some reason, Louise picked that moment to wander off.

"Hey, Ronnie," Karen said, joining us, "you know what Louise just told me?"

"No, I don't."

"She was up on campus today after we left, and it turns out there was a huge arrest, just like Eva said there would be."

"No surprise there," I said.

"Right, except that now the Chancellor's feeling all bad about everybody getting beat up, and Louise thinks he's getting pressured to mellow things out, or whatever, so anyway they agreed to form a commission of inquiry into the matter. Plus, there's going to be a big debate between the admin and the students, just to kind of cool things down. It's going down the day after tomorrow at five at Stevenson dining hall."

"No," I said, immediately, "it's got to be at Deerpark."

"Oh, no, it can't be, really. It's not a protest. It's a formal debate, like with microphones and everything."

"They should set it all up at Deerpark," I insisted, "don't you see that? They can move the microphones and put a PA in the trees. Not that I give a shit where they hold it, I suppose."

"What? Aren't you going?" Karen asked.

"To some debate? What for? Give me one good reason why I should go."

Karen opened her mouth, closed it, then opened it again. "Because, don't you — Ronnie — they bombed you with tear gas! Aren't you pissed off about that? I mean, what more do you need to convince — God, sometimes I don't know what it is with you, Ronnie Shorenstein."

I sighed. "Yes, Karen, Sherpa, darling, I'm slightly pissed off about being tear-gassed," I said. "But that was the cops, not the administration. I can tell the difference. The cops were fucked up."

"There's an understatement," Eva said. I hadn't noticed, but she

197

and Benny abandoned their conversation for ours. Boy, theirs must have gotten pretty damn dull for ours to seem preferable. "They tore my speech right out of my hands," Eva said to no one in particular.

"Tear gas?" Benny asked. "No one tells me anything."

"Yeah," Hal said, "it was like Kent State Jr. up there today. I'll fill you in later."

"O.K., but Ronnie," Karen said, with a voice indicating she had marshalled her thoughts anew, "O.K., but what you don't get is that the cops and the administration are the same thing. The cops are just the ones with the guns. But the administration is totally on their side. They're even worse. They give the orders. They're the ones who want to destroy Deerpark, and that's going to last forever. This is just one small incident."

"Ha," I said, "tell that to my sore lungs."

"You know, Karen," Benny said enthusiastically, "I believe you've hit squarely on one of Ronald's major imaginative shortcomings."

I tisked with great irritation. "Don't you mean, 'you know what your problem is'?"

"Exactly that," Benny said.

"Then say so," Hal growled.

"You know what your problem is?" Benny asked, accommodating us cheerfully.

"Yes, I do know. I know exactly what my problem is. Thank you for asking. Thank you all for your interest. Good night. God bless. Drive home safely."

"He cannot make connections," Benny explained to Karen. "He understands individual political situations with reasonable clarity, but he sees no linkage between one event and another."

"Oh, that's totally true," Karen said.

"He's never really been much of a systematic thinker," Eva pointed out.

"Hey, hey, hey!" I said, "what is this, a roast? Screw you all. I think as systematically as the next guy."

"I am the next guy," Hal said, "and I sure as hell don't think systematically. Big deal. Just admit they're right, Shorenstein. It's not like you burned down a church."

"I was just thinking about churches," I said. "In fact, I was thinking about them quite systematically, if you must know. Why are we talking about this, anyway? What am I, a lab specimen? Christ. Go pick on somebody else, will you? I feel like a bunch of aliens abducted me and now I'm up in your spaceship, getting probed. Systematically."

"But this is important," Karen said. "I feel like I've been trying to explain this to you forever. Say what you were saying, Benny."

"Just this: politics is not a sequence of random events. Everything you encounter, everything you aspire to, every obstacle you face involves politics in some way, so for you to delude yourself into pretending politics doesn't matter is really a way of denying your own existence. The road on which you push Great White was paved by someone who was hired by some delegate of an elected official, who was elected by actual common individuals — which could include you but likely doesn't. The cops on campus sprayed you with tear gas you paid for."

"Exactly," Karen said.

"Hey, kids, I already know I got tear-gassed," I said. "Thanks for the reminder, though."

"But it's not just about you," Karen said. "Tell him, Benny."

"The topic is linkage, Ronald. Look at it this way: if a man is born into poverty, he is more likely to receive a poor education. If he has no education, he is more likely to commit a crime. If he is locked up, he becomes a fiscal drain on the government, which means more people will be born into poverty. Education, poverty, crime are all interrelated."

"Well, no shit," Hal said. "I thought you had something new."

"It is new for Ronald," Benny said. "It requires political imagination to understand that linkage; imagination he seems to lack."

"Not just imagination," Eva said, "it requires sympathy for the suffering of others and a willingness to see them as equals. He can't make that stretch."

"You know," I said, "I just love it when you assholes speak of me in the third person when I'm sitting right here."

"Ronnie, honey," Karen said, "I'm sorry, but I think it's true. Every time something happens in the world, you treat it like it's got nothing to do with anything that happened before. Like it's got nothing to do with you."

I said, "You know —"

"She's right," Eva said. "You never want to take responsibility for anything."

Well, now. This was getting pretty fucking strange. I was being accused of not taking responsibility from — well, from a person who had just tried to kill herself. That was an irony so thick it felt like a telephone book slammed against my forehead. Goddamn Eva. I wanted to tell her where to shove her self-righteous older sister insights, her precious pearls of monotone wisdom. But I resisted. I don't regret that choice.

"Listen," I said, "I don't know how we got on this topic. All I was trying to say was that the damn debate should damn well be held at goddamn Deerpark Meadow, not in some damn dining hall, and that I'm damn well not going."

"Damn straight," Hal said.

"Why does it have to be in the damn meadow?" Benny asked.

"Because we're reclaiming it," Karen said. "We want them to know it's our land, the people's land, so they won't build on it."

Benny thought about that for a moment or two. "But if I may take the devil's advocate position," he said, "the land already does belong to the people. They have duly delegated decision-making power over to their democratically elected officials, who appoint the Regents, who have decided to develop this land. Their decision, however poor it may be, is therefore, in effect, the people's decision. The administrators are acting within their defined role. It is their decision to make."

"Of course it's their decision," I said. "Any idiot knows that. We were trying to demonstrate in a dramatic way that the land only belongs to the State of California because they swiped it from the Indians. So we went out to the actual spot to show our solidarity with the indigenous folk. It's a symbolic thing. A metaphorical thing. You're an artist, you ought to understand such things. Even Hal gets the symbology of that, don't you, Hal?"

"Duh, maybe, I guess. Gee boss, I dunno," Hal said in a mock stupid voice, which was actually fairly convincing.

"It was Ronnie's idea," Karen said proudly. "God, Benny, you missed out. It was a totally cool protest today, before the cops started up. Best protest I've ever been to. And we were like the total team. Ronnie was the idea man. Eva was the lawyer. I was the organizer."

"And I was the mascot," Hal said.

"No, you were the awesome driver," Karen said.

"That was a nice piece of driving," I admitted.

"Sorry I missed it," Benny said. "I've just been absorbed in this writing project. Parsing through Foucault's layers of meaning is —"

" — whoa, look at the time," Hal said.

"Getting mighty late," I said, grinning.

"It has been a long day," Karen said to Benny, who shrugged. "Maybe you can explain it some other time," she said.

"Maybe," he said.

We went out to the parking lot behind the cafe and Great White finally let us down. He just acted like he'd never seen that ignition key before in his entire life. I suspect he was upset because I had abandoned him for a few days, but whatever his motive, he wasn't budging.

Hal and Benny were within walking distance of the old apartment, but the three of us were stuck a light year from home. We five stood around for a minute as though GW might burst into spontaneous internal combustion.

"Hey, Mr. Awesome Driver," I said to Hal, irritably, "what'd you do to my car?"

In reply, he heaved a great sigh and then simply walked to the back of Great White, placed both hands on the back window and leaned forward as though being frisked. I selected and released a few choice curses from my vast collection, then went and joined him. We stood there side by side and waited for things to get rolling. Karen finally got the point and jumped into the driver's seat to do her bouncy ghost-driver thing. With the help of a mighty groan from Hal and me, Great White began to roll down Cedar in search of Ocean and its oases of midnight gas stations.

Eva walked along the sidewalk as though she might or might not be a party to our particular predicament, which pissed me off significantly. But again, I said nothing. Benny trotted up and tried to help, but had difficulty finding a useful handhold.

"Are you familiar with the myth of Sisyphus?" he asked, breathing heavily for no good reason. Neither Hal nor I wanted to waste energy answering him.

"He was cursed by the gods," Benny said, "to roll a rock up a hill for eternity until —"

"— shut the fuck up and push," Hal said with clenched teeth.

Benny shut the fuck up and tried to push. He was still having difficulty finding a spot, so he moved around to the driver's side to establish his own domain. He ran right into the path of an oncoming car.

Before Benny could react, Hal jumped out, yelled "Ben!" and grabbed him by the arm, yanking with all his strength. The screeching car hit Benny, and there was a shattering of glass.

The human mind can race at incredible speeds at times. Out of the corner of my eye I saw the car hit Benny, and I caught a shadow of his closed eyes as he fell; and in that instant I remembered a painful conversation he and I had once had about the inexplicable, miserable duty of attending funerals. Before I had a chance to react to the accident, an image of a younger Benny flashed through my mind: standing atop a grassy slope in terrible heat, wearing a heavy wool suit, his hand supporting his mother's elbow as they watched the first clump of dirt land on Benny's father's coffin.

Great White rolled gently out from under my hands and stopped. I raced over to find Benny on the ground, moaning. Hal still held a ferocious grip on Benny's arm.

Karen and Eva came running up. We all crouched in the middle of the street to determine Benny's condition.

"Benny!" Karen said, "Benny, are you O.K.?"

"What happened?" Eva asked.

"He got hit," I said. I turned my head to look for the car. It was gone. When I looked back at Benny, he lifted his head. He shook it once, shuddered as though cold, and sat up.

"Are you alright?" Karen asked.

"I think so," he said. "Hal, could you please let go of my arm?"

Hal looked startled, then let go.

"That's better," Benny said. He flexed his arm muscles, testing his reality. He stood up. "Ouch," he said. "Son of a bitch. My leg's killing me."

"Did they hit you?" Eva asked.

"Yeah," Benny said, "here." He motioned to his hip and waist.

"Look," Karen said. She picked something up off the ground. It was a broken car mirror, snapped off at the base.

At that moment we were all blinded by headlights. A car slowly pulled up to the scene of the crime. It was a low, sporty vehicle, cherry red, and it was missing the mirror on the driver's side.

The driver pulled over, stopped the car, and stepped out. He emerged from the glare of his headlights and we saw that he was a young guy, younger even than the rest of us. He was thin and sharply dressed, with freckled white skin, curly red hair, and a beginner's mustache.

"Uh, shit," he said, looking all around, "what happened?"

"You hit him," I said, "can't you fucking watch where you're going?"

"I was watching," the guy said, "he just jumped out at me."

"Bullshit," Hal said, even though it was more or less true.

The guy seemed startled by the hostility. I noticed he was shaking. "Well, uh, is he alright?" he asked.

"I'll live," Benny said, his voice in pain.

"Well," the driver said, exhaling heavily, "O.K., cool." He took a few steps backwards and pulled his keys from his pocket.

"You going somewhere?" Eva asked.

"No, I just —"

" — you have to give us your name and license and everything," Karen said. "We should wait for the cops."

"Good point," I said, as though cops and I were old friends. "Why don't you call them, Karen?"

"Wait a second," the driver said, nervous. He scanned the streets. "Why do we have to call the cops?"

"Because you just hit a pedestrian with an automobile," Eva said. "You could be charged with assault with a deadly weapon. If you fail to report it and leave the scene of the crime now, that constitutes hit and run, which is a felony. I might add that I've noted your license plate number."

Boy, she sure knew how to pour it on sometimes.

"Fucking shit," the driver said, and he seemed to mean it. His hands began to shake vigorously. I decided to take a shot.

"You know what happens when the court finds out you were fucked up when you hit him?"

"What? No, man! Come on, he's alright. What do you guys want? Oh, shit, goddamn it," he said, his eyes nearly popping out.

"An apology would be nice," Benny said.

"You come here," Hal growled. He grabbed Benny by the arm again and walked him over to the sidewalk, where they both sat on the curb.

"Karen, weren't you going to call the police?" Eva said in an even voice, staring the driver down.

"Oh, man, shit, you guys don't have to do that. No, come on, for real." He looked around again. "Uh, listen," he said, "hold on a second. I'll be right back."

He ran back to his car and jumped in. I thought about blocking his escape path but I wasn't sure he would stop for me. He didn't start the car, however. He rummaged around inside for a minute. We squinted to see him through the glare of his sporty headlights. There was no telling what he might pull out of the car. With safety on our minds, we all moved out of the street and over to the sidewalk, keeping a wary eye him.

After a few moments he ran quickly back toward us with a dark object in his hand. My knees went completely weak and my heart lurched into overdrive. Surrounded by the ghostly penumbra of his headlights, he was almost impossible to see. I wanted to move, but my molasses limbs were paralyzed.

He stepped right toward us, pulled out a leather pouch, looked around, and unzipped it. He then proceeded to unroll an enormous wad of one-hundred dollar bills. He peeled off ten and gave them to Benny, who looked as mystified as I felt. The wad was still thick. The rest of us stood there frozen like deer in headlights.

Except Eva. "Two thousand," she said in a quiet voice, "and five hundred for each witness. Then we all walk away happy and no one needs to know anything."

The guy swallowed like he had a pig stuck in his throat.

"Come on," Eva said, "let's get this over with."

Rich Kid hesitated for a few seconds. Eva gave him a hard stare, and then he seemed to collapse. He gave Benny a thousand more. Then he handed each of the rest of us five crisp hundreds, took one last look at Benny, and started backing away.

"Wait, you forgot something," Hal said, and tossed him the mirror.

Money Boy tried to catch it, fumbled it, and let it fall to the ground. He took one glance at it, then turned and raced back to his car. He screeched away, his tires peeling out for a good twenty feet. Still, I got a good look at his two bumper stickers: "Practice random kindness," the first one recommended, "and senseless acts of beauty." The other thing this fine young cannibal wanted to make sure the world knew he believed was this: "Shit happens."

I have never understood what that particular insight is supposed to prove. I coughed a few times, choking on the smell of burning rubber from his peeled tires and a clutch released too late. My lungs were still sore from tear gas.

The stench in my nostrils spoke to me. Until that moment it had seemed to me that the malice the police had displayed towards us was somehow a generational thing; the revenge of the beaten-down beat cop against the carefree wiseass jobless youth, as though we were the ones who had handcuffed them to their careers.

But if this drug dealer in his deathmobile proved anything, it was that you can find assholes in any generation. Ain't diversity wonderful that way? And while I had spent the evening daydreaming about the charming and unlikely ways in which our generation forms steely bonds of interdependence, our cokehead friend was out on the streets, doing his best to disintegrate those bonds.

Karen broke our stunned silence.

"Wow," she said. "Oh, my God, did you see how much money he had? Where did he get that kind of money?"

"Cocaine," I said.

"Crystal meth," Eva said, just to prove she knew everything and I nothing.

I have heard that more than thirty per cent of the one hundred dollar bills in circulation have some trace of cocaine on them. That figure may well be apocryphal, but I'd be willing to bet these particular bills had more than a speckle of white dust.

"Hey," Hal said, trying to dispel the weird gloom that had come over us, "hey, we're rich. Who cares where he got it?" He fanned his five hundred dollar bills. "Look at that. I think that's more money than I've ever had in my hands at one time. Whoowee! Come to papa! Hey, thanks, Eva."

"No problem," she said, with an air of sullen superiority.

"Wow," Karen said, still overcome by the whole experience. "How do you feel, Benny? You just won two thousand dollars!"

"I didn't win it," Benny said, "I got hit by a car for it."

"Oh, God, how's your leg?" Karen asked.

"Oh, it's fine," Benny said. "I'm feeling much better."

We all studied the street and ourselves for a long moment.

"This," I said to Benny, "has been one weird day. First I spend the morning getting tear-gassed by bloodthirsty cops, then a cokehead with a Camaro runs you over."

"Porsche 924," Eva said, purely to piss me off.

"He never did apologize," Benny said.

"Funny," I said. "Neither did the cops."

Chapter 25

I awoke from angry and violent dreams, unnerved. It was seven o'clock in the morning, and my day was already in turmoil.

I want to tell you of my dream. Patience! I know the dreams of others are torture to hear. When permitted, Karen Anne could go on for twenty minutes with tiresome, detailed descriptions of some truly senseless, pointless dreaming. But bear with me. I have a hunch this one is important.

The setting of the dream was exactly that of my reality. I dreamt I was asleep on my back, in my own bed with Karen beside me, and Eva on the couch in the other room. Within the dream, Eva awoke. She opened the front door and Mom and Dad walked in.

Then they were in the kitchen at home in Camarillo, arguing. They demanded that Eva come home and commit herself to the insane asylum in Camarillo. They argued for a long time, with great cruelty. I remember that Mom kept using the word "sanatorium," as though Eva were some nineteenth-century Russian princess who needed to "take the cure" at a Swiss retreat for rich consumptives. Dad kept saying, "there's a time and place for everything," whatever the hell that means. I felt a rare and burning fury.

Then Eva was holding me down, or I was holding her down. This part of the dream was very peculiar, and somewhat unclear. We were not in the bed, and although there was a sensation of wrestling on the ground, we were standing up. We appeared to be in her teenage bedroom, as evidenced by her Talking Heads posters, but otherwise we seemed to be standing in the middle of Deerpark Meadow.

Then I dreamt a brief but precise replay of the riot scene from the day before. I watched the cop swing his arm high in the air exactly as he had; and suddenly I woke up, heart thumping, tear gas choking me.

Karen's arm was slung over my chest like a barbell. I pushed it off more angrily than I intended, but she did not wake up. Then I lay there, thinking hard, for the better part of an hour, wondering what the right thing to do might be. This has always been a difficult question for me.

Maybe Mom and Dad were right. Maybe Eva did need professional help. At the hospital, she had been scheduled for all kinds of visits with a social worker, but I didn't know if she had ever attended them. I was far too wary of her to ask.

I had not even thought about the question in days, and I knew why. I had let all responsibility for Eva's condition fall to Karen. Karen's heart was kind and true, and she had worked the minor miracles in her power, but dreams seldom lie: Eva needed professional help. Maybe I was contributing to a worsening of her condition by not insisting on it, however difficult doing so to her face might be.

I stared for a long time at Karen's sleeping face, neither angel nor child, but simply herself, eyelids aflutter. After a time she awoke, her eyes suddenly staring into mine. For a long, bizarre moment I had a premonition that she had dreamt the same dream as I had. In fact I was certain of it. I knew without a shred of doubt that she was going to tell me the answer to the questions that were troubling me.

She stared at me for a minute, hovering between sleep and speech. Then she yawned like a circus lion and stretched mightily. I watched her in close anticipation of her first words. She made a few sticky-tongue clucking noises, and then, in a voice of boundless wisdom and deepest insight, she asked: "Ronnie, could you get me a glass of water?"

Actually, it did serve as an answer of sorts. I went and filled a tumbler of water from the kitchen tap. Eva was still asleep on the couch, scowling, and when I returned to the bedroom Karen was smiling, and it was an instructive contrast.

Karen's thirst was greater than it had ever been. I knew then that her measure from the cup of human burden had been too great. What I owed her, what Eva owed her could neither be measured nor repaid, but Karen was never supposed to be Eva's nurse, shrink, sister and mother all at once. What she was supposed to be, I did not know. She drank deeply, like a camel arriving at the oasis of respect after walking across the Sahara of neglect.

She handed the empty glass to me, smiled, and fell back asleep. After that early morning hour of inappropriately heavy thought, I lay my head down beside her, soothed by her presence and the knowledge that I was, after all, one of the nouveau riche.

When I awoke much later, Karen was gone. She had left a cutesy note on the pillow beside me, telling me she had gone out with Maria. I had no idea then, and I have no idea to this moment who or what Maria was. Karen had decided to skip classes that day because she and Maria had important business: they were going to test out Maria's new kite. Karen drew a picture of this event for me: two small female figures with long hair, one with a prominent butterfly on her belly, standing in front of curving lines which could only have been ocean waves, and above them a large diamond-shaped kite with a perfectly lovely tail flowing in the western wind.

I showered, dressed, and putzed around for an hour until Eva woke up. She sat up bleary-eyed on the couch and watched me eat the last of the cereal flakes with an expression I mistakenly assumed was one of amusement.

I really should have known better than to bother her just then. Eva wakes grumpy, grumpier even than her normal self.

"I know it's not really my business," I said, "but I kinda wanted to ask you something."

Powerful opening line, Ronnie.

Eva stared at me as though I might be an unusually fascinating bug squashed on her windshield.

"It's just," I went on in a rush, "in the hospital, they gave you that schedule, and I was kinda wondering if you've been meeting that schedule."

She must have taken forty-five seconds to review the question. I studied the special toy offer on the back of the cereal box with the desperate interest of the truly uncomfortable.

"Correct," she said at last, "none of your business."

"Well, yeah, see, that's true," I said, scratching the silver off of my prize match number, "except that it kinda is in the sense that you're here, and everything, and it is pretty much my apartment and of course it's cool however long you want to stay but I just wanted to know if there was — you know, some schedule I should be aware of."

"None."

"But —"

"What do you want, Ronnie, rent money? Here," she said, and threw her hundred dollar bills at me. "Take that, I'll get you more."

"No, no," I said, "it's not the money."

"Then what?"

"Well, you know ... "

She pinned me under her glare. "Are you trying to say I should go to some fucking shrink?"

"Well, no, not exactly. But — I mean, would that be, like, such a terrible idea?" Boy, there's a compelling argument.

"Hey, Ronnie, here's a piece of news: I've already got one mother. I don't need another."

Well, that was a fruitful conversation. I may not have won a set of authentic Indy Car Hot Wheels off the cereal box, but at least I learned how many mothers Eva has.

Eva got up and went off to shower. I don't remember what I thought about while she was gone. When she returned she seemed in a better mood, or at least closer to human.

"Why didn't you go with her?" Eva asked.

"She left before I woke up. Kite-flying emergency, I guess."

"Don't be snotty."

The phone rang.

Eva ignored it. "Would it kill you," she asked, "to treat women with a little respect?"

I picked up the phone.

"Hello."

"Ronnie, honey," the voice said, "it's so good to hear your voice. How is everything?"

"Hiya, Mom," I said, "how you been?"

Eva immediately began making frantic gestures, shaking her head, waving her hands sideways, mouthing the words, "I'm not here."

"I'm fine," Mom said, "as is Dad. Have you had any luck finding work?"

"Nah, not really. It's been kinda slow since the last temp thing died."

"Oh, I'm sorry to hear that. What do you do with yourself all day long?"

"I stay busy. You remember Benny and Hal?"

"Sure, of course I do. They're lovely boys."

I nodded, which is useless in a telephone conversation. Eva's stare was making me achingly nervous.

Mom asked, "What about girlfriends? Have you been going out? Have you met anyone special?"

"I go out," I said. "Listen, how's Dad?"

"He's fine. He's putting up a nice shelf for the tools in the garage."

"Didn't he do that about six months ago?"

She laughed. "Yes, but you know your father. Listen, Ronnie, I'm calling because I'm a bit worried about Eva. Has she called you?"

"No," I said, and Eva could immediately smell the topic. She leaned forward, her eyelid twitching malevolently at me. "No," I repeated, "she hasn't called me."

"It's strange. I haven't heard from her for quite some time. I spoke to her friend Heather, who claimed Eva was no longer living with her. Do you know anything about that?"

"She's not? I — uh, I never talk to Heather."

"What do you suppose Eva is up to now?"

"I haven't got the vaguest idea, Mom." This was the truest thing I had said up to that point.

"Well, I certainly hope she's alright. She acts so very strangely sometimes."

"Yeah, I know. I'm sure she's fine."

"You'll let me know if she calls you?"

"Yeah. I'll do that. Listen, I'm taking off here in a minute. Say 'hi' to Dad."

"Very well. I love you, Ronnie. Be good."

"Take care. Bye."

"What did she say?" Eva demanded as soon as the receiver hit the hook.

"Hey, if you want to find out what's on her mind, why don't you talk to her?"

Eva snorted. "Yeah, right," she said, with all the contempt she could muster.

"She's worried about you."

"Oh, don't make me puke. She doesn't give a shit what happens to me."

I had to laugh at that. "Then why did she call me looking for you?"

"It's called guilt, Ronnie. She's a fucking guilt factory."

"Oh, Christ, Eva, she's just — just concerned."

"Yeah, right," she snorted, "concerned. Concerned about manipulating everyone so they come out just right, like we're all living in her little American dollhouse."

"You don't know what you're talking about," I said.

"Huh. Don't I? Didn't she bug you about getting a job and a wife?"

"Nah. She was just —" I stopped myself. "Listen," I asked, "would it kill you to treat women with a little respect?"

Ooh, good one, Ronnie.

"Oh, fuck you, Ronnie," Eva said, enjoying the irony less than I. "Don't get all self-righteous on me." With that handy bit of advice she strode over to the door and yanked it open. She gave me a look as though she had one more thing to add, but instead walked out and slammed the door.

I stood there for a moment, wondering how it all got started, why Eva was no longer speaking to Mom. I could remember no good reason, but the hostility between them had become a sad, twisted, loathsome and loathing umbilical cord. What exactly had Mom done to deserve that? I stood there, a bit off balance, wishing I had said something to Eva, when the door flew open again.

Eva walked back in.

"Eva," I said.

"Forgot my purse," she said. She grabbed it and left again, which afforded her the deep pleasure of slamming the door twice in one minute.

I went into the bathroom to find some aspirin. Coated ibuprofen, my favorite. Yum, yum. I buy them by the gallon jug at the discount drug store. It took me twenty seconds to pop off the damn safety cap and poke my fingers in there to remove the damn cotton. Why they put cotton in the damn aspirin I have no idea. I then learned that some damn ants had somehow infiltrated the hermetically sealed bottle. Upon further inspection I discovered that they had eaten all the auburn-colored coating off the medicine, proving once again that an ant will eat almost anything, no matter how disgusting. I fished out a few of the naked pills and stood there for a minute, trying to remember what diseases ants carry. I filled my mouth with tap water, and swallowed the pills. Judge me not. With that headache you would have swallowed the ants, if necessary. In the end the whole ordeal gave me a worse headache than when I started. Which would probably have made a good metaphor for Eva's presence in my life, but my head hurt too much to think about it.

Instead, I went out to the mailbox to see if I had won any sweepstakes. I win all the time. I'm a big winner. Says so right on the envelope. I average about a million dollars a week. The contest folk expect this is an event I'll no doubt announce gleefully to all my "NEIGHBORS ON 14th AVE." Boy, they sure understand my relationship with my neighbors. We're tight, the neighbors and I. We're like family. They're always lending me a cup of flour for my delicious homemade bread, which I naturally share with them. I babysit all the cuddly neighborhood children constantly.

I'm not sure if I could ever cash in my winnings, because the sweepstakes people are convinced my name is Donald Snorenstein. I'd correct it, but that would imply even the merest crumb of hope that I would ever actually win a single solitary buck. And it's amusing to let all the sweepstakes snake-oil hucksters share one incorrect list.

The amazing thing to me is that the sweepstakes people are still using the decades-old trick of sticking my name and address every-where in the letter and on glossy certificates and other assorted colorful materials. It makes me wonder: are there yokels out there so clueless they have never heard of data entry? Do they see their names in a letter and jump for joy, thinking someone, somewhere, took the time to type in their special name and their special address because this is the actual winning entry?

Sometimes I picture people — well, white trash, anyway — all over this country, finding their own names in giant print next to big numbers with lots of zeroes, and jumping up and down in ecstasy, practically destroying the trailer, believing all their pathetic dreams have come true because it says so right there in crappy quality jet printer black on white.

In the words of the immortal P.T. Barnum: "No one ever went broke underestimating the intelligence of the American people."

As usual, the mail included a massive pile of recruitment information from every branch of the United States armed services. Someone had sent my name to them as a prank months before. I could never get anyone to talk, so I'm not certain who did it, but I have a powerful hunch his name rhymed with "pal".

I spent the rest of the day waiting for Great White to call from the repair shop to which we had brought him late the night before. After the hundred dollar bills had started flying through the air, we decided to just get GW towed to a garage and take a taxi home. Man, money is good. It has a way of just cutting through problems. Too bad it's such an annoyance to acquire.

Finally, GW got himself straightened out. Turns out it was carburetion. At least that's what the repair guys told us. Whatever. No point disputing their analysis. I wouldn't know a carburetor from a carbuncle. It's sorcery to me. Dad has always been severely disappointed in me. I can't take care of repairs on my own. I let mechanical objects degrade, never oiling anything, adding only gas, and that reluctantly. Mostly his disappointment stems from my obdurate refusal to acquire even the smallest shred of his vast storehouse of mechanical knowledge.

That was my teenage rebellion, OK? Everybody's got one. Mine was learning nothing about automotive repair. What a rebel. People used to scatter in fear when I walked down the street.

For my penance, I had to take an actual bus to the repair shop. A bus! Is there no limit to the suffering one mortal must endure?

Actually, I learned this: Santa Cruz busses aren't so bad. If I were European, I might even have enjoyed the experience, which was punctual, clean, roomy and speedy. But I'm not European. I'm a goddamned American. I'm a native Californian. I was born with a steering wheel in my hand.

Great White and I had a tearful reunion. He even admitted he had missed me, the big lug nut.

GW and I decided to hit the open road to see how the bypass operation had affected his ticker. It was astounding. The old boy started zipping around like the pace car at the Indy 500. We got on the freeway for no good reason, just to feel the rumble of the open American road and not have to worry about getting towed home.

The road affected us at it always did. It relaxed the mind and manifold, and permitted some heavy thinking. We wandered for a while without aim, pondering the hidden meanings of physics and history, of past and future. A vague notion of possible importance had been lurking for days at the outskirts of my thinking. It had something to do with the past, the future and the nature of history. I tried to pluck the eggshell of idea from the egg yolk of thought; but every time my fingers neared, the sliver of shell floated away.

Thoughts of past and future led Great White and me to means and ends. And one of us, I forget which one, remembered that Gandhi had said something about means and ends being like the seeds of a fruit on the vine, or something like that. That led me to a sudden hunger for fruit. Finding myself back in town, I stopped at the supermarket and splurged on some nectarines. Ahh, the nectarine! If only human beings could hybrid as sweetly and beautifully as the peach and plum.

At that moment I wanted very much to speak with Karen, to be with her, to revel in the sweet taste of ripe nectarine. But a call to her house proved fruitless. I was told she was away for the evening, spelunking in the dark with the alleged Maria and some hiker dudes. I recognized the names of the culprits. I had met them a few times at Karen's house. They were the sort of overbearingly fit creeps who lead whitewater rafting expeditions.

Great White, the nectarines and I all headed back to my apartment. I entertained a brief fantasy that someday we would do so in the company of a job. Silly me.

I unlocked the door and swung it open, and time began to compress again. I saw everything with great and awful clarity. There, on the floor, lay Eva's motionless body.

A massive queasiness surged up within me in the space of a sickened heartbeat. The top of her head faced the door, and her face was stuck in the carpet. Her pale arms were spread out wide, as though crucified. Her knees were bent and unmoving.

The sack of fruit fell from my hands. In terrible and extreme slow motion, a nectarine rolled across the carpet, tumbling and bouncing cheerily. It struck Eva's still head with an obscene, dull thud.

I remember so very clearly the only thought that went through my head at that moment: I could have. I could have.

What was it that I thought I could have done, or not done? Did I think I could claw at the hands on the clock of tragedy? Did I expect to stop or even slow their inexorable sweep through the terribly brief and endless day and into the midnight that awaits us all?

I could have.

"Hey, Little Guy," Eva groaned, looking up at me.

"What?" I cried out, stunned. "Eva? Are you ... ?"

"Am I what?" she asked lethargically. "What'd I do? Why are you throwing fruit at me?"

I began to breathe, as though it were a new and very good idea worth trying for a little while.

I said, "Sorry, I thought you were ... "

Eva yawned for five seconds. "Is there more to that sentence?" she asked.

"What? I'm sorry, I'm just a little confused. Why are you on the floor?"

"Just napping." She stretched and sat up. "Damn. I'm still tired from last night. I've just got no energy lately. No fucking energy, I swear. Why'd you have to throw a peach at my head? Is that supposed to be funny?"

"It's a nectarine," I said, clinging to the security of the one thing I knew to be true.

"Whatever," Eva said, and sank her fangs into the fruit. I sat down, my knees weak from a trauma that had never occurred.

"Hey," Eva said, "Hal called for you."

I nodded. "Listen, Eva, I've been thinking about what we talked about earlier."

She sighed. "Great. Is this a lecture?"

"Eva, I want a Closet Summit," I said. "Remember?"

It was an obscure reference. During high school, when Eva and I had grown closer again, we had sought to confide in each other the deepest secrets and greatest fears of a time that seemed to consist of nothing else. The door to Eva's bedroom was too rattlesome and thin for us, too near the eavesdropping outside world, and so we retreated deeper in the room to Eva's closet to whisper our confessions. It was a very brief period, a fleeting instant of boundless trust which never could have lasted very long. In all, we may have convened five Closet Summits, at most. I wasn't sure if Eva even remembered them.

"Yeah, of course," Eva muttered. "What do you think I am, senile?"

The significant element of a Closet Summit, the critical rule which distinguished it from all other conversations, was an absolute prohibition on interruption. When Eva needed to tell me exactly how degraded and utterly stupid she felt when her evil boyfriend Dave had slapped her; when she felt compelled to relate every thought that went through her head when she slapped him right back, crying fiercely through a haze of barbituates and vodka, I had to listen without comment until she was done.

When I confessed the upsetting fantasy I had of killing my Algebra teacher, who had never wronged me in any way, Eva had to listen. It was actually an extremely serious fantasy, a daily obsession which extended into planning what weapon to use, where and when to assault him, and what I would say to the police. I could not then, and cannot now explain the cause of that obsession, but I know it consumed me for months, and I know Eva listened without judgment.

A closet is a small place, highly constricting, and in Eva's case, piled three feet high with thousands of shoes. In the end, like all closets, it proved too small.

I remember well the last Closet Summit. Eva had spent twenty minutes crying into a crumpled T-shirt, confessing that she was late, three weeks late; and that she was terribly afraid that if Dave found out, he would kill her. When she was done, I asked, confused, what it was she was late for. Eva stared at me for a minute, in deepest disgust, trying to decide if I was somehow trying to be funny, or just a complete moron. Suddenly she sprang up, clawing at the closet door, sliding it open frantically.

I believe we both learned then, finally and irrevocably, that no amount of well-intentioned sibling intimacy could ever bridge the gender gulf between us. We had come as close to the ends of that bridge as possible. We could tease each other about boyfriends and girlfriends, we could lament the absence of sex in our lives, or the poor quality thereof, but we never went into details. There are some things a sister and brother simply cannot discuss. I could provide Eva with a listening ear, perhaps sound advice on rare occasions, but I could never be her sister; and that limitation ended the Closet Summits.

On the open highway, cruising with Great White, my thoughts had wandered to Karen; to her kind, open heart and gentle nature, and her devotion to caring for Eva. I decided that more than anything else she had been like a sister to Eva; the sister Eva had never had. That was the thought that reminded me of the Closet Summits.

"You haven't got a closet," Eva said, smirking.

"I know," I said, unsmiling. "Can't we just do it right here?"

She shrugged. "You want to talk, talk. It's a free country, except for the multitudes of legal, cultural and economic restrictions on personal freedom."

"Eva," I said, "I want you to listen, O.K.? This is serious shit. I've been thinking about this all day. All week. I've got to say — I know you don't want to hear this — that you have to go see a social worker, or psychologist, or someone like that."

I glanced at her nervously to see if she was going to interrupt, but she was devoted to the laws of the Closet Summit with a deadly fanaticism. There was, however, nothing in any of the laws, rules, codes, or by-laws which prohibited vicious sneering.

"Just now," I said, gulping for guidance, "when I came home I ... I saw you on the floor, asleep, and I thought you were ... I thought you were dead, Eva." A terrible lump in my throat began to choke me. "I thought you were dead, and I was so goddamn afraid like in the hospital and I don't really know of what or wh —" and I just could not, could not, could not stop myself from crying. All at once, some barrier within me was destroyed, like a sudden wildfire in untended underbrush.

A face which has held tears in check for twenty years does not let go of them easily. It contorts and chokes, it twists away and it hides in trembling hands.

I wiped snot from my nose with my sleeve. "Sorry," I said. "I guess I'm just trying to say that your head's too big, and it just needs shrinking." It was a pathetic attempt to sail from the ocean of untested emotional depths to the mainland of humor. It was an absolutely lousy joke, and we both knew it.

"I'm sorry," I went on, "this is serious shit. Didn't I already say that? I don't know. Listen, I don't like having to remind you, Eva, but you tried to — tried to commit suicide, and I don't want to know why, and I'm not asking why at all, but I really, really don't want you to do it again. Because — well you know why. I mean, think about if our roles were switched. Wouldn't you say the same thing to me? Wouldn't you try to help? Wouldn't you tell me to go to see that social worker? What kind of brother would I be if I didn't say this stuff?"

I wiped my face again and took a deep shuddering breath. Eva watched me for a minute.

"You done?" she asked at length, and I steeled myself for the inevitable onslaught.

"O.K.," she said, "my turn. You know, it's funny, but I've been asking myself some of the same questions as you have. 'What kind of a sister am I if don't tell him what he needs to hear?' I ask myself that one all the time. And I know it's none of my business, but goddamn, you're a fucking idiot, Ronnie. You were even ready to give that guy last night his money back."

Not true.

"If someone walked up to you," she continued, "and gave you a million dollars, you'd try to figure out a reason not to take it. Don't give me that squint. You know what I'm talking about. You've got someone, Ronnie, someone who really cares about you. Don't ask me why, but she thinks you're the most amazing thing since sliced fucking bread. She worships you. And you treat her like shit, you fucking idiot. You treat her like absolute shit. Don't shake your head at me, you know exactly what I'm talking about. You treat Karen like a fucking dishrag. I don't know why she stands for your stupid, childish, sexist bullshit. If I was her I'd be long gone. But she's still around, and if you had an ounce of intelligence you'd realize she's the best thing that ever happened to you — way better than anything I have ever managed — and you'd get down on your fucking knees and treat her with some respect."

Wow. The things that people store within them, unsaid. Like a mute trying to sing opera.

"Shit," Eva said, "stop looking at me like that. I'll go to the goddamn social worker, if it'll shut you up. It's completely pointless, you know. What the fuck do they know about me? I know exactly what they're going to say: 'Here, have some Prozac, and why do you hate your mother?' I've got enough problems without having to explain it all to some idiot with a B.A. in Psych., but if it'll make you happy ... "

She paused and looked at me. I blew my nose forcefully.

"Hey," she said, more quietly, "thanks, Ronnie, for what you said. Don't get too freaked out about me, O.K.? I'm alright. I told you, you've always been a good baby brother. If I knew how to say it, I'd tell you I love you, but I'm not really good at that kind of stuff. Hey! Wipe your face. You look like a mess, Little Guy. Listen, I'll make you a deal."

She seemed to be waiting for me to speak.

"What deal? Or can I not talk?"

"Yeah, of course. Fuck that closet shit. This is the deal: I'll go check out the social worker if you'll go up to the Deerpark debate tomorrow."

"What?" I asked, confused again. "Why do you care if I go up to Deerpark?"

"I don't. But Karen does."

"Yeah," I said, "I know that. But I'm not her. That Deerpark shit doesn't matter to me much either way. And I've already done her a favor ten times over up there. And got tear-gassed for it. And — my God, it's so ridiculous — me giving speeches and whatever like I give a shit. You have no idea how much I hate all that political bullshit."

"Goddamn it," Eva said, exasperated, "you haven't understood a word I've said. Let me clue you in on a little something about women, you clueless wonder. We like it when a man exhibits evidence of strength, of power. It's our little way of buying into traditional sexist bullshit, but there it is. That's why Karen likes seeing you up there, giving speeches, or whatever. She cares about the politics, but what she really likes is seeing you getting off your ass and doing something productive. So maybe you don't love giving speeches, but she loves seeing you do it. You think you can sit around on the couch all day and expect her to stay excited about you?"

"So what are you saying? That I have to become the next Jesse Jackson if I want to keep her around?"

"No, stupid. It's not politics. It's anything you do with power, with passion. If you became utterly involved with — say with writing, and devoted yourself to it, and took a million workshops and met people and brought them around, Karen would love it."

Suddenly, Eva broke out into a throaty chortle.

"What?" I demanded.

"It's just," she said, shaking her head with an ironic grin, "it's just that you must be pretty pathetic to need a lecture about ambition from a woman who just tried to kill herself."

I chuckled for a second, and then we both fell into a long, hard laugh. It lasted for a few minutes. We both knew it was more out of relief than anything else, but that was as good a reason as any.

"O.K.," I said, still chuckling, "it's a deal. You go to the bullshit social worker, and I'll go to the bullshit protest."

"Wonderful," Eva said, "and what a happy family are we."

It's difficult to continue with the ordinary routines of humdrum living after a great confrontation or confession. Eva and I had endured both kinds of catharsis in the space of an hour. The apartment seemed even smaller than ever. Like lost bear cubs in the motherless wilderness, we turned on the T.V. and suckled on it for the rest of the evening.

Somewhere out there must exist people — well, Neilsen families, at any rate — who find the sitcoms offered between six and nine o'clock on a weeknight entertaining. Eva and I turned off our brains and watched several mind-numbing offerings, starting things off with a Plot Three: Oh, no, Junior can't find a date for the prom, and he doesn't want Mom and Dad to find out because it will spoil their image of him, so he lies to everyone about everything, almost at random. The Beautiful Girl agrees to date him because the plot needs stretching, but it goes to his head and he mistakenly tries to take advantage of the situation. He learns the error of his ways thanks to a climax scene that is hideously embarrassing, poorly acted, and drenched in laugh track. Because he is properly remorseful, Girl kisses him on the cheek and exits, only to make a surprise cameo in the intervening commercial as Grandpa's Antacid Buddy. Back in the show, Junior hugs Mom and Dad a few times to thank them for their heavy-handed moralizing lecture, but not before Baby Sister says something abominably cute. Wacky Neighbor trips over the couch, and let's roll them credits.

Comic wizardry. You wouldn't believe how many hours of that crap Eva and I can watch together, in a kind of dull, familiar haze. It serves as a base paint over which we layer heavy brush strokes of sarcastic running commentary. With all due modesty, we're a hell of a lot funnier than our source material. From the time we were little kids, Eva and I have played an endless television game, the only point of which is to predict the exact phrasing of select dialogue before the actors can remember their lines. Eva has an absolutely uncanny talent in this department, and always wins this contest, unless sports are involved.

We sat there for hours, racing to yell out our lines. From the moment I flipped the T.V. on, my neighbors were forced to endure periodic shouts of, "Come on, you guys, let's dance anyway," and, "I sorry, Señora Phillips, I clean up that closet last week," and, "Has anybody seen Buttons since we fumigated?"

Late in the evening I remembered that I owed Hal a call. I always dreaded calling over to the old apartment, because Carl — you remember Oatmeal Carl Davies — usually answered the phone. In fact, quite a few times he had picked up the phone and I had hung up at the sound of his voice. Oh, do you think that's a rude thing to do? Gosh, I do hope I've not been ill-mannered. That would be so unfortunate, and so out of character. I happen to know it unnerved ol' Carl, because he kept asking Benny and Hal if they had been getting crank calls.

Luckily, Benny picked up.

"What's the good word?" I asked him, as I often do.

"Actually, this time there is a good word," he said. "Looks like I've been invited to do a poetry reading at the Chameleon, in the City."

"Hey, that's not bad," I said.

"Yeah, it's alright," Benny said, with false modesty. "It's certainly better than a poke in the eye with a burnt stick."

"Have you decided what to read?"

"Probably *Apocalypse of the Fellahin*."

"I don't think I know that one."

"It's recent. It's a meditation in epic narrative form, revolving around the events of a single mythic day in which the poor of every nation spontaneously rise up against the rich without knowing their own motivation. As I'm reading it, I intend to project intercutting images of a variety of indigenous peoples and cattle at a slaughter-house on a screen behind me. The title is stolen from Kerouac," he said, and I couldn't tell if that was a source of pride or chagrin.

Eva, in the background, suddenly yelled, "Honey, this soup is fantastic! What's in it?"

"What's going on over there?" Benny asked. "Your sister sounds like she's having a good time."

"No, not really," I said. "She's talking to the T.V. She's never that enthusiastic about real life."

"I heard that," Eva muttered, but then let out a quick blast of, "I don't think these are garbanzo beans!"

I talked to Benny longer than I intended, partially because his enthusiasm for the new direction his art was taking, while absurd, was nevertheless infectious, but mostly because I was dreading my conversation with Hal. In the last twenty-four hours, Hal had more or less saved my life, and Benny's as well, and now I was going to deny the only request he had made of me in living memory.

At length I congratulated Benny one more time.

"Well, Benjamin," I said, "go out there and kick some epic ass."

"A lovely turn of phrase," Benny said, and went to fetch Hal.

There was an unusual tone to Hal's greeting. He seemed out of breath, which was out of character.

"What's up?" I asked Hal.

"Well," he said, "kinda big news around here. We finally got a new housemate, a guy by the name of Paul. Still in school. Actually, he says he knows you."

"I don't know anyone," I said.

"I told him that, but he insisted. Anyway, this friend of his has been helping him move in the last couple of days. The weird thing is, Ronnie," and he lowered his voice, "I think she's into me."

"Oh, this is a she we're talking about? Is she cute? What's her name?"

"Brenda. And she's completely, just — yeah, totally cute. Like beyond."

I couldn't recall having heard Hal more excited.

"Well, ask her out," I said, enthused, "see what happens."

"I want to," he said.

"Then do."

"It wouldn't be that hard," he admitted. "She's around all the time."

"Then ask her," I said.

"I should, shouldn't I?"

"Yes," I said, "you should. Except, what gives with her and this guy Paul?"

"Just friends," Hal said. "Brenda's single."

"So ask her out," I said.

"I should, shouldn't I?"

"Didn't we just have this conversation" I asked, amused.

"Out, like where?" Hal asked.

"Out, like dinner and a movie."

"Oh, that's original."

"You don't get points for originality," I said.

"What do you get points for?"

"Cleanliness," I said. "Punctuality. And a large penis helps."

"Where would you take her?"

"Go nuts," I said. "Blow your five hundred bucks on something useful."

"Like where?"

"It doesn't matter, take her anywhere. Girls don't eat on a date anyway."

"Yeah, that's true," he admitted.

"Listen," I said, "what's the big deal here anyway? It's not like you're Benny or something. You've been around the block and up the stairs a few times."

"Yeah, I know, but this is different. She's all that, Ronnie. She's prime time. She is really — well, anyway. Who knows if she'll even want to? Hey, what time are you picking me up for the show?" he asked with sudden enthusiasm.

"Well, that's the thing," I said. "Kinda why I called."

"Don't tell me you can't make it."

"Well ... "

"Oh, come on, Shorenstein! Jesus Christ! I thought you were psyched about this."

"I am —"

"You know how much bullshit I had to go through to get you backstage?"

"Not that much," I said, refusing to be bullied.

"A lot," he insisted. "Now what am I supposed to do, have Benny be a bouncer?"

We stopped for a brief chuckle at that absolutely absurd thought.

"I'm writing an epic poem in Sanskrit," I said in a mocking tone. "It's about the indigenous cattle rising up to slay the dairy farmers."

Hal laughed, but stayed on message. "Why can't you come?" he demanded.

"I'm going up to that Deerpark debate."

"What? You're shitting me."

"I shit you not."

"How late does that go?"

"Karen said after six probably, and you're leaving town — what?"

"Like two o'clock, in order to get there and set up. Fuck, Ronnie, what is all this hippie protest shit? This isn't you."

"I know," I said.

"You think you're impressing anybody?" he asked. "You think they'll stop building their whatever because you asked them to?"

"Nope," I said.

"Then why bother? Give me one good reason why you should care."

There was a long moment of phone silence.

"I don't get it," Hal said. "It's not like you just met Karen. Why do you keep trying to impress her with your dedication to saving the planet, like she doesn't know you're totally faking it?"

"I'm not completely, one hundred per cent faking it," I said. "You know they're planning to build —"

"Oh, don't start that bullshit with me," Hal said. "I know you. You don't give a shit about politics, just like Benny said. You're like me. You don't give a shit about anybody but yourself. And that's good, goddamn it! That's the way it should be. If more people just mellowed out and minded their own business, the world would be a far better place. All these hypocrite politicians running around trying to save the world, just to blow up their own egos, it's such a bunch of bullshit."

"Yeah," I said, "I know." And I did know. Or thought I did. "But I gotta do this,' I said. "Don't think I'm not bummed that I can't go to the show."

"Whoa," Hal said. "You lost me. Too many negatives."

"I am bummed," I said. "I want to go to the show."

"Then go."

"But I want to not go even more."

Hal sighed. He waited out a phone second or two, which feels like an hour, to give me a chance to change my mind spontaneously.

"Well," he sighed again, "guess you're not coming."

"Guess not."

"You can't have everything," he lamented.

"Where would you put it?" I asked.

"If you had everything," he said, "you'd have a place to put it."

It was an old routine. We sought it out deliberately, hoping its comforting rhythms might smooth over the disagreement that had come between us.

Sometimes the freeway offers a lane which travels for a mile or two under the label of two different highways. Traffic is always worse in that lane, because the decision to switch freeways is not one to be taken lightly, and most people choose to postpone it as long as possible. It seemed then that Hal and I were following each other in that lane, trying to determine whether to merge left or right.

Chapter 26

In the forest clearing, the tribe quivered in small groups, weary, bruised and battered. The battle with the enemy had left the clearing in smoke and ruin, and the tribe seemed little better off. There was pain in every movement and hesitation in every word.

But the sun had barely moved in clear blue sky when the tribe started growing. It doubled and then tripled in size. Soon the entire clearing was full of the new arrivals to the tribe, who seemed almost indistinguishable from the original members.

It was good to be in the tribe.

A long table with chairs behind it and microphones atop it had been set up during the day by the enemy's soldiers.

Ha! You gotta give me credit for that one.

I sat with Karen on the grassy hillside and waited for the show to begin. She kept uprooting grass in a most unenvironmental manner and tossing it down the back of my shirt, for which I gave her a well-deserved Indian wrist burn — very popular among Indians, I suppose.

At the far left end of the table sat Gregory Thompson and M'Bopape whatever-his-name-was, each looking like he'd been flattened by an asphalt steamroller. I suppose a long day or two of tear-gas in the woods and unpleasant frisking in the county pokey had taken their toll.

On the far right side of the table sat our old friend Vice-Chancellor Meyers, and an old guy in a suit I did not recognize. The guy, I mean, not the suit. I'd know that suit anywhere. It was the Suit of Authority. Ann Capriati-Mentzinger the adult hippie sat directly in the middle of the long table. New day, new vest for Ann C-M. There were a few empty seats on either side of her, just in case someone important showed up, I suppose.

On the near side of the table and off to the right a bit, space had been set aside for the throngs of media, which seemed to include not only a bewildered yet haughty campus newspaper reporter, but also a video crew for the local cable access channel, the sort of people who air shows like "Wayne's World" to obscure audiences with Nielsen ratings somewhere in the .000001 range.

There were cops everywhere, spilling out of the mothership, polluting the damn field like armed lice. It was absurd to imagine that the students were expected to present rational arguments in the presence of those thugs. Karen and I sat near a small tribe of the clean-cut predators. The soldiers had soldered themselves into an immobile line facing the field. They looked at me through mirrored sunglasses as though I was the lowest form of life they had seen since humanity crawled out of the primordial ooze.

Here's a lesson of the Vietnam War from a guy who took a whole course on it: give a young guy a gun and complete power over some peasants, and you end up with a fucking mess. The My Lai massacre jumps to mind as a handy example, don't it? For those of you who missed that one, go rent *Apocalypse Now*, *Platoon*, or *Casualties of War*, or any of twenty other films in that genre. The movies have a fascination with American soldiers going berserk. It's terrific theater.

What was truly fucked up about My Lai was not just some peasants getting slaughtered. It was the transformation of the American soldiers. After endless sweaty months of wading through swamps and bullets, chasing, hating and demonizing the enemy, they had lost their own humanity. War does that. Happens all over the world. Those who would take on the role of the aggressive or occupying force for a prolonged period risk corruption of the national soul.

And that is precisely what's happening with cops in our own country. Walking around with guns and the power to intimidate and arrest is a perfect formula for losing one's humanity. Ever notice the sway of complete arrogance with which cops interrogate jaywalkers, speeders and other heinous felons? Ever notice the paternalistic glee with which they force kids caught with beer to pour it out in the gutter? Ever notice that cop protocol is to leave those kids sitting handcuffed on the curb for a half hour while the cops mosey back to the car for a chat with the dispatcher? Ever notice how cops insist on expressing themselves in a quasi-military officialese? Ever notice they have to say "step away from the vehicle" and not "get out of the car"? Ever watch cops flip on their sirens, cut right through traffic, and then turn the sirens off at the donut shop three blocks later? O.K., listen: they're not supposed to do that. Them sirens is up there for emergencies. But are you going to tell them to stop?

Didn't think so, punk.

"Ronnie," Karen said, "let's travel. I want to go on a trip."

I turned my attention away from the granite statues of malevolence and toward the lithe, blithe dancer who lay sprawled on the grass before me. It occurred to me then that Karen could never, ever be a cop, and that was about as high a compliment as I could imagine.

"Where would you like to go, Sherpa? The Himalayas? A nostalgic trek to meet your long-lost Sherpa brethren?"

"Where were the Incas?"

"Peru?"

"I want to go to Peru."

"O.K.," I said, "Peru for you."

"Really?"

"Anything your heart desires, Sherpa. I am at your service. Your wish is my command. What's mine is yours."

"Aww," she sighed, like a sap, "that's so sweet."

"Not really," I said, "I don't actually own anything."

Karen rolled over so her tummy was facing the sky and her eyes were pouring into mine.

"Ronnie," she said, "what would you say if I asked you to give me your PowerBook?"

This confused me. "You want to borrow my PowerBook?"

"No, I'm asking if I could have it, to keep."

I shrugged. "Well, I don't use it much. What do you want it for?"

"O.K., one last question," she said. "What if I asked you for Great White?"

That was a much more difficult question, and we both knew it. GW and I were two of a kind. We had been through much together, and we trusted each other with our lives daily. I hesitated only for a moment. "I would give you Great White," I said.

It was quite clearly the right answer. Karen pulled my face down to hers and kissed me like exceptional fiction, right there in front of ten thousand hippies, and I didn't stage a protest.

I will now divide the world's population in two by means of an abstract contrast. I am well aware I am not the first person to perform this exercise, but I have a purpose, and I believe I may be the first to employ this particular distinction: there are people who make buildings happen, and there are people to whom buildings happen.

Building people run the world. They built the Pyramids, the great cathedrals, the Sears Tower and the Panama Canal. They get ideas and they act on them. They wake up early. They make lists and cross off the tasks they've completed. They score well on standardized tests. They study. They have two sharpened No. 2 pencils. They fire thousands of employees before lunch. They golf. They engineer palace coups.

The rest of us, the half of the world to whom buildings happen, wake up late. We go fishing and catch nothing. We tear your ticket and squirt butter flavoring on your popcorn at the movie theater and we suffer miserable acne. We get stuck in the slow lane every single time. We mixed the mortar for those Pyramids. We got yellow fever digging that Panama Canal. We died by the dozens building that Hoover Dam.

Building people love to plan buildings. They love the sleek, cool feel of reinforced concrete. Show them an acre of grass and they see unsprouted condos just under the surface. They adore blueprints. They hate regulatory restrictions. They are the engines of commerce, the pioneers of progress. They innovate machines to make our lives easier, soaps to make our skin softer, and television shows to make our brains spongier. They demand to know why the impossible can't get done.

We demand to know if you'd like fries with that. We are unable to comprehend stock market listings, no matter how many times they are explained to us. Show us an acre of unbuilt grass and we get sleepy. We buy lottery tickets on obscure numerological whims. We get lost immediately in big office buildings and hospitals. We have poor elevator etiquette. We are genetically incapable of calculating square footage. If civilization depended on us, it never would have happened.

What is the opposite of a building? Grass? Sky? Termites? No, I submit to you that the precise opposite of a building is a mole. Those of us to whom buildings happen are moles, burrowing pink and hairless in a tiny dark universe without reason, plan or eyesight. From the moment of birth, the mole digs and pokes at the earth one inch at a time, never cognizant of the world one foot away.

Building people raise the sky. Mole people move the earth with our faces.

And yet, under every building there is a mole, chewing away, ruining the lawn, destroying the foundations. Without intention, without malice, without conscious design we tear down everything the building people erect. We embody everything building people detest.

Consider some example from people we both know. Mom is a builder. Definitely a builder. How about Hal? Hmm. Take a wild guess which type he is.

Then you've got your borderline cases. Take Gregory Thompson — please! Heh heh heh. Did you know that the original version of that fine joke was first uttered by Henny Youngman in a Catskills resort in upstate New York, more than four thousand years ago?

Where was I? Take Gregory Thompson. Gregory is a building person masquerading as a mole. Then there's my father, who actually builds buildings but doesn't really mean it that way. In a sense, Abe Shorenstein is Gregory Thompson's alter ego.

And then there's Eva. Mondays, Wednesdays and Fridays she's a building person. Tuesdays, Thursdays and Saturdays she tears down the buildings she has built. Sundays she rests.

Janis, the deceased guppy that spent her fifty-eight hours of life circling our childhood aquarium, was a building fish. Great White was a mole car, but in the best possible way.

Being a person on whom buildings fall does have its up side. If you have to have sex, don't choose a building person for your frolic. They're chock full of hang-ups and taboos.

If you want to get properly laid, stay on this side of the fence. Our finest example: Sweet Ms. Karen Anne "Sherpa" Bellamy, a cute little mole who wouldn't know an inhibition if it walked up and landed on her like a building.

We moles are funnier. We do stand-up. They react to jokes by saying, "Hm, that's funny." If we find something funny, we laugh. They actually laugh rather loudly, but they're faking it.

We curse better. They buy too much insurance. We have better rhythm. They collect stamps, coins and baseball cards in mint condition. We can't find a stamp when we need one, nor a quarter for the meter.

We moles can watch movies on airplanes without purchasing headsets, and be content. Building people are big on fidelity. They love the latest hi-tech gadgets; the stereos and high-definition TV's and parallel processing computer chips so powerful they approach sentience.

They buy new cars. We sell used cars.

Building people make history. Moles burrow through it.

Building people prepare detailed itineraries when travelling and follow them without deviation. Moles are the last to board the plane.

I must emphasize that this distinction is not just about haves and have-nots. The building-mole duality crosses gender, ethnic, geographic, age and income boundaries.

There are wealthy moles, people who grind out a meatloaf of a life in daily scoops of ground-round.

There are poor building people, the kind that win extraordinary scholarships or build small empires by distributing beer in the run-down neighborhoods they once called home.

The West was colonized by poor building people, traveling across a mysterious, mythical and majestic land cooped up in disease-infested conestoga wagons. Along the way many of them were attacked by warring Apaches, a building people if ever there was one.

Then you've got your Spanish and your Ohlone, and if you can't figure out which is which, you need more help than I can give you.

Modern building people feel most comfortable surrounded by tons of steel mass. Picture the bank basement buried in the financial district in San Francisco, where I spent one hellish summer. Fix in your mind the image of guys in suits tugging at the doors before this dumb mole got a chance to push the Green Button, and you know everything you need to know about the great void that separates us.

Why am I bothering you with all of this? Because I want you to know that at its core, away from all the distractions, the Deerpark debate was a fight between building people and moles. And there's one more thing I wanted to mention: building people always win.

Chapter 27

After twenty more minutes of general milling about, the wheels of the Deerpark Debate finally started spinning. At that point the meadow grass was getting trampled by at least five hundred students, more than fifty cops, a variety of functionaries and staff, and two press hounds. Among the mass of students were the usual tribelets: hacky-sack idiots, guitar players, massage fetishists, shy types pretending to study, and a fairly large group of politico diehards front and center. Many of the diehards I recognized from that miserable night in the woods I had endured a mere two days earlier. It seemed more like two decades.

The diehards held a few signs and banners of significant size but crappy quality. I could not read them well, because I was behind them, but I did catch sight of a few which read, "Amnesty for Deerpark 50!" and "Free M'Bopape!" which was patently absurd, as the man was sitting right there free as a freebird, his nose unshackled, ready to debate his anarchist little heart out.

Ann C-M spoke first. "Good afternoon. I'd like to welcome everyone and thank you for coming to this debate on the University's proposal for development at Deerpark Meadow."

"Sellout!" one of M'Bopape's minions yelled out suddenly. This was so unexpected, unnecessary and poorly timed that Ann seemed more embarrassed for the guy than upset. The look on her face seemed to say that she would have known when and how to yell "sellout!" far better than he. She smirked and continued.

She introduced the speakers. The old guy in the suit turned out to be the head honcho hisself, the big man, the top dog, the sweet cheese, A-Number-1, the commandante: Chancellor Perkins.

"As some of you may know," Ann said, "in recent days the debate over the Deerpark proposal has become more contentious, leading to consequences no one, neither administration nor students, anticipated nor desired."

"Pigs go home!"

Ann laughed. "Thank you for that contribution. This seems to be a good time to mention that there will be time at the end of the debate for further comments from any interested parties."

As she was concluding her remarks, another old friend, Fred Miles, joined the debate squad. Ah, so now the scales were going to get a bit more balanced. At least we had an adult on our side. He sat down on the administration side by mistake.

Ann indicated that the debate would give ample time to both sides, and that the students would speak first. They would likely need all the head start they could get.

M'Bopape started things off with a whimper. The entire focus of his microscopic life had been reduced to the question of police brutality. He detailed the events of the "cop riot", as he kept calling it, demanded that the police be held accountable, demanded a full inquiry into their crimes, demanded that all charges against protestors be dropped, demanded this, demanded that. The guy did a lot of demanding. It was hella boring. Christ, I was as upset as he was about militia malfeasance, but I have other things to do with my life. I have interests, I have hobbies: I like water-skiing, sky-diving, horseback riding on the beach at sunset, and men with beards.

M'Bopape had nothing to offer the crowd in the way of useful debate on the actual merits of the development proposal. Intellectually, his remarks were not particularly — well, demanding.

Chancellor Perkins had a great baritone which rumbled across the wild woods and down to the bay to compete with the foghorn at Lighthouse Point. "In an effort to show our good will in this matter," he rumbled, "the administration is provisionally prepared at this very moment to drop all charges against students arrested in the disturbances of earlier this week."

Scattered, distrustful applause.

"I trust that arrangement is favorable to the students?" he asked Ann. She looked over at Gregory and M'Bopape. The two of them whispered to each other momentarily, hands over their microphones, conferencing like Oliver North and his lawyer.

"Yeah," M'Bopape said, "actually, that seems O.K." Those few words betrayed a childish potpourri of emotions, obvious to anyone who had ever met the man or been harangued by him. He was thrilled at the proposal on its merits, but wary of accepting any offer proffered by the enemy. Most of all, he was heavily disappointed that the soapbox had just been pulled right out from under him. He had been yanked off the crucifix, the glory of martyrdom denied him. He looked a bit sheepish as he concluded, "Yeah, we'll take you up on that offer."

For that incisive and witty remark, M'Bopape was rewarded with a great rumble of applause and cheering. The militants up front waved their signs and hugged one another as though they had just won the soccer World Cup. Karen managed a sloppy whistle with her fingers, a skill I had been teaching her for months.

"In exchange," Chancellor Perkins boomed away, pleased with himself, "we ask for some assurance that those disturbances be the last of their kind. It is impossible to conduct the proper and legitimate business of higher education in an atmosphere of Luddite hooliganism."

Scattered, uncertain booing. No one, myself included, was sure who or what the Luddites might have been.

"We have demonstrated our good faith," Perkins said. "Accordingly, we request that the students, as a sign of your good faith, pledge permanently to vacate Deerpark Meadow as soon as this debate has concluded."

Heavy boos and jeers.

"Um, look, I'm sorry," Gregory said, "but we can't really do that. We've sort of, uh, pledged to continue our protest here until the University abandons its plans for a nuclear processing facility, plus promises not to build on sacred Native American ground."

Meyers responded immediately. "As we have told you before, the University has absolutely no intention of building any nuclear processing facility here."

"The very idea is ludicrous," Chancellor Perkins boomed. "We have neither the interest nor the resources to maintain a facility of that sort. Now, some of you may know that prior to taking this position, I taught particle physics for many years at Cal. I have long been on the advisory board of the Bulletin of Atomic Scientists, which has received a Nobel Prize for its work in advocating on behalf of social responsibility in the use and disposal of nuclear weapons and waste. I don't think it is a great stretch of credibility to suggest that I know as much about the dangers of nuclear proliferation as anyone present. I assure you that, as Vice-Chancellor Meyers has said, we have no intentions of building any sort of nuclear facility on Deerpark Meadow."

He was rewarded with a great deal of uncertain murmuring of the sort that swells in the courtroom when a particularly damaging piece of evidence goes on display.

"Ann," Gregory said into his microphone, "mm-hm," clearing his throat, "could I say something?"

The noise died down.

Ann looked over at Chancellor P., who nodded. Ann passed the nod on to Gregory.

"O.K.," he said, "I just want to read something to everybody. It was sent to me by an anonymous source."

"Ahh," I whispered to Karen, "the legendary smoking gun from

232

Gregory's speech outline, or I'm a monkey."

"You're a monkey either way," Karen whispered back.

"What this is," Gregory said, "is a memo addressed from Ms. Meyers to the Chancellor. At the top of the page the anonymous source has written, 'I thought the E. Club might find this useful, so I hacked it out of Infoslug,' which of course is the campus e-mail system. The memo says this: 'Dear Chancellor Perkins, I've been thinking about the Deerpark development alot. i think its important for p.r. purposes that we try not to let anyone know about the nuclear part of the development until later, after it gets approved. I think the students will be very upset about it.'"

A roar of anger went up from the crowd. The cops got fidgety in a hurry. I like fidgety cops even less than I like the garden variety.

"Let me see that," Meyers demanded. She glanced at it quickly and viciously. "What does 'For KAB' mean?" she asked. "It's typed at the bottom of the page."

Gregory did not have an answer to that question, nor did anyone else in that vast throng, except perhaps two small, innocent and inconsequential moles, one throwing grass down the other's back.

Now, whom do we know who might leak an anonymous e-mail message to the Environmental Club? Whom do we know who might dedicate such a stunt "for KAB"?

While we ponder that question, I remind you: your e-mail is not safe. You've been warned before. Stop writing love notes at work. Depart that nasty sex chat-room right this instant. Nothing is secret. Your computer is not a shield. Anyone can crack into it, provided they have the proper tools and the technical skill, the kind of skill that — yes — Carl Davies held in abundance. Not the Carl Davies that I used as my *nom de guerre*, but the real Carl Davies, my erstwhile roommate, who worked long hours at a high-tech company like a monk laboring over illuminated manuscripts, patiently offering up some obscure talent in the service of the almighty Internet. Turns out the guy was an environmental sympathizer, or so it seemed to me.

No one ever verified my theory, but I believe that's as good a guess as any to explain how Gregory eventually gained possession of what became known as the Meyers Memo.

I was a bit stunned by the development. Meyers had been caught red-handed like a Watergate burglar. And that good ol' oatmeal-sloppin' schmuck Carl was Deep Throat; or, since he wore the shameful horns of the cuckold, a more fitting name might be Deep Goat.

Very interesting. But a little too cozy for me. "For KAB," my ass. You lost her fair and square, chump.

I tried not to establish eye contact with Karen during this portion of the evening's entertainment, so I have no way of knowing if she ever pieced it all together. One would imagine she would have recognized her own initials, but logic and Karen were never the closest of allies.

"This is a fraud," Meyers said vehemently. "I never wrote this. I don't know how it got into my computer files, but I didn't write it. I give you my word I did not write it."

She was jeered mightily, suggesting what the value of her word was considered to be.

Fred Miles spoke up. "May I suggest ... " he waited for the noise to die down. The cadre of students who recognized him cheered heartily. "May I suggest we not jump to any conclusions? We have no way of knowing if this memo is what you claim it is, Gregory. Anyone can plant an e-mail note, or manufacture a copy of one. Do you have anything else more tangible that might help substantiate your claim of nuclear development?"

Ach, that Miles. Always the peacemaker. And just when we had a nice little war going.

"It was proposed in the 1990 General Plan," Gregory pointed out.

"That is hardly relevant," Meyers snarled, comfortably back in her element. "In 1990 a 'nuclear physics research facility' was one of a long list of alternative proposals for this site. I remind you that the General Plan is called that for a reason. It does not approve specific projects. It merely outlines broad goals and guidelines. Any subsequent proposals must be approved separately, which is the process the Deerpark Proposal is currently undergoing. The nuclear research component was never put into this specific proposal. And I reiterate that I did not write that memo."

Gregory and M'Bopape leaned their fool heads together, like Moe and Shemp formulating a housepainting strategy.

"Well," Gregory said, "we don't really know about all those nuclear details. But the fact remains that we have pledged to continue our protest here because you are building on sacred Native American ground, and we're not going to stop."

Wild cheers erupted for Gregory from a crowd sufficiently supportive they were willing to overlook his incredible incompetence and poor preparation.

"Now, look, we have extended our good faith," Perkins said, "but I must say that your presence —" he was drowned out by the noise of cheers fading and jeers swelling. He waited a moment, then began again. "Your presence ... excuse me ... please ... your presence here is illegal."

Massive booing. This was getting a bit pendulous. Cheer, boo, cheer, boo. It was like a very boring, poorly played basketball game. Some contest. Gregory was on crutches, M'Bopape was a lousy shot, and they were lined up against the Dream Team.

"O.K.," Gregory said, a stapled paper report in his hand shaking, "O.K., you say our presence here is illegal, but the truth is, it's the University's presence here that's illegal. Um, let me read from the Santa Cruz County Code, Chapter 16.40, the basic law about building on any land which has Native American cultural sites on it. I made copies," he said, and passed them down the table.

"Thank you," Meyers said, smiling nastily and displaying a thick notebook, "we already have the relevant information."

This unnerved Gregory considerably. His crutches began to sweat. "Well, Section 16.40.080 says: 'It shall be unlawful for any person knowingly to disturb, or cause to be disturbed or to excavate, or cause to be excavated, any Native American cultural site ...' O.K., so the administration has acknowledged that there are Native American remains here. So, because of that rule, the Deerpark proposal has to be cancelled."

Wow, did the kids cheer for that. I thought they were going to get up and do the Wave.

Meyers leaned forward like a cobra. "I'm afraid you are citing the regulation out of its full context to make it seem as though no development may ever take place near a Native American site. In actuality, the purpose of the regulation is to require that any artifacts on the site be treated respectfully, excavated for study if appropriate, or reinterred in the case of human remains. I refer you to Section 16.40.035, entitled 'Project Approval'. It lists the mitigation measures the project developer must take, including, 'preservation of the site through project design or restricting improvement and grading activities to portions of the property not containing the resource, or covering the site with earthfill to a depth where the site will not be disturbed by development.' I want to assure everyone present here today that the University has every intention of following these guidelines."

In response, Gregory just sat there, his mouth open to every fly in the known universe. One hundred feet up the hill, my feet began to twitch with nervous indignation. Noises of aggravation and impatience issued uncontrollably from my tonsils. Karen turned to look at me and squinted, confused at my agitated exhalations.

Perhaps you are aware that the rock band Pink Floyd suffered a bitter breakup. If so, you may remember that bassist Roger Waters considered himself the creative leader, and was mighty wrathful when the other musicians went on a live tour under the old band name. Commenting on the news that his former colleagues were continuing the Pink Floyd tradition of staging elaborate productions, Waters noted scathingly, "That's my giant pig up there. That's my airplane. The dry ice is theirs."

Which explains exactly how I felt. Digging through the County Code was my giant pig. Finding the restriction on construction on Native American sites was my airplane. And Gregory was blowing dry ice over the whole damn thing.

His resolve was wilting before our eyes. I could see him melting once again like a sorbet in a solarium, ready to give in as soon as he was challenged. He was missing the whole goddamn point, neglecting the great loophole I had discovered in my research, which had given me the original idea to bring the protest to Deerpark and not the base of campus. I must say that I knew exactly what I was doing, but I had not the vaguest notion why I was doing it, when I got up, walked through the mob and down the hill, and sat down next to Gregory and M'Bopape.

"May I say something?" I asked Ann, speaking into the microphone. Once again I was taken aback by the volume of my own voice. The crowd seemed puzzled, although I must report with all due modesty that a hardcore group recognized me and cheered like three-year-olds at the sight of Barney the purple dinosaur.

"Your name is Carl, isn't it?" Ann asked me.

"No," I said, "Ronald Shorenstein. I'm an alumnus."

"He's with us," Gregory explained, although it sounded as though he would have been more pleased if I had boiled away into vapor in front of his eyes.

"May I speak?" I asked.

Ann peered at the administration delegation for approval. They greeted my vital arrival with a shrug of collective boredom.

"We have established," I said, "that it is illegal to build on a Native American site. You have correctly identified the section of the code which nevertheless permits development as long as that development is properly mitigated. I applaud the University's intentions of doing the right thing. In that light, I want to turn your attention to —" I swiped the paper from Gregory's hands, "—to Section 16.40.020., which defines a Native American cultural site as 'a location containing either human remains or artifacts of Native Californians which are at least one hundred years of age.'

"Now, I submit to you that what you see in front of you," I extended my arm out to indicate the hillside of hippies, "is in fact a Native Californian youth culture which is at least one hundred years old. What are we if not Native Californians? We were all born in California. Our language, our behavior, our belief system, our rituals are all rooted in a distinct Californian culture which is more than one hundred years old. Under the provisions of this statute, the administration can no more move us from this spot than it could uproot a tribe of Ohlone Indians from their homes."

Oh, them hippies love to cheer. It's part of their native culture.

It took the administration poobahs a few moments to react to this unexpected tactic.

"This is preposterous," Chancellor Perkins said, but didn't finish the thought.

"Completely ridiculous," Meyers agreed.

Fred Miles spoke up. "What you are doing, Ron, is playing semantic games. Not even the broadest interpretation of the statute could permit such absurd conclusions."

I was stunned by this attack. Not because the substance of it was so very imaginative, but because it finally occurred to me right then and there what Fred Miles was up to. He was on the administration's side, not ours, the rodent. He was a double agent who had defected to the Soviets, and if I am any judge of faculty motivation, he probably did it for larger office space, a better parking spot, and insubstantial increases in departmental privilege. This — this would have been the appropriate moment for someone to yell "sellout!"

He smiled at me with the teeth of a shark. "This is serious stuff," he said, as if he and I were sharing a quiet office moment between student and advisor. "You may be getting into serious legal trouble."

I had to chuckle at that. I'd learned a few things about the law not long before from a morose relative of mine. She taught me this: they only threaten you when they're worried. Had we actually been in serious legal trouble we'd be in it, not talking about it.

"Fred," I said, because I knew the guy, "if I'm not mistaken, you're a history professor. Is that right?"

"That's right."

"But you're not a qualified legal expert, are you? Or am I mistaken? Are you acting as legal counsel here? Are you a lawyer at all?"

I have no idea where I got the guts. Partially it came from a certain familiarity with Fred, and partially from utter contempt. And if Eva could stand up on a car and declare her independence before God and all the world, I could certainly take on Fred Miles, traitor to his people.

"No, I'm not a lawyer," Fred admitted, "but neither are you."

"Very well. Then let's have a nice debate and not threaten one another, shall we?"

The crowd had been following this exchange very closely, and now they erupted again into applause, loud and long enough for me to gather my next thoughts.

"The point is," I said, "if I'm right, you are surrounded by Native Californian culture. Not only is it illegal to build here, but you may actually be trespassing on *de facto* sovereign territory."

Here's a quick tip for public speaking: use Latin whenever possible. It wows 'em.

"But your premise is nonsensical," Chancellor Perkins said. "If we follow it to its logical conclusion, nothing could get built anywhere in this state without the approval of the local youth."

And that remark, my friends, got the biggest applause of the whole damn day. Boy, for a guy who rose pretty high in the ranks of a hotshot university, Perkins sure was a moron. He walked right into that one. I let the roar play itself out.

"Let's be reasonable," I said at last, feeling emboldened. "Whether or not you accept my definition of Native Californian, we've established that this is a sacred Indian burial ground. Now, isn't there somewhere else, somewhere on this campus where the University might consider moving its proposed development?"

"I'm sorry," Fred said, "I don't mean to offend anyone, but I must point out that anywhere you build on this campus, in fact anywhere in this country is Indian burial ground. Naturally. The continent was occupied for tens of thousands of years by Indians, all of whom died and most of whom were buried. What's the big deal? The whole damn country is one big sacred Indian burial ground."

Whooowee! Fred Miles, losing his cool right there in front of five hundred of his biggest fans. With that last statement, enrollment in his Social Movements class for the next quarter shot down by fifty per cent. The other fifty per cent needed it for credit.

Perkins and Meyers shot Fred a tag-team dirty look and seemed fairly ready to hop on the booming "boo" that was rolling down the hill. With friends like him, they didn't need enemies.

"That remark does not represent my thinking on the matter," Perkins said venomously, and you could just see Fred's plum parking permit getting handed over to some junior math teacher who kept his head lowered and his mouth shut.

"This University," Perkins said, "is absolutely, one hundred per cent committed to the protection and preservation of authentic Native American historical, archaeological sites. In that goal, I believe we are in complete agreement with you, the students, and I applaud you for your devotion to this important issue, and for your scrupulous research. However, I believe it is sophistry to suggest that the students who sit here today, who have been gathered here only through the efforts of the University of California, somehow form a distinct historical culture to which accrue certain special rights. You may feel solidarity with one another, but you do not therefore form a culture, and you do not belong on this land."

Meyers nodded her head vigorously. Then, for a moment, no one at the table had a thing to say, except ol' Ronnie. As it happened, I had a great deal to say.

I held a certain advantage. Unlike the rest of them, I had thought a great deal about this question. In the three days since my conversation with JLP and my subsequent discovery of the supporting statute, I had been turning the concept over and over in my head. Most of what I had to say I had already rehearsed, talking it over with Great White. Some of my thoughts I had bounced off of Hal, which was exactly like playing tennis against a wall. Good practice, but not much human reaction. I wasn't sure how the crowd would take it, and I hesitated a few moments, fearing the worst and rehearsing the words.

But then I could delay no longer. It was time to speak up. I had become, after all, the unwilling oracle of oratory. "A man's gotta make his reputation, and then live up to it," Dad always said.

"Do we belong on this land?" I began. "I ask all of you: who is a true Californian? I was born and raised in Camarillo, and ain't I a Californian? As a child, I played every single day in the haze of the dense brown security blanket we southern Californians call air, and ain't I a Californian?"

That got a nice laugh, giving me added momentum.

"Before I was ten, I had gotten sunburned eleven times at Lifeguard Tower #7 at Zuma Beach, and ain't I a Californian? I learned how to drive before I learned any geography, and ain't I a Californian? I've been in so many earthquakes I rather enjoy them, and ain't I a Californian? I've worked with immigrants, played with immigrants, hated immigrants, berated immigrants, dated immigrants, and ain't I a Californian?"

This last bit garnered a mixed humming, an uncertain insect noise of confusion, part support and part distrust. It unnerved me a bit, but seeing that Meyers and Perkins were conferring, I pressed on.

"Before I ever left this great state, I had been to the lowest and highest point in the U.S., and ain't I a Californian? I've spat on the stars on Hollywood Boulevard and smelled the fresh and ancient Sequoia air of the tallest tree in the world, and ain't I a Californian? I've laughed at the bodybuilders at Venice Beach, and I've dropped acid at Haight and Ashbury."

Acid! Whoo-whoo! Shrieks and applause! Suddenly it's a rock concert! Them hippies love talk of acid.

"What exactly is the point of this diatribe?" Perkins demanded.

"Ms. Capriati-Mentzinger," Meyers said, "is there a program to this debate?"

"He doesn't represent —" Gregory began, but I shut him up.

"Tell me I'm not a Native Californian," I barreled ahead. "I've gotten in free at Disneyland 'cause I knew a dude who worked there, and ain't I a Californian? I've ridden my skateboard through first, second and third degree smog alerts, I've dyed my blond hair green with youthful summers of swimming pool chlorine. I've called into rock 'n' roll radio shows to get my free stuff. I can judge the quality of a strip mall from three exits away on the freeway, and ain't I a Californian? I've uttered the word 'totally' more than two million times and I totally intend to continue. I've observed police brutality in three different counties. I've watched enough hours of sensationalized T.V. trials to qualify me for the Bar. And so I say to you that I am in fact a Native Californian, and by law you may not build on this meadow without my permission."

Oh, they cheered like clapping monkeys, that great wide field of my fellow natives, that tribe of silly, serious, beautiful buffoons.

As I looked out at them, what I beheld sprinkled on that slippery slope seemed like it just might have some worth, like a great collection of stray change that has collected at the bottom of the sock drawer. Most of them were drab pennies, but every once in a while there was a nickel or a dime with serrated edges. And there, high on the hill, sat my lovely Susan B. Anthony dollar, blowing a kiss across a perfect palm.

"Well," Ann Capriati-Mentzinger said after a few moments, "that's a very interesting position. Would the administration care to respond?"

"I see no need to amend my earlier remarks," Perkins said, pissed. "This is sophistry. It changes nothing. Frankly, it seems to me that this debate has gone backward. We began with a compromise and have headed toward intransigence. Earlier I pledged to order the police to withdraw from the field. I did so in the expectation that the students would withdraw as well. I cannot say that I have any enthusiasm for that agreement now."

It took Gregory a minute to get it, since Perkins used big words.

"Wait," he said, "I don't think we have to go back on everything."

"Yeah," M'Bopape said. "We want the cops gone."

"Well," Perkins said, "this gentleman is making it very difficult for us to do that."

"Well, he's not a student," Gregory said, studiously avoiding eye contact with me. "He's an outside agitator, and I don't think he necessarily represents the student interest."

"If you can't agree amongst yourselves who will speak for you," Perkins said, "it becomes very difficult to conduct a rational conversation."

"Wait a minute," I said, truly angry at that weakling Gregory, "why don't we ask the students if I represent their interest? Could the audience please applaud now if you thought I was making a valid point?"

They applauded like mad. Maybe they were just trying to stay warm in the late afternoon shadows.

"I don't think stunts like that are very helpful," Meyers whined.

"I don't think it's a stunt to ask students what they think," M'Bopape said. Thank God Almighty, someone up there was on my side, even if it was beak-boy, the armchair anarchist.

"May I propose a compromise?" Ann said. "We have been here for almost two hours, and we've heard a lot of interesting and fruitful discussion. The day is getting late. I suggest we adjourn the debate and schedule another session. In the meantime, as a truce, both the police and the students will vacate Deerpark Meadow."

Absolutely everyone agreed to that so fast my head was still spinning when I found myself back in the adoring crowd, with Karen at my side. And, at her side, Eva Anne Shorenstein.

"What are you doing here?" I asked. "Aren't you supposed to be at —"

"Lay off," Eva said, "I'm getting around to it."

"I held up my end of the bargain," I said.

Karen scrutinized us quizzically for a moment, but seeing that no further debate was forthcoming, she jumped up gracefully to kiss me. "God," she said, "that was an amazing speech, Ronnie. All that stuff about being a Californian. It was great!"

"Well, thankya, thankya very much," I said in an Elvis voice resonant with utterly false modesty.

"I like to surf every day, and ain't I a Californian?" Karen asked, giggling, in a feeble impression of my phraseology.

"He stole the whole thing, you know," Eva said. "Sojourner Truth. She was a seminal feminist who asked 'ain't I a woman?' at the first women's rights convention in 1861. He swiped her whole schtick."

"An infamous suggestion," I said, grinning at the old sis. She was probably the only one in that crowd of undereducated yokels who caught it. "Never even heard of the woman," I said. "Sojourner Truth, you say? Quaint name."

"Uh-huh," Eva said, with a semblance of a grin. "Just watch it, kid. I could sue you for libel."

"Please don't. Ours is an overly litigious society," Karen said, throwing Eva's words of a week earlier right back at her.

We all laughed at that one. Cuddly Karen was catching on.

"Besides," I said, "imitation is the highest form of —"

"— plagiarism," Eva said.

Chapter 28

"Ronnie," Karen said, "there's someone over there who wants to talk to you."

I looked through the scattering crowd in the direction indicated.

"Oh, Christ!" I groaned, "not him!"

"Wait, he really wants to make up with you. Go on, Ronnie. Do it for me. Come on. Come on."

I grimaced, then made my heroic way across the mine field. Karen and Eva pretended to make conversation with a herd of hippie yearlings who had gathered around them.

John Lone Pine slouched on that grassy knoll shrouded by a cloud of attitude so dense I could barely see him. His arms were crossed in defiance of some imagined offense. He chewed on his lower lip and stared stonily into a make-believe distance.

"Uh, hey," I said, because that's what I tend to say.

"Hey," he said, "so I guess you were gonna apologize?"

"No, actually, I thought you were."

JLP tore away from his obstinate stare and looked at me, confused. After a moment or two it occurred to us, simultaneously, that we had both been tricked by Karen. We each had been told the other wanted to talk. It was the old third grade stunt: "Janie says she would kiss you if you asked her to." "Gosh, really? O.K., tell her I asked."

JLP and I had to laugh at the ambient childishness.

"Lovely fucking speech," JLP said.

"Oh, did you like it?"

"Hated it."

"I figured. Look," I said, "there's really not much point ..." My voice trailed away. At that moment we both suddenly lost what little interest we had in the conversation. Our attention was seized by a developing situation, some twenty feet down the hill. A very beefy cop, trying to usher the crowds, had just knocked down a young woman the size of an Olympic gymnast by placing his hand on her back.

"Fucking cops," I said.

"He had no cause to touch her," JLP said.

The cop was surrounded at once by twenty vigilante punks overly ready for some action. Never surround a cop. They get nervous fast. Before anyone had a chance to react, before backup could arrive, the cop had pulled out his gun, the idiot.

I don't know who made it down the hill faster, JLP or me. Call it a photo finish. Without exchanging a word nor even a glance, we pushed our way through the crowd.

"Easy, now," JLP said.

"Let's everybody mellow out," I said, pulling my way to the center.

"He's got a gun," some idiot hothead said.

Of course he's got a gun. He's a cop. What do you think he's got, a shillelagh?

"I need all of you to back up right this instant," the cop said.

"Let's do what he says," I said.

"Backing up," JLP said.

Space developed.

"O.K.," I said to the cop, "we're cool."

"Everybody stand back," JLP said. "More."

"He didn't have to knock her down," the hothead said.

"Maybe not," I said, "but we don't want any more violence, do we?"

Christ, the cop had a gun drawn, and these yahoos wanted to prove some stupid point of pride.

"Looks O.K. to me," JLP said to the cop. "How about holstering the firearm, then you won't have to file an incident report? Situation seems under control."

The cop looked at JLP as though he had spoken the first English the cop had heard in three weeks. Warily, he put the gun away.

"O.K.," I said, "let's be reasonable. He didn't mean to push her. Did you, officer?"

"Of course not."

"Are you alright?" I asked the young woman, who had been nearly trampled in the excitement.

"Cool beans," she said, proving once again the unrelenting capacity of the hippie to utter the most obscurely cheerful remarks at the most unexpected moments.

"Fine," I said, "it's been a long day. Why don't we all just head home and forget this happened?"

There was grumbling, but they dispersed. The cop actually thanked JLP and me. What a difference a day or two makes in cop relations.

"What a bunch of fucking idiots," I said when JLP and I were alone again.

"Can't corner an officer," he said. "Big mistake."

"Hey," I said, "where did you get all that 'incident report' lingo?"

"My dad's a cop," he said.

"Oh," I said. Then I added, "Well, nice work there."

"Yeah, you too. Kinda scary."

"You ever think about taking over the family business?" I asked him. "You seem pretty cool under pressure."

"Nah," he said. "It's a dangerous life. My dad works in Oakland, and the shit they have to deal with — it's unreal. It's messed up, what goes on out there."

"He's your Indian side?" I asked.

"Yeah," JLP said. "Why? Did you think we're all deadbeat alcoholics?"

"Never said that," I sighed, gearing up for another fight.

"My father never drinks."

O.K., I said to myself, just get it over with. Karen will be happy. Happier than usual, that is. It's the right thing to do. Dad always says, "A real man firmly admits when he's wrong," a saying I believe he stole from Dale Carnegie's *How to Win Friends and Influence People*, Dad's personal bible. But that's another story.

"JLP," I said, "I'm sorry if I offended you, the other day."

"O.K," he nodded.

"I guess I shouldn't have popped off. Christ, I don't even remember what it was about."

"I do. Same bullshit as your speech, just now. Speaking for other people." He gave a half-laugh. "You're just getting worse, you know. Maybe I should have stuck around and explained it to you, before you went and made a fool of yourself in front of all these people."

"A fool of myself? They seemed pretty pleased with it."

"Then they're as clueless as you."

"Yeah, well. Why don't you tell me all about it?" I asked, sarcastically. Stupid! I just refuse to learn. Got a skull like a bowling ball. The last time I had extended an invitation of that exact nature, JLP had ended up hectoring me for a fortnight or two.

"I could explain, but it would take time." JLP said.

"Yeah, well," I said, "I'd love to stick around, but I have to give Karen and my sister a ride home."

Talk about your bad timing: Karen had just come up, and had heard my last words.

"Oh, no, it's cool," she said, "we've got a ride with Marcia. Why don't you take Great White and we'll meet later?"

Oh, that's real good. Oh, thanks, Karen. Thanks so very much for abandoning me. Oh, boy, are you gonna get it later for that one.

She jaunted off, leaving me alone with the man who has pledged to spend the rest of his days following me around, correcting my thinking.

Karen and Eva went off with two young women. I actually recognized them both. Marcia was the co-facilitator from the original E. Club meeting, and Marianne was my moronic press release sidekick. I confess I felt a surge of nostalgic apathy at the sight of those old comrades.

"Who's Great White?" JLP asked.

"My car."

"What's so great about white?"

I frowned. "Look, it's just a car, it's not a campaign slogan."

"Strange name."

"Jesus. Why don't you just get over it, JLP?"

"Why Great White? As in Great White Hope?"

"As in Great White Shark. As in, it guzzles a lot of gas. As in, I just got it fixed. As in, it runs great now, and if you need a ride somewhere I could give you a lift if you can manage to sit inside something named white."

"I could use a bite," he said.

"Well, Great White is always happy to bite."

We drove slowly down the hill into town. GW was now capable of greater speeds, but I knew the whole campus was crawling with cops ready to arrest me for sneezing with my eyes open.

"You know," JLP said, "you really have hotspa."

"I have what?"

"Hotspa. It's like nerve. Like, the guts to say stupid stuff in front of a bunch of people."

"Oh," I said, "you mean 'chutzpah'?"

"That's it. Weird word."

"It's Yiddish," I said.

"Oh," JLP said. He looked at me for a moment. "Sorry. I didn't realize you were Yiddish."

Believe it or not, that was not the first time someone has uttered that oddity in my presence. It always gives rise to an obscure, uneasy lump in my manly Jewish larynx. Now, I'm no Lubavitcher Chasidic Orthodox type guy in a long black coat in the sweltering summer, but Dad's Jewish, and we used to go to my Aunt Rosie's house for Passover, until she died of breast cancer. It was quite sad, which I suppose is no great new insight on death; but what I mean is that Dad suffered terribly for a time. I was under the age of ten, but I remember one image of his back, shuddering violently as he cried, alone in the kitchen. And I remember Aunt Rosie. She was kind to kids, and she cooked tremendous amounts of chicken and potatoes. I think she and Eva had a particularly strong bond, but I could be wrong about that. I was rather young. We had to travel to Seattle to visit Aunt Rosie. She lived alone, and I just now remembered she used to give each of us kids a twenty dollar bill every time we visited, at the moment of our departure. Pretty cool.

That was about the extent of our Jewish upbringing: yearly Passovers with Aunt Rosie. And I certainly know the difference between being Jewish and speaking Yiddish.

Back to JLP — ugh, do we have to? Back to JLP and his tangled terminology. I hate that sort of confrontation, because I never know which offenses to let slide and which to correct.

"I'm not Yiddish," I said. "I'm a person, not a language. A member in poor standing of the Tribes of Israel."

"The tribes of what? Is this that white power thing of yours?" he actually asked.

"No, I said, the twelve Tribes of Israel. I'm Jewish. Not," I pointed out, "that one would need to be Jewish to know how to pronounce 'chutzpah.' It's something most educated adults pick up."

"Listen," he said, utterly uninterested in my distractions, "the point is you've got a lot of hoot-spa, or whatever, and it pisses me off. And now you go claiming to be tribal and all. What I want to know is, where do you get off speaking on behalf of Native People?"

"I never did that."

"You think I can't speak for myself?"

Actually, I do think he can't speak for himself, at least not in public, but that would probably have been impolitic to mention.

"I never said that."

"Where do you get the right? All that bullshit about being a Native Californian."

"Hey, it's true. Born and bred. A lot of people out there seemed to agree with me."

"A lot of people are full of shit."

Well, now we finally had our common ground.

"How dare you?" JLP said, like some society matron. "How dare you expropriate our culture, our name, our identity?"

Expropriate! Well, la-dee-dah.

"Listen," I said, "refresh my memory: wasn't there a time, like a million years ago, when you and I were on the same side?"

"What's your point?"

"Just this: I never even wanted to get sucked into this Deerpark horseshit, but since I'm in it, I'm trying to do what I can. I don't even have a good reason, but I'm on your side. I'm with the good guys. I'm trying to help you."

He laughed at that, cruelly. "Oh, yeah," he said. "I'm so glad another white man in a white hat has come along to try and help us by wiping out our history."

"Hey, you know what? I'm sorry if I offended you, but I'm trying to get something done. I've put myself way out there trying to stop this Deerpark development, which I never even minded much in the first place, and which is sounding better every minute. As far as I can tell, all you do is walk around with a chip on your shoulder, shoveling Indian guilt all over people. I slept out in the woods and got tear-gassed by cops, but I stuck it out with the Deerpark tribe. I never saw you during all of that. As far as I'm concerned, you're the one who's not in the tribe."

"Wow," JLP said, "wow. *I'm* not in the tribe? That is just *unbelievable* hotspa. Man! I gotta hand it to you. You sure know how to piss a guy off." He actually stopped and laughed at me for a minute as I pulled the obligatory left onto Mission St., the main thoroughfare. That would be Mission as in Franciscan Mission.

"You know what a 'wannabe' is?" JLP asked. "That's somebody who wants to be something else so bad, they can taste it. That's you, man. You want to be Native American so bad you had to dream up some fake tribe to make you feel like you belong to something, because you don't have any community of your own. What am I supposed to do, stand up and applaud while you insult my heritage? You want me to get tear-gassed in the name of your so-called youth culture tribe? What am I supposed to do, pretend I believe in your perversion of a law meant to protect Native remains?"

"I don't know what you're supposed to do," I said, "but I do remember you saying, less than two weeks ago, that you were going to give your life for this struggle."

Ha! Gotcha, punk.

"Yeah, well," he shrugged, "I guess a lot of people said a lot of things."

So they did.

Great White interrupted. He seemed puzzled. I agreed. "Where am I supposed to be going?" I asked.

"Somewhere cheap," JLP said, without hesitation, "and filling."

My thoughts turned immediately to the old standby, Golden West Pancakes. It was really more of a two-in-the-morning-because-nothing-else-is-open kind of place, but it was cheap and filling. It would serve.

And then an odd thing occurred. After five years of frequenting that charming bistro, after hundreds of burgers and thousands of fries — but not one pancake — it finally occurred to me what the restaurant logo portrayed. I could see the giant red sign above the restaurant displayed with perfect clarity by the projector in my mind's eye.

I used to inhabit a hovel a block east of Golden West. I'd driven past the eatery hundreds of times, and gone inside scores of others. The visual details were fixed in my mind like Polaris, the North Star by which we navigate. I knew the rock garden outside as though I had planted that gorgeous white and auburn landscape myself. Everything on the Golden West menu is either golden brown, piping hot, or both. I could visualize the logo on the sign in the sky exactly: it portrays a smiling little Indian girl, with a little headband sporting two feathers. In her hands she holds a plate of four giant pancakes, with butter melting over them. Looks delicious, but one quick question: what the hell does it mean? An Indian, with pancakes? Is that supposed to be some kind of native delicacy? Moronic. You don't have to be JLP to be offended — but it sure helps.

You have to figure that long ago someone, somewhere in a faraway advertising boardroom stood up and said, "How are we going to convey our concept of the Golden West visually?" And, rejecting sunsets, beaches, a sparkly golden nugget, the Golden Gate Bridge, Sutter's Mill, a golden compass, and old west conestoga wagon imagery, our advertising executive said, "I know! An Indian girl with a goofy smile and a plate of pancakes!"

Sheer genius. Probably the same guy who had the old Sambo's account. You may remember that, after public outcry, they changed the name to Season's. It was probably the story of tigers melting to butter in the old Little Black Sambo story that inspired the butter melting off the Golden West pancakes.

"How about Denny's?" I asked JLP.

"What about Golden West?" JLP said. "I feel like pancakes. You ever go there?"

"Yeah, sure," I said.

And that, my friends, was that. Go figure that with a slide rule.

"So that was your sister standing next to Karen?" JLP asked, flooding his pancakes with a pool of maple syrup the size of the county reservoir.

"What?" I asked.

"Was that —"

"Yeah, it was. What about her?"

"Well," more syrup, "don't take this the wrong way, but she's righteous."

"She's what?" I could barely down my cheeseburger bite. I chased it with some Coke to clear my throat.

"Righteous. Wasn't that her who gave that speech from the top of the car?"

"Yeah," I said, confused, "but I didn't see you there."

JLP gave me a weird little grin. "I was there, but I was hiding out. I wanted to check it out, but I was kinda keeping a low profile. I really didn't want to get arrested. My dad would kill me. Know what I did?"

"What?"

"Climbed a tree."

He seemed to think that was the cleverest deed any mortal had ever accomplished. He grinned at me like a diseased killer whale.

"Watched the whole protest from that tree," he said.

Trees. That was it.

"Listen," I said, "I've been meaning to ask you something. Do you remember that night we went out tripping?"

"Yeah, of course. That was only like five days ago."

Good God, he was right. It only seemed like a century. A really shitty century, like the Fourteenth, when the Plague was all the rage.

"No," I said, "what I mean is, do you remember what happened? I mean when you and I climbed that big oak tree. Do you remember what you were thinking?"

He shrugged. "I was just tripping."

"Do you remember saying anything to me about trees?"

"No, nothing special. Excuse me," he said to the waitress, "could we have more syrup, please?"

"You don't remember saying something about all the trees disappearing? Because I think we both saw the same thing."

He thought about that for a moment. "That doesn't happen," he said, "two people can't have the same trip."

"I know, I know! That's why it's so weird. I could swear there was a moment — you don't remember anything like that?"

He thought for a minute. "No. I'm a blank slate."

No sense arguing that one.

"It's just," I said, "that I thought it might make it a little easier to explain — about what I was saying about tribes."

Actually, there was a great deal more to it, a shadowy, furtive movement across the darkened caverns of thought. That hallucinatory moment in the tree had moved me in some peculiar, profound way. Images from that night had been following me everywhere in the intervening days, popping up in odd thoughts, in dreams, at intersections.

Incidentally, I don't mean to imply that the only path towards meaningful insight is through the judicious ingestion of recreational chemicals. Perhaps you've found some other way which suits you better, America. God bless. Mushrooms worked for me at that time, and I wanted someone, even if it had to be bonehead JLP, to validate the experience. It had led me to a silverlode of unusually heavy thought, spinning in every direction like the small dust twisters that start up in the vast dead farms along the great California artery of Highway 5, winding first one way and then the other, eventually petering out without purpose.

"Listen," I said, trying to get a handle on things, "I've been developing this theory lately. Do you know anything about physics?"

"No."

"Me neither. But I do know that Einstein worked his whole life on something called the 'Grand Unifying Theory.' It was supposed to explain everything in the physical world, all in one formula that accounted for everything."

"So?"

"So lately I've been thinking about that, and whether there there could ever be some kind of analogous theory for human beings. Kind of like a Grand Unifying Social Theory. Not that people haven't tried to make up theories like that, God knows. But I think they're all outdated, because they were all theories based on traditional moral structures. And I've been thinking about connections between people in the modern world, and the ways they are formed, in the absence of those traditional structures. It has to do with the negation of history. Plus it has something to do with the past, the present and the future, and two different people witnessing the same vision of trees disappearing. It's hard to explain. I feel like it's all kind of floating around in my head, and I can't really grab a hold of it. I wish I could put it into words. Damn."

"Sounds interesting," he said, unconvincingly.

"I'm not saying it right," I said. "I'm not sure what the point is anyway—except I'm sure it would help me explain better what I said about Native Californians being a tribe."

"Oh, man," he said, "don't get started on that again. I told you, to me you're just another white man speaking for me. Is it so hard to understand that Native People don't need you speaking for them?"

"I'm not speaking for anyone," I said. "I'm barely speaking for myself. I wouldn't really call it speaking, anyway." I wiped my greasy mouth with my greasier napkin. "I'm just muttering a few muddled thoughts before mortality comes to claim me."

"Are you going to eat all of those fries?"

"No, go nuts. Listen," I said, "what about you, JLP? Do you speak for every Indian in every tribe in the United States and Canada?

This took him aback. "No, of course not," he said.

"Yes, you do. You just said that Indians don't need me speaking for them, as though you know what they're all thinking at eight o'clock on a Friday. Well, maybe some of them would be happy with what I had to say today."

"Yeah, right," he said, shaking his head, not getting it in the least. "If it makes your big ego happy, you go ahead and think that."

I'll say this for him: the man really knew how to irritate. "Look," I said, "we're all on the same side. That's what I'm trying to say. It's my theory of history. I wish I could explain it more clearly."

"Listen," he said, "one tribe conquers another. That's my theory of history. Everybody knows that. All I'm saying is that you don't have to add insult to ignorance, or whatever, by pretending you have some kind of special visions so you have some kind of special connection with native history and native culture, when you don't. You can't save a culture by replacing it."

"I didn't say I wanted to save it, or replace it. I just said I felt some kind of connection with the past."

"You want a connection with your past, swim back to England."

"England?" What in the name of Prince Phillip in a can was that supposed to mean?

"Or wherever your ancestors are from. Because you're not a Native Californian."

"Look," I said, "I've spent my whole life in California. What does it matter where my parents come from? How long do you have to be somewhere before you get to be native? Two generations? Ten generations? Ten thousand? Your so-called indigenous people of America all came over the Bering Strait from Asia."

"That's in dispute."

"Doesn't matter. The point is, when did history start? That's the real question. Ten thousand years ago? When the Spanish arrived? When the state was formed? After World War II? Ten minutes ago?"

"I don't know."

"I'll tell you when I think it started. Remember when you recommended that I read *The Ohlone Way*?"

"Yeah. That's when it started?"

"No, I meant —"

"—just kidding," JLP said. "Take it easy. You're hyperventilating."

Wow, was that a peculiar remark. It wasn't even from left field; it was from the parking lot outside the ballpark, where wise guys in satin windbreakers do their ticket scalping. Whoops! Did I say scalping?

"Listen," I said, refocusing, "we know the Ohlone had no reading and writing, right? And we know they were completely wiped out in under a hundred years."

"I told you, they weren't completely wiped out. There are still families who trace their lineage back to the Ohlone."

"But they're not the real thing, you know that. They don't practice the old ways. They don't speak the language. They don't hunt and gather the same way. There's nothing but blood connecting them with the past."

"Blood is the strongest connection of all."

"Is it? I don't think so. Anyway, putting aside a couple of families, will you grant me that the Ohlone were essentially wiped out?"

"Of course."

"O.K, so in that sense, their history stopped about a hundred years ago, right?"

JLP nodded reluctantly.

"O.K.," I said, pressing on with a full head of steam, "that's what we think, but that's wrong. Remember that we know — or more precisely, the guy who wrote the book is guessing — that the Ohlone had an absolutely rock solid taboo against speaking of the dead. If your father died, you buried him, and then you never spoke of him again. Odds were, therefore, that you never knew much about your grandparents, or anyone before them. It wasn't like some African tribes, where they've got oral historians who could tell you the names of everybody that ever was in the tribe and what day of the week they were born. Sure, the Ohlone had stories about the world and animals, Creation myths, that sort of thing, but they never talked about what happened fifty years ago."

"So? What's your point?" a pancake-weary JLP asked.

"This: not only have the Ohlone disappeared from history in the last one hundred years, they never had any history in the first place. Everything in the universe existed for them in present tense."

"O.K.," JLP said warily, "all of which proves?"

"That I've got as legitimate a claim on this land as they ever had. Hold on. O.K., imagine if you transported an Ohlone guy in a time machine to right here, and told him we were having a huge debate about how to preserve remains of somebody from two hundred years ago. You think he'd have any idea what we were talking about? You think he'd understand what archaeology is? If he did, he'd probably be totally offended by the concept, because the past is taboo to him. So my whole point is this: I think it's the greatest irony in the world that we're working like mad dogs to preserve the history of a bunch of people who would have been insulted by the whole idea of preserving history. We should just leave well enough alone."

After that, JLP was quiet for quite some time. At some point he got up and went to the bathroom, leaving me to my thoughts.

"That's pretty depressing," he said when he sat down.

"What's depressing about it?" I asked.

"It just makes me sad to think that you actually want people to know even less than they already do about the history of Native people. People are so ignorant already, and you don't want to let them know the truth about what happened here."

Truth. No kidding, the guy actually wanted Truth. Before me sat one more foot soldier in the timeless, naive campaign on behalf of that fairest of abstractions, the pure and shining one that has absolutely no earthly body or content.

"Look," I said, "I majored in history. If there's one thing they teach you in that discipline, it's that there is no such thing as objective history. History is just what the people who write it down say it is. Sometimes they have a specific agenda of how they want to mess with history. Sometimes they try their hardest to be objective, but their biases will always come through."

"That's also depressing."

"No, what I think is that we should just accept this problem as a given, and use it to our advantage."

"Our advantage? Who's 'we'?"

"You and me. Hear me out. Instead of trying to figure out exactly what Ohlone history was like, we should just accept we can never know — and in fact, that we'd be insulting them by trying to know their taboo history. So I say we just make it up, with no guilt about it. We fabricate their history for them."

"Why? Assuming for a second that's not the most disgusting, most fucked-up thing I've heard yet, why would you even bother to waste your time making up history?"

"Well, I figure it's like this: if you accept a static past, you accept a static future. But, if you can change the past, you can change the future."

"Bullshit. Anyone who doesn't learn from history —"

" — is doomed to repeat it. I've heard the saying. But that's my point, not yours. I think it's a whole lot easier to learn from history if you make it up yourself. And if you can change the past, which seems so irrefutable and completed, what about the future? Why do we despair of changing it before it has even occurred? In about twenty years, when what is happening today becomes the past, everyone will no doubt argue about what really happened, right? So we might as well start now."

"You know," JLP said "you lost me about an hour ago. I thought we were talking about that bullshit native white power youth culture you invented."

"I didn't invent it. I identified it. It grew up on its own, organically. I inherited it." Oh, dear God. Now I was using the word "organically" in sentences. There was no doubt: the Karen virus had infected me. I should have used better protection.

"So, um, speaking of inheritance, about your sister ..." JLP said, as though it might be a complete thought.

And that was the golden moment — call it the Golden West moment — and we must give credit where credit is due. It was JLP who, at that very instant, utterly unwittingly, made the vital connection for me.

From the moment of Eva's arrival aboard the jumbled jetliner of my life I had been descending from a great height, the tremendous pressure building in my ears. And suddenly, pop! I could hear again.

If you can change the past, you can change the future.

"What about her?" I asked.

"Well, do you think she would go out with a guy like me? I mean, I think she's really fine."

Yeccchh. What a thing to say to her brother. I'll tell you, that JLP sure had hotspa.

"I don't think she's right for you," I said.

"Is she with anybody?" JLP asked.

"Oh, no," I said. "No, she's all alone."

I wish I could tell you that John Lone Pine and I concluded our long, disagreeable evening with some final, loving reconciliation, and marched on Washington together in some joint cause. I'd like to report that we even made the slightest bit of sense to each other for a tenth of a second, but that would border on fiction.

However, just before we departed Golden West, there was one small, hopeful bit of overlap, a linkage between us. And although it might not have sustained the emotional depth of a shared vision, it was something on which to hang the slim hopes for our future friendship. You see, JLP, God bless him, was an even worse tipper than I, and he pocketed all the free jam packets shamelessly.

Yes, there was hope for the man.

Great White and I dropped JLP off at his house, and I'll say this for the guy: at least he didn't slam the fragile passenger door. In fact, he shut it so meekly that I had to reach over and finish the job. I watched JLP walk up the long driveway to his house for a minute, knowing he had never really listened to a word I said, and was still convinced I was just another white man on the warpath.

It's amazing how people can continue to deceive themselves, convinced of the validity of their beliefs, despite the best evidence to the contrary.

Chapter 29

By now, Great White was like an ancient horse on a well-trod delivery path. He knew the way so well I barely needed to hold the reins. Clop, clop, clop, and on up to campus once more the wagon wheeled its way.

Karen did not have to beg me much this time, because I must admit I too was curious to witness the day's events. Karen seemed a bit nervous, or apprehensive. When I confronted her regarding this condition, she said only, "It's a sad day."

Ann Capriati-Mentzinger was there, standing alone to one side of the meadow, and she too seemed to me more mournful than celebratory.

"Hello," she greeted us as we walked up the familiar path to the familiar field. "Ron and Karen, isn't it? Welcome."

"Thanks," I said. Suddenly sullen Karen said nothing.

"Quite a turnout," Ann said with a sweep of her hand and a smirk of her features.

The gesture indicated for us a Deerpark Meadow teeming with men in suits. The suit material was wool. The temperature exceeded eighty degrees. These facts afforded the three of us a quiet measure of satisfaction. The suits stood facing an inappropriately formal podium, chatting quietly. There were also some press people, a clump of students to another side, and many cops.

"Who are all the guys in suits?" I asked.

"Mostly U.C. officials. You see those five over there?" Ann indicated a group of old white guys standing in the muddy meadow who looked about as comfortable as a pig in a parka. "Those are Regents."

"Wow," I said. "Quite a coup for you."

Ann lowered her voice. "Quite a headache for me." She nodded to us and stepped away to observe the pageantry.

The speechifying began. There wasn't much variety, nor skill in public speaking. Trust my expert opinion.

"It's an honor to welcome all of you to this groundbreaking ceremony," Chancellor Perkins began, and the rest of us immediately suppressed a yawn. He yammered on at the podium for ten more minutes, taking special care to register his pride that this particular development project had enjoyed what he termed "the closest possible public scrutiny from faculty, staff and students."

From the student wing, slowly, steadily and loudly, M'Bopape began to clap, steadfastly building a dramatic tempo. It seemed to me applause in its most ironic form, but the suits didn't get that and energetically joined in.

Of students in attendance there were perhaps twenty, demoralized and downcast. They did not join M'Bopape in applauding. They hardly seemed in an applauding mood. They hardly seemed in a conscious mood. Of police in attendance there were probably fifty, which was comically excessive. Deerpark was a done deal. No one was going to riot for the sheer masochistic pleasure of it.

Unexpectedly, Ann walked back to join Karen and me.

"This is completely off the record," she said quietly, "but you guys were right. They shouldn't be building in this beautiful place."

I was rather taken aback by the admission. I was somewhat at a loss for words, which occurs with the frequency of lunar eclipses. Karen awakened from her torpor, took a step toward Ann, and kissed her on the cheek. They smiled like long-lost cousins greeting at the airport.

"Whistling in the graveyard," I said.

"Oh, did you guys hear?" Ann asked. "There was a real screw-up. It turns out the human remains weren't Ohlone Indian."

"What?" Karen asked. "Who was it?"

"It was much fresher than that. Apparently, some serial murderer in the seventies dumped one of his victims here. Did you know that in those years Santa Cruz was called 'the Murder Capital of the World' because of the unusually high incidence of serial killings?"

"God," Karen said. "How awful! Who was the victim?"

"A college student. She's been missing twenty-five years. Dental records," she said grimly.

Karen was visibly upset by this revelation, as was I, although it's hard to say why. We had already known that some human had died. Why should it have mattered who, how, and when?

"Wait a minute," I said, "I thought the archaeologists had identified it as a male body."

"I know," Ann said, shrugging. "People make mistakes."

As if on cue, Gregory Thompson stepped up to Perkins' side, walking without crutches now.

"Why is he up there?" Karen asked in all her innocence.

"Now I'd like to introduce Gregory Thompson," Perkins said in reply. "Gregory has recently been appointed to the position of Chancellor's Special Assistant for Student Affairs, and has been invaluable in aiding the completion of this project."

"Thanks," Gregory said into the microphone. "I just wanted to say a few words on behalf of the students. As some of you might know, I was initially opposed to this project, but then Chancellor Perkins and I had a good long talk about it. Let me tell you why students are behind Deerpark one hundred percent."

"Uhhh ... my ... Gaahh ..." Karen gaped, so stunned she was unable to complete the final syllables of her exclamation.

"Ann," I said, my eyes steadily fixed on Gregory, "does a Special Assistant receive any money?"

"Fifty bucks a month," Ann said.

At this point good ol' M'Bopape pulled an absolutely enormous sign from some hidden cache and held it above his head. On both sides, in gigantic red block letters, it read subtly: "GREGORY THOMPSON IS A MOTHERFUCKING SELLOUT!!"

From the students there arose a mighty cheer as they suddenly awakened, motivated either by the defamatory content of the sign or by the plucky public presentation of profanity. It's hard to say definitively which. They began to clap with great force and rhythm as M'Bopape marched back and forth right in front of the podium. This went on for a few moments, and was so loud and disruptive Gregory was unable to continue speaking.

Five cops shot forward towards M'Bopape, reaching for the sign. M'Bopape held it away from them exactly as one would hold a ball away from a child. I took a step forward, but I was distracted by a glimmer of light glinting high in a tree at the edge of the meadow, like a VCR flashing midnight at noon. I squinted, and suddenly I knew I was looking directly at JLP's watch.

"Hold it!" Perkins said into the microphone, his face to the press. "Let the man hold his sign. This is a university. We do not suppress free speech. We encourage it."

A press camera flashed at Perkins twice. The cops backed away. M'Bopape held his sign high for all to see.

"Wait a minute —" Gregory began, but applause drowned out his words. He stopped, and the applause died down. Then he began again, and once again the censorious clapping kicked in. Suddenly I noticed that Karen was applauding, and that I was as well. And then I saw that Ann Capriati-Mentzinger was applauding with fierce conviction, staring sneeringly straight into Gregory's serpentine heart.

Gregory was never permitted to finish his speech. After a few more false starts he simply slunk away, like a properly beaten dog. He walked in the direction directly opposite M'Bopape and the student wing, which brought him straight toward us.

Karen stepped in his path. "Gregory," she said, her voice a bit pleading, a bit insistent. "Why'd you say that stuff? I thought you were against Deerpark."

"Hey," Gregory shrugged, "shit happens."

He stepped around her and walked away down the far side of the meadow, shamefaced. He had been cast out of the tribe, and in that verdict was our vestige of victory.

Perkins pulled out a ceremonial shining silver shovel, at which point every single student got up and walked away. Without conferring, Karen and I joined them and walked down the hill, hand in disconsolate hand.

Ann alone was left behind to clear a good spot and hold the Chancellor's jacket as the shovel struck the earth.

Chapter 30

The next few weeks were a teleologist's dream come true, by which I mean only that certain coffees which had long been percolating were finally brewed.

While Karen, Eva and I seemed stuck in a pointless but acceptable rut, the winds all around us began to swirl.

Benny got lucky. People liked his poems and slides and obscure dog-and-pony show so much, he got accepted to S.F. State for the fall in the Artsy Bullshit Department. I believe that leads to an M.F.A.

Hal got even luckier. Brenda and he got engaged. Shocked? Not half as much as I. Knocked me off my chair, out the window and halfway down the block. They have yet to set a date, but they have moved in together. I'm not sure it's entirely a coincidence that Hal got his life together as soon as Benny declared he was leaving.

The few times I've met Brenda, I was not utterly overwhelmed. She's too skinny, for one thing. But Hal always liked them skinny. Her heart seems to be in the right place, which I suppose means inside her chest. And it's plain she adores the man, God help her.

A stroke of good luck seems to have struck that apartment. And don't think I've forgotten my old oatmeal-slopping buddy Carl. He apparently has been bumped up one entire rung on the computer corporate ladder and is making even more money he doesn't know what to do with than before.

I wonder about Carl and the Meyers Memo sometimes. It was such a colossally poor tip, such an obviously phony and useless bargaining tool, that I wonder if he might not have faked the whole thing. Maybe he knew that passing the Meyers Memo along would only make the E. Club look bad. So here's my theory: he did it on purpose, because he knew that Karen and I were involved with the E. Club shenanigans. He planted disinformation with which we could only make utter idiots of ourselves. He did it for revenge. He did it to sabotage the team of Ronnie and Karen. What do you think, is that completely paranoid? Or should I go buy a bullet-proof vest?

As for the beloved Gregory, the rumor mill has churned up the following: he now has a job lined up at his father's Wall St. brokerage. I pity the poor minnows when that shark arrives.

I have spent no further time debating the Deerpark debacle with any of the particular participants. But I have finally decided which side I'm on, completely and irrevocably. Maybe someone needs to stick a thermometer under my tongue or somewhere even less pleasant, because lately I've been thinking that I may have been wrong. Yes, I, Ronnie Shorenstein, may have erred. I know, you think that highly unlikely, but bear with me, because it gets worse: I think JLP may have been right.

You see, it's a binary situation: either I was right, and young Californians form a neo-tribe, or they do not. If there is such an association, well, then, I suppose I belong to it, as I proclaimed in front of God and Chancellor Perkins. I sure as hell don't belong to Perkins' tribe, the Building People. I am a mole, and them Deerpark kids were all moles, except for traitorous Gregory. And if I belong to their tribe, then I ought to behave as one of them. People in tribes do what other people in their tribe do. That's what makes them tribes.

Although it seems to me that even in actual primitive type of tribes, the kind with neck-stretching rings and mud masks and little thong thingies, there must have always been guys who bucked the system. There must have been random misanthropes who cherished their own terminally low opinion of just about everyone in the tribe, and despised its cloying, boring traditions. If I had been born fifty thousand years ago, that would have been me. But let's be honest: you can't pick and choose if you want to part of a tribe like that. Either you're in, or you're dead. Without the luxury of leaving, I would have found ways to tolerate it. Ways even to like it. Brrr. Makes me shudder.

And now I find myself doing odd things. It's still a mystery. In the past, when confronted with puzzling abstractions and counterintuitive situations, I would have asked Benny to help me sort it out. But he's in the Big City now. I am forced to speculate what he would say, or waste a buck on a phone call. I'll save the money. "Introspection informs behavior," would probably be the essence of his much longer diatribe.

M'Bopape called me a day or two ago. I should get an unlisted number. He's off the Deerpark schtick now. He's organizing a protest of Lockheed, Inc. According to schnoz-boy, the company makes triggers for nuclear weapons, just up the road from UCSC, and that's a mean thing to do. Of course, his information on that could be wrong. Hell, his first name is probably a deceit of some sort. He asked if I would write a position paper, and possibly speak at their protest next month. Sounds only a trifle more fun than javelin catching.

But hark! Awoooo! Awooooo! What's that noise? Do you hear those howls? My tribe is calling. And maybe I will do something to save their sorry, illiterate hides once again. Awoooo! One position paper, coming up. Because the truth is, when you get right down to it, that Alex and Marianne were right all along: p;utonium is a very bad idea.

On the other hand, maybe I was wrong, and there is no such thing as a neo-California youth culture. Maybe we are all wandering the streets and alleys, solitary hunters in an anarchic and hostile urban forest. Maybe there is no tribe. It's a bit of a lonely thought.

But if there is no tribe today, then logic dictates that the old tribe still applies. And I don't like the implications of that possibility much either. It means the Ohlone and friends are still running the show, and it's time to honor all the treaties, turn over all of Santa Cruz and San Francisco and Chicago and New York back to their rightful owners, grease up with vaseline, and start that long cold swim across the Atlantic.

The ocean calls. If there is any meaning to being a Native Californian, in any era, surely it must involve an intimate understanding of and relationship with the great deep sea.

Late one American evening along the Pacific Coast, when Letterman had already tucked all the funny bits into bed and there were just some obscure, unwarranted and unwanted minor celebrities clogging the airwaves, I asked Eva if she wanted to take a walk to the beach. She looked at me as though I were Philo T. Farnsworth, inventor of television: completely nuts, but with an idea so peculiar it just might work.

"It's cold out there," she said.

"I'll lend you my sweatshirt," I said. "We need the fresh air."

Eva shrugged and let the tide carry her out the door. In an oversized XXL Harvard sweatshirt and her nighttime glasses she looked like an overeducated ragamuffin. Her hands were hidden deep inside the floppy sleeves. The sweatshirt was the only keepsake I had retained from a very brief encounter with a young woman who — ah, never mind, you'd just think I was bragging.

Seven blocks from my apartment there is a beach I like to visit at night when the foam and moon are at their phosphorescent best. A long jetty of piled boulders extends far out into the ocean, to protect the yacht harbor. At the end of the jetty I long ago discovered a boulder now known far and wide as the Most Comfortable Rock in the World. I'm suddenly certain that Hal proposed to Brenda there. The rock was naturally formed so that the rear end of a human being of moderate size fits perfectly on a wide horizontal platform. There is another smaller platform below for one's feet, and the entire rock is pitched at a perfect angle so that one can lean back and relax and yet enjoy the view in all its beauty. Underneath the jetty, the boulders echo with the sound of troubled waves crashing and swirling. When one has been out to sea for a very long time, it can be a very comforting rock.

It was this rock I sought when I took Eva to the beach that night. She complained bitterly every step of the way, but that was generally a sign of a decent mood. In her worst moods, she is deadly silent.

We finally arrived, and I let her sit on the Most Comfortable Rock in the World all she wanted, because that's the kind of brother I am. She grudgingly admitted that it was comfortable, but too cold, as though I could provide a rock that was both comfortable and heated.

"Eva," I said at length, "I've been thinking."

"Don't hurt yourself."

"Listen, I had a long talk with JLP. You know who he is?"

"Yeah, Karen filled me in."

"She did? Did she tell you he thinks you're — and I quote — 'righteous'?"

"No," she laughed, "what is that supposed to mean?"

"Search me."

"'Righteous'. Does he imagine that maybe I sin less than others? Boy, is he in for a disappointment."

"The reason I mentioned it, is that he and I were talking about the past, present and future, and there was something in the conversation that made me think of you."

"Oh, was there? Did it involve my righteousness?"

"No. It was an entirely different context. We were talking about Indian history."

"Did he tell you how utterly full of shit you are with your youth culture tribe theory?"

"Yes, thank you. He filled me in on that completely."

"Good," she said, with satisfaction.

"We were talking about history, and the ways in which contemporary historians reshape the past according to their own arbitrary biases. And I had this theory that came to me: essentially, the past does not exist. The past is what we make it, and so, therefore, is the future. Are you following this?"

"Duh. It's not rocket science."

"Do you agree that the past is what we make it?"

"Sure. That's old news."

"O.K.," I said, my heart pounding a bit faster, "then why can't that be true for you too, Eva? What I mean is, why can't you make your own past what you want it to be, instead of what it was? That way you can create a future you want."

It's hard for me to explain how difficult it was to utter these simple thoughts to Eva, and I don't know why it had to be so hard. When we were younger, Eva used to be the only friend and confidante the world offered me, and such words would have come more readily. But that was many moons ago.

I watched in the moonlit dark, waiting for her response. This was the reason I had brought her out onto the jetty, and forced her to sit comfortably at the far end of a mass of boulders stretching halfway into the Monterey Bay. There was nowhere to run.

"Ronnie," she sighed, "are you saying I need to go to a shrink? Is that your little point?"

"We had a deal," I said in a miserably whiny voice. "I went up to campus and you didn't —"

"I went to the social worker," she blurted out.

"Oh ... oh, you did?"

"I did. You want to see my note from school? I went."

"Oh," I said, still rather stunned, "well, how was it?"

"Fabulous. Miraculous. I'm cured. Praise Jesus. God, what a fucking joke. Anyone who goes to a psychologist ought to have her head examined."

"Come on, what did she say?"

"Well, if you must know, if you must pry into private and confidential conversations which don't concern you, she said I need to confront my demons. Which is a hideous cliche, but I believe that's what you were trying to say just now in your own inarticulate way."

"Exactly! Create the past —"

"No, Ronnie. Sorry, but you're wrong. We can't create the past. We can only confront it."

"But —"

"You're wrong, Ronnie. You're pretty much always wrong when you try too hard. I can't just ignore the past, or efface it. Listen, just because I'm a suicidal manic depressive doesn't mean I don't know exactly what's wrong with me," she said in an unnervingly straightforward manner.

"I even know how to fix it," she said. "At least I think so. I just don't have the energy, the will to do it. We talked about that a lot, my zookeeper and I. She thinks I need to get out. Truth is, I think she's right."

"Get out? Like how?"

"Like leave town."

"Where are you going to go?"

"I don't know. It all depends on whether I have the willpower. I just

265

keep wavering, minute to minute, you know? I go from feeling pretty O.K. to feeling like a bowl of yellow jello. Nurse Ratched is trying to pop me full of meds to slow those swings. I don't know. When I feel good, like tonight, when I'm strong and clear, I don't want to start popping some downers. I know what I need. I have to head back to Eugene. I've got some past to confront."

"And Camarillo," I said, thinking only of Mom's face, and the way she always used to give Evie the spatula to lick whenever she made chocolate cake.

"Oh, yeah, Camarillo," Eva scoffed. "Don't push it." There was a long lull, during which four waves swelled, curled and broke in a thunder of foam, just as they have done since the past began.

"I don't know," Eva said in a quieter voice. "Maybe someday, Little Guy. Maybe someday in the future."

Chapter 31

Real jobs having proven themselves completely out of my stunted reach, I migrated back to my nesting home at the determinedly guy-style temp agency. Girl temp agencies provide high-paying, polite jobs in air-conditioned offices, answering phones that don't ring. Guy temp agencies provide menial labor for recovering drug addicts, wayward deadbeats, and the terminally stupid.

I ended up stacking boxes for slave wages at the Wrigley Chewing Gum factory, an ugly low building fringed with large stretches of the pointless grass fields that characterize modern industrial parks. I ask you: why do they bother? No one ever sits on the grass, and the company is forced to hire a guy to mow the lawn all day long.

I'll wager you thought they have a machine to stack boxes at such places. Fool! That's just what the enemy is expecting!

As a job, stacking boxes surpassed each of its predecessors in mind-numbing, soul-crushing simplicity. I stacked boxes, I grew homicidal, I got paid.

The entire factory stank of sugar, a disgusting syrupy miasma that seemed to ooze from the ducts and stick to my skin. There was no cafeteria, just a lobby with snack machines, and that's what got me worst. After every few hours of breathing sticky sugar-air, the workers would shuffle off to the lobby to buy a chocolate bar and a soda from the machines. Sugar, sugar, sugar.

The horror. The horror.

Blecchh. I worked my five-hour part-time days and got the hell out of Dodge.

When the school term ended, poor Karen found herself with neither education nor troublemaking to occupy her time. Many of her friends had migrated home for the holidays. I was now busy most days, and there was only so much time Karen could spend in Eva's company without her own formidable hippiness losing a bit of its hop.

And so Karen decided to make good on an earlier threat, and declared her intention to travel, to heed the call of the open road, to visit the great national parks of the Golden West without reservations. Upon this trek I was supposed to embark at her side.

Unfortunately, she had already spent her five hundred dollars on a new futon she had been craving, and on a wide array of diversions including the usual assortment of drugs, and tickets to shows put on by bands claiming the mantle of the extinct Dead. She also lavished an obscenely massive pile of gifts on her friends. Nor was I immune to her carefree generosity. She bought me a thick cardigan sweater, ethnically decorated and imported straight from a Peruvian sweat-shop, knit by hand by wizened, exploited latter-day Incas with bad teeth and no dental plan, I have no doubt. This lavish expenditure she justified with the excuse that the sweater matched my eyes, whatever that means. My eyes are not made of itchy wool.

Carless and coinless, desperate and down on her luck, Karen did what any self-respecting, freeloading hippie would do. She turned to her parents for help. Two days later they bought her a Japanese econobox with about two thousand miles on it. Oh, the joy! Nothing like buying a car to reunite an American family. It ran perfectly, drank no gas, and could have towed Great White up Mt. Everest at eighty mph if Karen ever exceeded the speed limit.

Great White was pleased at first. He had a little red minnow to chart the seven seas alongside him. But Karen's car had no name, and Great White could never be close with an anonymous box of tin. We tried to name the little red wagon, but it had no character, nothing to distinguish it from the masses of reliable red two-door functionality roaming the highways. The truth is that there is an inverse relationship between reliability and character. No car can have both.

Karen tried, slapping hippie slogans on her bumper as though it were an oxcart festooned for the fall festival. But it was no use. The car ran far too well for anyone to believe in its individuality.

But in the end, the little red wagon served an absolutely vital purpose. It may have even saved a life.

"You're sure about this?" Eva said.

"No," I said, "but I'm never sure about anything."

"Just take it," Karen advised Eva. "He wants you to."

Eva shuffled her feet for a minute or two in the gravel of the car lot below my apartment, and squinted at me for reassurance.

"Dammit, I'm going to do it," Eva said with a sudden grin. "I'm going to go call Heather right now. I think I can stay with her."

Without the slightest warning, Karen pounced on Eva with a Karen hug.

When Eva came up for air fifteen minutes later she seemed to be beaming, but in a very subtle way, which no spectrograph could have possibly detected.

"You're absolutely sure about this?" Eva asked me.

"Positive," I said.

"No Indian giving," Eva said.

"I never give like an Indian," I said.

I had thought long and hard before making my decision. Eva had spent the better part of two months in my orbit. She had oscillated from the very depths of despair to unusual little spikes of enthusiasm, and now she seemed to be leveling in some way. Was she coming away from the experience sane, adjusted, happy and married? No. Had she restored a sense of her own worth, and regained her faith in humanity? In some small measure, I believe she may have done so.

I do not claim to know what is really wrong with Eva. I do know that in some ways it has been there all her life. I don't know why. I'm certain she would feel her privacy violated if she learned that I have spent endless hours speculating on her condition. I know she spent much more time than I internally diagnosing her condition. And while I found myself a sudden and unexpected advocate for a profession I have always found highly suspect, I'm not sure if Eva has ever truly benefited from the sort of help mental health practitioners provide. I do know this: the finest help she ever got was from an unlicensed, untrained prodigy, a graceful dancer who never ceased insisting on the validity of astrology and decorated her car with bumperstickers of the extraterrestrials who will soon be shepherding us all onto a higher plane of existence.

Once Eva left town, she would no longer be under Karen's watchful eye, nor under the care of a so-called trained professional. But if she was going to make it alone in this gray cold world, she could have no better guide than Great White.

"I'll tell you what," I said to Eva, "I just want to take him for one more spin, for old times' sake. Why don't you call Heather, pack up your stuff, and you can start in the morning."

"Me and Ronnie are starting in the morning," Karen said, repeating information we all knew. "Maybe we could caravan out of town."

"Righteous," Eva grinned.

"Wait," I said to Eva. "Two things you have to promise me,"

The look of brief happiness in her eye immediately turned to suspicion.

"First," I said, "don't let people slam the passenger door. GW just hates that."

"Do-able," Eva said. "What's number two?"

"You can never change Great White's name."

In reply, that perennially cheerful, eternally sappy sister of mine gave me a big, sloppy kiss on the cheek. It took me a long, sheepish minute to wipe off all that yucky black lipstick she favors.

For our final tour in the belly of the beast, Karen and I chose a favorite sunset excursion. We took Highway One, the grandest of all Mother Nature's great grand highways. From Santa Cruz it glides north between fields of brussel sprouts and meadows on one side, and the ocean, the endless ocean on the other. As the highway rises toward the inland pass to San Francisco, there is a spectacular stretch of cliff-hugging mountainous pass known as Devil's Slide, which soars up to dizzying heights to survey its own grandeur. Far below, waves originating thousands of miles out to sea finally come to shore to crash majestically against boulders which have undoubtedly been there since the earth's crust cooled.

GW pulled over at the lookout point and we clambered out. It was incredibly windy, a steady gust that tossed Karen's hair and her long skirt into a billowing confusion and threw us both a little off balance. I held my arms open to the gale, and for the first time in weeks my skin felt clean of the sticky sugar factory feeling. After a few moments of twisting and turning her head into the wind, Karen managed to find the angle that allowed her hair to flow behind her and let her sweet child woman face taste the salty windclean spray and the air so fresh and clear it seemed pure oxygen and sunlight. Far below our floating bodies, the waves were splashing and rumbling ecstatically and the sun was burning orange and blue on the water. It was as though time and all of creation had stopped to admire itself. If you've ever seen beauty, or held it in your mortal hands, you know how I felt just then. It was a moment of rare perfection, glorious and free; and yet doomed. The moment would not last, not in this fleeting, transient existence, and it would never repeat itself until the end of all things came to pass.

The joy of the moment and the sorrow of knowing it could not last overwhelmed my meager soul. It was such a melancholy, aching beauty; I could not hold the moment close to me and capture it, because time would take it away from me, and even from my memory. And all I could think to do was to breathe the moment, taste it, exhale it, and then destroy it; capture it and annihilate it with a grim sense of purpose, so that it could not be tainted with any imperfections.

Karen was looking out to sea with a rapturous smile absent of any guile, and it was at that moment that I was allowed a sudden insight into the great gift she had been granted by the benevolent and capricious gods of human nature. Karen was not remotely concerned with destroying the moment. She was content to live it. Karen could feel joy and not suspect it of ulterior motives; and it seemed to me then that if I could learn that simple lesson I might not have lived entirely in vain.

Without pulling her gaze from the blustery waters, Karen held her hand out to me. It was neither a request nor a demand, but simply an expectation. I reached out to take her hand, and as I did so she slid comfortably into position, wrapping my arms around her from behind, and I warmed her shuddering form with a fierce, comforting squeeze. She leaned her head back; her neck, her throat and bosom all open to me. With closed eyes, her lips found mine. She lavished her moist, warm tongue over mine and breathed a lifelong kiss straight into my undeserving heart. Then she opened her eyes, stared into my soul, and said something; something vitally important and intimate, but the wind carried her words away, and I could not be sure if I had heard her correctly.

I knew as the words gusted away that it might have been the Immaculate Utterance, the three sacred words so fraught with meaning and depth and implication, the golden syllables Karen and I had been avoiding from the moment we met.

The words, the words! Words are important to me. I choose them carefully, and I do not use words whose meaning is unclear to me. How then, could I use that certain word, so laden with connotation and consequence it has almost lost all meaning?

From the first weeks of our uncertain dalliance, I had led the way in a childish verbal tiptoeing, scrupulously avoiding speaking the forbidden, as had Karen. That reluctance was uncharacteristic of a woman who played free and easy with any expression of affection. Perhaps she was just following my lead, unwilling to risk standing naked in the spotlight as the only one opening her heart. Or perhaps, as I often feared, she had nothing to say.

I muzzled my trembling snout into her windswept hair and, without rational thought, without worrying about mistakes or losing myself in labyrinths of analysis, I whispered into her chilled ear. And I may have responded with the same words, but again the wind blew heavy and loud, too loud for either of us to be certain of any meanings.

As the sun died away, Karen and I walked back to Great White, hand in hand, like children in the morning of the world.

I opened the rear door, and we jumped in with both comfortable familiarity and breathless excitement. Like the mighty ocean pounding below her, Karen could be both a being of quiet calm and a tidal adrenal rush. Ocean and Karen both held the power of the storm to flood the senses and the power to cleanse, as sand does on a windswept terrace.

We lay in the back of Great White, and for a time we simply huddled together, trying to restore warmth to our windswept bones. But as the winds howled outside in the great darkening star-sky, we began to move against one another with the playful pressures of a demanding passion.

My hands pulled her skirt up, and tugged at her periwinkle panties. She gave that comfortable, knowing twist, permitting them to slide off her toes in the easiest way, and I could already scent her earthy inner self exuding its erotic essence. I ran my tongue along her knees, against her thighs, and breathlessly found the shapes and contours of her greatest pleasures.

After a time she stopped me, and in the dark gave me a blessed smile. She pulled me into a kneeling position, and pressed her nude form against me from behind. She slipped my shirt over my head, kissing my back and caressing my aching chest. Slowly, maddeningly, she slipped her slim hands down the front of my jeans, caressing with her soft strength until the pants became too tight and she pulled them off, her fingernails tracing down with the slightest of scratches. Then the full warmth of her body was on top of mine, feeling as though it had always belonged just there, weighty with the fullness of humanity, light as a song.

I twisted her over, and in the dark I found her butterfly tattoo and kissed it again and again. I could feel the wings trembling, glowing hot and red. She began to tug at my hair on my head with a relaxed rapture, her fingers twining and pulling against the grain, playing up from the nape of my neck, circling and circling around my head like thoughts of breathless ecstasy. The light of the fullest of moons had begun to shine through the window when her butterfly began to tremble violently, uncontrollably, until it took wing at last in a great burst, and flew away into the unimaginable night sky that has always been ours.